Nyght
& Daie

Part 2: Nyght Tyme

I0660556

PAUL W. GIBBS

SonWright Books

SonWright Books

ISBN: 979-8-218-96573-0

Library of Congress Control Number: 2023919696

Cover Illustration by Victor Guiza © 2024 Paul W. Gibbs.

PRINTED IN THE UNITED STATES OF AMERICA

To my sister Tamara, who has always supported me in my writing and who has shown me that even when life is challenging, you do not give up. Thanks.

Glossary

Sun-cycle: One day

Moon-cycle: One month

Sun-mark/mark: One hour

Moon-mark: One week

Season: One year

Land-mark: One mile

Blessed Day: Birthday

Handbreadth: Three inches

ONE

Nyght was the last to enter through the doors to the Guild, which meant she was the one standing closest to them when they closed behind her. The sound echoed with a loud metal bang and all of the children turned to look at them, except for Nyght; but now, all the children were looking at her as well. She tilted her head up enough so that she could see under the top of her hood, but the children were not able to see her face, which to them made the child seem more unsettling.

They all turned around and walked further into the room with Nyght bringing up the rear. When the others came to a halt, she moved into the position at the far right of the line of children. In front of them, they saw a wall stretched across the room, and on that wall, there were seven doors.

The children looked at each other, except Nyght. They kept their eyes off her, and she kept hers on the doors in front. She did not even listen to what a couple of the children started talking about. All she did was begin to figure out what she was supposed to do next.

As soon as she moved to where she was standing, she knew that unlike outside, there would not be any of the Masters coming through those doors. It was a test, and she had to figure it out. If one of the other children came up with the solution first, then she would follow their lead. However, she was not going to wait until one of them did.

She began to think about the situation she was in, "*I am in a room with seven doors. There are seven of us. One door for each of us.*" She moved her eyes only, because she did not want the others to see what she was doing. She saw that on each of the doors, there was an emblem. Each one of those was different. She then thought to herself, "*Which one for me?*"

She came up with the idea that the emblem was the key, and most people carry a key on them. She raised the arrow she had brought into the room with her, the one the Master made sure she brought with her. She looked at the part of the shaft just beneath the arrowhead. She did not see anything, so she adjusted the arrow in her hand so that she was now looking at the end of the shaft. There were three feathers, each of them gray, but that did not give her any indication as to what door she should choose.

She then thought the arrow would point the way. She raised the arrow up so that it was at eye level and pointed the tip toward the wall with the doors. It was not the tip of the arrow she now saw; it was the small hole at the end of the shaft and the small piece of parchment rolled up inside.

She brought the arrow down in front of her chest, placed her dagger Umbra in the top of her trousers, and then pulled her dagger Full from under her cloak. She lowered the arrow a bit, inserted the tip of her blade into the small hole, and placed enough pressure on the side of the opening. She then pulled the blade up, bringing the piece of parchment out past the edge of the shaft. She was now able to pull it out the rest of the way with her fingers.

She did not have to look to her left to know that the other children had been watching her, and they all started to do exactly what they had seen her do.

Nyght unrolled the piece of parchment and saw on it a drawing of two snakes. One of the snakes had its head and the top part of its body positioned so that its lower half supported the top half of its body. In its mouth, it had the second snake. The first snake's fangs had impaled the second one just below its head.

She adjusted her head so that she was looking at the seven doors. She saw the same emblem on the second door from the right.

She placed her arms back inside her cloak and returned Umbra to her left hand while keeping Full and the arrow in her right. She then walked over to the door with the same emblem on the parchment, opened it, and stepped through closing the door behind her. Before it had completely shut, she heard the other children rushing to whatever door matched the emblem on their parchment, but they did not concern her.

She was now in a hallway and began walking because she knew that standing at the door was not where she was to remain. She noticed there were no torches in the hall, but that did not bother her or interfere with her moving forward. She had spent most of her life traveling at night and had long ago been able to see clearly even with no light at all. Only now she could see even better, and she knew it was because of how Moon transformed her last night.

As she moved forward, something inside her told her to stop. It was not Moon; it was something else. Her instincts told her that if she took another step she would be in danger.

She was about to bring out her daggers but decided that most likely, whoever had wanted her to be there would be watching somehow. If they saw her resort to her daggers, they would think that was how she would solve all of her problems. No, she knew that whatever the reason was that she was in the hallway, it was just like the previous room with the doors. Like then, this was a test, one that she would have to pass without the use of her weapons.

She could see well enough in the dark, but all she could see were the walls surrounding her. She looked to her right and to her left but did not see anything that would make her feel as if she was in danger. She looked upward and thought something could come out of the ceiling and fall on her, but if that happened, then she had a feeling many of the recruits who came through there would not make it to whatever waited at the end of the hall.

She decided that whatever danger there was, it would be coming from in front of her, which was the direction she needed to go.

She began walking again but moved slower than she had been before. She also cut the distance of her steps by half. She moved one foot forward, and when she had it placed securely on the floor, she moved the other ahead of the first. After performing the act three times, she brought her left foot forward. It went further downward than it had before. She held her position for a moment to get her balance so she would not fall forward. When she was ready, she pulled her foot back and placed it next to her other one.

She then knelt down and placed the tips of her fingers on her right hand against the floor. As soon as she felt it, she placed her palm on it, then slowly slid it forward. When she reached the spot where her left foot had not made any contact, she once again felt the empty space. She pulled her hand back so that she was able to feel the edge where the floor stopped. Nyght could not stop the grin from appearing on her face.

She could see very well in the dark, but what she had trouble distinguishing was depth. With no light, the gap in the floor was the same color as the floor itself. If she had kept walking without being cautious, she would have walked over the edge and straight down to whatever waited below. She doubted that the gap was so deep that if she had fallen in, it would have killed her, but to test how deep it was, she dropped the arrow into the gap. She did not hear it land.

The Guild had set these tests to see what the chosen children were capable of even before they started their training. Straw covered the bottom of the hole, which was why the arrow made no sound and it lessened the chances that one of the new recruits would come to serious harm. Someone might fall and break an arm or a leg, but they would survive, and the Masters would remind them that they should always be aware of their surroundings, but at least they would live to remember the lesson.

Nyght could not tell how wide the gap was, so she did not try to jump it. She realized that like the test with the arrow and the door, the Masters had provided a solution; she just had to find it.

She knew she could not go over the gap and the ceiling was too high for her to grab onto. She decided she would have to go around it somehow leaving her only option the walls at the sides.

She walked over to the left wall, making sure she kept her feet just at the edge of the gap in the floor. When she reached the wall, she placed her hand on it. Like the gap on the floor, she would not be able to see any difference if there was one, so she had to rely on her sense of touch.

She bent over and used her right hand to feel the wall. She started at the bottom where the gap began and moved her hand upward but did not feel anything different. She then moved her hand back to the bottom of the wall, but this time she moved it outwards, sliding it against the wall. She stopped moving it when she felt her hand enter into a hole, only this one was only big enough for a person to place their toes and the balls of their feet in. "Footholds," she thought to herself. *"And if there are footholds, then there might be handholds as well, so a person could use their feet and hands to get across the gap in the floor."*

Nyght kept her hand against the wall but slid it from the foothold upward. When she had moved it some, she had to stand to continue her search. As soon as she did, she felt a second hole in the wall where a person could place their hand.

She knew the next part of the test would be a little more difficult. She had found the first two holes and figured there would be others not far from these. The only problem was that she could not see them, and the distance was too great for her to stretch out to find them.

This was another part of the test. The Masters wanted to see if the recruits would give up and turn back or even decide to risk jumping the hole. If they did the first, then they did not deserve to be at the Guild anyway. If they attempted the second, then they would learn the lesson that all risks come with a cost, so before they take it, they need to make sure there is not a less costly way.

Nyght prepared herself to make the crossing. She positioned her cloak so that it was completely at her back along with the hood so that it would not get in her way. She placed her daggers down the sides of her trousers. The length of the blades ran past her knees, but it would assist her with what she was planning.

When she was set, she placed her left hand in the upper hole remembering where it was. She had already positioned herself as close to the edge of the gap in the floor so that the tips of her boots were over the edge. She then moved her left foot and placed it in the bottom hole, also remembering its position. The next part of her plan was going to be more difficult.

With her left hand and left foot secured, she pulled her body toward the wall and placed her right hand in the hole with the left and on top of it. There was enough room for both of her hands while she put pressure against the bottom of the small hole so that she could hold herself in that position. The hole she had placed her left foot in was not big enough for both of her feet, so her right was hanging over the gap in the floor. As with her hands, she put as much pressure as she could on the bottom of her left foot to support her weight.

It was now time to move on to the next part. She placed the tip of her right boot against the wall and up against her left foot. She then moved her right foot away from her other one while making sure the tip of her boot kept in contact with the wall. As she slid her foot across, the tip of it found its way into the next foothold in line.

She now had both her feet secured. Making sure she had enough pressure on the bottoms of the footholds, she slid her right hand across the wall to find the next handhold. She located it directly over the second foothold, only at the height of where her left hand was.

With both her hands and feet secured, she now was against the wall; but at the same time, over the gap in the floor which she now had to make the journey across.

The holes where she had her hands were about four handbreadths apart. As were the ones her feet were in. Figuring that the distance to the next free holes would be the same distance from the second set of holes, she made sure her left hand and both feet still supported her. She then slid her right hand away from her. Four handbreadths away from the second hole, she found the third one which she placed her right hand in. She then secured her position with the new hole, then removed her right foot from its hole, and moved it away. Even with her limbs spread further apart, she had no problem with holding the position. However, she did not hold it for long.

She moved her left hand out of the first hold and slid it across the wall until it reached the second hole. As soon as she had her hand secured, she moved her left foot out of the first hole it was in and positioned it in the second one. Now that she knew the distance between the holes, she did not have to keep her foot against the wall to find it. She just moved it out of the hole and placed it in the next one in line.

She had figured out how to get across the opening on the floor.

She continued to move across the wall, adjusting one hand or foot at a time, and securing it in the next opening in line. As she did this, she counted how many sections she crossed. When she reached the count of twenty and moved her hand to find the next hand-hold in line, she did not find one. When she started her crossing, the first hole was a handbreadth away from where the gap started on the floor. With no more holes, she would have to jump the rest of the way to get over the edge of the gap on the other side.

Just as she was about to push off from the wall, she thought that she should put enough force into her jump to make sure she cleared the distance and more just in case the Masters had decided to make the last bit of the test a little more difficult. If these last holes were the same distance away from the edge as the first set, then it would be nothing to clear the distance. If they were farther from the edge and she tried to cover the same distance as at the beginning of the test, then she could fall into the hole and everything she had done would be for nothing.

She moved her left hand and placed it in the hole with her right. She then put as much pressure down on them to give her the support she needed to hold herself in that position. The next part would be the most difficult maneuver out of everything she had done since she began the test.

She removed both of her feet out of the footholds and let them and her legs dangle in the air. While using her hands to hold her over the gap in the floor, she began to swing the lower part of her body from the left to the right and back. When she was ready and believed she had enough momentum, when her legs swung toward the right, she used her hands as much as she could to push against the inside of the handhold to give her a little more momentum. She then let go and allowed her body to swing her to safe ground.

She did not quite make it.

She underestimated the distance. When she landed, only the top half of her body struck the solid surface.

As soon as her body collided with the floor, she started sliding backward. More to the point, when she struck the edge of the gap, the momentum she had built up was not enough to get her to safety, but it was enough to cause her body to hit the edge of the floor, which caused her to bounce enough to take her into the gap itself.

As she was slipping, she did not try to stop her fall. She stretched her arms out with her palms against the floor, but the surface was too flat to grab hold of. Instead, she let herself fall and even allowed her upper body to go over the edge. As her hands connected with it, she grabbed hold of the edge to stop herself from going any further. She then pulled herself back up and out of the gap.

When she jumped and landed, she knew that since the beginning of the gap was at her midsection and below the point where her hands were, if she tried to use her hands to grab a hold of the edge, she would only end up twisting her body causing her to tumble into the gap itself. She waited until her body had entered into the gap and used her hands to stop her fall.

The Masters had made the last part of the test to see if a person would be able to save themselves, and more importantly, to see if they would panic when faced with the unknown.

After Nyght pulled her body clear of the gap, she stayed on her back for a moment. She was not doing this to rest but to reach into her trousers to pull out her daggers, where she had placed them before she began to cross. Since the length of the daggers was past her knees, she was not able to bend her legs. This helped as she traveled across the wall because it forced her to keep her legs straight which aided her in what she had to do. Before she stood, she had to remove them or else when she did stand, they would either cut her or at the very least slice her trousers.

When she had her daggers in hand, she stood up and turned away from the gap. She had passed the test so there was no reason to look back at it.

She only had to walk another ten paces when she saw a metal handle. Since the handle was a lighter color compared to the surrounding walls, she was able to see it in the dark. She immediately thought that wherever there is a handle, there is usually a door.

She looked at the handle, but before she opened the door, she took a moment to think if there might be something on the other side waiting for her. She decided that if there was, she would deal with it when the time came. If there was nothing waiting to harm her, she did not want someone to think the last test had gotten to her, which they might, if she had her daggers drawn. She once again placed her cloak around her body and had her hands and arms inside concealing her weapons.

She moved the dagger in her right hand to her left so that she could take hold of the handle. She then turned it and opened the door. She stepped out into an area with torches. Wherever she was, it was not what she expected.

She had looked at the building of the Assassin's Guild for over three seasons. She could tell anyone how many windows, doors, and especially the number of floors it had. It was four. Now, when she raised her head and looked upward, she saw that the ceiling was so high she could not even see it.

"Confusing, isn't it?"

Nyght turned her head to look in the direction she had heard the voice come from. She saw a young woman standing off to her left about fifteen paces away. From what Nyght could tell, the woman looked very young; maybe only a few seasons older than herself.

She wore a red dress that went all the way to the floor covering her legs completely. The sleeves of the dress ended at the woman's wrist, but where they stopped, red leather gloves began.

The only part of the woman the dress did not cover was from her shoulders to the top of her chest. The dress caused the woman's bosom to make more of an appearance than a normal dress would allow.

When Nyght took her eyes off the woman's breast and looked up, she saw the woman's hair. She had it styled so that it was up off her neck and rested on the top of her head and was the same color as the dress.

The last thought Nyght could think to describe the woman she was staring at was that she was probably the most beautiful woman she had ever seen. It was the first time Nyght had ever thought about her own appearance. It was not that she was ashamed of how she looked. Even before Moon had changed her skin to white, Nyght never cared about her looks. When Moon gave her the gift to look as Moon did, she called herself beautiful as well. The woman walking toward her was not just beautiful by appearance, beauty was radiating from her. As if every bit of her would make a person stop and look at her, whether they wanted to or not, and very few would not want to.

The woman walked over to Nyght and stopped when they were a pace apart. "My, your skin is so beautiful," the woman said. Any other person would have returned the compliment to the woman, but Nyght remained silent. "I can see Master has chosen wisely." Nyght still remained quiet, so the woman continued, "I am Crimson," she said then tilted her head downward to take a look at her own clothing, then looked back at Nyght. "I figured I should let you know my name before you began calling me Scarlet because most women who dress in this color and have their hair the same go by that name."

"So why don't you?" Nyght asked.

The woman smiled, then gave her answer, "Because the name *Scarlet* is used by common whores..." she paused, made a devious smile then completed her sentence, "...and I am not common." Nyght knew the smile she had ended with meant that the woman might not be common, but it was clear she and whores had one aspect they shared. "And you are?"

Nyght was only fifteen and shorter than the woman standing before her, so she still had to look upward at her. "Nyght," the child said to answer the question.

"It is so nice to meet you Nyght," Crimson said

and extended her hand to shake. Usually, Nyght would not even accept the gesture of the greeting but since she did not want to offend anyone who was part of the Guild, she took hold of Crimson's hand and shook it once, then pulled her hand back. If she offended the woman, she did not show it in any manner. "If you follow me, I will escort you to your quarters," Crimson said and once again ended her sentence with the same smile she had been using ever since the two had met. Nyght saw that even the woman's smile was so beautiful any man would do anything just to get her to give them a glimpse of it.

Crimson turned away and started walking. Nyght walked a pace behind her guide. She looked around and saw that the area she was traveling through was very wide. There were a number of torches placed around the circular room to supply light and Nyght saw that the walls were made from some type of gray stone. There were different paintings on them, but since Crimson did not take her near any of them Nyght was unable to see what images they portrayed.

Crimson led the new arrival to a set of stairs and as they began to ascend, she started the conversation, "So Nyght, what do you think of the place so far?"

Nyght moved her head to take in the surroundings then answered the question, "It is too big to be situated in the building I entered."

Crimson stopped on the step she had reached then turned and looked at Nyght who was two steps below her, "When you exited the last door, you entered into another building. One that is far away from Sarzanac." She turned and once again began her climb up the stairs, "We are located in a group of mountains far, far to the north of the city you were in. Just to let you know, if you were to step outside of our little home, you would be dead in less than a day if you were not prepared to endure the freezing temperatures that are hazardous no matter what season the rest of the world may be in at the time." Crimson's statement did not bother Nyght. She may not be in Sarzanac, but she was in the Assassin's Guild, which was where she wanted to be.

Crimson did not say anything else until they reached the sixth floor. Nyght noticed that the stairs continued to higher levels but figured this was where her quarters would be.

Crimson walked down the hallway and came to two doors, only two. "The room on the left is mine. This one is yours," Crimson said and turned to open the door on the right side of the hallway.

Nyght stepped into the room and saw that it was nothing like what she thought it might be. The entire room was the same size as the distance of the hallway she had traveled to get to the room which was sixty full steps. Inside the room, there was another door off to the left, but since it was not open, she could not see what was behind it.

There was a desk across the way, and next to it, there were three bookcases, each having five shelves, and each one filled with books. Since Nyght did not know how to read, she did not think anything about the books. Over against the wall to the right was a bed. Of course, she had seen beds before but none that were as big as this one. It looked as if four adults would be able to sleep in it and still have space where they would not touch someone else lying in the bed.

Halfway between where Nyght was standing and the far wall with the bed, there was a fireplace. There were two chairs placed in front of it with their backs facing toward the wall behind Nyght. Between the two chairs, there was a small table; although, nothing was on it.

The only way Nyght could describe the room was that it was too big. She had always lived in places where she could cross it within four or five steps, but with this place, she would have to run if she wanted to cover the distance in the amount of time she normally dealt with in her small lodgings.

"Lovely, is it not?" Crimson said and Nyght turned her head to look over her left shoulder at the woman. "The lavatory is off to the left behind the door." With the look that appeared on Nyght's face, Crimson could tell the child did not know what she had been referring to. "Forgive me. You are probably unaware of the fine luxuries that come with being selected. Do not feel embarrassed. I myself did not know what a lavatory was when I first arrived. I to use to call it a relief shack."

Nyght was not embarrassed about not knowing what the woman was referring to. She did not know what one was, and to her, not knowing something was no reason to be embarrassed. If this woman had been when she arrived, then that was something she had to deal with. Nyght turned to look at the door to Crimson's left. She had never heard of a relief shack inside a building. Normally they were outside at the back of a house, but since it was not important to Nyght, she did not mention it to her escort.

"I will leave you to freshen up, while you wait," Crimson said and turned to leave.

"Wait for what?" Nyght asked just before Crimson had closed the door behind her.

"Why for Master Viper of course." Crimson gave Nyght one more smile then closed the door with her on the other side.

Nyght moved her head so that she could look at the room one more time. She did not like it, and she also decided, she did not like the smile Crimson always seemed to be giving her.

She walked further into the room and over to the chairs in front of the fireplace. She sat down in the one to the left of the table and waited, hoping that when Master Viper arrived, he would take her to a less luxurious room because this one was too much of everything.

Nyght did not know how long she had sat in the chair. There were no windows in the room so she could not see outside. "Moon, can you see me?" she asked, knowing that if Moon could, it would mean Moon was in the sky and it was night.

"No child, I cannot."

It was still day but that did not give her every-thing she needed to know. "Moon, can you see Sarzanac?"

"No child, I cannot."

Now she knew that she was at least on the same side of the world as the city she was in. Crimson had told her that the Guild was far, far to the north, so Nyght knew that if something were to happen, she would have to head south to get back to Sarzanac. Not that she was planning to leave any time soon, but she felt it would not hurt to be prepared.

She was sitting in the chair not doing anything when she heard a knock on the door. She stood and walked over to it. Before she reached it, she thought once again that the room was too big. When she opened the door, she saw the second person she had seen since her arrival.

She had noticed how Crimson stood about a head taller than she did. The woman standing out in the hallway stood about a head taller than Crimson. Nyght took two steps back into the room to allow the woman to enter. Once inside, the woman closed the door behind her and the two exchanged looks, inspecting each other.

When Nyght saw Crimson, she could not help but think of how beautiful the woman was. Now, seeing this woman standing two paces in front of her, Crimson was nothing but ordinary. She remembered what Crimson had said about waiting for Master Viper. From what she was seeing, Nyght did not think that the woman in the room with her had anything in common with any type of viper.

Not only was the woman tall, but because the dress she wore was sleeveless, Nyght noticed the woman's arms and how well-toned they were. Most women with the height of the one in front of her were thin and gangly. That was not so with the woman standing before her.

Unlike Crimson, the woman wore her hair down; it was the color of brown but the shine that came from it made it look like silk. She had the hair on her left side flowing behind her, but the hair on the right side of her head fell in front of her across her shoulder and down across her ample breast. The dress Crimson wore caused her breasts to rise higher on her than if she did not have the dress on. This woman needed no dress to show that her cleavage was something any man would die for, just to rest his head on while they slept together. Like the dress Crimson wore, the dress this woman wore left her shoulders bare, but the top of the dress started farther down her chest than the one Crimson wore, which caused this woman's bosom to protrude more out of the dress than in it.

Yes, Crimson was very beautiful, but this woman, the one standing before her, did not only have beauty, nor did it just radiate from her. This woman was the word "beauty" in living flesh.

The woman took another step toward Nyght, and to her own surprise, she took a step backward away from the woman. The woman then smiled, and if she meant to use it to calm Nyght, she failed. It was the smile that finally made Nyght realize that this woman might have more in common with a true viper than what Nyght had thought a moment ago. "Your petitioner did not mention the color of your skin." The woman then closed the distance between them and since Nyght did not move from where she was, the woman raised her right hand and with the back of her fingers, ran them down the side of Nyght's face. "It is so beautiful," the woman said then removed her hand.

Before either of them could say another word, there was a knock on the door, and then it opened. Crimson walked in with something in her hands. "The refreshment you requested Master," she said and waited for her next instructions.

"Place it on the table by the fireplace, my dear," Master Viper told the young woman, but all the while kept her eyes on Nyght. Crimson did as commanded, then walked back to the door and out, closing it behind her. "Come, let us take a seat by the fireplace." The woman turned and walked to where she had just mentioned. Nyght was glad the woman had gone first because she did not want to have this woman at her back.

Master Viper took the seat to the right and Nyght returned to the chair she had been using before the woman knocked on the door. As soon as Nyght took her seat, the woman spoke, "This is Richwood wine," the woman said and gestured her hand toward the glass container on the table along with an empty glass. Nyght noticed that there was only one glass sitting next to the bottle. "Every night, before you retire to bed, you will need to drink a glass of the wine." Before Nyght could say that she had never drunk wine before, the woman continued, "It will not cause you to feel intoxicated in any way, but even if you wish to drink more than one glass, you must not. Is that understood?"

Nyght was a child of few words and when she was growing up in the first town she lived in, she never replied to questions an adult would ask her. She had a feeling that this woman would not appreciate "no reply" at all, but at the same time, she was going to make sure the woman realized that she was not going to be forthcoming with a lot of words, so she nodded her head.

"Crimson will begin your training tomorrow. She was my pupil before you, and the last of her training will consist of preparing you for what I will be teaching you. Crimson will have a month to prepare you; then I will release her to the status of True Assassin. Afterward, you will have very little contact with others until your training with me has come to an end, which will be five seasons from now. Then, you will remain for one moon-cycle with me, training the next girl I choose." Even though she did not ask a question, Nyght nodded her head to let the woman know she understood what she had said. "You are a child of few words," Master Viper said then smiled, "I will be able to teach you to use that to your advantage." Nyght was not sure what she meant, but she had a feeling that whatever the woman was referring to was not something she would like.

"Now, please stand and remove your cloak so that I can see what I have to work with."

Nyght was not sure what the woman was talking about, but she did as the woman had told her to do. She stood and faced Master Viper then took off her cloak. Even doing so, all the while, she did not let go of her weapons.

"I see that you have chosen the fighting daggers as your weapons of choice." The woman looked at the blades and Nyght was not comfortable with the way she was eyeing them. "They are quite beautiful but when I am done with your training, you will not need them."

For the first time since the woman stepped into the room, Nyght spoke, "Then how will I kill the ones I am supposed to?"

Master Viper stood and moved two steps to put her in front of Nyght. "My dear, with what I am going to show you, you will bring death to a man and even a woman with just a look." Then the woman raised her arm, reached out in front of her, and ran her hand through Nyght's hair. "The color of your hair is so beautiful and with your skin, you will be my most precious achievement." Nyght allowed the woman to continue to run her fingers through her hair. All the while, they both stared into each other's eyes.

Master Viper could not stop thinking about how she would enjoy training this child. She had chosen wisely and spent many marks debating with the other Masters as to why she should be the one to take the girl as her pupil. Three other Masters wanted the opportunity to train the girl Dodge had told them about. In the end, those three conceded to Master Viper. Of course, they only did so after they spent a night in her bed. Each of them was willing to give up any interest in the child for one night with the woman who could make a man kill his own mother, just by smiling at them.

While Master Viper had her own thoughts, Nyght did as well. She did not like the way the woman touched her which she had now done so twice. First, on the side of her face, and now, she was stroking her hair.

Just before Nyght was about to use one of her daggers, the woman stopped what she was doing and walked away heading back toward the door. "The kitchen is on the first level. You will be responsible for preparing your own meals. There are breads and other foods that do not require any cooking skills, though part of your training will consist of preparing a proper meal. For one way to a man is through his stomach." The woman reached the door, opened it, and then turned to look at Nyght, "Of course, the other way in which I will be educating you is a lot more fun." The woman smiled at Nyght, "Goodnight my dear Nyght, and remember to drink one glass of the Richwood wine, only one." Master Viper closed the door behind her.

Nyght kept her eyes on the door for a few breaths longer to make sure the woman would not be returning. She then turned and picked up the container of Richwood wine and removed the glass stopper. Nyght had never tasted or even smelled wine before, but when she brought the bottle up to her nose and took in its aroma, something in her told her that whatever was in the dark red liquid was not something she wanted inside her. She placed the stopper back in the bottle then placed it back on the tray and turned back to look at the door.

She had not waited all those seasons to enter the Assassin's Guild just to end up in the hands of Master Viper and subjected to her touching. The feeling she felt was as if she was back in that small closet and was watching the girl and that man. The same memory came to her when she had made it to the landing in front of the Assassin's Guild. She did not like the feeling then and she does not like it now.

Nyght thought about the two times Master Viper had touched her but only long enough to conclude: there would not be a third.

TWO

Nyght sat back down in her chair. She thought about how she had waited so long to enter the Assassin's Guild, and now that she was there, she saw it was not what she thought it would be. Something awakened in her all those seasons ago when the boy had said the words, "Assassin's Guild." She did not know why but she knew it was what she was meant to be. She did not have a problem with taking someone's life. She had done so before, but with the way Master Viper had spoken, she felt that if the woman were to teach her, it would be herself who died.

Nyght knew she had to do something. She would not let the woman teach her and she definitely would not let the woman ever put her hands on her again. Nyght had waited so long for this and now she felt as if she would not be able to train at the Guild. She was going to have to find a way to leave. If there was one. She thought about going back down to the first level to see if she could re-enter the door that brought her to the Guild. Crimson said that when she stepped through, it brought her to the true Guild. Nyght could only hope that by going back through, she would return to Sarzanac and away from her dream.

"No!" she thought to herself, *"I have waited too long for this, and I will not let some woman make me into something she wants. I am in control of my life, and I will not surrender that control to anyone."*

Nyght remembered that there were at least six other Masters at the Guild. They had chosen the other children and it was Master Viper who chose her. It did not take long for Nyght to realize that Master Viper was the obstacle standing in her way of becoming what she wanted to be.

Nyght was still sitting in the chair, but she raised her daggers out of her lap and brought them up to look at them. She quickly determined that she would not be able to use them to solve the problem. The reason was because if she did, someone might be able to tell that her weapons ended the woman's life and the others who ran the Guild might force her to leave or they might even do something worse. If she were going to leave the Guild completely then her daggers might be an option, but since her goal was to stay but only after removing that woman, then she would have to find a way to solve her problem without her daggers.

She stood up and looked around the room. As she took in everything present, nothing came to her. When she saw the door to the room Crimson had told her about, she decided to inspect it to see if there was something in there to help her out of the situation.

When she opened the door, she saw that the room was not as big as the outer one. She stepped inside and looked at what was around. Over to the right was a metal bin that rose off the floor to about the height of her knees. It also had a wooden cover on it. She walked over to it and when she looked down, she saw that in the center of the piece of wood was a hole. Inside the metal bin, there was water. Nyght raised her eyes and saw that behind the bin, hanging away from the wall at about eye level was a chain. It had a wooden handle attached to the end of it. She grabbed hold of the handle and pulled. There was a rushing noise from inside the metal bin, and when she heard it, she looked down and saw that the bottom of the bin had opened up and all the water rushed out. She did not know where the water went, but once she let go of the wooden handle, the bottom of the bin closed back up and water flowed back into the bin, from a metal pipe located inside. Nyght decided that this was what an inside relief shack was.

Nyght was a little impressed with what she had seen but knew it was not going to help her solve her problem. She did keep in mind that if it came down to it, she might be able to use the opening at the bottom of the bin to get out of that place. She might not know where it leads, but it was an option.

She turned her head and looked over to her left

noticing a metal tub against the wall and walked over to it. She had seen something like this before in the first place she lived. People would use it to bathe. They would heat water over a fire and fill the container with the heated water, then wash themselves. There had only been one in the entire building where she first lived and very few people ever used it. From what she understood, it took too much time to heat enough water to fill the container so that a grown person could use it.

She remembered the woman she used to live with used a very small tub to give her a bath the morning the man came and took her.

Nyght had not thought about that moment for a very long time. So long, that she could not clearly remember what the woman or the man fully looked like. She did remember that the man had deep eyes.

The tub in front of her was metal and grayish but it had different designs on it that looked like flowers and birds to make it fancy; not something anyone would normally have in their home, only someone who cared about bathing on a regular basis. She also thought that it would be too much trouble to fill the tub with water. It would take many buckets, and since she did not see any other rooms on this floor, the water had to come from somewhere else.

She looked at the end of the tub that was against the wall. Hanging over the edge of it, there were two pipes coming out of the wall with the ends angled down and into the tub. Nyght moved closer and saw in the middle of each of the pipes was a piece of metal sticking up out of it with the end of the metal pieces stretching out to the front and back of the pipe. That part of the metal was not as wide as her middle finger, but it looked as if a person could grab a hold of the metal piece going into the pipe.

Nyght used her right hand to grab hold of the piece of raised metal coming out of the pipe on the right. She tried to move it back and forth, but it did not budge. She then pulled up on the metal piece, and when she did, water started flowing out of the pipe and into the tub. She looked into the tub and saw that the water was exiting out of a small hole at the bottom but also saw a cork floating near the hole. Nyght figured that if she were to place the piece of cork in the hole, it would cause the water to fill the tub. She now knew how the water got into the tub.

As she was watching the water go down the hole, she noticed steam from the water. She moved her hand to feel the water coming out of the pipe and when she touched it, she felt that it was hot. Hot enough to where she quickly pulled her hand away.

She let the water run for a couple of breaths more, then reached over and pushed the piece of metal back into the pipe causing the water to stop flowing. She then reached over and pulled the piece of metal attached to the left pipe. Water started flowing out of the pipe and Nyght slowly stuck her hand into the stream of water and felt that it was very cold. While the water continued to flow, she once again pulled on the metal piece on the right pipe and the water started flowing from it as well.

As both streams of water went into the tub, it gathered at the bottom and exited into the hole. Nyght bent over the edge of the tub and touched the water that had not exited yet. The water was not too cold or too hot, it was just right.

Now that her experiment was over, Nyght pushed back down on both metal pieces in the pipes and the water stopped flowing. What was in the tub went into the hole at the bottom.

Nyght then looked at the wall on the other side of the room and saw a table and a long-cushioned bench. There were some items on the table, so she moved over to inspect them.

She saw a lot of bottles and boxes. There were also some brushes and combs. She picked up one of the bottles and pulled out the small glass stopper. As soon as it was free of the bottle, Nyght could smell the strong scent coming out. She knew the contents inside were what women would put on to make them smell good. The women in the brothel, where she had first lived, did not use items like this because it cost a lot of coin, which was something they did not have to spend on the scents. When she was on her own and came to the first city, many shops sold these items. Since Nyght never had any interest in making herself smell different, she replaced the bottle back on the table.

She then looked up and saw a reflection of herself. She had seen mirrors before but only in shops. In the brothel where she first lived, the women would make themselves as presentable as they could without one. She had heard that in brothels in other cities, every woman had a mirror in her own room. Now, Nyght was looking at herself in one.

She finally saw what her face looked like since Moon had made her skin the color of Moon. She knew that her body, legs, and arms were pale white, but she never had the opportunity to see her face. Now that she could, she saw just how black her hair and eyes were, compared to her skin. She never thought about how she looked, but now, looking in the mirror, she thought that she did look beautiful. Maybe others would think she was a freak, thinking of the word the boy had used to describe her, but he was dead, and she was not. Since she did not care what others thought of her appearance, then it did not matter.

As she continued to look at her image, she once again focused on the way her face appeared in her reflection. She noticed that the color of her skin brought out the darkness of her eyes. Others have looked into her eyes, and they would have said that her eyes were deep. Others would have seen something else. To Nyght, her eyes did not reveal anything to her. Maybe it is because a reflection has no soul.

She remembered that both Crimson and Master Viper liked the way she looked. Not that she cared, but if two women as beautiful as they were thought she was also beautiful, then she must be.

She took her eyes off the mirror and looked around the room. That is when it came to Nyght on how to deal with Master Viper, and when she put her focus back on the mirror, she saw the smile her reflection was making.

She could not use the daggers Moon had given her. Others might be able to tell that it was those weapons she used to end the woman's life.

Nyght bent down and pulled up the right leg of her trousers revealing the top of her boot as well as the handle to the knife she had ever since she was on her own. Dodge told her that she had to acquire a different weapon other than the one she had. He never said she had to get rid of the weapon, so she tucked it inside the top of her boot and brought it with her into the Guild.

She could use it to kill Master Viper. She then turned around and walked back over to the relief bin. She stretched out her hand and pulled on the handle attached to the chain. Once again, the bottom of the bin opened, and the water rushed out. Nyght knew that after she used the knife on the woman, she could place the knife in the bin and let it fall into the hole at the bottom.

She let go of the handle and looked at the knife in her right hand. It had been with her ever since the day she left that town. A town that she did not even remember the name of. That night she had also taken the waterskin and the bag where she kept food and other items. She had left them back in Sarzanac. The knife was the only thing she had left. She looked from the knife to the bottom of the metal bin, then back to the knife. A part of her, a big part of her, did not want to lose the item, but a bigger part of her knew that she was going to have to do what she was planning if she wanted to stay at the Guild and not have to be with that woman. She did not say it, but in her mind, she spoke to her knife, *"I'm sorry."* She had never used those two words before.

Nyght turned around to look back at the room and to take her mind off her knife. She took in the table and bench on the other side of the room then looked toward the tub. She now came up with another part of the plan. "Moon?"

"Yes, child," Moon thought to Nyght.

"Can you see me yet?"

"Not yet."

"Can you let me know when you can?"

"Yes."

Nyght said one last thing, "Thank you, Father."

Nyght went over to the table. She ignored the bottles because even with what she had planned, she refused to use the scents. She picked up a comb and started running it through her hair. Since she normally would only use her hands to work her hair, with the teeth of the comb so close, she had to use enough force to get it through the tangles and knots that had built up over the seasons it had grown. For the first time in her life, Nyght felt real pain. Since Master Viper was fond of her hair, she would make sure that when she saw the Master again her hair would look even better.

Nyght worked on her hair for a while and by the time she had finished combing and brushing it, Moon had told her that Moon could see her. She also had a very big pile of her own hair which she had pulled out with the comb. Nyght did not worry about what she had done. Since her hair was so thick, the small amount was nothing and the result was that her hair never looked better. Just with brushing and combing, it brought a gloss to it which made it shine. Just like Master Viper's.

Nyght asked Moon to let her know when Moon was at the midpoint in the sky. When the time came, Moon did, and Nyght began the next part of her plan.

She filled the tub with water and then for the first time since she left the first town where she lived, Nyght took a real bath. She had bathed herself in rivers, streams, and lakes, and when she was in Sarzanac, she always made sure she had enough water in her bag to wash up at least once a week. When she came into the time of her womanhood, she did as the woman she had first lived with taught her and made sure she kept clean during her cycle.

When she submerged herself in the water of the metal tub, she could not help but feel that a bath was something she enjoyed. She used a small cloth to wash herself and even used the scented animal lard. After she finished, she rested a moment in the warm water. It felt so comfortable she did not realize that she had dozed off until her head went under the water causing her to swallow some. She immediately popped back above the water and when she had cleared her eyes, nose, and mouth, she spoke to Moon, "Moon, can you still see me?"

"*Yes, child*," Moon replied.

Nyght thought she had fallen asleep for a longer period of time than she really had, and if so, she might not be able to continue with her plan. She wanted to do what she needed to while it was still night, and everyone was asleep. Since Moon had told her that Moon could still see her, she knew she had not dozed off for too long.

She climbed out of the tub and removed the cork to allow the water to drain. She noticed that as it was leaving, it looked a lot darker than it did when she had filled the tub. The existing water was not black, but not far from it.

What Nyght did not know was that no matter how filthy she might become, her skin would always be the color of Moon.

She used the bigger cloth to remove the bit of water still on her. When she was dry, she put her own clothes back on. She realized they were probably just as dirty as she was. To cover up the smell of her clothes, which she could definitely notice now that she was clean, she could have used some of the scents on the table but decided she preferred the scent of her clothes. She then ran a comb through her hair again to make sure it was looking its best.

Before she left the lavatory, she picked up her daggers which she had placed in the tub with her while she bathed. She then picked up her cloak and went into the other room.

She was still trying to decide if she was going to go through with the next part of her plan. She laid her cloak across one of the chairs because she was not going to need it. As for her daggers, she had not made up her mind about what she wanted to do with them.

She thought it would be best if she appeared defenseless. She was just as hesitant about leaving them behind as she was about getting rid of her knife after all of this was over. She had not had them as long as the knife, but she still did not want to be apart from Moon's gift. So much, she had even bathed with them.

She finally decided to leave them behind. She remembered when she had taken her knife from under the man's mattress. She walked over to the bed in the room and was going to place them under the top mattress but stopped before she did. She thought about the fact that the man had hidden his weapons in the same place she was planning to which might mean someone else might think the same thing.

She went to the other side of the room to where the bookcases were. She knelt down on the floor, pulled out enough of the books on the lowest level, placed Umbra at the back of the bookcase, and then replaced the books. She then moved over to the bookcase to her right and did the same thing, only leaving behind Full.

As she stood, she started to wonder if it would be best to take the blades. She could use Umbra to hide in shadow, and even though she had never tried to use it, she thought it might be for the best.

Reluctantly, she decided to leave the weapons behind. They might come in handy, but Nyght knew that like the test with the arrow, door, and the gap in the floor, the daggers would not help her. Besides, she still had her knife tucked into the top of her boot. At that thought, she felt an ache inside her when she realized that it would be the last time she would use the item.

She checked with Moon one more time, "Father, can you see me?"

"*Yes, my daughter. I can still see you.*"

With that answer, Nyght went over to the door of her room, opened it, and exited into the hallway. She closed the door behind her making sure she did not make a sound.

She looked across the hall at the door to Crimson's room. She did not go near it to see if she could hear the woman inside; she just hoped she would be.

Nyght walked down the hall and when she came to the stairs, she had to decide on which way to go.

She looked to her left where the stairs would take her to the lower floors. She then turned and looked to her right where the stairs rose to the levels above. Since she was on the sixth level, she decided she needed to go up. That would be where she would find Master Viper. Nyght herself always sought out the highest place in the buildings where she stayed so she figured Master Viper would as well. Another reason Nyght chose the direction was because she could smell the scent Master Viper had been wearing when she came to see her. That was another reason Nyght decided that she would never wear something that would allow someone to track her.

Nyght climbed the stairs and went all the way to the tenth floor which also happened to be the floor where the stairs ended. Nyght looked upward and saw the open area off the stairs continued upward to the ceiling which she still could not see.

Nyght walked down the hall and came to the only door on the level so she figured that was where Master Viper must be.

Nyght knocked on the door and did so in a way to make sure that whoever was in the room would hear it, but at the same time, it sounded weak as if the person knocking might be afraid of something. Even though Nyght was not afraid of being in front of the room, she wanted Master Viper to wonder why someone would be at her door in the middle of the night.

Nyght had to knock one more time before she

heard someone moving toward it. She was not sure if the person in the room had not heard the knock the first time or if it took them two knocks to cross the distance of the room.

When the door opened, Nyght saw Master Viper standing in front of her. The Master had looked beautiful when Nyght saw her earlier, and even at this time of night, she looked no less exquisite. "What are you doing here?" Master Viper said and Nyght could tell that she was not happy to be seeing the child at her door. "You are not to come to my room unless I summon you."

Nyght did not panic at the woman's reaction to her being there. She had a plan, but she also knew she might have to adjust accordingly if the situation called for it. "Forgive me, I did not know," Nyght said, while at the same time looking up at the woman standing in front of her and making sure she smiled. "I could not sleep and had some questions."

The two stood there for only a few breaths and when Nyght thought the woman would send her away, she lifted her right hand and brushed back her hair bringing attention to it. The woman had said she had beautiful hair, so Nyght was using it just like a knife or a dagger, as a weapon.

"Come in, child, and we can talk for a few moments," Master Viper said and stepped aside to allow Nyght to enter, which she did. Once she was in the room and heard the door close behind her, Nyght turned around to face the Master.

When she put her eyes on the woman again, she noticed what she was wearing. When she saw her before, Master Viper's dress left something to the imagination. With the clothing she had on now, there was no need for anyone to imagine. Nyght could see through the article of clothing the woman was wearing. It was black but with her skin being a lighter color, it showed every bit of the woman's body a dress was supposed to conceal. As Nyght had thought, the woman did not need a dress like the one Crimson wore to lift up her breast to entice a man.

Nyght realized that the woman was looking at her so when she lifted her eyes upward, she smiled. The same way she remembered the women who worked in the place where she first lived smiled at men. They seemed to like it, and apparently so did Master Viper, because she returned the smile exactly the same way.

Nyght turned around to make sure she did not hold her smile too long; it might cause Master Viper to suspect her. When she did, Nyght saw something that made her make the second adjustment to her plan. She quickly turned away from what she saw and focused on something else, "You have a fire going," she said with her back to Master Viper.

"Why don't we take a seat in front of it and warm you up a bit," Master Viper said. Nyght heard the woman start walking toward her. She did not want to be within arm's reach of the woman, so she made her way over to the two cushioned, high-back chairs and sat in the one on the left. She chose that one because she wanted to be in view of what she had taken notice of a moment ago. Master Viper sat in the remaining chair and Nyght was thankful for the space between them so that the woman would not be able to touch her.

When Master Viper sat down, she crossed her right leg over her left knee, and with the split running down the side of the outfit she was wearing, it revealed her entire leg from her thigh to her foot, and Nyght was sure she had intended for it to be that way. "Now, what has brought you to my door at such a late mark?"

Nyght noticed that the woman was talking in the same manner she had earlier. She pronounced her words so that every syllable that passed across her lips would entice whoever might hear them. Nyght thought that if the woman sitting across from her were to talk about cattle, she could still entice a man by how she spoke to the point that he would do whatever the woman asked of him.

Nyght looked down at the floor in front of her to keep her eyes off the woman. She wanted Master Viper to think that she was afraid of even being in the same room with her. "I am not sure if I understand why I am here."

"What do you mean child?" Master Viper asked, with a slight, but alluring laughter.

"I wanted to join the Guild so that I could be an

assassin," Nyght adjusted her posture so that she was looking directly at the woman before she continued, "So I could learn to kill." Nyght held her gaze for two breaths then returned her eyes to the floor. "I do not think I can be like Crimson." Nyght raised her head again to look at Master Viper, "Or you." She then placed her eyes back on the floor.

"My child, do you think Crimson was any different than what you are now when she first arrived?" Nyght looked back at Master Viper but did not answer. "Crimson came to me with more dirt on her than you have probably ever seen in your life. And her breath reeked of the foulest of spirits." Nyght did not think what the woman had said was funny, but she smiled anyway to show Master Viper that she was beginning to relax, even though she was before she left her room.

"But you said I would not need my daggers to kill and that is what I thought I would be trained on."

Master Viper sat back in her chair, placed her hands across her midsection, then began speaking. "Almost anyone can be made into an assassin. All they need is the will to take another's life and the intelligence not to be caught." Master Viper then leaned forward. She did not leave the chair, but she was now closer to Nyght. "For most contracts, an assassin takes on, they kill only one person. With what I will teach you, you will be able to eliminate entire regimes. It is easy to kill a king or any other monarch, but when you leave the Guild, you will know how to bend them to your will, and they will beg you to do so. You will be able to bring a young boy out of the worst part of a city, make him into whatever ruling figure we choose to make him, and when we are done, you will cast him aside, and not once will he fault you for it."

Master Viper stood and walked over to stand in front of the fire, with her back to Nyght. "Will that require me to go to their bed?" Nyght asked. She waited for the answer to her question. Depending on how Master Viper responded, Nyght would decide if she needed to follow through with the rest of her plan.

Master Viper turned around and faced Nyght, "My dear child, it is in a man's...or woman's bed, where most of life's decisions are made. A person will lie in bed awake or even while they are sleeping and contemplate what the best way is to handle a certain situation. And you my dear will lie next to them and whisper into their dreams." Nyght now had her answer, and she had no doubt that Master Viper was not the one to teach her how to be an assassin.

The woman took two steps forward so Nyght turned her head to the right to look at what she had noticed when she was over by the door. "You have a window," Nyght said, and stood to move away from the woman coming toward her. She went to stand in front of it. When she reached it, even though it was night, she could see the snow falling in the sky. She knew that it was not the season for it, so she reasoned that being so high in the mountains it snowed all the time.

Nyght placed her right hand on the glass. Surprisingly, she could not feel the coldness of the outside. She moved her hand to the latch that held the two windows in place, though to the woman behind her, it appeared that she was only inspecting the window. With the slightest movement of her finger, she pushed on the latch which kept the windows secured. She then gently pressed on the glass and saw that the windows were now able to move. She did not allow them to swing open, she kept them only slightly ajar; just enough so they did not even appear that they had been adjusted. What pleased her even more was that to work them they swung outward.

"Our wizards have placed a spell on the windows to keep the cold out," Master Viper said from across the room.

Nyght turned her head to look at her. She started to wonder just what else the spell did. If it keeps the cold out, does it also keep anything else inside? What if there was a spell on the window that made it impossible for something to exit through it? Nyght forced herself to stop thinking about what might be. She decided to continue with her plan and if the situation called for her to make a change, then she would.

"Would you like to know how I chose to go

by the name Viper?" the woman asked, and even though Nyght was there to make sure the woman would not be the one to teach her, she supposed it might be an interesting story, so she nodded to the woman. As she started walking toward Nyght, and the window, she began her story. "There is a species of viper which lives in the lands to the south. Very far, far to the south, across the great water. When it was first discovered centuries ago, they captured some to breed them. No one knows if they did it to keep them as pets or for food but that is not important. What is, is that they would put pairs together: one male and one female. The individuals breeding them would discover that the male always died before the female, but in a short amount of time after the male's death, the female would lay a cluster of eggs. One of the breeders decided to watch the vipers constantly to see why the male would die first. It did not take long for them to find out." The woman stopped telling the story.

"What caused the male to die?" Nyght asked in an inquisitive voice and saw that Master Viper had paused just so that she would ask the question.

"The female killed it," Master Viper said and smiled when she finished. She paused for just a breath then continued. "It has been known for quite some time that there are a number of insects that when a pair has finished mating, the female kills the male. She does this so that she can receive nourishment to bring her offspring to life. It is a sacrifice the male has to make for his bloodline to survive." Master Viper had been moving closer to Nyght and was now standing not a pace away from her. "As for the Ama Viper, named after the one who discovered it, the female of the species does not kill her mate so that she can feed on its body to give her nourishment; no, she kills it because she can. She uses the male for what she needs it for, and once done, she has no more use for it so ends its life by puncturing its body with her fangs, injecting her venom into it. It was also discovered that even though the male of the species has venom as well, it has no effect on the female of the species."

After hearing the explanation Nyght realized what the picture drawn on the piece of parchment placed in the end of the arrow had meant as well as the emblem on the door she entered the Guild through. Two vipers, one with the other in its mouth. Nyght knew which one represented the woman in the room with her.

Master Viper took a step to close the distance between her and Nyght. As she did, Nyght stepped to her left and turned her body so that the window was to her right. Master Viper positioned herself so that she was in front of Nyght, and the window was to her left.

"That is why you go by the name Viper; because you kill your mates?" Nyght asked.

Master Viper smiled at the simplistic way Nyght spoke the moral of the story. "Like the female

Ama Viper, I kill that for which I have no more use. Whether it is a man, two men, a woman, or an entire country."

It was the way she said the statement that made Nyght begin to rethink about going through with her plan. If she failed, the woman in front of her would no doubt end her life. Then Nyght thought that if she did not go through with it and accept the way Master Viper would train her, she would suffer something worse than death. She wanted to be an assassin from the moment she heard the word, but she would not kill in the way the woman wanted her to. Nyght wanted to be an assassin, not a whore.

Nyght took one step to her left, then turned to face the woman, who also positioned herself to face Nyght. "Do you think I will be able to be like Crimson, like you?"

Master Viper smiled knowing the answer, "My dear child, I will make sure you become exactly as I am."

Nyght did not like the answer but smiled, nonetheless. She then lifted her left hand and ran it through her long black hair, "I combed my hair for you," she said and then smiled at the woman as the woman in the brothels had to their customers.

"It is very pretty," Master Viper said with the same type of smile.

"Would you like to run your fingers through it?" Nyght asked.

Master Viper did not say anything. She just

raised her right hand letting Nyght know that she would love to take her up on her offer.

Nyght took a step closer to the extended hand of Master Viper, but before she allowed her to touch her hair, Nyght quickly moved forward, placing her own hands on the woman's midsection, and pushed. She used enough strength to force the woman to take one step backward, and when she reached the window, she continued to push, causing Master Viper to fall through the opening and to her death.

Nyght looked out the window but the distance to the ground below was too great for her to see if the woman had come to the end of her life. She could not see her, but she knew who could. "Father, is she dead?"

"*Yes, my daughter, she is dead*," Moon thought to Nyght. Moon had watched the entire scene from beginning to end and Moon was very pleased with the outcome.

Nyght believed Moon because she had no reason to doubt Moon. She quickly left the room, traveled back to the level her room was on, and entered it. Before she climbed into bed for the night, she retrieved her daggers from the bookcases. She did take off her clothes before she got under the covers, but she kept the daggers with her and placed them at her sides while lying on her back.

She did not know what was going to happen when the morning came. She still might have to learn from some other woman like Master Viper. If that happened, she would have to figure out what she was going to do. She also thought that the other Masters might realize that she was the one who had ended Master Viper's life and if so, she was sure she would not survive long. Then again, she might learn from a Master who will teach her how to be a true assassin.

For Nyght, at the moment, it did not matter. She had removed the one obstacle she knew about which was in the way of what she wanted. All the other things she would deal with when and if they came upon her.

For now, she would not have to have that woman ever touch her again, and what was best of all, she still had her knife which she placed under her pillow before she laid her head down, to get some sleep. Sleep, which came quite easily to a girl of fifteen seasons who had just killed a Master of the Assassin's Guild.

THREE

High-Master Wraith quickly sat up in his bed. He had been asleep, but when his next breath had not entered his body, he woke and brought himself to an upright position gasping to send air into his lungs. This was not the first time this had happened.

Once he was breathing normally, he swung his legs to his right over the side of the bed. He extended his right hand out to grab the small tumbler which held a swallow of his tonic. He drank it down completely and even though the taste made him want to spit it out, he did not. The tonic would make the pain he was feeling throughout his body end at least for the moment. That is until another of the spasms he suffers from while sleeping comes upon him. Though not this night, for with the way the incident made him feel, he would not be able to return to sleep.

He looked to his left and saw the time-marker sitting on its stand. The top piece was a wooden rod four handbreadths wide. Another rod was located at the bottom about three handbreadths from the first one. Stretched between the two were fifteen wires and on each of those was a wooden bead. The beads on the first three wires were at the bottom and the bead on the fourth wire was over halfway down. It told the High-Master that it was almost the fourth mark of the new day. He had not planned on rising so early but he had no control over the spasms that came to him in his sleep so he could not do anything about being awake.

He would have been up in a little over two more full marks, but he could have used all the sleep he could get since the times between spasms had gone from a moon-cycle to a moon-mark. He also remembered that there had been a point in his life when the interval between the spasms was a full season. Yes, they were coming closer together, and he knew what it meant.

High-Master Wraith rose out of his bed. Since he would not be going back to sleep, he decided he would review what he would be discussing in the morning meeting he would be attending at the eighth mark just like every day.

High-Master Wraith, along with the other two High-Masters of the Assassin's Guild, met with the seven Masters twice a day, at the eighth mark and twelve marks later at the twentieth mark. The first meeting was to discuss what was on the agenda for the day and the second was to discuss anything that had risen during the day between the two meetings. In between them, the Masters were responsible for the training of their pupils while it was the High-Masters' job to make sure the Guild ran efficiently.

They were the ones who made sure every member of the Guild was doing their part. That is from the people responsible for purchasing supplies to the cooks who prepared the meals for all the members; with the exception of the pupils, who were responsible for fixing their own meals. Since the Guild had the Masters, the High-Masters, the staff, and of course, the many assassins currently residing at the Guild, they all needed to be fed.

Another task the High-Masters were responsible for was to assign the assassins their contracts; the people that would become their next target. The High-Masters would base their decisions on a number of factors. If the person the contract was for was of royalty, the assassin would need to be able to get past more security than a person with lesser standing. If the person who placed the contract wanted the person to suffer in a certain way, then that would call for a different type of assassin to handle the contract. There were a couple of other factors but the final one to determine who the contract would go to was how much the person wanted to pay the Guild to put an end to someone's life. Of course, there was always a bare minimum of what a person would have to pay, but as the price increased, so did the expertise as to the handling of the contract, the higher the price, the better the service. Even the cheapest person, paying the lowest cost, had the same guarantee as all other customers who called on the Assassin's Guild; a contract taken, is a contract fulfilled.

High-Master Wraith rose from his bed, and after the dizziness from the spasm and the nausea of the tonic lessened, he walked over to his desk on the other side of the room. Only stopping at the fireplace to stir up the cinders to raise the fire in the hearth to raise the temperature in the room, and hopefully, the temperature in his bones and soul.

He sat in the chair and picked up the first piece of parchment lying on the stack in front of him. He had organized them before he went to bed so that he would be able to look at them when he rose closer to the sixth mark of the day, but since he was awake, he would get an early start.

The first document was about the eggs the farm had raised over the last full cycle of the moon. The figures showed the number of eggs and the size of the yokes produced by the hens that laid them as well as which city, town, or village held the feed the chickens fed from.

All of this was code of course, but having been part of the Guild since he was fifteen, and a High-Master since the age of seventy, High-Master Wraith understood what every word, number, and symbol meant without even thinking about translating the code. Any documents the Guild dealt with were in code, and only the Masters, High-Masters, and the ones who wrote the documents knew the code. The average assassin did not learn the code unless they chose to become a Master or took on one of the duties required to run the facility.

It had been that way since the beginning of the Guild. The original founders developed the code, and even though no one knows how long it has been in existence, the Guild uses the code to this day. Of course, every few seasons, someone would suggest the code was no longer needed and outdated and the Guild should just write everything in the standard language, but the High-Masters politely declined the suggestion. Not only because the code has always been in use, but also because everyone was so used to reading and understanding the intricate code, they figured it would be more trouble and harder to understand a document if they eliminated it. It was always a person who had just taken over a new position in the Guild to suggest the change, but after a full season of using the code, they felt the same as everyone else. The code has always been around, and it always will be.

There was only one piece of information never written in code. That was the name and last known location of the person who was to become the next target of an assassin. When the Guild representative and the buyer of a contract finalized the details, the High-Masters receive the information. Then they would write it down on a piece of parchment and meet with the assassin they felt would be best suited for the assignment. All three High-Masters would sit behind a table and the assassin would come before them. Then one of the High-Masters would slide the piece of parchment across the table to the assassin. They would see the name, the last location of the target, and one more piece of information, which was how much the full contract was for, even though the assassin would only receive a portion of that amount. The Guild did have expenses, and even though it was in the business of killing, it was still a business.

If the assassin did not want to undertake the contract, which they had the right to decline, they would slide the parchment back to the High-Masters, turn, and leave the room. The High-Masters would take no offense to the assassin refusing the contract. They were the ones taking the risk, and if the assassin decided it was not worth the price they would be receiving, then they would pass, and the High-Masters would move to the next person they would decide on. If the assassin did accept the contract, they would pick up the piece of parchment, turn to their right, and place the parchment in the fire, burning it in a stone brazier to their right. This was their way of accepting the contract. At no time was the name of the target mentioned in the room, and there was no trail of parchments that would lead to the name of the soon-to-be-dead person.

The assassin had the name and the last known location of the person. It was the assassin's duty to retrieve whatever other information they would need to fulfill the contract, and of course, a contract taken, is a contract fulfilled.

High-Master Wraith continued to go through the few remaining parchments to prepare himself for the morning assembly. It was the typical information he had been seeing for the last forty-seven seasons of his life, and since it mostly always consisted of the same information, he only looked over the documents at a glance. As usual, they told him that the yokes were up to standards, the eggs were up to standards, and the chickens were producing according to standards. That translated to the amount of gold taken in was up to standard, the coffers were up to standard, and the assassins were performing to standard. That was what the reports have always said ever since High-Master Wraith took on the position as one of the three High-Masters. In fact, that is what the reports have said since the Assassin's Guild first came into existence and began the task of assassinations. The Guild was in the business of killing and they have always been efficient at their task.

Even with the mundane reports, High-Master Wraith did not grow sleepy to the point where he would return to his bed. Even if he had, he would not. After one of the spasms which he suffered from came upon him, he would not try to go back to sleep. With the feeling the spasm brought over his body and soul, he felt that if he returned to his bed that same night he might not wake up in the morning.

High-Master Wraith sat at his desk and recalled the meeting he had with the other High-Masters and the Masters the previous evening.

The new recruits entered the building bringing them to the Guild and as usual, all the recruits made it to their correct door. Of course, there were magic wards in place to show the Masters which of the children were the first to solve the test.

When given the update from the Masters on the particular part of the test, High-Master Wraith did not put much concern into the information. There was always one or two of the children to come up with the solution to which door they should pass through, and the remaining children followed their example. It was not until he and the other High-Masters heard that the same child who had come up with the solution to the door was also the only one who had solved the obstacle of crossing the gap in the floor.

When the High-Masters heard the particular update of the new recruits, they all paid more attention to the meeting and the conversation. That is because no recruit in over fifty seasons has passed the test. This season, two of the children obtained fractured ankles, and one even broke their arm, but one child, the same child who was the first to come up with the solution to the doors, crossed over the gap and made it safely to the other side.

One of the other High-Masters asked which Master the child belonged to, but High-Master Wraith knew the answer before she even spoke. The smile Master Viper was wearing was more revealing than the dress she had donned to attend the evening meeting. A dress showing everyone in the room that she had no weapons on her or at least none she was not born with or developed when she grew into her womanhood.

All eyes in the meeting were now on Master Viper, and being the woman she was, she liked it that way. Even though the others were looking at her because it was her new recruit who had passed the test, after a couple of breaths, more than one of the Masters were looking at her in more than a professional way. Even High-Master Wraith thought that if he was maybe forty seasons younger or even just thirty, he would take Master Viper up on her offer to join her in her bed for a night. High-Master Wraith knew that with his age, as well as other reasons, he probably would not survive into the morning, but he also thought it might just be worth the risk.

Without any questions from the other members of the Guild, Master Viper began giving an update on her new pupil. That was one of the items on the agenda for this meeting. On the day of recruitment, all the Masters would give an update to the High-Masters on the ones they had chosen. Since their job was to make sure the Guild ran efficiently, the High-Masters did not deal with the ones chosen to be the next line of assassins. In fact, the High-Masters never saw a new recruit until five seasons after they had come to the Guild. That was when the High-Masters would offer them their first contracts. Of course, since it was their first, they were always eager to make their first official kill. The newly appointed assassin never turned down the first contract offered to them.

Master Viper, with everyone's eyes on her, continued with her report. She had sent her last pupil Crimson to make first contact with the child. Since the child did not give her name to the assassin that recruited her until just before she entered the Guild, Crimson was to find out that bit of information, and take the girl to her quarters, two tasks below any of the Masters. When Crimson learned the child's name was Nyght and she passed it on to Master Viper, she also told her teacher about the child's skin. There was also one more bit of information Crimson had noticed but kept to herself.

Master Viper had then met the child, and briefly discussed a couple of items. The main one was to have the child start taking the Richwood wine, something very important since the child was going to be under the tutelage of Master Viper.

After the Master met with Nyght, she then went to the evening meeting knowing that since the pupil she had chosen, and bartered for, was the only one to pass the test of the entrance hall, she would be the one smiling the most out of all the Masters. She also believed that with the child she had under her wing, Master Viper would be smiling long after the child graduated from the Guild and set off to partake in the vast world of political affairs and everything that came with them.

High-Master Wraith listened to the rest of Master Viper's report, and when she had finished, he asked her if there was anything else she had to say about the child before he allowed another of the Masters to speak. Master Viper said that she had finished but she did keep one bit of information to herself. She did not know it, but it was the same information Crimson had kept from her.

The other Masters gave their reports, but High-Master Wraith allotted very little of his attention to the discussion. He was still interested in knowing more about the child who had passed the second test. He also had a great desire to go and see the child, not just because she was the only one who had succeeded at the test in over fifty seasons, but he wanted to see if what Master Viper had said about the child's appearance, about her pale white skin, was actually true. It was not that he thought Master Viper was exaggerating the truth for her benefit, but with the test and her appearance, High-Master Wraith was intrigued.

He had been a member of the Assassin's Guild since he was fifteen seasons old. When he turned forty, he took on the position of Master, to train others to be part of the Guild. When he turned seventy, he accepted the position of High-Master, to replace one who had passed away after having lived for eighty-five seasons. Now at one hundred seventeen, High-Master Wraith was the oldest of the three High-Master and had held the position longer than any of them. With the exception of the Guild's Weapons-Maker, he was the oldest member of the Guild.

In the time he had assumed the duties of a High-Master, his life had changed greatly. When he was an assassin in his younger seasons, he had the thrill and excitement that came with the position. As a Master, he was responsible for teaching others the duties that came with the profession and it brought great satisfaction to him, especially when one of his former pupils would perform a task that would make any father proud. However, when he took on the role of High-Master, he no longer had to take a life or nourish one. He had to make sure that all the numbers added up and that everyone was account-able for what they were responsible for.

It might not have been so bad if every now and then someone did something that would cause him to reprimand or even take out some small form of punishment on someone. Not that he would enjoy it, but the old assassin would welcome anything that got his blood rushing through his veins or a reason to open his eyes in the morning. Alas, everyone who was part of the Guild performed their task very effi-ciently. The assassins, the bookkeepers, the commu-nicators, and even the cooks performed their duties to Guild standards. The Assassin's Guild was very efficient, but from a certain aspect to High-Master Wraith, there was no joy.

High-Master Wraith brought his thoughts back

to where he was at the moment. He had not realized that he had sat at his desk in his chamber for
so long that the time-marker was showing he did
not have long before it was the eighth mark of the
day. He had read over the reports and had started
thinking about the meeting that had taken place the
evening before. He could not help but chuckle at the
fact how that little bit of change the new recruit had
brought to the Guild had given him a bit of enjoy-
ment even though it was only brief. He had even felt
as if he could go back to bed and get some sleep
without having to worry about not waking up.

He looked at the time-marker again and decided
that if he went back to bed now, he would not want
to get up for the morning meeting with the other
High-Masters and Masters. In all the time he attended them when he was a Master as well as when he
took on his current position, he has never missed a
meeting because that would not be efficient.

Usually, he would take his breakfast in the outer
room of his chamber, but since he was feeling a bit
sprier this morning, he would take his morning meal
in the dining hall with some of the other members
of the Guild. Yes, he decided that was what he was
going to do.

After his morning meal, which did seem better when he had company to talk with while eating, High-Master Wraith went to the gathering hall
where the morning meeting would take place. He
would normally be the first one to arrive, but since

he had met two of the Masters in the dining hall and walked with them, others had arrived before he did, and more than one person found that unusual. Everyone did notice how High-Master Wraith seemed to be in a very exceptional mood this morning and everyone was happy for the elderly man.

They all had respect for the High-Master who had lived past a hundred seasons, something very rare, not just for an assassin, but for a human as well. High-Master Wraith had given both of the High-Masters their positions and he trained four out of the current seven Masters as well. Of course, Master Viper was not one of them, but a couple of the Masters and both High-Masters thought that maybe High-Master Wraith had finally taken up Master Viper on her offer to join her for a night of entertainment. More than one of the Masters and both High-Masters would not turn down her offer if she happened to make it to them. It was well worth it even for the elderly High-Masters who had to use a couple of elixirs from Master Force. He was the Master who trained the Guild's assassins with magical capabilities and used those abilities to go after their targets. Some of which were wizards themselves.

High-Master Wraith finished talking with the two Masters and entered the gathering hall where all three took their seats. The other two High-Masters gave their mentor a questioning smile as to why he seemed more alive this morning, but since he had no idea what they were smiling about, he just smiled back at them, then turned to look around the room to the others attending. When he saw the empty chair, he asked his question, "Has anyone seen Master Viper?"

The other two High-Masters exchanged glances at each other, each knowing what the other was thinking. High-Master Wraith seemed to be a lot more active this morning and it just so happened that Master Viper was running late for the morning meeting. They nodded to each other thinking that they were correct about High-Master Wraith's private meeting with the woman of everyman's dreams, and since he was there and she was not, their respect for the man grew tenfold, because if he had outlasted Master Viper, then he had done something no man had ever done before, including themselves. They continued with the meeting without Master Viper, who never arrived.

After the meeting, High-Master Wraith told the other two High-Masters that he would go to Master Viper's tower and see what her reason for her absence was, once again, their respect for the old man grew another tenfold. To them, not only had he placated the woman who had no rival in the bedroom, but now he was going to make sure she was still able to perform her normal duties. Their respect grew, as did the smiles on their faces. Which High-Master Wraith noticed just before he walked away from them, still not knowing why they were smiling so much since he had first greeted them.

He walked down the long corridor connecting the Guild's main tower to the tower situated on the east wall of the complex. He could not even remember the last time he had taken one of the passageways to the personal towers of each of the Masters where they trained their pupils in private. The best he could recall is that it had to be the last time he had held the position of Master himself.

When he reached the door to the exit of the long passageway, he did not have to open it himself. There were wards placed in the passageway to let the ones in the tower know someone was approaching. It was the responsibility of the current pupil to meet the individual and learn the reason for their visit. Usually, it was one of the other Masters, and for this particular tower, they came because of an invitation from Master Viper. If they came uninvited, the pupil would relay the reason the person had come to the tower and take it to their Master. Then the Master would decide if the person would be allowed to enter or not. If they were not, then the Master would simply leave with no ill feelings. Masters respected other Masters' privacy because they wanted their own respected.

When Crimson opened the door to the passageway, she was surprised at who was standing on the other side of the door. It took her two breaths to grasp just how ill-mannered she had appeared. When she realized her Master would be unhappy with the way she received a High-Master she quickly made up for her lack of hospitality. "Forgive me, High-Master, I was just so surprised to see that you have graced us with your presence." To add to her apology, she placed her hand just above her bosom, not only to show the High-Master that she was at a loss of breath due to his arrival, but also to help guide the man's eyes to her ample and protruding breast. She did it exactly the way Master Viper had trained her.

She had never seen this particular High-Master, since he never accepted any of Master Viper's personal invitations, but since she was a pupil in the Assassin's Guild, she knew all of their policy and protocols. One of them was that a High-Master wore gray robes which ran all the way to the floor and had a red sash running from their left shoulder to their right hip. The color of the robe was in honor of their seasons lived and wisdom. Gray represents both of those attributes. The red sash was a symbol of the blood they had drawn to obtain their seasons lived and wisdom. If they wore the grey robes and red sash, they had to be an assassin who had lived long enough and drawn enough blood to obtain them both.

"Please, High-Master," Crimson said and took a step back and to her right to allow the High-Master to enter. To add to her greeting, she bowed her head slightly and closed her eyes as he passed by. This was not something she or any of the other pupils or assassins performed because of their training or Guild

protocol. It was something many of the younger assassins did to show the respect they had for those
who came before them. The High-Masters did not
require or ask any of the other assassins to bow to
them, but with the respect they had earned in their
lifetime, others felt obligated to perform this small
gesture.

"I am High-Master Wraith," he said to introduce
himself to the woman he had never met. When he
announced himself as the oldest of the three High-
Masters and the one who has been with the Guild
for over one hundred seasons, Crimson could not
stop herself from taking a slight breath or stop her
eyes from widening a bit. There was even a part of
her that wanted to show this most honored man just
what Master Viper had taught her over the last five
seasons, and if he accepted the offer, she would do
everything to make him, Master Viper, and herself
very proud.

"It is an honor to be in your presence," Crimson
said once the High-Master turned around to face
her. He was not sure if she actually meant what
she had just said or if it was part of her training by
Master Viper. He quickly decided it was a little of
both. "What may I do for you?" she asked and he
saw the right corner of her mouth raise to make it
look as if she was offering him the world, but the
left side of her mouth lowered just enough to tell
him that it would sadden her if he did not take her
up on her offer. He was sure the smile was part of

her training because she had made it the same way Master Viper had done so many times to him.

"I wish to speak with Master Viper if she is available," he said to get their meeting moving along before he grew any older or the woman ninety-seven seasons younger than him tried to remove his clothing.

"I am sorry High-Master, but Master Viper is not here at the moment. I have not seen her this morning, so I do not know what she has planned for the day, nor do I know when she will return." She moved so that she was less than an arm's reach away from the senior assassin. "If you wish to remain here until she returns, I would be more than happy to make your stay pleasant." Once again, she was using the weapons Master Viper had trained her to use. Her eyes, her mouth, her bare shoulders, her breasts, and even the words she spoke. High-Master Wraith knew this pupil of Master Viper was going to make the Guild very proud as well as very profitable.

High-Master Wraith had come to the tower to see about Master Viper's absence, so he decided to put an end to the soon-to-be True Assassin's attack. Yes, she was good, but High-Master Wraith had not survived by caving into his physical lust. In his younger seasons, he was more than willing to take a woman like the one before him to his bed and show her what true passion and desire were. Of course, there was also a woman or two who tried too hard to bed him and to end their games he ended their life, before they ended his.

He could not do that now, neither the bedding nor the killing, but he did not want the young woman to continue to waste her womanly charms on him. To decline her last offer, he simply gave her a look to let her know that he was not interested. His expression had more of an effect on her than all the things she had tried on him since she opened the door. A man had turned her down. A part of her felt as if she had not learned a thing from Master Viper.

High-Master Wraith turned away to let the young woman come to grips with the fact that no matter what weapons Master Viper trained her to use, some men would not succumb simply by a pleasant word or two. Nor by one, who batted her eyes, licked her lips, or took a deep breath to allow her breast to rise seductively.

He looked around the area he was standing in. Over on the other side of the room was the door used to bring the new recruits in from Sarzanac. He immediately thought about the girl Master Viper had told him about the previous night. "And how is our newest member?" he asked and turned around to look at Crimson who still had a wounded look on her face from his rejection.

It took her a couple of breaths to realize he was speaking to her, and when she did, she stuttered trying to get herself to focus on the person with her, "She...She is someone Master Viper believes will bring great promise to the Guild, High-Master."

Master Viper had used the same words to

describe the child. "Is it true about her skin? That it is pale white?"

"Yes, High-Master, it is true. And with her dark hair, it is all the paler, but now that she has cut it, it does not bring out the color as strong as before."

"Cut it?" the High-Master asked, remembering Master Viper had said that the child's hair flowed over her shoulders and down her back.

"Yes, High-Master. When she arrived and when I last saw her yesterday, the child's hair was long. When I went to her room this morning to begin with her training, I saw that she had cut it and it now just reaches the top of her neck."

High-Master Wraith thought for a moment, then asked his next question, "Did you ask the child why she cut her hair?"

Crimson did not hesitate to answer the question because she thought that maybe he was testing her, "No, High-Master. I left the child last night, while Master Viper was with her. I presumed she was the one who instructed the child to cut her hair and I would never question a decision that my Master or any Master of our Guild has made."

He nodded to let her know he believed her in all aspects of what she had just said. He looked around the area again, but did not see the child, "Where is she now?" he asked when he returned his eyes back to Crimson.

"I have her performing the very same task I was given the day after I arrived."

High-Master Wraith could not stop the smile from appearing on his face. He knew exactly what the child was doing. It was the same task every new recruit did on their first full day at the Guild. Himself included. The child was scrubbing every step on the stairs that went from the ground floor of the tower all the way to the very last step at the top of the stairs. There were ten floors in each of the Masters' towers. There were nine flights of stairs that led to the floors above. Each set of stairs had twenty steps. That was a total of one hundred eighty steps the child had to clean. They would do this for the first ten days they were at the tower. If they complained even once, they would receive an additional ten days of the chore. The task was to see if the child would do as instructed without question. It was an important lesson for them to learn and pass. Even for the ones trained by Master Viper and the ones who came before her. Maybe even more so because of what they would have to do to accomplish their task.

High-Master Wraith brushed his own distant memories of the task away and focused on the present. "And how did the child react when you told her what she would be doing?"

"She took the bucket and brush I had in my hands and immediately began to clean the steps." Crimson paused for a breath then continued, "Without a single complaint." She concluded the last statement with a smile because she knew that with the child going at the task the way she had with no complaints, it showed that the child had what it took to be part of the Guild. With the way the child has performed so far, it would only make Master Viper happier and Master Viper being happy was important to Crimson.

As much as High-Master Wraith wanted to see the child, he knew that he was not to interfere with her training. He still thought that maybe Crimson would be able to tell him a little bit more about the child who had passed the test in the hallway, "So is there anything else about the child that shows she will be an asset to the Guild?" It was not much but to the High-Master who had spent the majority of his life watching and studying others, he saw the slight motion Crimson made with her eyes toward the direction behind him to where the stairs were. To where the child was somewhere going about the task assigned to her. "What is it?" he asked.

"Nothing, High-Master."

She only hesitated for less than a breath, but it was enough to let the High-Master know that the young woman had something she was not saying. He took a step closer to Crimson, and since he was a bit taller than she was, he looked down and gave her a stare to make sure she knew he was not going to ask again.

Crimson had to swallow before she answered. High-Master Wraith did not know if she did this because he had scared her or because of what she was about to say. "It's her eyes," Crimson said, and since High-Master Wraith was still looking directly at her, she explained what she had just said, "They look like death."

As soon as he heard the words he turned away from Crimson and looked over his right shoulder in the direction of the stairs. He had heard those same words before and even used them himself at one point in his life. He turned back to face Crimson. He did not speak but the look in his eyes and the expression on his face asked the question, "Are you sure?"

Crimson did not speak either. All she did was nod her head to let the High-Master know that what she had told him was what she saw when she looked into the child's eyes. She trained for five seasons to become an assassin. She was not supposed to fear death; she was to deliver it. Nevertheless, when she saw the child's eyes when she first met her yesterday, it took all of her training to restrain herself from giving away what she was feeling. It bothered her so much that she did not even tell Master Viper what she had seen in the child's eyes, afraid that the Master would think she was not ready to become a True Assassin.

High-Master Wraith held his gaze on Crimson for a moment then turned his entire body to face the stairs leading to the upper levels. If what Crimson had said was true and he believed she was honest with him, somewhere on those stairs there was a child with eyes that looked like death.

"You will begin to train the child with other tasks." He turned around to face Crimson, "Stop her with the cleaning of the steps…"

"But High-Master," Crimson said, interrupting him, something no one had ever done in his time as Master or High-Master and when she saw the look he was giving her, she knew she might not make it to True Assassin. "Yes, High-Master," she finally said in hopes he would forgive her of her defiance and not end her life where she stood. "The child, like most of us when we arrived at the Guild, does not know how to read, or write. I can begin with those lessons." Crimson hoped that since she now presented the High-Master with a plan then maybe she would live to begin what she had suggested.

"It will suffice for now," High-Master Wraith said, and walked past Crimson to head for the door that would take him back to the main tower of the Guild.

"Forgive me High-Master," Crimson said, and he turned to look at her before he reached the door. Yes, she was afraid of him and had much respect for the man who had been with the Guild for so long, but she also had a duty to Master Viper which she was still technically under and did not want to get between these two. Crimson did enjoy breathing. "What shall I tell Master Viper?"

High-Master Wraith looked over the top of Crimson's head at the stairs behind her then back to her, "If I see her, I will explain why I have altered the child's training." He then turned, opened the door, and walked out.

Crimson was so relieved when he left, that she never noticed the word the High-Master had used to start his sentence which was "If." She only turned and headed to the stairs to retrieve the child and begin training her to read and write. Something Crimson was not thrilled about doing because it meant she would have to be face-to-face with the child for an extended period of time and did not want to have to look into her eyes and see death, again.

High-Master Wraith walked hurriedly back down the passageway. *"This could not be a coincidence,"* he thought to himself. *"The child passed the test in the hall. Something no one has accomplished in over fifty seasons, and now, the way someone described her eyes, that they saw death."* He ran over the meeting of the previous night in his head, and he was sure Master Viper had not mentioned anything about the child's eyes. Then again, if what Crimson had said was true, not even a Master of the Guild would be able to not look at those eyes and not think that they were looking into death.

This brought two more thoughts to the High-Master, *"I have to know more about this child and where she came from,"* was the first thought. The second was, *"Now I have the beginning of the answer as to why Master Viper missed the morning meeting. Something she had never done, at least not until the child arrived."*

FOUR

When he returned to the main tower, High-Master Wraith sought out any of the other Masters. It did not matter which one he came across first; they would have the answer he was looking for, and since Master Viper was not available, he would ask one of the other six.

When he found one, he asked them his question and when he received an answer, High-Master Wraith was not surprised. The one who had petitioned the child for the Guild was always able to spot the type of person the Guild was looking for. Dodge was good at everything he did, and High-Master Wraith would be glad to speak to the assassin on the matter of the child.

With this bit of information, he went to the communications room of the main tower. It is where people would send others to run messages to wherever the messages needed to go. The Guild was serious about keeping Guild business between Guild members only. If someone needed to contact another member in another town, city, or even on the other side of the world, the message would travel by courier and be delivered in person. The courier was of course an assassin, but even an assassin who had been with the Guild for a long time would take on the task of courier. Being an assassin meant a person served the Guild whether it was when they were fulfilling a contract or delivering a message.

Since it was the High-Masters who assigned the assassins their contracts, High-Master Wraith knew Dodge was not on one. That did not mean he was presently at the Guild. He could be staying in the Guild House in Sarzanac, or he might have gone to another city. The people who worked in the communications aspect of the Guild always knew where every assassin of the Guild was located at all times whether they were on assignment or not. It was a rule that every assassin informed the communications division with information of where they would be. If they were in another city and decided to leave, they would have to give the information about where they were going to the city's Guild House, so if anyone from the Guild came looking for them, they would know where to go next. If there was no Guild House in the city, there was always a point of contact that could relay the information.

This time, the communications operator informed High-Master Wraith that Dodge was still staying in the Guild House in Sarzanac. High-Master Wraith was happy to hear that because it meant he would be able to speak with Dodge soon. He might be staying at the city's Guild House, but he could be anywhere in the city though it would not take much time to locate him. The communications operator informed High-Master Wraith that he would send a runner out immediately to find the assassin and relay the message requesting his presence.

Once finished, High-Master Wraith went back to his own chamber. He needed to meet with the other two High-Masters, but he knew they were probably also taking care of some matter requiring their attention. Since all three of them respected one another, he would not request their presence even though the situation he was monitoring was probably the most important event to happen at the Guild in an exceedingly long time.

For two marks, High-Master Wraith sat in the outer chamber of his quarters, seated in his chair close to the fireplace letting the flames warm his body and soul. The entire Guild had magical spells placed on it, so even though its location is within the highest peaks of the mountains and snow constantly fell, the temperature in the tower remained comfortable for all those within. Even the towers of the Masters stayed warm including the passageways leading to the main tower. Most people who use the fireplace in their quarters only do so because they enjoy seeing it or like to hear the crackling of the flames. High-Master Wraith kept a fire going in the hearth in the outer chamber of his quarters as well as the one in his bedchamber. The spells might keep it comfortable for most, but High-Master Wraith needed the heat from the flames to lessen the chill in his soul.

He sat there looking into the flames thinking about his life and all he had done in his one hundred seventeen seasons. He had lived a long time and had not one regret. Not in choosing to join the Guild. Not in the fact that he never married or sired any children. Not in the fact that he knew he would die at the Guild and more than likely his death would come to him in the room just off to his left where he took to his bed every night.

It was a knock at his door that brought him out of his thoughts and even though the heat from the fire was warming him greatly, he knew the person knocking on his door may be able to add warmth to his soul which the flames could not.

The person did not enter after they knocked, waiting for High-Master Wraith to grant them permission. He stood up from the chair and walked across the room to stand ten paces from the door. As he walked by the small table located next to the side of one of the chairs, he picked up the three throwing daggers he had placed there earlier for when his guest would arrive.

It was possible that the person on the other side of the door was not who he was expecting but if it was not, he could slip the daggers into his robe with no problem at all. "Enter," he said loud enough for the person in the hallway to hear him. When the door opened wide enough and he saw who was there, High-Master Wraith made sure he controlled himself to keep the smile from his face.

"You wish to speak with me, High-Master?" Dodge said as soon as he saw High-Master Wraith standing across the room. Even though he did not receive an answer, he stepped completely into the room and closed the door behind him. He knew what was coming but still turned enough to face the door so that the High-Master would be able to perform the same act he always did when Dodge came to his chamber.

Without saying a word, High-Master Wraith brought his hands from behind his back. In his left hand, he held one of the three throwing daggers and as soon as his arm extended to the proper distance to release the dagger, he did so, and it went flying across the room toward his invited guest. A breath after the release of the dagger in his left hand, High-Master Wraith brought his right hand out in front of him, which held the last two daggers, which he released simultaneously toward the assassin on the other side of the room. All three daggers were in the air before the assassin had even put his eyes back on the High-Master.

Dodge knew the daggers were coming toward him. Not just because he heard them flying through the air but because whenever High-Master Wraith wished to speak with him, he would perform the same test which was to see if the assassin Dodge still lived up to his name.

The younger assassin's back was toward the High-Master, and he kept his eyes on the door. He did this to show the elder assassin that he was not worried about the daggers coming toward him. Before the first dagger reached him, Dodge adjusted his position so that his left side was now toward the High-Master. With the distance between his chest and back, Dodge's body was still too wide to avoid the dagger coming toward him. He thrust his arms out in front of him, pulling his chest in more to allow the first dagger to pass by his upper body just barely missing his shirt.

The other two daggers were coming right behind the first, so to avoid them, Dodge, with speed quicker than the High-Master could believe, dropped to the floor spreading his legs so that one stretched out in front of him and the other behind him. This allowed the last two daggers to fly over the assassin's head and land in the door with the first. Knowing that the test was over, while he remained in the position on the floor, Dodge looked across the room at the High-Master; both smiling at one another.

Dodge adjusted his body so that he was facing the High-Master but was still on the floor with each of his legs extended to his sides. He then placed his hands on the floor in front of him, and while pressing down, he pulled his legs toward his body which allowed him to rise upward. When his legs were together, he raised his upper body and was now standing looking at High-Master Wraith; both were still smiling.

Dodge turned around and faced the door. He

reached out and retrieved the daggers embedded into the wood which was better than them being in his body if he had not been fast enough to dodge the weapons to let the High-Master know that he could still go by the name Dodge. As he pulled the blades out, he also noticed all the other marks on the door made by the previous daggers from the previous tests the High-Master always gave whenever the young assassin came to see him.

He walked over to High-Master Wraith and handed him back the three throwing daggers. "One day, you are going to have to pull those blades from my body yourself High-Master Wraith."

The High-Master's smile grew a bit then he gave his reply, "From what I just observed, you are as fast as you were when you joined our Guild, and no doubt, my throws have slowed down since that time."

"But your aim is still perfect, and I am sure one day your blades will never make it to the door," Dodge said this to show his respect to the High-Master. They both knew that what he had just said was more than likely not going to happen, but the young assassin would never think of speaking words to the High-Master regarding his age or the fact that with every test, the blades did come toward Dodge just a bit slower than the last, though not by much.

"Thank you for coming," High-Master Wraith said to take them to the reason he had requested to see the assassin.

"It is an honor," Dodge replied and meant it.

The High-Master motioned with his left hand for them to move closer to the fire and take a seat before they continued with their meeting. Dodge extended his right hand in the same direction to allow the High-Master to proceed before him, in the position of honor, which the High-Master did. Even though it did not matter to him which of them went first, he knew that it meant something to the younger assassin, and he would show the respect the young assassin was showing him.

When they reached the chairs, High-Master Wraith continued forward a bit to stand closer to the one he had been sitting in close to the fire. He then turned around to face Dodge and gestured for the young man to sit which Dodge was waiting for because to sit down before the High-Master had sat or before he had given the young assassin consent to do so would be disrespectful. "Thank you," Dodge said to show his appreciation.

"Help yourself to something to drink, if you like," the High-Master said.

Dodge noticed the bottles of liquids sitting on the table in front of him, centered between the three chairs before he even sat down. Since the High-Master offered him a drink, he knew that he could pour one but not before he did what was proper to him, "May I pour you one as well, High-Master?" The High-Master simply shook his head to decline the offer. Dodge took up the container of drink he preferred over anything. He had never tasted a single drop of any spirit, not even ale. There were only two items Dodge would drink. One being water and the second was the one he was pouring now, milk.

At his age, High-Master Wraith's stomach could not take the drink any longer, but since he knew Dodge would be the other member of the meeting, he made sure he had a fresh bottle sent from the dining hall. The younger assassin had told him a long time ago that spirits, and even ale, would slow down his body and it would be impossible to dodge a weapon if he was not able to stand on his own two feet.

Sitting in the chair and with drink in hand, Dodge put his eyes on the High-Master waiting for him to begin. "You were the one who petitioned for the child Nyght, were you not?"

"Yes, High-Master. Is there something wrong with her?" Dodge asked.

He did not know how to answer the question. There was nothing wrong with the child but at the same time, she was not normal. The High-Master thought to himself then spoke to the assassin. "She was the only one to pass the test of the hallway." When he said that, he could see Dodge trying to hold back his smile. All assassins are trained to keep their emotions hidden, so as not to give any information away, but the High-Master knew the news he had just passed on pleased Dodge greatly.

It could have been for a couple of reasons. One

was probably because no one had passed the test in over fifty seasons, including Dodge, and it reminded him of his own failure for which he did not fault himself. Another reason was probably because he was the one to petition the girl's admittance, and when she began to bring coin to the Guild, he would receive a percentage of each contract the child accepted. It was a finder's fee.

"Is there anything you can tell me about the child that you might not have told the Masters?" High-Master Wraith asked him in order to lead the meeting down the path he needed it to go.

"No, High-Master."

Dodge hesitated. It was for less than a half of breath, but he did, and the High-Master noticed it. If he had paused for a few breaths more, High-Master Wraith would have thought that maybe the assassin was trying to decide if there was something he had forgotten to mention about the girl, but with the amount of time he took and his reply, the High-Master knew he was going to have to lead the assassin further down the path.

He turned around and faced the chair he had been sitting in. It was facing toward the fireplace, but the High-Master turned it so that it was now facing the other assassin, and then High-Master Wraith sat down staring all the while at the other one in the room. With that stare, Dodge could tell that the High-Master knew there was more to the story of the child he had sent there.

High-Master Wraith could not fault the young assassin. If the girl was what he suspected, no assassin who looked into the child's eyes could not see what those eyes revealed. Now he just needed to get the assassin to tell him what he saw. "Tell me about her eyes." He decided that the direct approach would move the conversation along.

Dodge could not keep the expression off his face. To try to cover it, he raised his glass and took a drink of his milk. When he brought it back down, he was not looking at the High-Master even though he knew the High-Master was looking at him.

Once again, High-Master Wraith held no ill will against the young assassin. The eyes of one like the child could affect anyone who has taken the life of another. Dodge performed his Guild duties exceptionally well, and for that, he received quite a few contracts per season. He had fulfilled many contracts, and because of that, if he looked into the child's eyes, they would have affected him even more than Crimson or even Master Viper. The more lives a person took, the more those eyes would affect a person when they encountered them. High-Master Wraith, even after all these seasons, could remember the first time he looked into eyes like the ones he believed were like the new recruit.

He knew he was going to have to walk the assassin down the path. "If you were to use one word to describe the child's eyes..." High-Master Wraith waited to continue until Dodge was looking at him,

"...would you say they were deep?" The High-Master used the word most people would use to describe what they saw in the eyes of one like the girl. Those people had never taken the life of another. An individual who has killed before would use a different word.

"No, that is not the word I would choose," Dodge said.

"Then what is?" High-Master Wraith asked with authority in his voice to let the assassin know that he would not be waiting much longer for his answer.

Dodge lifted his glass and finished the last of his milk. The High-Master allowed him this pause, and for a moment, he thought the assassin might switch to something stronger than what he had been drinking. Then the young assassin looked at the High-Master and gave his reply, "Death."

He had his answer now, and even though he had never seen the child, he knew she was what he thought she was. "Have another drink," High-Master Wraith said to Dodge, who did not hesitate to accept the offer. If anything could force the man to take to drinking spirits it would be what they saw in the child's eyes; however, Dodge poured himself another glass of milk.

High-Master Wraith stood and walked over to the fireplace. He did it to give himself some time to gather his thoughts but also because even thinking about the time he had come across eyes like the one who is now at their Guild had brought a coldness to his bones. When he was ready, and when he thought the younger assassin was as well, he spoke. "I need you to find out everything you can about where the child came from." He turned around and looked at the assassin. Dodge nodded his head to let the High-Master know he would do as asked. "She was not born in Sarzanac that I can tell you because I would have known, so she must have come from another city. I need to know where she came from. When you have the information, I need you to find out who her parents are."

"But as a child on the streets of Sarzanac, her parents may not even be alive."

The High-Master knew the assassin was not trying to get out of completing the task. He was just bringing information to the conversation and the High-Master had no problem with that. Since they are both assassins, they know that obtaining information is the first step in completing any mission. "What I am asking of you will not be easy," the High-Master said and walked over to stand in front of his chair, "But it is very important." The young assassin nodded to let the High-Master know he understood. "Her parents might be dead, if they are, then try to confirm it. If they are alive, then bring me that information, as well as their location."

Dodge stood up and faced the elder assassin, "Yes, High-Master. I know the child was staying with the one called Selby in the lower district. I will start there."

Hearing Dodge's plan, High-Master Wraith remembered that this was not the first time that he heard of the name Selby. "Is he the same one who is making a name for himself in Sarzanac? In fact, it was you who informed the Masters of what the boy has been up to over the past few seasons."

"Yes, High-Master. One night, I followed the girl back to where she was staying." Dodge remembered the night well, "Over the seasons, as I kept an eye on her, I also paid close attention to what the boy was doing. It seems that with the business of killing rats, the girl helped him obtain quite a bit of coin for himself which he used to advance his holdings."

High-Master Wraith remembered the accounts brought to him and the other High-Masters about the boy named Selby. He did not know about the girl because she was just a child with the possibility of recruitment into the Guild; the Masters would handle her part, so he did not have to be involved. However, he did receive reports about the boy named Selby, and over the past few seasons, he was still receiving reports on how the boy, now seventeen, was making a name for himself. He looked at Dodge, the one who had recruited the girl named Nyght as well as reporting on the boy named Selby. It appeared that Dodge had been keeping a watchful eye on what was going on in the city of Sarzanac. Of course, he had always been an efficient assassin of the Guild. The High-Master would not even hold it against him for not mentioning the girl's eyes.

He finished gathering his thoughts together and then asked a question, "Do you still feel the boy Selby would be an asset to the Guild?"

Dodge gave his answer, "At the moment, he is still gaining ground, and from what I can tell, he is not going to get ahead of himself and will wait until he has a stronger force behind him as well as a stronger hold on the city. However, I do feel that in two or three seasons, the name Selby will be well known in the city of Sarzanac and to lands further away."

The High-Master could tell that Dodge was pleased with the one called Selby, and since he was going to the boy to discuss the girl Nyght, he might as well cook two eggs with the same fire, as the saying went. "Very well. Let your visit to the boy serve two purposes. Find out what you can about the history of the child Nyght, and while there, get a more personal assessment of how the Guild might benefit from dealing with the boy. Since this will be first contact, make sure you do not give too much away that will make the boy think he has a future with us. It just may be that instead of being a benefit to our Guild, the boy might become a burden and will have to be dealt with."

"Yes, High-Master, I agree as well," Dodge said and gave a slight bow to show that he truly did respect the High-Master's way of handling the situation.

"Your main goal is to find any information about

the girl. There is nothing more important. You may take any amount of coin you feel you will need to accomplish this task and I will guarantee that you will be paid full price of your highest contract."

"High-Master?" was all Dodge could say. He understood what he had just heard. Usually, an assassin obtained only a percentage of a contract; but now he would receive the full amount of whichever contract had the highest amount that he had ever taken. He knew it was more than he would make in two seasons. He also knew that his assignment would not be easy, and it might just take him two seasons or longer to find the information the High-Master was looking for.

"I will guarantee the amount. If the other High-Masters decide to not agree with me, then I will pay you out of my own holdings." With the look on his face, Dodge knew the High-Master meant what he had said. A part of Dodge was about ready to tell the High-Master that he would perform the task free of charge because he respected the elder assassin so much. Of course, Dodge was an assassin and since the Guild was in the business of making coin, so was Dodge and he would take the High-Master's offer graciously.

High-Master Wraith walked over to Dodge and stood in front of him. "Find out if her parents are alive and if they are, I need to know. The task I am giving you is extremely important, for the Guild as well as for me."

"I understand, High-Master. I will not fail."

With the meeting over, Dodge gave one final bow to show his respect and then left the quarters of High-Master Wraith. He had a job to do, and he knew it was not going to be easy. The Guild always selected children who had no parents or any other family ties. Now he had to find a set of those parents. Difficult, but possible. He would start in Sarzanac with the boy named Selby. Captain Selby is what the ones following him call him. Dodge would see what he could find out from him; afterward, he had no idea where he would go.

After Dodge left, High-Master Wraith remained in his chamber. He had been going over everything he had heard or thought of since last evening. It all started with the child passing the test in the hallway but since then the entire situation has grown rapidly. The High-Master did not believe he could slow it down, or if he even wanted to.

He was getting old and soon he would leave this world due to his age or for another daunting reason. Before he did, maybe he had one more chance at bringing a bit of spark back into his own life. With what he was planning, he would be able to leave the Guild with something very few, if any, even knew about. He did, but since he was the oldest assassin alive, and as far as he knew, the only one who knew what the ones with eyes like the child were, he would have to be the one to guide her into what she was to become.

He had given Dodge the task of finding the parents of the child. If it was the mother she inherited her eyes from, then he was sure he did not know the woman. If the father was the one who passed the trait along, then it was possible the two had known each other in the past. There were others out there, like the girl, but he had never come across any after the first one he met so it is possible he knew neither parent of the child, but he had to find out.

When he heard the knock on his door, High-Master Wraith turned to look at the time-marker in the room and saw that it was going on the fourteenth mark of the day. He had been awake since before the sun came up or at least came up in the normal world, because in the mountains where the Guild is situated, the sun never made the morning sky more than the color of gray.

"Enter," High-Master Wraith said, and when the door opened, he saw the other two High-Masters. He was glad they had come because now after he had talked with Dodge, he was ready to let the two know what he had planned. "Come in my friends; we have much to discuss."

The other High-Masters came into the room and over to where High-Master Wraith was sitting in his usual spot in the chair closest to the fireplace. The other two sat in their usual locations, one in the chair at the far end of the small table across from High-Master Wraith, and the other sat in the chair at the side of the table to the left of High-Master

Wraith and to the right of the High-Master, he had entered with.

"Did you speak with Master Viper?" High-Master Grave asked.

High-Master Wraith exchanged looks with his two counterparts and then answered the question. "I believe none of us will speak to Master Viper again." The two did not say anything because they understood what High-Master Wraith had just told them.

For the past two marks, he had been going over everything he had heard since the circumstances all started. As for what happened to the missing Master, he knew there were very few scenarios that could have taken place and since he was not just a High-Master but an assassin as well, he believed he knew what happened to Master Viper and possibly where she might be. "I think we should make a sweep of the exterior of our fair Guild. The search should begin on the eastern wall close to the tower which belonged to Master Viper."

Both of the High-Masters heard the word "belonged" which would state that Master Viper was no longer in charge of the tower.

"I would suggest we ask our Weapons-Maker to take on this task. He is about the only one who would not be susceptible to the cold temperatures of the outside of our Guild." High-Master Copper said.

High-Master Grave added his own opinion, "Not

only that, but we can trust in his secrecy to ensure he reports what he finds to us and us alone."

"I agree," High-Master Wraith said to let his counterparts know they had both spoken wisely.

"And if our Weapons-Maker happens to find Master Viper, what shall we tell others?" High-Master Grave asked.

They all looked at one another but it was High-Master Wraith who gave the answer. "Simple. That Master Viper is no longer with the Guild." They once again exchanged glances but the other two nodded to agree with High-Master Wraith. They all knew that no one would question what the High-Masters told them.

"We will need to grant Crimson, True Assassin status," High-Master Copper said. "Master Viper was prepared to do just that within the moon-cycle and there will be no need to have her wait."

"I agree," High-Master Grave said. "We can give her True Assassin status and she can still train the pupil until Master Viper's position has been filled. Then her replacement can continue with the training."

"And what of the rule?" High-Master Copper asked but did not receive a reply from the other two, so he continued, "The rule is clear that no assassin is to take the life of a fellow assassin and clearly that is what this pupil has done. Surely, it was not Crimson who caused Master Viper's parting."

High-Master Wraith noticed that High-Master Copper was very quick to come to the defense of

Crimson, and he was the one to suggest she receive the title of True Assassin. High-Master Wraith suspected that maybe High-Master Copper had his eye on the latest student of Master Viper. The soon-to-be True Assassin was taught by the best and even though she would never be as great as Master Viper, Crimson was sure to be a close second like the others trained by the missing Master. At the moment, High-Master Wraith did not care about any of those details. Although, since High-Master Copper mentioned the rule in the discussion, High-Master Wraith had an answer. "The rule does not apply in this instance."

"How so?" High-Master Copper asked.

"The rule was created to stop one assassin from killing another assassin," High-Master Wraith stated.

"And is not that what we suspect has happened?" High-Master Copper asked.

High-Master Wraith did not take offense to the questioning his counterpart was doing. This was how the three High-Masters resolved matters concerning the Guild. They would discuss a topic and if there was a difference of opinions, they would debate over the subject until they came to a decision, whether it was a compromise, or they came to the decision to discuss the matter at a later time. As for the current topic, High-Master Wraith was prepared to bring this line of questioning to an end. "The rule states that no assassin can take the life of another assassin." High-Master Wraith saw that High-Master

Copper was about to speak, so he raised his hand to stop his counterpart. High-Master Copper nodded to let High-Master Wraith know that he would listen. "Thank you, my friend," High-Master Wraith said to let the other High-Master know there was no animosity between them. "The rule does not apply at this moment for two reasons. One is that if the child did have anything to do with our missing Master which we have no proof of," he added the last part to remind the others of just that fact, "the child is not an assassin, so therefore since she is not an assassin, she could not be an assassin who killed another assassin."

The other two looked at each other and even though what High-Master Wraith had said was a very weak interpretation of the law, it was the truth. The child had only been at the Guild for two suncycles, and it took five seasons to obtain the title of assassin. The two other High-Masters nodded to each other to let each other know that they could accept the first reason. Then both looked back to High-Master Wraith. "And what is the second reason?" High-Master Grave asked.

High-Master Wraith smiled just before he answered, "The child has only been here for one day in relation to the disappearance of Master Viper and we all know that the rules which govern our Guild are not taught until the tenth day a recruit has been with us."

High-Master Copper continued with what he

thought his counterpart was leading them to. "Since she did not know of the rule then she would not have known she was going against the rule."

"Correct," High-Master Wraith said and smiled.

The other two could only smile as well. Even though they have been High-Masters for ten and twelve seasons, they knew they were out of their league when it came to dealing with the one who has been a High-Master for over forty seasons. They had no animosity toward the way he obtained his desired outcome, in fact, they respected him even more and hoped that if they happened to reach his age, their minds would work at least at half the speed as the eldest High-Master.

"It appears that Master Viper's death was an unfortunate accident," High-Master Grave said, not even hiding the point that all three of them knew that if they did find Master Viper, she would not be returning to her duties.

"I agree," High-Master Copper said, "A horrible, and unfortunate accident."

"Very well. Then I suggest we discuss who will replace Viper," High-Master Grave said using only her chosen name without the title of Master which only applied to the ones currently teaching at the Guild. "I believe Lady L is next in line for the position. She is of the age requirement and has shown remarkable success in the ways the previous Masters of the vacant tower are trained in."

"Yes, Lady L would be my choice as well," High-Master Copper said, and High-Master Wraith could hear the excitement in his statement. He spoke of Lady L the same way he had spoken of Crimson at the beginning of their discussion. High-Master Copper always loved to live dangerously. Crimson was just a budding student, and even though Viper was deadly, Lady L was certainly not someone any smart man would jump in bed with.

There were quite a lot of rumors as to why the assassin of discussion had taken the name Lady L. Some say that when she took a man to her bed, if he had not pleased her, she would slice the man's throat and remove his manhood. Then she would carve an L in his body that began at the top of his chest and went down to his stomach. Supposedly, the L stood for the word "Lousy" which was in reference to his love-making skills. High-Master Copper had better make sure he had plenty of potions to help keep his stamina up if he chose to meet with the legendary Lady L.

"Very well, I will have a runner sent to bring her back to the Guild so that we can discuss the position with her. Until then, Crimson can train the child," High-Master Grave said.

"I agree with the choosing of Lady L," High-Master Wraith said to add to the conversation, "but as for the child, I will be the one to take over her training." He had put his eyes on the floor before he spoke, so he did not see the look on the other two High-Masters' faces until he looked up because they had not said anything about what he had just told them.

The two exchanged looks, then put their focus

back on High-Master Wraith. High-Master Copper asked the question they both had, "Why?"

He was ready for the question. When a Master stepped into the position of High-Master, their duty was to run the Guild. They did not have to deal with training anyone ever again. A Master had to give at least thirty full seasons of their life to the teaching of others before they took the position of High-Master. Thirty seasons is a long time to train others so when a Master became a High-Master, they could leave the painstaking task of teaching behind them. Never before has a High-Master taught another individual.

High-Master Wraith stood up from his chair, turned, and walked over to stand in front of the fireplace. He was ready to give the speech he had begun to work on when Dodge had left earlier. "It is time for you to start looking at finding my replacement." He heard the other two High-Masters stand and begin to walk over to him. He turned around and lifted his hands to let them know he still had more to say. Since they respected the man so much, they kept silent. "I have outlived more than any of our members, not counting our Weapons-Maker, but technically he is not a member of our Guild, he only works here. Nevertheless, it is time the both of you to begin your search for the one who will fill my vacancy. Since there are now only six Masters at the moment, you will only have to choose from them."

"Yes, High-Master," the other two said at the same time.

"I have taught you both and I am certain that whomever you choose, the three of you will ensure that the integrity of our institution remains long after I have left this world."

"Yes, High-Master," they both said at the same time.

"But what do you mean you will train the child?" High-Master Grave asked.

"And if you have assigned us to find your replacement, do you intend to..." High-Master Copper paused for a moment because he had to come up with the best way to say what he wanted to, "...remain with us for the time it will take for the child to be granted True Assassin status?"

High-Master Wraith smiled at the way his counterpart gracefully referred to his death. "I will be around to make sure the child becomes an assassin. For that, I am sure. But I will step down as soon as you have made your decision as to who will take my place."

"That, I cannot allow," High-Master Copper said forcefully. By the way High-Master Wraith and High-Master Grave were looking at him, he knew he had to explain. "A High-Master has never stepped down from the position. If you wish to train the child then I will support your decision, but you will remain a High-Master until..." He paused to find the right words, "...until you are no longer a member of our Guild." Once again, High-Master Wraith smiled at the way his counterpart gracefully referred to his death.

"I agree," High-Master Grave said, "You are a

High-Master, and you will remain so. We will do as you have suggested and begin the task of selecting the next High-Master, but we will not grant them the title as long as you are a member of our Guild."

High-Master Wraith knew that he would not be able to change their minds. Another way they resolved a difference of opinions between the three was if two of the High-Masters agreed against the third as the two had just done.

"Very well, I will keep the title of High-Master even though I will be training the child. I have a feeling she will not be taking up a lot of my time." The two other High-Masters did not know what High-Master Wraith was referring to but did not question him. "I suggest we conclude this meeting. I am sure we all have other tasks we need to attend to."

"Yes, High-Master," the other two said and turned to leave.

Before they reached the door, High-Master Wraith said one last thing. "Please make sure you have our Weapons-Maker check outside the east tower, especially under the previous Master's window."

"Yes, High-Master," they both said, then left.

High-Master Wraith turned and looked into the flames in the fireplace. He was sure he had time to train one more assassin.

FIVE

Dodge took every assignment given to him as if it was his first. He treated it as if it was his opportunity to show the Guild what he was capable of and that he would not fail them.

He left High-Master Wraith a little after midday, and even though he wanted to immediately begin his new task, he knew he would have to wait until the latest marks of the night before he could put the first part of his plan into action.

It was way past the midpoint of the night before he would speak with the boy named Selby, although the assassin had been waiting in the boy's bedchamber for over a mark.

Dodge had been observing Selby for almost as long as he had been watching the girl named Nyght. During his time watching the two, he had come to their building on a number of occasions and had taken a tour of the interior without anyone ever knowing. He was an assassin trained by the Assassin's Guild and an assassin not seen, was an assassin still alive. Dodge could dodge more than just daggers or other weapons forced upon him.

He knew Selby did not retire to his bedchamber on the fourth floor of the building until the late marks of the night. Some of those times, the boy would only make it to his bed just as the sun was rising into the sky. It did not matter when he came to the room on this night because Dodge had already prepared to remain until the boy joined him for the meeting he had planned for the both of them.

Dodge only had to wait until the fifth mark of the new day. He heard the door open to the room and made sure he remained motionless while standing in the corner to the left of the door but across from the bed where the boy would make for. Yes, Dodge has watched the boy for the past few seasons, and he knew the boy's routine. He would come into the room and walk over to the far side of the bed.

Selby did exactly as the assassin had suspected. The only thing the uninvited guest did not calculate was that Selby sensed that someone was in his room the moment he stepped through the doorway.

When he made his way over to the side of the bed he tossed back the covers as if he was preparing to turn in. He sat down on the bed, bent over, and removed his boots. Once finished he sat back up and stretched his arms upward making it appear as if he was tired and was about to rest. When he brought his arms back down, he placed his hands on the bed at his sides but moved his left hand to the pillow at the head of the bed and slid it under to grab the small hand crossbow he kept there just in case.

When he had a hold of it, he quickly stood up and turned to face the direction he thought someone was hiding. Now that he was facing the intruder, he was able to see him clearly, even though it was still dark out and Selby had not lit a candle when he entered. His eyes were used to the night, and he was prepared to defend himself or die trying.

"It won't do you any good without this," Dodge said, and before Selby could ask the intruder what he meant, the assassin tossed the small bolt that had been set in the hand crossbow onto the bed just out of Selby's reach.

Selby looked at the small weapon he was holding and noticed that what was on the bed was what he needed for the weapon to be of any use. He looked down at the bolt and tried to decide if he could grab the item and set it in the crossbow before the man on the other side of the room made another move. It was a risky plan, but Selby thought he could make it.

Dodge has had the title of True Assassin since he was the age of twenty. Now at twenty-eight, not only is he still just as fast as he was a few seasons ago, but he also has confronted enough people who have been in the same predicament as the boy is now, so Dodge knew exactly what Selby was trying to decide. Dodge came to talk and did not want to cause the boy any harm but at the same time, he had to show the boy he was not dealing with just any intruder.

Dodge waited until a breath before he knew Selby was going to make a move for the bolt, but before he could even move a finger, Dodge thrust his own hand out and sent a throwing dagger across the room. It passed just in front of the boy's face.

Selby, being able to see better in the dark than most people, saw the blade pass before him, and as it did, he turned his head to follow it in the direction it had been moving, and when the dagger stopped, it was less than an arm's length away from his head embedded in the wall to his right. "I have more than just one of those and yes, that was only a warning. I did not have to miss," the man said to him, and Selby was sure he was telling the truth.

He tossed the small useless weapon on the bed so that it was lying next to the bolt. He then saw the man across the room step out of the corner and walk over to stand on the other side of the bed. They looked at each other, not saying a word, but each thinking their own thoughts.

Selby was wondering that since he did not see any other daggers in the man's hands or on his body, then maybe he had been lying, and just maybe, he could make a grab for the crossbow and bolt.

Dodge was thinking that maybe he would let the boy try what he knew the boy was thinking but decided he needed to move this meeting along. He leaned over enough to grab a hold of the two items on the bed but kept his eyes on the boy to make sure he did not try something that would cause the assassin to have to defend himself because when the assassin defended himself, someone ended up dead.

Dodge had been watching the boy for a few seasons and on the first night the assassin made his way into the building and inspected the room where he was now, he found the crossbow under the pillow. When he made it into the room this time, he removed the bolt but left the weapon to make sure the boy did not make a very costly error on his part by trying to kill the assassin. Dodge had nothing against the boy and did not want to kill him if he did not have to.

Dodge placed the two items on the stand to his left at the side of the bed. He did this without taking his eyes off the boy, and of course, Selby did not take his eyes off the assassin. "Now that we each know where I stand, I have a matter I wish to discuss with you," Dodge said to let the boy know why he was truly there.

"And why would the assassin Dodge wish to talk with me?" Selby asked while still looking at the man standing on the other side of the bed. Since he never took his eyes off the assassin, he saw the expression that came across the man's face and was glad he was able to cause the look which was a mixture of confusion and astonishment. Exactly what Selby was going for.

Dodge did not know what to say or do. For it was not often the assassin came upon a situation that would cause him to have to think about how he made his next move. The boy had called him by name. His assassin's name "Dodge." Every assassin used a name they would only tell other assassins. This was to make sure their identity was only known to the members of the Guild. This child, who was not a member of the Guild, had called him by his name. Even though his desire to end the boy's life had increased because he wanted to protect himself as well as the Guild, his respect for the boy increased also, and because of that, he would hold off on killing him. At least until he got the information he had come for as well as how the boy knew his name.

Selby was the one to make the next move. He turned around and walked over to the other side of the room. Putting his back on the assassin showed the uninvited guest that he was not scared of what the man could do. At least he wanted the assassin to think he was not scared, because since Selby knew who the man was and what he was, there was a good chance he would not be alive after this meeting was over. He called the assassin by his chosen name to put the man off guard. Selby knew that an assassin's name was something only known by other members of the Guild. Of course, that was the reason he had chosen the task as his personal project. Not just to learn the names of the assassins living in Sarzanac, but to learn the names of all the assassins in the Assassin's Guild. Selby knew it would take most of his life to find out the information, but information was what he was good at finding.

When he reached the desk against the wall, Selby turned around and to his surprise, he saw the assassin standing at the foot of the bed. It was not the fact that he was there that bothered him, but the fact he had not heard the assassin move. The building Selby had lived in for so many seasons was old, and with that, the floorboards creaked with every step anyone would take. Selby did not hear any noise while he had his eyes off the assassin, so he thought that since he did not hear the floorboards, the assassin was still on the other side of the bed. Since he was not, he had moved and never made a sound. His respect for the assassin increased.

"It appears that we both are well trained in the line of work of our choosing," Dodge said to give a compliment to the boy as well as a warning. "But as I said, I only came here to talk and to gain some information."

"So, you wish to barter?" Selby asked. It was the question he would use when someone wanted something from him.

Of course, Dodge knew this was how the boy began all his transactions. "Yes, I wish to barter," Dodge said.

"Your offer?" Selby asked to find out what the assassin would barter with.

"Your life," Dodge said, and he made sure there was no smile on his face when he did.

Even though Selby knew the assassin was being serious, he did not show any signs that the assassin's reply bothered him and continued with the meeting, "Your desire?" Selby asked to find out what the assassin wanted.

"Information on the girl who was with you for over three seasons."

Many girls stayed in the building, but Selby knew there was only one girl the two in the room had in common, the girl with the deep beautiful eyes. "We cannot barter," Selby said to let the man know that there would not be an exchange of any kind. He did not care if the assassin threatened his life, he would not tell anything to the man about the girl he had just seen walk into the Assassin's Guild two sun-cycles ago. Into the Guild and out of his life.

Part of the assassin's training consisted of being able to read every type of reaction a person would make when he spoke to them. It was no different now. When the boy said they could not barter, the assassin heard in the boy's voice that he would rather die than give any information about the girl. Dodge also knew why. Selby was in love with her. Love was something no assassin could ever defeat. They could torture a person until they died from it, but if what the assassin wanted would harm someone the person loves, truly loves, they would die to protect that person. A mother and father would protect the child they love. A child would protect the parents they love, and a man would protect the woman he loves.

What he heard in Selby's words was that he was a man in love and not a boy. No, he could not defeat love, but he could go around it.

High-Master Wraith said that the Guild, and even he, would cover all expenses. He could offer the man a large sum of coin, but Dodge knew that like torture, Selby would not give up any information concerning the girl even for all the gold the Guild had. He had been studying the young man long before this night and he knew the only thing this one wanted more than anything. Maybe not as much as he wanted the girl known as Nyght, but it would be something the assassin could use to barter with. "I suggest we stop the flaunting of our skills and talk man to man," Dodge said and walked to the side of the bed where Selby had been standing. He then sat down.

"No offense, but I am not going to let you bed me to get the information either," Selby said jokingly.

Dodge always enjoyed a person with a quick wit, and he was beginning to like Selby even more than what he had before he came into the room. "No, I think that maybe we can work together." When he saw he had Selby's attention, he continued. "That is correct; you and I pull our resources together so that we can find out what we both want to know."

"And what is that?" Selby asked.

"Information," Dodge said.

Selby did not hesitate to give his answer, "I told you we cannot barter. I will not tell you anything about the girl."

Dodge was not too sure about that, especially once he finished telling the young man what he had in mind. "You will tell me what you know about the girl, and you will do so willingly. Without me even threatening your life or paying you a single coin."

"And why would I do that?"

Dodge stood up from the bed and took three steps toward Selby. They were still over two arm lengths away from each other but closer than they had been since the meeting began. "Because you want the same thing I want." Selby did not say it, but Dodge could see that Selby wanted to ask, what that thing was, so Dodge told him. "You want to know more about the girl. You want to know everything about her. Especially, her past and where she came from and what made her the way she is now." As soon as Dodge finished, he could tell that he had used the one item the young man could not turn away from, information.

They stood there for a moment; it was Selby who spoke next, "I will not tell you anything or do anything that will bring harm to her."

Dodge took a step forward to close the distance between them. "Believe me when I tell you that neither I nor my Guild wish the girl any harm."

Since they were so close to one another, Selby saw in the assassin's eyes that he was speaking the truth. "Why didn't you ask her what you wanted to know?"

Dodge had thought the same question when

High-Master Wraith had given him this assignment. He never asked it though because he thought he knew the answer, and probably so did High-Master Wraith. The child would never say anything she did not want to. He had only spoken with the child three times, but in all those incidences, the child said very few words. "Since you have known the child, has she ever talked about her past to you?" he asked Selby.

He took a moment before he answered. It was not that he did not have one. He was trying to decide if the assassin was trying to trick him into giving information that would cause problems for the girl. He did not see any harm in answering the question. "She never talked about her past. In fact, she never talked about her future. The only reason I knew she wanted to join your Guild was because she asked where it was."

"She never said where she came from or anything about her parents?"

Selby shook his head to answer the question and then added his opinion. "She would talk only about the present and whatever job I had brokered for her."

"The rat killing," Dodge said as a statement and not a question. He wanted to show Selby that he had information concerning the two of them and what they did before the child entered the Guild."

"Yes," Selby said, then turned around to face the desk. When he turned back to the assassin, he had a bottle of hard spirits in his hand, and he made a gesture with the bottle to offer the assassin some. Dodge thought the man was now a lot more relaxed with the assassin in the room but turned down the offer. He would never drink something that would dull his senses and slow his reflexes.

Selby turned and picked up a glass and poured himself a drink. He then sat the bottle back down on the desk, took a sip of his drink, then continued talking about the girl. "She always kept her thoughts on the present. At least the ones she spoke and that was whenever she did decide to speak. I have a feeling the thoughts she kept to herself were always about her future. It is my guess that she didn't have much use for her past." Selby raised his glass to take a drink but before he did, he added one more thing, "Not like we do."

The assassin knew that he now had this young man captured in the intrigue of the girl. With what he ended with, Dodge knew that like him, Selby wanted to know about the girl and where she came from. He wanted to make a proposition to the young man; but first, he had to make sure that Selby would not be more of a hindrance than help. "How did you know my name?" Dodge got straight to the point. Depending on the answer he received would decide how the meeting ended. Whether or not they both would walk out of the room or just Dodge himself.

Selby sat the glass down behind him on the desk without taking his eyes off the assassin. He then stepped around Dodge and headed back over to the bed. At first, Dodge thought that he was going to try to make a grab for the weapon on the table on the other side of the bed, but when he saw Selby stay on the side he was on, he decided he was after something else.

Selby went to the foot of the bed, knelt down on the floor, and placed his hand on the wooden rail the mattress rested on. He then slid a piece of wood toward the foot of the bed revealing a hidden compartment. One that not even Dodge had come across when he previously searched the room on a number of different occasions.

He did not see what Selby had in his hand until he turned and faced Dodge and tossed the small book to the assassin who had no problem with snatching it out of the air as soon as it was within his reach. He opened the book and started flipping through the pages. As soon as he came to the first page with writing, he stopped and read what was on it. He moved his eyes down the page and only took them off the book when he had completed going over the contents written. He then put his eyes on Selby who was still standing at the foot of the bed with a big smile on his face.

Dodge kept his eyes on the young man for a couple of breaths then put his focus back on the book in his hands. He continued to turn the pages and quickly glanced at some of the information on them. He then skipped further ahead in the book and came across a drawing that covered both the left and right pages.

It was a drawing of the entire section of the parcel where the entrance to the Assassin's Guild was. Not just the building where the recruits entered that took them to the true Guild, but the houses around the building the assassins used while in the city. There was a total of twelve buildings. Three on each side of the parcel. The center building on the north side was just like the one the recruits entered into. Instead of taking an assassin to the doors and the passageway the recruits had to get past, this building transported an assassin to the main tower of the Guild land-marks away, high up in the mountains.

The Guild owned every house on the parcel. They had five of the twelve buildings set up to run their operations in the city of Sarzanac. The remaining ones were nothing more than decoys. Now, it appears that this young man knew more about the Guild than anyone who is not a member.

The drawings of the buildings were shocking, but it was what Dodge had read on the first few pages that disturbed him. It was a list of names. Names of assassins along with a description of what they look like, as well as dates, and times they walked out of which building and on what day, and times they left the city including which of the three gates they used or whether or not they left by ship. If that were the case, there was an entry of what the name of the ship was and the destination the ship was making for.

Dodge did not know which bit of information

bothered him more. The fact the young man had mapped out some of the coming and goings of the assassins or the fact he had the names of nine assassins. Names no one should know. For the second time that night, Dodge was not sure what he should do next. Just by knowing his name, he should kill the young man, but because of the book he had been handed, it proved that the one called Captain Selby was more efficient at gathering information than anyone the assassin had ever come across. He also could not help but think that Selby might have made a good assassin himself. If the Guild was anything, they were efficient.

As he was going over everything he had discovered in his thoughts, Dodge could not ignore what his instincts were telling him. Normally they would tell him to kill the young man to protect himself, other assassins, and especially the Guild. At the moment, his instincts were telling him that a live Captain Selby would be more beneficial to the Guild than a dead one. Of course, his respect for the young man increased when he realized that no information was out of this young man's reach.

Dodge tossed the book across the room and Selby snatched it out of the air. Not as gracefully as the assassin of course. Even though the assassin did not ask why he was making notes on the Guild, Selby began to tell him. "It is a personal project I have taken on." He made sure the assassin was looking at him before he continued, "No one who works with me knows about this book or the fact that I have been studying your Guild for a number of seasons. I am the one who watches the buildings and follows whoever leaves them and where they go."

Dodge understood why the young man had told him the last part. The Guild prefers to keep their secrets, secret. Because of that, Selby did not want anyone else punished for what he had taken on himself. Even if what he was doing was something that could end his life, Selby wanted to make sure others were safe. Dodge's respect for the young man increased for the third time that night. "You do it because you want information. Not necessarily on the Guild but information pertaining to everything. You have taken on this task as a personal training exercise. You know that if you can find out the secrets of my Guild, especially our names, you know you will be able to always find out what you want to know." Selby nodded to let the assassin know he was correct. "So why tell me? I am sure you are aware that by knowing my name, let alone having that book and information, I should kill you."

"To let you know that I am not afraid of you. You may be an assassin and yes you could kill me before I even thought about killing you, but information to me is worth more than any amount of gold you could offer or even my own life."

Dodge's respect for the young man continued to increase. He knew he would not kill this man, at least not tonight. In fact, he would not even mention the book to anyone else. Not even to the Masters or High-Masters. He had a better way of making sure the information the young man had collected would not hurt him or the Guild. "Keep that book out of the sight of others and keep what you find to yourself."

Selby nodded, turned, and replaced the book to where he had it hidden, covering the compartment in the frame once again. He then stood and faced the assassin, "So where do we go from here?"

Dodge knew exactly. "We find the past of our mutual friend." To make sure he did not let his friend slip away, he added a bit of bait to keep him interested. "By the way, she now has a name she goes by." Dodge saw Selby's eyes go wider.

"What is it?" Selby asked with way too much enthusiasm.

Dodge showed him the bait, but he was not going to let him have a free meal, and he could not go against the rule of the Guild which states an assassin is not to reveal their chosen name or the name of any assassin to someone outside the Guild. "It is her name, so it is hers to give to you if she chooses." Dodge could tell that the young man wanted to know more than anything else what the girl went by. "Maybe some night, the two of you can talk about it." Dodge made sure he did not say his statement to give anything away. Of course, if the young man was as good as he thought he was, then maybe he would notice the hint. "Where did she stay in the building?" Dodge asked, thinking that if she had left anything behind, it might lead him in the best direction. Even when he had searched the building previously, he did not know which room the girl had been staying in.

"I promised her that I would not let anyone enter her place. Just in case she decides to return," Selby said.

Dodge wanted to reply with, "Just in case she returned to you," but did not. He himself had no need for the love of someone. His love was what he did, but he did not fault others for having the weakness. Yes, a person might protect the ones they love, but to love someone truly, a person must sacrifice a part of themselves to have love. Dodge needed every bit of who he was to do what he does. "So, you won't tell me where she stayed in your building because you made a promise."

"Yes," Selby said, and Dodge knew he meant to keep the promise.

Dodge still wanted to look at the place and he was not going to let a silly promise stop him. He had not gone completely through this building, but he knew the girl was staying there. Now he just had to figure out which room was hers. It did not take him but two breaths to come up with the answer. He was an assassin like the girl, and he knew that the best place to defend would be the highest ground. He smiled and looked at Selby, "She stayed in the attic." Once again, it was a statement, not a question.

"I can't let you enter it," Selby said and took a step closer to the assassin.

"The fact is you cannot stop me." Dodge did not like what he said but he had no choice. He had a task to complete, and he would see it through. As much as he was growing fond of the young man, he would not let him get in his way. Of course, there is usually a way around every promise. "You said you promised to not let anyone into her place is that correct?"

"Yes," Selby said, wondering where the assassin was leading him.

"And you will not let me in. I will make my way into the place myself. If you wish, you have three options." Selby did not say anything, so Dodge continued. "You stay here, and I go to the attic, or you can come with me." Dodge stopped there.

Selby asked the question the assassin was waiting for, "What is the third option?"

Dodge answered right on cue, "You try to stop me. I kill you here and now and I still go to the attic; your choice."

Selby took a moment to think over his options including the third one, if he thought it would protect the girl, but he chose to go with the second offer. "I will go with you."

"Good choice, but to keep this little expedition to just the two of us, why don't you go out and make sure no one else is around with open eyes."

Selby thought it was a good proposal. He knew that if anyone were to see this man in the building then they might start asking questions and the answers to those questions could be awfully bad for

them. He turned away from the assassin and headed to the door of his chamber, but before he opened
it, the assassin gave him one more bit of advice. "A
smart man would only do as I instructed which is to
make sure our way is clear. A dead man would bring
in a few of his associates to try and end my life."
Dodge paused for two breaths before he continued.
"I trust you are a man of the first type."

Selby did not turn to give his answer. He just
nodded his head to let the assassin know he understood. The truth was that Selby never thought
of going against his uninvited guest. The lives of his
people would be in jeopardy and Selby would do
anything to protect them. Also, like the assassin, he
wanted to know more about the girl he had known
and had left. The final reason Selby would do as the
assassin instructed was because even though he was
an assassin, Selby trusted him. Just because of the
profession he had chosen did not mean the man did
not have honor. Something Selby could tell Dodge
had and respected him for it.

Since it was almost morning, no one was around
the part of the building where the two needed to
go. Selby had turned the fourth floor into his place
of operations and living quarters, and even though
he used to have guards posted at the door to whichever room he was using at the time, he always dis-
missed them when he went to bed. There were still
guards posted on the lower levels but none on the
fourth floor. Since he had an uninvited guest stop by

this evening, he decided that he might start having guards posted constantly on this level just in case someone else tried to make their way into his living quarters.

When they reached the fifth floor, it was still completely vacant. Selby wanted to make sure he kept his promise to the girl but now it seems that he had to break it. Of course, just as the assassin thought, he was only bending it a little. It was not that he let the assassin go into the room, he just could not stop him.

They made their way up into the attic and even with the hatchway open, there was very little light entering in. Selby had only been up there once when he first acquired the building, but since there had been so many rats, he never returned. When the rats left, the girl had taken up residence and wanted her privacy which Selby gave her. Since both he and the assassin wanted to look around, he walked over to the small window and opened the shutters. Some light entered the room, and it was enough to allow the two to begin their search. Both had spent a good majority of their life wandering around at night and in dark rooms. They just did not know that the girl they were so interested in could see in the dark better than both of them put together.

The day Nyght entered the Guild, she had left four items behind in her room. One was the majority of the coins she had saved over the past seasons, which she hid inside one of the walls. Another was the blanket she used to sleep on. It was the last two items Dodge spotted almost immediately and when he did, it only led him to more questions.

He walked over to the wall where the blanket was lying on the floor. On top of it, laid a black waterskin, and another bag of the same color. This was not the first time the assassin had seen items like these. He himself had a set of them back in his room at the Guild House in the city. He received them on the day he accepted his first contract, as it was with all assassins.

The Guild's wizards spelled both bags. They would keep water and food fresh. Water would stay cool in the waterskin, and no matter how long a bit of food was in the other bag it would not go bad. Assassins would use these items when they went out to fulfill a contract. As long as they had water and food to place in the items, they did not have to worry about it not being usable. The question Dodge did not know the answer to was how the girl would acquire these items. As soon as he thought of the question, he remembered his assigned task. To find the parents of the girl. They were, or at least one of them was an assassin and High-Master Wraith wanted to know who those parents were. "Do you know how long she had these items?" he asked Selby.

He knew the answer but before he spoke, Selby thought if responding would harm the girl in any way. He decided it would be safe, so he answered the assassin's question. "The first time I saw the bags was the first night she had come to the building. I would say she had them when she arrived but kept them hidden under the cloak she always wore."

Dodge was bending down toward the floor examining the items and Selby was standing behind him. He did not turn to look at the young man, but he did agree with what he had said. The girl always wore that cloak of hers and she could have had them the first night she arrived. More than likely, she did.

After seeing the two bags, Dodge knew the answers at the end of his journey were going to be greater than he could even imagine. He stood up and turned around to face Selby who would also enjoy seeing this to the end. The only problem Dodge could think of was how much could he trust the young man. He may respect him, but trust was something quite different. He alone has killed more than one person he respected but did not trust. One more name to the list would not bother the assassin at all. "How did you find out what my name was?" he asked Selby, who was surprised at the sudden change of topic.

Selby gave his answer by asking a question first, "Does someone else, other than you, know you go by the name Dodge?"

"Of course," the assassin replied.

"Then your name is not a secret. A secret is something that only one person knows. If more than one knows, the secret becomes information. Secrets are kept; information is shared."

Dodge understood the statement. The saying was that if you wanted to keep something truly a secret tell only one other person. That way, if someone else mentions it, then you would know who told the secret. To Selby though, even telling one other person was one person too many. Dodge was sure he would be able to trust Selby. "I will be leaving the city. Come with me if you want to find out about our friend."

Selby looked at the assassin with amazement. Asking himself, did the man just ask him to join him in whatever task he was undertaking? Selby could not deny the fact that he was more than intrigued with everything that had happened since the assassin entered his chamber. "I cannot," he said to turn down the offer. "I have plans that are in the works and I cannot just walk away from them."

The assassin was not ready to accept his answer, for he wanted the young man to come with him no matter where the path led. Not only did he have respect for the young man, but he liked him in a way that reminded the assassin of a younger him. "I know what you have planned and so does the Guild."

Selby was not surprised at what he heard. He knew the Guild had informants all over the city. He even knew who some of them were, and even obtained some information about the Assassin's Guild itself from those informants.

"I cannot," Selby said and turned to leave the room.

Dodge spoke before he left. "I know what you have started in Sarzanac is only the first part of your plan. When you are ready, you will increase your reach to other cities." Dodge walked over to stand in front of the young man. "Come with me, and as we travel, you will learn of those places. You will be able to see some of what you will be reaching for in the future, and from what I can tell, what you will grab a hold of." Dodge was using Selby's own desire to get him to join the assassin. He also had another piece of bait he could use. "You know the girl better than anyone, yet you still do not know the majority of her story. This is your chance to find out what you do not."

Selby could see what the assassin was doing. He could also see that it was working. He wanted information. He needed information. All information. Even though his feelings for the girl were strong and he did not want to bring any harm to her, his need to know something pulled hard on his soul. There was only one thing he felt more strongly about; protecting the people he was responsible for. "I cannot. I must stay in the city until I am sure the ones I leave in charge are able to survive on their own. I will not abandon them."

Once again, Dodge's respect for the young man increased. He still wanted Selby to join him, so he had a solution to the last problem the young man spoke of. "Come with me and I will guarantee that all those who are under your protection will not come to any harm by another's hand during the time you are away."

Selby heard what the assassin said, he just did not see how he would make it possible. "What will you do?" he asked to get an explanation.

Dodge was ready with his reply, "If I told you, it wouldn't be a secret." He smiled at the young man who was now smiling as well. "Inform your people that you will be going away for a period of time. I cannot tell you how long we will be gone. It depends on how much difficulty we run into looking for our answers. But if you tell them that if they do not act against anyone in the city that you and your people usually have quarrels with, I will make sure they are safe from anyone that wishes them harm." With what Dodge had planned, he would not let Selby's people use what the assassin would put in place to take out those who wish to see Selby and his organization disappear. That included other organizations, businesses, and even the people who ran the city of Sarzanac itself.

The offer the assassin was making pulled hard at Selby. He would love to get out of the city and not only begin to make plans for the next phase of his dreams, but he would love to find out more about the girl he knew nothing about but had taken his heart when she walked into the Guild. "Can you guarantee my people will be safe?" he asked to get verification of his biggest concern.

"I can guarantee that as long as they do not take

any aggression to others, they will be protected from anyone who resides in the city or anyone who comes to Sarzanac in your absence. You have my word."

That phrase coming from an assassin might not mean much to others, but Selby knew the man was sincere about what he was offering. "I will join you," Selby said and even smiled. Dodge as well was glad the young man accepted his offer.

"Very well. You speak to your people and let them know you will be away for an undisclosed amount of time. Just remember to keep my name and anything that took place tonight out of your conversation."

"I had not planned on mentioning you," Selby said, and the assassin knew he was being truthful.

Dodge continued to relay the next part of the plan. "While you take care of your people, I will do what I need to do to...take care of your people." Selby chuckled at the comment. "We will then need to decide where we need to head next."

Selby already had the answer, "North," he said, and the assassin gave him a look as if to ask why that direction. "The night the girl arrived in the city I sent someone to find out which gate she entered through. One of the guards remembered her and he was at the northern gate. So that is where we will leave the city. Afterward, we will have to see if we can track her path and if we can find anyone who had contact with her."

Dodge could only nod to agree with what his

new partner had just said. Not just because it was a good plan, but because he was amazed at how fast the young man had come up with it. Or maybe the young man, who wanted to know all, had thought about finding out where the girl had come from long before the assassin had made contact.

"Very well, we will leave by the north gate," Dodge said. "How long will you need to get ready?"

"Give me until the eighth mark. I will meet you at the north gate at that time."

Dodge turned his head and looked out the small window in the room. With the way the light was shining outside, it was just at the sixth mark of the day. That would give him two marks to make the necessary arrangements for their journey as well as what he had promised the young man he would do. He turned back to look at Selby, "I will meet you at the north gate at the eighth mark."

Selby nodded then turned to walk out of the room. When he reached the top of the ladder, he turned around to say one last thing to the assassin, but he was not there. Selby looked toward the window, the only other exit to the room. When the assassin had left, he even made sure he closed the shutters behind him just as they were when they had entered the room.

Selby went down the ladder and closed the hatch to the attic. He had a lot to do before he had to meet his new partner and little time to do it. He figured that he should start by gathering his top five lieutenants together and letting them know that he would be leaving. He trusted the assassin to keep his word to protect the ones he was responsible for while he was gone. That was what was most important to him. That and finding out information.

After Dodge left the building through the window, he immediately went to the Guild House in Sarzanac. He had already made plans for him to have supplies and a horse ready for him so he could leave that morning. Even though he did not know what direction he would be traveling in when he had, but now after talking with Selby, he knew the beginning of his path.

He also arranged for an additional horse and double the amount of the supplies he had first requested. Since the Guild ran so efficiently, there were no problems fulfilling his requests.

He went to the people who managed the Guild House in Sarzanac and asked for a Mantle of Protection for the people under the supervision of the one known as Captain Selby. The only question asked was how long the Mantle was to remain in place, and Dodge told them, "Until he returns." The Guild agreed. Any assassin could request the Mantle if they felt that the protection of a person or persons would be in the best interest of the Guild. Since the ones operating the Guild House in Sarzanac were well aware of Captain Selby and his people, they understood the Guild's interest in the young man and what he was attempting.

With the Mantle in place, the Guild would make sure that everyone under it would not come to harm. That is unless the ones under protection tried to take on someone themselves. They were assassins, not soldiers. The Guild would make sure the necessary ears, including the people who ran the city, knew that as long as the Mantle was in effect, the Guild would deal with anyone who took an unfriendly interest in the Guild's interest, which was not a wise thing to do.

At the eighth mark, Selby arrived at the north gate. The question he wanted to ask the assassin before he went out the window was, "What supplies would they need?" Selby decided to pack the things he thought he would need for the trip and that the assassin would take care of his own supplies. When Selby met up with the assassin, he saw that not only did the assassin have supplies for both of them, but he also had acquired two fine horses to ride.

Being the person Selby is, he had learned to ride a horse a while back, so when he reached the one with no rider, he placed his supplies at the rear of the saddle and then swung up onto the back of the horse with almost as much grace as the assassin had. When they had each other's attention, Selby added one more point to their joint venture. "I'm sure your friends will cover all expenses."

Dodge was impressed with how Selby used the term "friends" instead of referring to the Guild in any manner to bring attention to themselves. He really did respect the young man, and only nodded to agree to the statement.

Selby then kicked his horse into motion and headed out through the north gate.

Dodge held back for just a moment. His task was to find out information about the child, especially who her parents are or were. In his travels with the young man, he decided that he would take on a second task: to nurture him into a man. Dodge had some idea of what Captain Selby had planned for his future and he would need to know more about the world than what he learned on the streets of Sarzanac.

Dodge did not have any family by blood, at least none he knew of, but a part of him had just adopted a younger brother.

SIX

High-Master Wraith had made it to the fourth set of stairs before he had to take a break to catch his breath. He realized that he had not made a trip up through one of the towers held by one of the Masters since he was a Master himself. That had been over forty seasons ago, and now at the age of one hundred seventeen, he could not help but think that teaching another is best suited to one who is greatly younger than he was. Of course, he did not think that for long, because he knew when he reached the sixth floor and talked with the child, he would be more than willing to train her. Just not in the tower he was currently in with all the stairs.

He began his climb again and thought about the events that had taken place in the Guild over the past few sun-cycles. The child passing the test, as well as the death of Viper, confirmed yesterday when the Guild's Weapons-Maker requested the presence of all three High-Masters in his private chamber located on the lowest level of the Guild.

When they arrived, the body of Viper was lying on the floor at the feet of the Weapons-Maker who had found her. She was still wearing her night-clothes, even though there was very little material to the ensemble to begin with, but there were obvious rips in the material that came from when her body landed on the ground far below her chamber's window.

From what the High-Masters and the Weapons-Maker could determine, she had been lying out in the cold temperatures for at least half of a sun-cycle. The blood in her body had frozen and caused her to remain in the same pose the Weapons-Maker had found her in. Even though the fire in the room was warm as well as the entire level the Weapons-Maker lived on due to the forge he continuously kept burning, the woman's body would still take a while to thaw to the point where she could assume a more respectable position.

Her left arm had frozen into place behind her along with her right leg which bent so far backward that the toes were touching the middle of the woman's back. Of course, all four thought to themselves that with the flexibility the former Master had when she was alive, as well as what she enjoyed doing in her bed, the position she was currently in at the moment was a memorial in itself to the life she led.

Since the Weapons-Maker's accommodations were below the first floor of the Guild, there were hidden tunnels that only he and the High-Masters knew of which allowed the Weapons-Maker to exit the Guild unnoticed and locate the missing assassin without anyone knowing what he was doing and what he had discovered. He entered back into the Guild the same way and let the High-Masters know they needed to meet with him.

The Weapons-Maker was loyal to the Guild and the High-Masters and would keep what he found to himself. The death of a Master could not remain a secret from the other members, so the High-Masters came up with her passing as an act of Creator. They would let everyone know that apparently, the dear woman suffered from an attack of the Richwood wine which she and all those she taught and all those who came before her drank on a daily basis. Unfortunately, she had developed a habit of the substance and after taking more than the dosage that even she knew of to be safe, she fell from her window to her death on the jagged terrain below. Since she had been out in the cold for so long, the toxins would still be in her blood or at least they would be once the Weapons-Maker poured enough of the wine into her. Just as soon as she defrosted enough to where he would be able to open her mouth without breaking off her lips since they were frozen shut.

The three High-Masters established a plan quickly and easily. Before they took on their current roles, they were very efficient assassins, and arranging the death of a person to look as if they died a certain way was nothing to them. As for the Weapons-Maker, he did not care what happened to anyone.

Whether they were dead or alive, just as long as he was able to continue to make his weapons.

Even the explanation of why they waited a day or two to inform the other members of the Guild would be easy to explain. They would simply tell everyone that the dear woman was not in a presentable manner and out of respect for the deceased, the High-Masters wanted to ensure her final memory was as the beautiful woman she was in life.

The High-Masters visited the Weapons-Maker before their eighth-mark meeting with the other Masters. At the meeting, they informed the Masters of the tragic incident but made sure the Masters did not speak to anyone about it as of yet because there were still some matters that needed to be addressed. Of course, the Masters agreed, out of respect for the dear woman as well as for the High-Masters.

When the High-Masters met again with the Weapons-Maker after the meeting, he had already poured three glasses of Richwood wine into the assassin's mouth. He had to prop her against the wall to make sure the liquid went into her system, and to make sure it traveled into her bloodstream even more, the Weapons-Maker swung around in a circle while holding onto the deceased arms. He kept that part of the plan to himself. Like everyone who was part of the Guild, even the Weapons-Maker was efficient, and he wanted to make sure the facts matched the story. More than likely, no one would even check the body or the blood to see if the death was due to the Richwood wine, but no matter what the Guild did, they did it thoroughly.

High-Master Wraith reached the sixth floor where the child's quarters were. Before he began walking down the hallway toward the door, he looked back at the stairs behind him and thought that it would be a lot easier going down them when he left. He just did not know how much easier it would be until he attempted the task. He was definitely feeling all the one hundred seventeen seasons he had been alive.

He walked down the hallway to the two doors. He glanced to his left and saw the door to Crimson's room. She was not there at the moment because the other two High-Masters had sent for her just before High-Master Wraith entered the tower. They would be the ones to tell the young woman about the unfortunate incident concerning her mentor. The young woman might take the news harder than others since they had spent so much time together in the past five seasons and the High-Masters thought it would be best if she heard the news directly from them, instead of someone else. Of course, to help with the loss, they would tell her that they would immediately grant her the title of True Assassin. It would assist with any grief she might have. If she was like her mentor, any emotions she might display were more than likely nothing more than a charade. She learned from one of the best.

High-Master Wraith turned to face the door

to his right. Before he knocked, he paused a moment to prepare himself. He took a few more deep breaths to get air into his lungs which had left when ascending the stairs and to make sure he was ready for when he saw the child.

He knocked on the door, and even though he was over a hundred seasons old, his sense of hearing had not lessened, so he heard the child walking across the room. Since he knew the size of the room, he did not knock again and waited for the door to open.

When it did, as much as he wanted to, he made sure he did not look into the child's eyes. It was the way he used to deal with being in the presence of the one he had known all those seasons ago. When he had to face the person, he put his eyes on their feet first and then lifted his head but stopped when his own eyes were on the person's chin. Making sure the two would not make eye contact. When he met the other person, he had already been an assassin for over forty seasons, and in that time, he had killed quite a few individuals. Back then, he was known only as Wraith, but he was well known throughout the Guild because there was not a single individual who knew of the way he would fulfill the contracts he accepted. Not even the Master who trained him or even the High-Master who had promoted him to Master, nor the High-Master who had selected him for his current position. He had fulfilled many contracts, but he was the only one who knew how he had accomplished them.

Now that there was another one with the same eyes as the first, High-Master Wraith did not want to look into those eyes. He had not taken a life in many seasons, but he was still responsible for the deaths of many by sending the assassins out on their missions. He may not have drawn the blood, but he had a hand in ending their life, so he still dealt with death every day of his own life.

The door opened and when he had his eyes set, he spoke, "I am High-Master Wraith," he said to the child, making sure he did not make eye contact with her. "May I enter?"

The child took a step to her right and turned so that she was still looking at the High-Master. When he stepped into the room, she closed the door behind him. He walked further inside and took in the surroundings.

He had not been in any of the chambers in this tower or any other tower belonging to one of the Masters since he had been a Master himself and occasionally took up the offer of Master Butterfly, the assassin who was the Master of this tower when he was one as well. After he became a High-Master, he was always too busy taking care of something important, so he did not have the time to take care of the needs his body desired, and after a few seasons, he did not care one way or the other.

He saw the bed across the room to his right and could not stop the small smile from appearing. When a new pupil came to one of the Master's towers, they were not supposed to have any substantial contact with anyone but the Master training them. That rule, even though it pertained to this tower as well, was not enforced when the Master of this tower invited another Master or High-Master to join her and sometimes her pupil as well. The way everyone looked at it, the students had to learn all styles of bedchamber recreation and sometimes it required more than two participants. Since the other Masters were part of those recreations, of course they did not say anything about the broken rule. It was for the benefit of the student's training as well as the benefit of the Guild.

To stop thinking of his past, he took his eyes off the bed and moved them to look at the wall to his left. It was the one with the fireplace but what he was focusing on was the bottle of red liquid sitting on a tray on the small table between the two chairs. He knew it was Richwood wine.

He walked across the room and stopped when he reached the small table. He turned enough to see the child behind him. She was still standing near the door so the distance between them was too great for the child's eyes to affect him. He still kept his gaze at a level where he did not look into them. It was what he trained himself to do with someone like her and to make sure he did not accidentally look at her eyes when they were close, the High-Master kept the practice up even at a further distance. "Did you drink any of this?" he asked the child.

"No, High-Master," Nyght said, and the High-Master noticed that she had said it with the respect others gave him. It appeared that Crimson had schooled the child on how to address one in his position. He turned back to look at the bottle, picked it up, and brought it closer to his face. "I would not drink that," Nyght said, and the High-Master turned his head so that he could see her. "I believe it has gone bad. I was going to inform Master Viper when I see her since she is the one who gave it to me."

The High-Master held his view of the girl for a moment longer, then turned back and placed the bottle of wine back on the table. As he did, he could not help but wonder about the whole situation. He had never intended to taste one drop of the liquid. Richwood wine was poison. In fact, it was thirty different poisons combined to make one. All the women trained in this tower drank it. The first Master of the tower created it and happened to go by the name "Richwood" herself. She had taken the thirty most potent poisons whether they came from nature or someone else had created it. She made the wine, drank it herself, and had all the pupils who came after her drink it as well.

What the poison did was make it so the women built up an immunity to not only the poisons the drink contained, but since they were the thirty most potent in the world, the person would be immune to every other poison known to exist. For an assassin, poison was a perfect way to remove someone. Since the assassin was immune to all poisons, they could put whatever they wanted into someone's food or drink as well as their own. The only difference would be that they would be the only person to enjoy another drink or meal. There have been times when an assassin trained in this manner was the only one to walk out of a banquet leaving everyone else attending lying on the floor or sitting in his or her chair, each of them no longer breathing.

There was some risk to taking the wine. One was that once a pupil took the first drink, they would have to continue with it. The poison acted in a way that even though an individual would be resistant to all poisons, their body became addicted to the wine and if they did not partake of one glass of the drink within one cycle of the sun, then the poison caused their entire body to shut down and they would die.

Another risk was that if the person could not control themselves, they could become addicted to the drink, and taking in more than one glass within a sun-cycle would cause the poisons to become too potent in their system which would also lead to their death, which was the story the High-Masters were proclaiming as the death of Viper.

High-Master Wraith did not turn to look at the child just yet. He was trying to figure out if the wine truly had gone bad, which it could, after the time of a moon-cycle, or was the child able to tell the drink would not have been good for her. He looked down at the bottle and from what he could tell, the wine looked as if it was still good, so he had to assume his second assumption was the truth. It was also the one he would suspect from one such as the child behind him.

He decided it did not matter. She had not consumed any of the liquid. If she had, she would have to continue to take in the substance and he would have to have one of the other women that partook of the drink to make it for him to give to the child or train her to make it herself. There are very few secrets between members of the Assassin's Guild but one of those is how to make the Richwood wine. The High-Master knew which poisons were used in the wine but only the women who drank the wine knew the exact amount of each poison to put into the mixture. It had something to do with balancing out the toxicity of each poison with all the others. If the measurements were off by the slightest, a person would die a very horrible death. Lucky for them it only lasted for the count of ten breaths, but it was the longest ten breaths the person had ever lived through and suffered.

He turned around so that he was facing the child, but before he could say anything, she spoke first, "Crimson did not come to get me for my training today and I have not seen Master Viper since the night I arrived."

For just a moment, High-Master Wraith thought the child could not have had anything to do with the death of Viper. It was the way she had said her statement. So innocent. He then realized that thought was not the truth. The child was making sure he did not think she had anything to do with what happened to the former Master. The child had spoken the truth, but she was covering her tracks and High-Master Wraith knew he could not let the child's manner make him think of her as something she was not, and that was a killer. "You will be trained by someone else," he said.

Nyght suspected that if she were to stay at the Guild, they would give her someone else to teach her. Now she had to decide what she would do if she ended up with someone like Master Viper.

"You will be leaving this tower," High-Master Wraith said and started walking toward the child, making sure he did not look into her eyes. "You will be staying in the High-Tower of the Guild for now until it has been decided who will continue with your training." High-Master Wraith had told the other High-Masters he would take on the child's training but even he was going to make sure she was worth his time. He was not going to teach a child who showed that she was no different from any other recruit they chose off the street. Since this was going to be his final act as a member of the Guild, he was going to make it beneficial to him. "Pack your things and follow me."

"Yes, High-Master, I am ready."

She had not moved from where she had been standing since he had entered, and she closed the door. With the exception of the cloak she was wearing, he did not see anything else she might be holding. "I was told you carry two fighting daggers, is that true?"

"Yes, High-Master," Nyght replied.

When she did not make a move to show them to him, which was what High-Master Wraith was expecting, he realized that besides the eyes, the child had another thing in common with the one he had known all those seasons ago. She was one who spoke very few words. "Show them to me," he said in a voice to let the child know that he was not going to be speaking every command to her. She had better learn quickly that his patience had its limits.

Nyght brought her hands out of her cloak, separating the two sides, pushing them out of the way. She then brought her hands up in front of her to show the daggers to the High-Master. He had been annoyed when she did not present them at first, but when he saw how beautiful the two weapons were, he was too amazed to even think about her hesitancy. If they were his, he would not let many, if any, get a glimpse of them because they might just want the two weapons for themselves.

The one dagger was black, and he could tell the metal was something he had never seen before because metal was just not that color. As black as the one the child held in her left hand, the other was just as white. High-Master Wraith immediately compared it to the color of the full moon. Which when he thought about it, was odd since the child went by the name Nyght. He noticed one last thing about the second blade. It matched the color of the child's skin.

She had her cloak covering her when she opened the door and he had only looked at her chin. When he was across the room from her, it was the first time he was able to get a good look at the child. Although her skin was unusual, for some reason he thought the child should look that way. Maybe since Viper had told him about the child's skin during the meeting the first night the child arrived, he had been prepared for it.

He also noticed the child's hair. It had been long, but as Crimson had told him it was now short, just barely reaching the top of her neck. He had a feeling that she had cut it after dealing with the woman who more than likely ran her hands through the child's hair too many times. He decided he would test that theory. "I was told your hair was longer than what it is now. Did you cut it?"

"Yes, High-Master." Once again, she answered with only a single word, and his title to show respect.

He had one more question concerning her hair. "Why?"

Nyght took two breaths before answering, "Because it was a burden."

Her response did not give the High-Master an answer that would offer him any insight into what happened to Viper, even though he knew the child had that knowledge. "Do you have any other weapons I need to know about?" He was an assassin and knew that an assassin, even one that had not earned the title yet might have a backup to their primary choice.

Nyght moved the blade in her right hand to her left with the other. She then lifted her right leg so that her knee came up with her leg bent downward toward the floor. She then used her right hand to remove the small knife she had concealed in the top of her boot. While still holding all three weapons, she lowered her leg back down. High-Master Wraith noticed how smoothly she performed the act. She was so balanced that she did not sway one bit through the entire process. "Is that all?" he asked.

"Yes, High-Master."

He had no choice but to trust her. If she was lying to him, there was nothing he could do at the moment. He would not think of searching the child; it would show a sign of weakness on his part. What High-Master would be afraid of a child? Even though he was not afraid, he was going to be cautious. He may not have proof that the child had something to do with Viper's accident, but he would make sure the other High-Masters and the Weapons-Maker did not have to come up with some story to explain why his body ended up on the outside of the Guild's perimeter. "Very well, I will take you to the High-Tower where you will remain until we decide where you fit in."

He walked to the door, but before he reached it, the child moved and opened it so that he could step through before her. Even though the child was showing him respect, he did not like the fact she would be at his back. When he entered the hallway, he waited until the child closed the door and joined him, he then gestured with his hand that she should go before him down the hallway and the stairs. She nodded to let him know she understood then started walking away from him.

He waited until she was a pace ahead, then began walking himself. It might have been difficult for him to climb the stairs, but he was hoping the trip back down to the first level would be a lot easier on his old body. However, he had a better chance of making the journey with the child in front of him instead of at his back. More than one person has met their death by descending a set of stairs. Whether it was an accident, or someone had assisted them, they still reached the bottom and did not get back up. He was not going to be one of those people. As far as he knew, he was the only member of the Guild who knew exactly what the child was, and what she was capable of. She may only be fifteen, but death has been with her from the day she came into the world. He had no doubt in his mind about that.

When they reached the lowest level, the High-Master wanted to stop for a moment to catch his breath. The descent, though not as bad as when he had to climb the stairs, still took a toll on his body but he did not want to show any weakness to the child. When they both had cleared the last step, he gestured with his hand in the direction the child needed to go. When they reached the door that would take them through the passageway back to the High-Tower, Nyght opened the door, but once again, the High-Master gestured for the child to go before him. She did not seem to have a problem with it.

When they reached the door at the end of the passageway leading to the High-Tower, the child opened it and stepped through, not even giving the High-Master the opportunity to tell her to go ahead of him. Since he did not ever really go for all the respect everyone would show him, he did not have a problem with the child taking the initiative to move the journey along.

When she stepped into the outer area, Nyght could not believe what she was seeing. The tower where she had been staying had ten floors, but the ceiling went so high she could not even see it. What she could see now was that the tower she was in had at least twice the number of floors and the ceiling went far higher than she could imagine.

"There is a total of twenty-five levels to the tower," the High-Master said when he saw the child looking up with her head bent back as far as it could go. She stopped looking up and turned her head so that she was looking at the High-Master to her right. He was just fast enough to advert his gaze so that he would not look into the child's eyes. "You are the first recruit who has been to the High-Tower in quite a long time." He started walking away from the girl. Since there were others around, other assassins, he did not have to be concerned about the child trying to have him join Viper. At least he had less of a concern than he had when it was just the two of them. "You see the circular metal platforms?" he asked and pointed at what he was referring to.

"Yes, High-Master. What are they?"

The High-Master was surprised at the tone of her voice. He could sense something in the way she asked the question. The child was inquisitive. "There is a total of twenty-four. Each one can take up to four people to a specific floor. They start over there," the High-Master said and pointed off to the left of where they were standing.

Nyght looked in the direction he was showing her and then turned her body to follow the lifts situated around the circular chamber. As she was observing the lifts in use by a few of the other members, the High-Master continued, "Each lift can only be used to reach its designated level. So, if you were to take the lift for the twenty-fifth floor, you would have to take the same lift back to this level if you wanted to go to a different one."

"Wouldn't it be simpler if each lift could stop at any level a person would choose to go to?" Nyght asked.

"Yes, that would be simpler and if you come up with a way to make that possible, then maybe

I should let you talk to the wizards who designed them because they have not been able to develop a method to do what you have suggested." The High-Master saw that Nyght was still looking at her surroundings, but he was sure she had heard him and continued. "Now if you are on a level and someone else has used the lift to return to the ground floor, there is a white crystal on each level next to the area where the lift stops. If you wave your hand over it, the lift will come back to the level you are on."

Nyght listened to the High-Master and understood. She thought that her idea about each lift stopping on every level would be more efficient but since they had designed a way to go from the lower floor to the top and every level in between, then it was more efficient than climbing multiple sets of stairs to reach the desired destination. Although she did not tell the High-Master what she was thinking she did have a question concerning them. "Has anyone ever fallen off one of the lifts?" she asked and High-Master Wraith was quick to respond.

"Certainly not! We are assassins my child and what good would someone be if they could not even keep their balance while riding one of the lifts." When he finished, he could not help but wonder why the child had asked the question and was she somehow thinking about how Viper had fallen from her window in such a manner that someone would fall from one of the lifts. He had to get past the fact that the child probably had something to do with Viper's accident. It was in the past and both he and the child needed to move forward. "Come, I will take you to the level where you will be staying." He turned around and walked off in the direction that would take him to the lift they would be using. When they reached it, he stepped onto the circular disc and the child followed his lead.

The lift did not rise as soon as the two riders were situated. The wizards who had come up with the spell to activate the lifts made sure there was a delay between the moment a person stepped onto one and it started to move so that it did not move while someone was still getting into position.

The lift started moving and to Nyght's surprise, she did not feel any motion at all except for the slight bit of air that went across her face as the lift rose. When it came to a stop, Nyght, who had been counting the number of floors as they passed them, ended at twenty-five. She was on the top floor and wondered why she was there. She always made sure she had positioned herself in the highest place where she stayed, even Master Viper had done the same, so she believed that whoever this level was for would be the highest ranked in the Guild which she knew were the three High-Masters. Crimson had begun her training with the basic information of the Guild itself. Although, in the time she had been with the woman, she had not told her much.

When they reached the top level, High-Master Wraith stepped off the platform and began walking around the circular hall which she saw was the width of the tower itself. Nyght fell into step behind him leading her to believe that the High-Master was now less worried about what she would do to him. She was not certain if he suspected her of having something to do with Viper's disappearance, but she was not going to let on that she did.

He never said anything, but Nyght could tell that the elderly assassin made sure he limited the amount of time she was behind him, as well as the fact that he never looked at her face any higher than the lower part. She did not know why that was, but since he was a High-Master and seemed to be well up in seasons, maybe he had some quirks about him that made him act wary around others. Nyght did not understand that his behavior was because he knew exactly what she was.

As they walked around the circular path, Nyght counted the doors she saw. She had only counted two when they came to the final door on this level. *"Three doors, three High-Masters,"* she thought to herself. She looked across the opening and saw the other two doors evenly spaced apart from the third door they had come to. She only stopped taking in her surroundings when she heard the High-Master speak. "Step inside." She turned her head and saw that he had opened the door and once again wanted her to go before him. For the first time since she had met the High-Master, she wondered if she was going to have to do something similar to what she had done to Master Viper. Not to give him any reason to be suspicious, she did as he instructed and stepped into the room.

She went in far enough to where she could get a quick look at the room but made sure she quickly turned around so that she could see the man who had brought her to what appeared to be a very secure place.

"These are my quarters. This is the greeting room and lounge. This is where I speak with others." He walked around Nyght, and she turned to make sure she had her eyes on him at all times. She also tightened her grip on her daggers. She had placed her small knife back in the top of her boot before she left her room, but she would have no problem getting to it if she needed to. "The door over there leads to my bedchamber." She saw the door he had pointed to and then he turned to face her. Once again, she noticed that he did not look any higher than the lower part of her face. "You are not to enter into that room under any circumstances. Is that understood?"

"Yes, High-Master." With what he had just said, she began to relax a bit more. If he did not want her to enter his bedchamber at all, he was nothing like Master Viper.

"Follow me," he said, then turned to his right and walked across the room. Nyght moved with him but stayed a pace behind. She thought it would make the man feel more comfortable although she did not understand why he was being so cautious around her.

She saw another door and when the High-Master reached it, he opened it and stepped inside, far enough to where he was still by the door, and held it open for her. She once again made sure she had a tight grip on her daggers in case when she entered, the man tried something she did not like.

Once through the doorway, she moved far enough inside and then turned her body so that she would be able to see the High-Master. "This is where I keep most of my books and items of study. I very seldom use this room anymore, but I have no desire to get rid of anything in here." He then walked past the child and across the room where she saw another door. Once there, the High-Master opened it, but this time, the door opened out toward him, so he held it open, and she knew he wanted her to step inside. Since there was light in the room, she decided she would be able to see if the man tried to do anything to harm her. Of course, he did not know she could see in the dark, just as well.

She stepped inside and saw that the room was about half the size of the room she had just come from. It was about the same size as the room she had stayed in when she found the building Selby and the other children occupied in Sarzanac. She saw in the room a bed against the wall to the right and a desk and chair against the wall across from where she was standing just inside the door. She realized she had taken her eyes off the High-Master and so she walked further into the room and turned to face him.

He stepped inside but did not close the door behind him. "This is where you will be staying until it has been determined who will be training you."

She started feeling more comfortable, so she stopped looking at the High-Master, turned around, and walked over to the desk. When she was standing in front of it, she turned back to face the High-Master. "When will I know who will be training me?" she asked.

"When and if you pass a test."

She knew whatever test they gave her she would be able to pass. "When will the test take place?" she asked, wanting to know so she could get it over with and begin her training.

"Now," he said and noticed that the child seemed to become a lot more alert. "Remove your cloak."

Nyght was not sure if she should do as he had told her. Maybe this man was just like Master Viper or maybe he was even worse. She decided she would do as he said for the moment, but no matter what his idea of a test was, she would not let him touch her. She removed her cloak and laid it across the chair at the desk.

"Now I want you to look at me." He waited until he was sure the child had her eyes on him, but he kept his eyes off hers. "No matter what, do not take your eyes off me, especially my hands. Do you understand?"

"Yes, High-Master," Nyght said, and he did not know it, but she was not going to take her eyes off his hands anyway. If he were going to harm her, it would be his hands that made the first movement.

"Are you watching my hands?"

"Yes, High-Master."

"Good, the test will now begin." As soon as he spoke the last word, Nyght felt a sharp pain in her right shoulder. She quickly looked down at the part of her body now hurting and saw a small dart that was about a handbreadth long sticking out of her right shoulder. She raised her left hand to pull it out, and even though she was fast, the High-Master had crossed the room and grabbed a hold of her left hand before she had a chance to remove the dart. She also noticed that if he had not been able to move so quickly, he would not have been there in time to stop her from falling to the floor.

While still holding onto her left hand, he reached around the right side of her body and used his other hand to guide her down to sit on the floor so that her back was resting against the desk. She had enough strength to keep her eyes open and she had to use them to ask the question, "What just happened?" She wanted to say it, but even though she tried, she could not speak a single word.

"Do not worry, the toxin the dart was coated with will not kill you. It will only put you to sleep for a few marks." Nyght was coherent enough to hear what he said, but she did not like the fact that she was about to fall asleep and had no way of stopping it. She had underestimated the old man and now she was going to pay for that mistake.

"I must hurry while you are still conscious," High-Master Wraith said, then he situated her head so that she was able to see the dart sticking in her shoulder, "You see the dart? That is the test." He then lifted his right hand and brought it into view of Nyght. She could see his hand and the dart; he used the first to remove the second. He then moved closer to her, she would be completely under the effects of the drug in just a few more breaths and he had to be quick. "This is the test. You watched my hands, and I am sure you did not see them move, yet the dart did end up in your shoulder. If you wish to continue with your training by me, you must tell me, from where did the dart come from?" He paused a moment, but he was sure she had heard him. "You have exactly until this time tomorrow to give me your answer. If you do not, not only will I not train you, but you will leave this Guild never to return. You have one cycle of the sun, to show me that you are worth my time." He paused again then continued, "Well not exactly a full sun-cycle because the drug will keep you asleep for the next six marks, and when you wake, you will not enjoy the pain in your head which you will have for the remainder of that time, but that also is part of the test."

The High-Master was about to stand and leave but instead moved even closer to the child sitting on the floor. So close that he was next to her left ear so that he could whisper one last statement he had to say to her. "I do hope you pass this test; it would be an honor to train you, but if you do, know that unlike the late Master Viper, I do not have any windows in my chamber to which I might fall from. Remember that." He then stood up and walked out of the room, closing the door behind him.

With the drug running through her body, she was losing consciousness rapidly. She did not know it herself but out of all the people who had suc-cumbed to the sleeping drug, she was fighting the effects better than anyone, although she could not fight them forever. She continued to think of what the High-Master had said to her, especially about the part referring to how she would have to leave the Guild never to return. Something she did not want to happen.

She could no longer think straight; the drug was affecting her too much. All she could do was look at the door to the room where the man who had placed her in this situation had left through. After a few more breaths, the door became fuzzy looking, and not long afterward, she did not see the door at all because she was asleep.

SEVEN

When she was finally able to open her eyes, Nyght forced the rest of her body to move as well and jumped to her feet. In less than a breath, she was back on the floor, only this time, instead of sitting with her back against the desk, she was lying on her stomach face against the floor.

She tried to push herself up at least to where she was on her knees but was not able to. When she first regained conscience, it was the thought of being defenseless that gave her the will to rise to her feet, but it was not enough to keep her there.

She stayed on the floor because she had no choice. She did not know how long she had been asleep, but when she was able to move her lips, she could tell that her mouth was dry, and was not able to say a word. With whom she wanted to talk with, it was not necessary for her mouth to work properly. She tried to think to Moon, but as she tried to run the words through her mind, she had to close her eyes tighter than they had been because the pain in her head was so great.

She could not move, she could not speak, and she could not even call to Moon. The only thing she could do was lay there on the floor until she regained control of herself.

She did not know how long it took, but eventually, she felt feeling return to her body. Even though the pain in her head had lessened some, she continued to lay there but tried again to call out to Moon with her thoughts, *"Fa...Fath...Father."*

"Yes, my child," Moon thought to her.

When she heard Moon's reply, Moon's response caused her head to hurt even more, but she immediately felt safer. Moon was still with her as Moon always would be. She still had to pause to force her thoughts together, *"Can you see me?"*

"No, my child, I cannot."

Nyght was not sure how to take Moon's answer. She had come to this room a little after the eighth mark of the new day. The High-Master, the one who did this to her, said that she only had one sun-cycle to pass his test. She remembered that he also said she would be asleep for at least six marks. What if she had been asleep longer? Long enough that the time of the test had already come and gone. *"Father, how many sun-cycles has it been since you have seen me?"*

Moon replied, *"Child, a full cycle has not passed since you were in my sights."*

Nyght understood. Moon could only see her at night so if it had not been a full cycle of the sun since

Moon had seen her, then Moon would have just left the sky a few marks ago. She still had time.

Even though Moon could not see Nyght, Moon knew the child was suffering from something. Moon did not know what happened to the child, but Moon did feel her absence for a time before she called out to Moon. *"Child, you must gather yourself."*

"I am trying Father, but I can barely move my limbs and the pain I feel in my head is great."

Moon did not care that the child was feeling any pain or suffering. Moon needed the child to pull herself through whatever was affecting her. Moon could tell that the child was vulnerable with the way she was and if she were to allow someone to harm her, then it would interfere with what Moon needed her for. It was not that Moon did not care for the child, but Moon did care for Moon more. *"I gave you the gifts you have. I gave you part of myself. I chose you because I thought you were worthy."* Moon paused to let the child prepare herself for what Moon was about to say, *"Did I choose wrong?"*

With the last statement, Nyght knew she would not make Moon think she was not worthy of what Moon had given her. "No Father, you did not." She spoke the words to make herself work through the pain which ran throughout her body. She then thought of a way to get her mind off the pain her body was feeling because of the drug. With effort and pain, she turned over so that she was lying on her back. She then brought her right leg up toward her body. Just the movement alone hurt, but she moved it enough to where she was able to grab the knife she kept in her boot. Even though she was still feeling weak, when she had the knife in her hand she felt better. There was still pain, but now she had a weapon she could use against someone, if necessary, but also for what she had planned.

With her hand still feeling numb, it took her a moment to position the knife in her right hand so that she was holding it by the handle with the blade pointing downward. She was still on her back but did not rise up to see the lower part of her body. With what she was going to do, she was not sure if she wanted to see it anyway, but since she was too weak to sit up, she remained lying on the floor.

She did have enough strength to move the hand with the blade and position it so that it was over the upper part of her right leg. After taking three breaths, she used the last bit of strength she had to raise the blade as high as she could. With her strength used up, she had no problem with allowing her hand to fall back down. With the way she was holding the knife, there was enough force to allow the blade to enter her leg.

She not only immediately felt the new pain, but it forced her to sit up. She did not know why she knew the new pain would help. Moon had not told her to do it and she did not think it was because Moon had given her the knowledge Moon had about fighting. Something deep inside her led her to stab herself to get her mind off the pain she had been feeling from the drug. The pain from the stab wound was something different, and even though it hurt, it caused her to focus on something other than the pain in her head and the fact that it came from whatever drug was in her system.

With the rush of pain she was feeling, she forced herself to her feet, and even though she swayed a bit she managed to stand. She was facing the desk and saw her daggers lying on the floor where she had been standing. She realized she must have dropped them when the dart entered her shoulder although she had not planned to let them go.

She started limping over to them. Her left leg quivered because of the drug, but her right throbbed because of the knife which she had not removed. She left it there so that the pain would continue to keep her focused on what she had to do.

When she was an arm's reach away from the desk, she let her body fall forward to cover the remaining distance. She now had enough of her senses back so as she fell forward, she used her hands and arms to catch herself before she fell over onto the desk itself. She took three more breaths and turned her head slightly to the right to see the small chair at the desk. She thought that if she could sit down for just a moment then she would feel better. It took her less than a breath to move her right hand to the back of the chair and forcefully push it away from the desk so that it went sliding across the floor and away from her. She knew that if she sat down to overcome what she was facing she would be allowing the situation to control her and she had to control it.

She took another breath then pulled herself closer to the desk. She moved her hands from the top of it, made sure she was not going to fall over, turned around, then bent over and picked up both of her daggers. Just like when she took hold of her knife, with the daggers in her hands, Nyght felt better. Maybe not physically, but she felt more comfortable with having the weapons.

She did not use the chair, but she did lean backward enough so that the desk would give her the support she needed to stay on her feet. She placed both daggers in her left hand then used her right to reach down and pull the knife out of her leg. She jerked it out fast, and with the pain that came from the act, she started feeling better. Through the removal of her knife, she did not scream out the slightest bit. She could still feel the pain in her head, but it was not as bad as the pain in her leg, the pain that came from the wound, which she had done to herself. If she was going to feel pain, then let it be from her own hands, not from someone else.

She could tell that the drug was starting to wear off, and with that, she began to think more clearly. The first thought she had was how she was going to make High-Master Wraith regret what he did. With him coming to her mind, she remembered that everything the man had done was because he was putting her through another test. A test she had to pass, or she would have to leave the Guild forever.

She brought the knife up to look at the blade and saw it covered with her blood. She then bent her head so that she could see the self-inflicted wound. She could tell the blade did not go the full two handbreadths of the blade into her leg, but it had been deep enough to cause her pain, as well as draw blood. She looked to her left and saw the bed against the wall.

With daggers and knife in hand, she limped over to the bed and pulled off the blanket on top. She saw that there was linen under it and decided it would be better to use it to wrap the wound. She pulled on the linen and when she had enough in her hand, she placed her daggers on the bed and used her knife to cut enough of the material to tie around her leg to stop the bleeding.

As she was working, she realized that this was the first time she had ever suffered a wound. She had killed animals, even a couple of humans, but in all those times, in all her life she had never received an injury like the one she has now. She could not stop herself from smiling because she was the one who had been the first to wound herself.

Once she had the piece of linen tied around her leg, she placed her knife back into her boot and picked up her daggers. She then turned to face the door to the room. She thought to herself that somewhere on the other side, the High-Master was waiting for her, either to train her or to force her out of the Guild. She knew she would not leave.

She took her eyes off the door and walked back over to the desk. She did not want to stay close to the bed because while she was next to it, she kept thinking that she should lie down for a moment to get some rest, which was something she did not want to do.

The High-Master had told her that she had one cycle of the sun to answer his question. She did not know how long she had been asleep, but no matter how long it was, she had already lost time. Time, she could not afford.

She remained standing but leaned back against the desk to support herself. Now that the pain from the wound in her leg was starting to lessen, she was feeling the pain in her head again. The High-Master had been correct when he said the effects of the drug would last for most of the day.

She was holding both of her daggers in her left hand, so she raised her right to rub her temple. She did this without realizing what she was doing, but when she did, she stopped and brought her hand back down. She was not going to let what the High-Master had done to her control her actions. She thought about using her knife again, but with one wound already in her leg, she did not think it was wise to put another in her body. Instead, she did something she did not know the reason why. It just came to her naturally.

She moved to the center of the room, the exact center. Once there, she sat down on the floor, and even though the wound in her leg caused her pain, she crossed her legs in front of her with her knees at her sides. She placed her hands on her legs then bent her head down and closed her eyes.

While sitting there, she did not try to find the solution to the High-Master's test. At least not at first.

Her mind was focusing on too many things at once. The pain in her head, the weariness her body was feeling from the drug. The pain in her leg from the wound she had done to herself, and the test. It was too many things, and she knew she had to put them all aside except for the last, which was not the first one she dealt with.

The weariness she was feeling was the first item she would remove. Not so much remove it but push it aside where she did not think about it. This was the easiest item to deal with because she told herself that she was now sitting down and in time, the weariness would go away especially after she passed the test. Once that was over, she would be able to rest. Because the weariness was something she could not take care of now, there was no reason to think about it. With that last thought, she thought no more about the weariness of her body.

The next item she was going to deal with was the pain she was feeling in her leg. This was going to be a little more difficult. Not that she felt she would not be able to, but it was the wound in her leg that took her mind off the pain in her head. Once she stopped thinking about her leg, she knew she would feel the pain in her head even more. She had to get the thought out of her mind so she could focus on the test.

To put the pain of her leg out of her thoughts, all she did was tell herself that she was the one who inflicted the wound and that she would never do something to cause herself any harm. Because of that, the wound was not an injury; it was just part of her. It worked. The pain in her leg, even though it was still there, was no longer in her thoughts. With that, the pain in her head seemed to double instantly.

This was going to be the most difficult item to remove from her thoughts. The pain a person feels in their head is always something they have trouble not thinking about. Their head and mind were together, so the pain was with every thought a person had.

Nyght tried to stop thinking about the pain, but she could not. It was so intense she could not think of anything else. It was there and it was not going to go away any time soon. When the thought came to her, she knew how she would deal with the pain. It was not going away, and it was in her way of concentrating on finding the answer to the test. The pain was against her; it was an enemy. To resolve the issue, she asked herself, "How do you defeat an enemy? Simple, you beat it."

She remembered that the High-Master had said she would have trouble trying to solve the test because of the pain she would feel. The pain was not something separate from the test, it was part of the test. Just like the gap in the floor was part of the test to get to the door. She could not get rid of the gap. She had to work with it and overcome the test before her.

She then knew that the pain in her head would not go away in the time she had left to give the High-Master an answer; the pain would stay but she told herself that she was still going to pass the test.

With the pain in her head, she began to concentrate on what the High-Master had said. Even with that first thought, she felt the pain increase but did not submit to it. The pain was going to be there, just like the gap in the floor, she could not remove it, so she continued to think about the task the High-Master had given her.

"How did he do it?" she thought to herself. She started replaying the entire incident in her mind and felt pain for it. He had told her to watch him and especially his hands. He had said "Do not take your eyes off my hands," and she had not. Still, the dart appeared in her shoulder. With that thought, she felt even more pain going through her head but continued to go over what she had seen.

She remembered the High-Master standing there looking at her and her at him. His hands did not move that she was sure of. *"So how did he get the dart into my shoulder?"* As she thought about the question, the pain grew even more but she would not succumb to it. She was determined not to close her eyes tighter to deal with the pain. She would not let the pain control her actions, she would.

She continued to replay the scene repeatedly in her mind, but every time she did, she could not see anything to let her know how he had made the dart enter her shoulder. She then started wondering if he had used magic to fire the dart across the room. What if he was one of the wizards in the Guild? He had mentioned them when he told her about the lifts. What if he had mentioned them to give her a clue to solve the test, which he knew he would be giving her?

"That's it," she said to herself and opened her eyes. She smiled because she believed she had discovered the answer to the test. She stood up and was about ready to move to the door to go find the High-Master to let him know she would be staying at the Guild, and he would be training her. She did not take a single step.

She felt as if she was missing something. The answer she came up with was a good answer, but deep down, she felt that it was not the correct one. She thought to herself, *"What am I missing?"*

She had an answer, but she felt it was not the one that would allow her to stay at the Guild. She then realized it was not the answer that was wrong, it was the question she had been asking herself. She then remembered what the High-Master had asked her. He did not ask, "How did the dart appear?" he asked, "From where did the dart come from?" She had the wrong answer and if she had gone to him, with the one she had, she would have failed the test. Suddenly the pain in her head was gone.

She did not even return to where she had been sitting on the floor. She would not find the answer there.

Nyght turned and walked back over to the desk. She stopped when she was standing in the exact spot she had been when the dart struck her. She then turned to face the door across the room. Closed now, but opened when the High-Master was in the room with her, and he had been standing directly in front of it.

She closed her eyes and once again envisioned the scene that took place when the High-Master was present. She did not remember seeing his hands move, but it did not matter. That was part of the question that would answer "How," and she needed to know "Where."

She replayed the whole scene up to the part where she felt the dart enter her shoulder. She remembered she had not taken her eyes off his hands until then. "The dart," she said, then continued to put the pieces of the puzzle together. He had asked "Where," which refers to a direction so the answer to the question was that she had to tell the High-Master from where the dart had come from. Even to her, the simplest answer would be "from him," but that was not the correct one because it was too easy and also because she was sure the High-Master's hands had not moved. She thought that maybe he had moved so fast she had not been able to see him throw the dart, but she put the idea away because she did not think the old man, whom she had noticed had trouble going down the stairs in the other tower, would be able to move so quickly.

She looked back toward the door to where she was visualizing the High-Master. She then looked down at her right shoulder. Even though the dart was no longer there, in her mind she could see it clearly. It was at that moment she had her answer. The answer to the test and even a little bit more.

At first, she wanted to rush out of the room, go to the High-Master, and tell him the answer she had and knew that it was correct. Instead, she decided she would wait a while.

She walked over to the bed, picked up the blanket lying on the floor where she had tossed it a moment ago, then climbed into the bed. She still made sure she had her daggers in her hands and placed them across her chest but kept them hidden under the cover. *"Moon,"* she thought.

"Yes, my daughter."

"Can you please wake me as soon as you can see me?"

"Yes, my child," Moon said and with that, Nyght went to sleep. Not because she needed the rest or

because of what she had been through just before High-Master Wraith had left the room. She knew she would need her strength to return to her because once she saw the High-Master again and gave her answer, he would begin her training to become an assassin.

Once Moon was in the sky over the Assassin's Guild, Moon woke Nyght. She still felt a bit tired, but she was not going to lie back down. Now that Moon was in the sky over her, she could tell just where Moon was and knew by Moon's position it was past the twenty-first mark of the day.

She stood up and when her feet touched the floor, she felt some pain from the wound in her right leg. She did not put any thought toward it, because that bit of pain was nothing compared to the way her head had suffered from when she woke from the dart's toxin. She bent down and removed the piece of cloth she had tied around the wound. Some blood was still exiting it, but she decided it was not enough to place another bandage over it. She would deal with it later. Right now, she wanted to find the High-Master and begin her training.

She walked out of the room and into the adjacent one where High-Master Wraith kept his books and other items he took an interest in. Since Nyght did not see him, she made her way to the door, opened it, and stepped into the outer room.

Her eyes went to the other side of the room and

saw that there was a fire in the hearth. She also saw a chair with a high back, facing the hearth as well as High-Master Wraith sitting in it. With the way the back of the chair was, she could not see his face, but she could tell that he was sitting with his left leg crossed over his right and he had his right arm positioned so that she could see his right hand and the goblet he was holding.

"Awake so soon?" High-Master Wraith said but did not move in his chair. He then lifted the goblet he was holding and even though Nyght could not see his face, she knew from the motion of his arm that he took a drink then brought his arm back down so that once again she could see the goblet he was holding. "Either you are prepared to give me an answer or you have decided my test is too difficult for you." He adjusted his position so that he was looking at Nyght but still seated in the chair, "Which is it?"

"I have your answer," Nyght said but did not give it nor did she move further into the room.

High-Master Wraith, while keeping his eyes on the girl but not on her eyes, took another sip from his goblet, then brought it back down, "But is it the correct one?" Nyght did not answer. He stood and turned to face the child on the other side of the room.

When he rose, Nyght noticed that the High-Master seemed to have trouble standing and when he had made it out of the chair completely, he appeared to stagger a bit. Not much, but enough for her to notice. She also observed that after he was standing, he took another drink from the goblet and as he lifted it up to his mouth, she saw his hand was trembling. After he finished swallowing whatever was in the cup, he lowered it and placed it on the small table next to the chair. To Nyght it appeared that his body had stopped the bit of trembling he had been doing as if whatever he had been drinking put an end to it.

"Well, give me your answer," High-Master Wraith said from where he was standing in front of the fireplace allowing the flames to warm his body and soul.

For Nyght to give her answer she wanted to be closer to the High-Master. In fact, she wanted to be the same distance apart from him as they had been just before she felt the piercing of the dart.

She walked across the room and noticed that once again, the High-Master was making sure he was looking at the lower part of her face. She did not care about that for the moment because it was not part of the test.

When she reached the desired position, she looked at the High-Master, "Well," he said in a demanding tone to let her know he was waiting.

"You asked, 'From where did the dart come from?'" she said.

The High-Master wanted to tell her that he knew what he had asked her but decided to say something else, "And do you know?"

Nyght did not say her answer. All she did was lift her right arm and point at the High-Master. He was about to tell her that she had failed the test, but before he could, she started moving her arm toward his left, her right. He watched her the entire time, and when she stopped, he saw that she was pointing a pace to his left. He looked in the direction then back to the child making sure he did not look into her eyes. The child's answer was correct.

The child still had her arm out. High-Master Wraith figured she was waiting for him to let her know if she passed or not. "Are you sure?" he asked to see the reaction of the child. He thought that maybe he would be able to put some doubt into her, but when she just nodded her head, he knew her answer was final. "How did I do it?"

Nyght lowered her arm and gave her reply to his question although it was not what the High-Master was expecting. "That was not the question when you presented the test to me, High-Master."

The High-Master wanted to reprimand the child for what she said, but he could not because not only did she make her statement with no hostility toward him for asking the question, but she was also correct. The test was not if she could tell how he was able to do what he did but where the dart came from. When he devised her little test, he did not make it so that the child would not have any possibility of passing, that would be unfair. The question he gave her had a very simple answer, if she simply did not overthink the question, which from the answer she gave, she had not. He was still curious to see if the child knew how the dart got to her. "You are correct. That was not part of the test and to let you know you have passed, and I will train you, but can you tell me how the dart got to you?"

Nyght did not hesitate to answer, "No, High-Master. I do know that I kept my eyes on you and especially your hands but did not see you move. I do know that the dart came from that direction." She raised her arm again to point in the direction she had a moment ago.

"And how did you determine that?" he asked but could tell that the child was thinking this was another test. "As I said, you passed, and I will see to your training. I am asking you to understand how you were able to come up with your answer." High-Master Wraith wanted to see just how she worked through the problem.

"It was the dart itself, High-Master," Nyght said but did not continue.

"Explain."

"It was the angle the dart was situated before you removed it from me. When I first felt it, I saw it in me but that was all. Then you positioned my head so that I could see the dart while I was sitting on the floor. You wanted to make sure I saw it because the way it struck me told me what direction it came from. If the dart had been straight in me, then it would have come from directly in front of me. Since it was at an angle and the end of it was facing to the right, it told me from what direction it came from." Nyght stopped, knowing that she had given more than enough information on how she was able to answer the question. It was also probably the first time she had said so many words at one time. There was one item she did not give in her explanation. It went to the question of how the dart got to her, so she did not feel she needed to pass the information along.

She knew that somehow the High-Master put the dart into her. Even though she did not see him move, it did not mean he had not. She remembered he used his right hand to pull the dart out of her. That means it was his right hand he used mainly. She was able to confirm this when she came into the room and saw the High-Master was holding the goblet in that hand as well. She believed the High-Master had somehow made it so she could not see him and that he was the one who had thrown the dart into her. Since he was right-handed and with the angle of the dart, she could tell where he had to be standing for his right hand to make the dart land the way it did. She did not know how but it was something she would keep in mind. She had a feeling the answer to "How?" the dart got to her would be very interesting.

The High-Master was not surprised that the child did not know the "How?" The answer was the same as to how he was always able to fulfill a contract.

No one in the Guild could ever figure that out so he doubted very much the child would be able to. Of course, if someone could, it would be her or someone like her. Since that was not part of the test, they both could move on.

"Very good. As I said, you passed my test so I will take you as my pupil." The High-Master walked across the room and stopped when he was two paces from the child. "There is more to being an assassin than just placing one of your daggers into someone and doing it in a manner as not to be seen." He said and smiled at the child, but she did not smile back so he continued. "An assassin is not just a killer. Anyone can kill someone. An assassin is not just a person who kills for profit. Anyone can do that as well. An assassin is a killer who is paid to kill, but does so because they are called to the profession."

Nyght did not say it, but she understood what the man had said. Ever since she heard the word, "assassin" she felt a calling, even if she did not know why.

"Our Guild has existed for over eight hundred seasons even though no one knows exactly how long it has been around but in all of its existence we have done what we are called to do."

"And what is that High-Master?" Nyght asked because she wanted to know everything there was to know about what she was going to become.

High-Master Wraith turned and looked to the other side of the room. He had a feeling this discussion was going to be a long one, and even though he did not mind, he figured he might as well take his seat by the fireplace to warm himself. He turned back to look at the child but kept his eyes low enough to not see into hers. "Let us move closer to fire," he said, then turned and went back over to where he had been sitting. As soon as he was in the chair, he picked up the goblet and took another drink.

Nyght followed him to the other side of the room, but since there was only one chair next to the fireplace, she stood off to the right of it. The High-Master did not offer her a seat and she did not take one. He did this as part of her training. There would be many times her training would consist of him talking at great lengths explaining many different topics. A pupil would more than likely fall asleep if they sat so having the child stand would ensure she stayed awake. He wondered just how long she would be able to stand though. He noticed the wound in her right leg, which had not been there when he had last seen the child. Since she was the only one in the room, then the High-Master knew she must have done it to herself, and he had an idea as to why. The phrase *"Pain removes Pain"* came to mind but he would not bring the wound up at this time.

"The world we live in exists because of one thing." The High-Master took another sip from the goblet. "Do you know what that one thing is?"

"No, High-Master," Nyght answered without hesitation which the High-Master was pleased to see. If she did not know something, then she did not try to hide it. He knew that as long as she continued in that manner, her training would proceed a lot smoother because she had no problem with admitting she did not know something.

"Balance," the High-Master said the one word, paused a moment for her to take it in then continued. "Balance is everything. There are always forces at work; forces we mere mortals do not see, but nonetheless, have a hand in them. An assassin's part of that balance is to ensure that neither good nor bad succeeds."

"But as assassins, do we not kill others, and even though that is something I do not have a problem with, others do."

High-Master Wraith was pleased with what the child had said, and she was right. "Yes, we kill but the question is why do we kill?" He stopped looking into the fireplace and turned his head to look at the child but only from her neck to her chin.

"I do not know, High-Master."

"The answer to my question is not even known by me." He was sure the child was a bit confused. Even one like her, where death was part of her life, would not know the mysteries of the world they both live in. "I do know that when we kill someone there is a reason. A reason other than the one given by the person wishing to see that person dead. There is a reason which no one other than Creator himself knows."

"So, we kill for Creator," Nyght said, and the High-Master had to force himself to look away quickly before he looked up into the child's eyes because of what she had just said. Which was the basis of what the Guild was for and why there was a need for assassins like himself and especially like the one the child would become.

The High-Master sat back in his chair and returned his gaze to the fire, "Yes child, we kill for Creator. Whether the person we remove from this world was one who walked the path of virtue or the path of malice, is not of our concern. Through Creator's direction, not by our own, do we receive our assignments and it is our job," the High-Master stopped to change what he was going to say, "It is our responsibility to do what Creator has charged us to do. And that is why our most precious and sacred rule is that 'A contract taken, is a contract fulfilled.'"

"Because not fulfilling a contract would not be fulfilling what Creator has given us to do," Nyght said to let the High-Master know she understood.

"Yes child, that is correct." Even though the child understood what he had just explained to her, he did not think she was any different from any of the many children who had come to the Guild for training. The reason for what they were meant to do with their life was the first lesson taught to them by their Master. High-Master Wraith learned it when he came to the Guild when he was fifteen and he taught it to others when he became a Master. Children understood it because it was so simple it had to be true.

Throughout his life, High-Master Wraith did not doubt the teaching he was now speaking to the child. He believed with all his heart that when he or any assassin took the life of another, there was a reason for it. One which he would never know or even try to find out as to why. He, like every assassin, was just one being in the grand plan of Creator, and what right did he or any other individual have to question what Creator had set in motion.

Some people might believe that the way the Guild thought was just their way of justifying what they did. Every assassin had one thing in common with each other. They did not choose to become what they are; they were born with it in them and eventually it rose to the surface and made them into what Creator needed them to be.

They talked for a few marks more, and even though Nyght appeared to be able to continue with their conversation, High-Master Wraith was feeling the effects of what he had done earlier and not even the tonic he had been drinking since he left the child on the floor in the room was helping him to recover. He needed to go to bed and rest.

He sent the child to her room, the one where he gave her the test, and the one where she would live for the next five seasons and then he went to his own bedchamber.

A part of him was concerned that if he did close

his eyes, he might not open them again but the strain on his body was too great and he would have to allow his body to make whatever repairs it could in the time he could rest. Hopefully, he would be able to make it through the night without suffering from one of his spasms. He had been taking in the tonic for the majority of the day and even though it made him sick as well, he needed it more since he gave the child the test.

He crawled into his bed, closed his eyes, and thought that maybe he would not live long enough to train another assassin one last time.

Nyght went to her bed, and even though she wanted to stay up and talk with the High-Master a while longer, she could tell that he was tired and that was probably why he suggested they continued their discussion in the morning.

Once she was lying down, she realized she was actually tired, but she felt that it was more from the excitement she was feeling from the topics they had been discussing. All pertaining to what she was to become. An assassin, and now she believed more than ever that this was what she was meant to do with her life. She went to sleep and rested very peacefully.

EIGHT

Nyght rose a few marks later ready and eager to continue her training. She walked out of her own quarters, through the next room, and into the outer room of the High-Master's chamber. She did not see him, and since he had not given her any instructions on what she was supposed to do, she decided that she would remain there.

She looked over to the door leading to the High-Master's bedchamber and remembered what he had told her about never entering his personal chamber. She did go over to the door and placed her ear against it to see if she could hear anything from the other side. If the High-Master was in there, he was either still in bed or doing something not making a sound.

She realized she had not relieved herself in at least a full sun-cycle, and now that the thought had come to her mind, she had to go more than ever.

She looked around the room and only saw the door to the bedchamber, the door leading back to the room she had slept in, and the door to the outer hallway. She did not need to go back to her room and High-Master Wraith told her not to go into the bedchamber. That only left the last option, but since the High-Master had not told her that she could leave his quarters, she did not think it would be a good idea to go wandering around the Guild.

To take her mind off of having to relieve herself, she went over to the fireplace and stirred the embers to get the small fire going. She then pulled two pieces of coal from the container to the left of the fireplace and placed them on the fire. Soon it was burning as it was last night when she and the High-Master had talked in front of it.

As she watched the flames, she remembered something the High-Master had said. It was after she had been drugged and fallen to the floor. Right before he left the room, he said that he did not have a window in his chamber from which he could fall. She could not help but smile and turned her head to look at the door to the bedchamber.

He knew. He knew she had killed Master Viper and yet he was still going to teach her to become an assassin. She then thought that on the other side of the door was the first person ever to best her. She did not know what she was feeling but for others it was admiration. She held her gaze at the door for a moment longer, then put her eyes back on the flame. To her, the man deserved her respect not just because he was a High-Master, but because he earned it.

There was a knock at the door and as soon as

she heard it, she turned her head to the right. She did not know who was there, but she was sure it was not High-Master Wraith. He would not knock before entering his own chamber.

She pulled the front of her cloak together, and once her arms were inside, she moved both of her daggers to her left hand. She then made sure her left arm was at her side. She walked over to the door and with her right hand she opened it making sure she did not let her daggers come into sight.

Once opened, she saw two men who wore the same apparel as High-Master Wraith. She knew these were the other two High-Masters of the Guild, but she also noticed when she looked at their faces, they had their eyes fixed on the lower part of her face.

"Where is High-Master Wraith?" the man on the left asked.

"I believe he is still asleep," Nyght answered.

The two men then stepped into the room with enough speed and force that Nyght had to step to the side and behind the door to allow them to enter. Once inside they did not stop and say anything else to her. They walked across the room toward the High-Master's bedchamber. She did not know the reason they had come, but from the way they were moving, they had a purpose for entering so abruptly. Nyght closed the door, then with both arms inside her cloak, she moved her dagger Full to her right hand just in case the two men decided to be a little more forceful toward her.

When High-Master Copper reached High-Master Wraith's bedchamber, he immediately raised up his fist and pounded on the door. There was no reply, so he knocked again and called out, "High-Master Wraith." There was still no answer. The two men looked at each other, then High-Master Copper faced the door, banged on it harder, and called out louder, "High-Master Wraith are you in there?" There was no reply and after the two men looked at each other one more time, they decided they had waited long enough and had shown the High-Master enough respect by knocking. High-Master Copper tried the handle to the door, and it opened. They both looked at each other one last time then stepped inside the bedchamber closing the door behind them.

Nyght did not know what they were so concerned about, but she did know that she was not going to go anywhere.

The two High-Masters walked further into the room. The fire in the hearth had gone down throughout the night so there was not much light. Even so, there was still enough to see that High-Master Wraith was lying in his bed. They also realized he had not heard them knocking, nor when they had entered. "High-Master Wraith?" High-Master Copper called out again, but there was no reply.

They walked over to the side of the bed and saw the candle sitting in its holder on the stand next to the bed. High-Master Grave reached over, picked up the flint stone, and struck it with the piece of metal to light the candle. He picked it up so they could see High-Master Wraith. When they did, they were more than pleased to see that his chest was rising and lowering. At least he was still breathing.

"High-Master Wraith?" High-Master Copper said, and this time placed his hand on the right shoulder of the one he was calling to.

With the touch, High-Master Wraith opened his eyes and saw the two men standing over him with looks of fear on their faces. "What is it, my friends?" High-Master Wraith asked, not knowing why his fellow High-Masters were disturbing his rest.

"We came to see..." High-Master Grave said then stopped.

High-Master Copper then spoke about the reason they were there, "We wanted to see if you were well." He looked at the man he walked into the room with then back to High-Master Wraith. "You did not show up for the morning meeting, and we came to see if..." Like the other High-Master, High-Master Copper did not finish what he was going to say.

High-Master Wraith had no trouble figuring out what the two were thinking, and even though he was surprised that he had slept so long that he had missed the morning meeting, he felt he should put the more important concern to rest for his fellow High-Masters. He tossed the covers off and swung his legs over the side of the bed. The two other High-Masters moved aside so that he could arrange himself. He sat there and had to catch his breath before he could speak. Out of the corner of his eye, he saw the two High-Masters exchange looks. "Do not fear my friends, I did not come to my end this night." He looked up from the floor to the two men, "By natural death or by the hand of my pupil." High-Master Wraith knew his two companions must have thought he had suffered from the same ailment Viper had. He could not help but smile at the thought. "I can assure you that the child has no interest in removing me. For if she did not attempt it after I had given her my test, then I am certain I am quite safe." He then forced himself to his feet.

"High-Master Wraith, we were concerned for your wellbeing. When you did not arrive for the eighth mark meeting, we immediately came to see if you were well," High-Master Grave said, and High-Master Wraith could see the distress they both had on their faces. He was delighted that they cared so much for him.

He turned to his left and then walked over to the two men. When he reached them, he placed a hand on each of their shoulders and patted them. "I apologize for missing the meeting but as you can see, I am well." He then stepped between the two. He had his back to them and did not see their looks of distress increase. It was not only because their friend had missed the meeting, but also because they saw how old and tired High-Master Wraith appeared this morning.

When he had come to them yesterday and told

them that he had given the child a test to see if she was worthy to be his pupil, they noticed he seemed a lot weaker than he normally was. They knew then that taking on this pupil might hurt their friend and that was something they did not want to see. At his age, at one hundred seventeen, High-Master Wraith would not have many more seasons. Even though he has lived longer than most humans and was still able to get around on his own, the two High-Masters did not think their friend would live to see one hundred twenty. It was still three seasons away, but most humans die before they are one hundred, and High-Master Wraith, had gone another seventeen. To them, it was only a matter of time before his body and health caught up to his age. By the way he looked this morning and the fact he had missed the meeting, something he had never done since he had been a Master, they thought his end was moving closer.

They kept those thoughts to themselves, but High-Master Wraith was thinking the same thing as he walked across the room. He had never missed a meeting and he definitely had never overslept. He had always risen before the sixth mark and now saw that the time-marker was showing it was after the eighth mark. It appeared his friends did not waste any time checking on him and for that, he was grateful; however, there was nothing they could do to help him. No one could.

He walked to the edge of the bed, picked up his

chamber robe, and placed it on. As he tied the sash, he composed himself then turned to face the two High-Masters. "I assure you that I will not miss any more meetings..." he was not finished speaking, but he saw the looks on the other two faces and knew what they were going to say. They were going to tell him that missing a meeting was not important, and High-Master Wraith agreed, but he did not want them to start treating him as if he was a crippled old man, so he raised his hand to silence them before they had a chance to speak. "The child and I were conversing well into the night. She seems to be very inquisitive and is quite willing to be my pupil."

He did not say it, but that was the reason he knew he did not have anything to fear from the child. While talking with her last night, he determined that if she did have anything to do with Viper's death, and High-Master Wraith was certain she did, the child wanted to become an assassin like him and not in the way Viper and others from that tower were trained. The child would kill with one of her daggers or a number of other ways but never with her body.

"High-Master, may I propose we assign another to train her," High-Master Grave suggested.

"Yes," High-Master Copper said to agree with his companion's statement. "The other six Masters have pupils, but in this case, we can allow one of them to take on the child as well or maybe have one of the other elder assassins train her. One who has been with us for the number of seasons required and has already been looked at to become a Master should the need arise."

High-Master Wraith knew the two only had concern for his wellbeing, but he could not worry about that now. "No, I will train the child, but once again I give you the opportunity to promote a Master to take my place which will free you from the worry of me handling my duties." He could tell from their looks they were not going to replace him.

"Our decision stands on you remaining as a High-Master," High-Master Copper said. "We will continue with the meetings as scheduled and if something should arise where you cannot be present, then we will continue with the meeting and update you at your earliest convenience."

High-Master Wraith smiled at his friends. They had too much respect for him to remove him from the highest position in the Guild as well as too much respect to stop him from teaching the child. They were both honorable men and he knew he had chosen well when he promoted them to the position of High-Master. It comforted him that when he was gone, the Guild would continue to operate with honor and integrity.

"I thank you both and if I do happen to miss another meeting then please give my apologies to the Masters as well as I give them to you both at this moment." The two High-Maters gave a slight bow for their mentor's comment. "But as I said, I will make the meetings. I know I have taken on more with the child's training, but the Guild must come first." He did not say it, but he knew that by training the child, he would be helping the Guild more than his two friends could understand.

"Yes, High-Master Wraith," the two men said together and all three of them knew the concern they had come in with had reached its end.

"Now, I hope you both did as I instructed you when we met yesterday."

"Yes, High-Master," they both said at the same time.

"As soon as we saw that she was the one to open your door, we made sure we did not look into the child's eyes," High-Master Copper said to verify what they were all discussing.

"Good. As I said, it is for the best. As for the others within the Guild, I think it might do them good to see just what the child brings to our home." The two High-Masters did not know what he was talking about, only that he had told them not to look into the child's eyes. Even though they both were curious. "Now I suggest we all go and see how my pupil is doing." He turned around to head for the door then looked over his shoulder, "Remember, concentrate on the lower part of her face only." The two nodded and they all started heading out of the room.

Since his two fellow High-Masters were up in seasons, they did not have long for this world unless they lived as long as he has, but High-Master Wraith thought he would do them the kindness of not having to live with what they would see if they looked into the child's eyes. As for the younger assassins, he thought it would be a good lesson for the ones who bring death to others.

When they entered the outer room, Nyght was standing next to the fireplace. All three of the men came over to her and stood two paces away. She noticed all three High-Masters kept their focus on the lower part of her face. She realized it was not just High-Master Wraith, and figured all three of them were up in seasons and maybe age was starting to get to them. In a way, she was correct. With age came wisdom and High-Master Wraith was wise enough to avoid her eyes and pass that wisdom on to his fellow High-Masters.

"Have you left these quarters child?" High-Master Wraith asked.

"No, High-Master," Nyght replied.

"Very well," High-Master Wraith said, then turned to his two companions. "She will be staying in the small room attached to my library. As for her meals, she will eat them in her room. I will have our preparer send them up to her. I still wish to limit the amount of time she spends with the other members of the Guild. Of course, she will have to use the lavatories on one of the levels below." All the High-Masters had their own lavatory attached to their bedchambers, but High-Master Wraith gave Nyght instructions that she was not to enter his inner private quarters. High-Master Wraith continued explaining his plans for his new pupil. "As for her training, I will schedule time with our Archivist to teach her to read as well as other academic aspects she will need. Our Weapons-Maker will be the one to train her on our weaponry."

"Excuse me, High-Masters," Nyght said and all three of the men turned to face her. Most pupils would not interrupt a Master when they were talking. Not even a Master would interrupt all three High-Masters when they were discussing something. Before any of them could reprimand the child, she spoke. "I do not need to be trained on how to use weapons."

The High-Masters all looked at each other, and since it was his pupil, the two were going to let High-Master Wraith handle the child. From where he was, he turned his body so that he was facing her. "Usually, it is the Master of the Tower who trains a pupil. I have decided that our Weapons-Maker will train you since my time is required elsewhere." He began to turn back to his fellow High-Masters to continue their conversation, but Nyght had something else to say.

"But I already know how to use my daggers." Once again, all three of the High-Masters looked at the child.

It was not uncommon for a child that entered the Guild to have some knowledge of one or two types of weapons, but none of the children knew how to use them to the standards of the Guild. High-Master

Wraith explained to her more of the Guild's ways, "Child, you may know how to use your blades like a common street hoodlum, but as an assassin, you will need to acquire a much higher skill."

"I have all the skill I need," the child said, and was about to end it there to show that she would not back down but realized that these men were the head of the Guild, so she added, "High-Masters," They all looked at each other. Nyght decided the three men did not understand what she was capable of doing. At least not yet. "If you will allow me, I can show you that I can wield my weapons to your..." she paused to change what she was going to say, "... to our Guild's standards."

The two younger High-Masters remained quiet and the looks they had on their faces showed that they thought the child was about ready to become the next victim of the assassin called Wraith. He had not killed in many seasons, and he may be older than every other person in the Guild, but that did not mean he was not able to put an end to the child's life.

It had been quite some time since anyone had talked to him in the manner as Nyght was. Not since he held the title of Master and took on the pupil with eyes like the child standing before him. He remembered how defiant the first child had been when told that he would receive training with his weapons. The child had not spoken like this one though, and even though he thought it would be best to show just who was in charge, he could not resist the urge to see what she wanted to show him and the others. "I will allow you to show me and the other High-Masters what you are capable of," he saw the child was about to nod her head in agreement, so he quickly continued. "However, if we all feel that whatever you demonstrate to us is not worthy of what you claim, then you will be sent out of the Guild." He paused for a moment to let the child decide if her staying at the Guild was worth her confidence in herself.

"I will be worthy," Nyght said, with no lack of confidence.

High-Master Wraith looked at the girl for a moment. As the one training her, he had the right to refuse her the opportunity. He thought that with the threat of her expulsion from the Guild, she would change her mind, but she was determined to show him that she knew how to use her weapons. If she failed, then he would have no choice but to follow through with the terms of her trial. Even if the other High-Masters had not been present and she failed this test, then he would force her to leave. It was a matter of integrity. He had made his decision and so had she. "Very well, you have one opportunity to show us what level of skill you have." Even though he was only looking at her mouth, he could tell from the slight smile she had, she wanted to reply with "I only need one," but she did not. "What method will you choose to demonstrate your ability?" High-Master Wraith asked.

"The Trial of the Circle." As soon as she had finished speaking, Nyght saw the look on all three High-Masters' faces. She was not exactly sure why.

The Trial of the Circle was a test used ages ago. Not even the High-Masters have seen it used before but each of them knew what it consisted of. An individual would draw a circle on the ground. It would be the width of both of their arms extended at their sides. They would stand in the circle while others would drop loose parchments over their head. The contest was a test of skill and speed. As the parchments reached the taker of the test, they would try to capture as many of the pieces of parchments as they could. If they were using a knife or a sword, they would use their weapon to stab the parchment before it reached the ground. If a piece of parchment touched the ground outside the circle, then that piece did not go against them because it was out of their range. Any falling within the circle and landing on the ground went against the total number of pieces they were able to capture.

"And what will be your allotted number?" High-Master Copper asked. The allotted number would be the number of parchments the participant could allow to get past them. Usually, a person gives themselves an allotment of five as a minimum, just in case.

"Zero, High-Master," Nyght answered.

All three of the High-Masters looked at each other and could not stop the smiles or the slight laughter they allowed to escape. They all knew that an allotment of zero usually ended with the contestant showing that their tongue moved quicker than whatever weapon they had chosen for the test.

High-Master Wraith, turned back to face Nyght, "Very well, we will give you The Trial of the Circle once we pull together enough of the parchment we need. It will take a mark so until..."

"We do not need to wait that long," Nyght said, once again interrupting the High-Master. She saw he was not pleased, so was quick to give her explanation, "I noticed that you have quite a few books in your study. We could use a few of them," she paused for a moment, "If you will be willing to part with them, High-Master?"

Once again, the High-Masters looked at each other. Another item they knew about the test was that the parchment used for the trial was thicker and a heavier weight than parchments used in books. By choosing to use such parchment that she suggested, the child would have a disadvantage, because with the lighter parchment, it would float down slower, but at any second, the slightest bit of change in the air could cause the paper to move off the path the participant had expected it to be.

"Very well," High-Master Grave said, and High-Master Wraith gave him a questioning look. "She has asked for the test and has stated the terms; I see no need to postpone the task."

High-Master Wraith was not sure if his fellow

High-Master just wanted to get the test over with or if he wanted to see the child fail. Or perhaps, like himself, he was eager to see the child's performance. "Very well," High-Master Wraith said as well and turned back to look at the child. "Let us go and see if we cannot find some books which I have no problem relinquishing."

Nyght nodded to him and led the way to the other room. Once inside, she entered enough so the High-Masters could join her. Since the books were not hers, she did not know which ones High-Master Wraith would be willing to part with.

He walked over to the table and started looking at the books he had lying on top. He read a couple of the titles and decided that they were the ones he enjoyed the most and did not want to use them for the trial.

He walked over to one of the bookcases lining the wall and started browsing. When he came to a book on plant life, he decided he could do without that one and turned to face Nyght, "This should do," he said.

Night walked over to him, "May I?" she asked while extending her right hand out for the book, which High-Master Wraith handed to her. She then walked over to the table in the middle of the room and sat the book down. She pulled out Full, and when it was clear of her cloak, she could tell that the two younger High-Masters were looking at it.

She placed the point of the blade on the table

so that the dagger was standing on its tip next to the book. With the book lying on its front cover, the height of the book was only a third of the length of the blade. Nyght turned her head to look at High-Master Wraith, "I will need enough pages to match the height of the blade. While she looked at him, he looked at the other High-Masters and they were all thinking the same thing. The more pages the child tried to capture, the longer the trial would last. The longer the trial lasted, the greater the chance was that she would tire out, and her reflexes would slow down making it harder for her to stop any of the pages from getting into the circle.

All the High-Masters nodded to one another. Each of them agreed to the child's request but now they were more than curious as to what the child would be able to do.

High-Master Wraith turned back to face the bookcase, browsed the shelves for a moment then selected three more books, also about plant life, then took them over to Nyght. When he handed them to her, she placed them on top of the first, and with all four books they reached from the tip of the blade to the cross guard of her dagger.

"I will find something to cut the pages free," High-Master Copper said.

Before he took a step, Nyght spoke. "That will not be necessary, High-Master," She inserted Umbra in the top of her trousers. She then held Full by the handle, with the blade away from her. She unstacked the books and placed the blade against the back binding of one of the books so that it was against the side facing downward and close to where the back binding ended. She then pressed down on the blade which had no problem cutting through the cover. She slid the blade down freeing the book of the top portion. She flipped the book over and did the same to the back cover. She then moved the blade so that it was directly against the last part of the binding of the book running along the spine. She pressed down on the blade again, causing it to cut through all the sheets and freeing them from the last bit of material holding them together.

She did the same with the other three books all while the High-Masters watched her. Only this time it was not just Nyght they were studying, but the blade she had in her hands. A blade that had no problem cutting through a stack of parchments which had about three hundred pieces of parchments each.

When she finished, she stepped back from the table, "Since I am the one partaking in the trial then it would not be appropriate for me to carry the parchments." All the High-Masters understood. She did not want them to think she might toss some of the sheets away to improve her chances. "I suggest we move to the lowest level of the tower. I will remain on the ground level and the three of you can toss the sheets from the third level." Without a reply, she turned and walked to the door to the room.

As she was making her way to the front door of the chamber, she heard one of the High-Masters ask someone else a question, "How did this child know about the trial?"

Nyght did not respond even though she was the only one who knew the answer. Moon had seen this trial done many, many seasons ago and Moon passed the knowledge to Nyght.

After High-Master Wraith changed out of his sleepwear, they all left his chamber and took the lift to the first level. Once there, the three High-Masters went to the lift that would take them to the third level but not before they assigned some of the Guild members to watch the doors on the first level to make sure no one walked into the area. By the time the three made it to the third level, a great majority of the Guild members were watching from other levels, as well as the ground level. They were the ones who wanted the best view of what the child was going to attempt.

Nyght waited until the High-Masters were on the third level. They were positioning themselves at an equal distance from each other, while three levels below, Nyght was standing in the center of the hall. When they stopped moving and were watching her, Nyght raised her right hand up and removed her cloak. She tossed it to the side well out of reach of where she was. She then moved Full to her right hand while holding Umbra in her left. She extended both her arms out to her sides as far as she could stretch them. With the tips of her daggers pointing toward the ground, she dropped them. To everyone's surprise, everyone except Nyght, the blades went into the marble surface of the floor a third of a handbreadth. Even with that small demonstration, she had everyone's attention.

She then bent at her knees and grabbed hold of both hilts of her daggers. She lifted them up enough so that their tips touched the floor. While still kneeling, she placed her left foot half a pace in front of her right, and then with balance and precision, she started rotating her entire body. While she was turning, she kept her blades against the floor causing them to cut into the marble, etching a circle into the floor as she turned. When she had finished and was facing the opposite direction from where she started, she had a circle drawn around her. Everyone looking could tell that it was a perfect circle. With the two starting points being where the tips of the daggers had begun. She had drawn it with no effort at all.

High-Master Wraith had seen the entire task, and even though it would cost the Guild some coinage to fix the floor, he could not help but be impressed. He also thought that maybe the circle could remain. Maybe they could initiate The Trial of the Circle into the Guild just to see who performed the best at it.

Nyght stood and looked to the third floor. She gave a nod, and two breaths later, the High-Masters began tossing the sheets of parchment each of them took. They knew the rules of the trial so they only threw a few of the pages out at a time, this would make the trial last longer, but that was part of it, so they only threw out about twenty pages at once. Since all three of the High-Masters were doing the same, there were about sixty pages going to the levels below. As soon as they were out of their hands, they would take hold of more of the pages and toss them as well. Even though there was a pause between the times they released some, it was not that long of one.

Nyght saw the pages coming over the ledge and down to her. The first thing she noticed was that the High-Masters had very good aim and they were not going to make it easy for her to pass the trial. They were after all assassins, and as assassins, they had precision and accuracy which allowed them to get the majority of the pages over her head and directly over the circle. She had to make sure none landed inside.

Moon had given her the images of all the battles and fights Moon had ever seen. These trials were also among those memories, so she had seen every one Moon had witnessed. Humans were not the first to put this trial into place. There were others who not only developed the trial but also performed it better than any human.

Nyght could see the memory clearly in her mind. The beings who perfected the trial looked something like humans but were taller, leaner, and had long hair. Nyght also saw their ears through their hair and the pointed tips. She had never seen these creatures before, but since Moon knew the word, Moon passed it to Nyght. They were Elves. It was the images of these beings that would allow her to pass because out of all her memories of the trial, they were the only ones who had ever passed it without a single piece of parchment entering the circle.

Since the pages had to come from the third level of the Guild, she had a few breaths before they reached her but when they did, she moved to intercept them.

She was holding her blades with the tips away from her. When the pages reached within an arm's length above her, she stabbed for them. She began immediately to puncture the pages directly in the middle of each one. The first pages reaching her were easier to handle but when the ones coming behind the first started making their way to her, she had to increase her speed to make sure none of the pages reached the inside of the circle. At times, she would have to adjust her stance or change the direction she was facing to make sure she caught hold of a piece of paper, but each move was executed with such precision that everyone watching was amazed.

As the pages in the air started to bunch up together, she had to change her tactics. It was something those who created the trial knew that others did not. The test was not just about catching hold of the pages falling and were within the participant's reach, it was also about guiding the ones the person knew they would not be able to take hold of.

When a page came into the area of her daggers, but she was not able to get to it, she had to maneuver her blades so that as they brushed past the page, there was enough force of air between the page and the blade to push it out of the circle. When humans performed this test, they always concentrated on getting every piece of paper coming close to them. The Elves knew that the test did not just pertain to the number of pages caught but also the number of pages that fell into the circle. There are two parts to the test, just like there are two parts to fighting: attack and defense. Using the weapon to slice into a page was the same as an attack on an enemy. Using the weapon to force one of the pages out of the range of the circle was a defense against an enemy, and in this case, the circle.

Nyght continued to either force the pages onto her blades or out past the edge of the circle. She moved so fast and efficiently that no one even understood she was using her weapons to push some of the pages away from her to clear the circle. She continued until she saw that there were no more pages coming from overhead.

She brought her weapons down to her sides but made sure the tips of the blades were still facing the ceiling since she did not want any of the many pages she had caught to fall into the circle. She looked up and it just so happened she was facing High-Master

Wraith. She knew, without a doubt, that she had passed the trial and that she would remain at the Assassin's Guild. She also thought that since she had proven herself, hopefully, they would allow her to use the lavatory. Something she had to do so desperately.

From where he was standing, he could see the lowest level, and he, as well as the other High-Masters and everyone else who had been watching the child, saw that all around her there were pages strung across the floor. Not a single one of those pages even came within a half of handbreadth to the edge of the circle.

Nyght did not look down to see if any of the pages were where they were not supposed to be, which would have caused her to fail the trial; she knew there were none. Even if she did not, when everyone who had been watching started applauding, she did. She turned her head enough to see the others who had been standing on the third level and noticed that the other two High-Master were clapping as well.

When she put her eyes back on High-Master Wraith, she noticed that he was the only one not showing any type of congratulatory reaction. It did not matter to Nyght; she passed the trial and had shown him that she knew how to use her blades.

As he heard the clapping of everyone around him, High-Master Wraith was not impressed with what the child had accomplished. Yes, she was good.

No, she was better than good when it came to wielding those daggers of hers but there was one thing she lacked. He decided there, at that very moment, he would not send her to the Weapons-Maker to learn how to use her blades, although there was one thing he hoped the Weapons-Maker would be able to teach his young pupil, humility.

NINE

Nyght walked down the stairs that would take her to the lowest level of the Guild. High-Master Wraith had brought her to the door but then told her that she was to go to the Weapons-Maker alone.

After the trial, High-Master Wraith told her that he still wanted her to meet the Weapons-Maker because even though she knew how to use the weapons she had, there were other things she could learn from someone with more experience with weapons than any member of the Guild: alive or dead.

As she descended, she could feel the temperature of the surrounding area getting warmer which to her seemed strange because she figured the deeper she went the colder it would be. There were torches spread out down the stairwell which provided light but even those would not provide the warmth she was feeling.

When she reached the bottom of the stairs, she stopped and looked behind her, "Two hundred," she said, referring to the number of steps she had counted when she started descending.

She put her focus back on the passageway before her. After walking a bit further, she began hearing noises although she could not tell what was making them.

Soon, she saw light coming from a room at the end of the hallway. The door to the room was slightly open and not only was that where the light was coming from, but the noise was as well. She had on her cloak, and within it, she had her daggers in her hands. She did not think High-Master Wraith would send her down there because he wanted to show her that she did not know how to use her daggers as much as she thought she did, but that did not mean that this was not some test. A test given by the Weapons-Maker of the Guild.

When she reached the door and saw it slightly open, she pulled it toward her. As soon as she was standing in front of the opening, she could feel the heat coming from the room. It was hot and with her cloak on, she was starting to perspire. However, it was bearable, so taking a tighter grip on her daggers she stepped inside, leaving the door behind her open just in case she decided she would have to leave quicker than she arrived.

"Shut the blasted door!" The phrase was spoken by someone whom Nyght could not see, but she knew it came from somewhere off to the right. Since she did not seem to be in any immediate danger, she turned around and pulled the door closed but only as far as she had found it when she came upon it. "All the way!" the voice yelled again, and when Nyght did as the voice had said, the door closed with a metallic bang. One that sounded to her as if she had just sealed herself in the room.

The voice did not say anything else, so she decided to find out just where the Weapons-Maker was. As she started walking through the room, she saw crates stacked three high, full of wood and ore. So many crates, they made up the walls she was traveling through. She realized it was not just a walkway but a maze. A maze that would take her somewhere.

When she came to the end of the walls of crates, she was still in the same room, but with the number of steps she had traveled, she was sure she was further from the door she entered through. The maze of crates did not have any intersections where she had to decide on which way to continue. She knew that to get back to the door to leave, she only had to start down the passageway in the opposite direction. If the Weapons-Maker was the one who had arranged the crates, he did not do it to confuse anyone who entered his chamber so she would be able to go back the way she came.

She could now see what was making the grinding noise she heard in the passageway to the entrance. She looked over to her right and ten paces away, someone was standing with their back toward her working on something. Their elbows were out to their sides, letting Nyght know that they were using their hands and she saw the person's right leg move up and down. With the motion, she could tell the person, this Weapons-Maker, was sharpening some weapon.

She decided she was going to stand where she was. She felt that there was no reason for her to be there, especially since she did not need any training with her weapons.

Neither of them spoke. She stood there while the person on the other side of the room continued with their work. Nyght could tell that the person was male. That she had known when she heard him tell her to close the door. Although, there was something about the person's body that did not seem right. She could only see his back and part of his legs and arms but from that little amount, she could tell that his physical appearance was different from anyone else she had seen before.

She did not stop her observation of the Weapons-Maker when he finished what he was working on and raised up from leaning forward. Once upright, Nyght saw that he had a sword in his hands and was inspecting it. Since he still had his back to her, she only saw the tip of the sword because it rose higher than the top of the Weapons-Maker head.

While inspecting the weapon, he turned around. He was still looking at the sword he was holding in front of him not once putting his eyes on Nyght, but this did allow Nyght to get a better look at him.

The first thing she noticed was that he had his hair in a single braid that ran down the front of him on his left side. His hair was brown and was so long it went past his waist. She also saw that at the end of the braid, there was something that looked like a piece of metal. From what Nyght could see, his hair was the most normal thing about him.

When she was looking at him from behind, she thought there was something different about his body. Now that he was facing her, she could see she had been correct. His arms, legs, and body were disproportioned to each other. She had seen weapon makers who had been working their forges for so long that the muscles in their arms were of good size and well-formed. However, their entire arm was proportioned to the rest of their arm. The man she was looking at now was not like that. His upper arms were wider and thicker than she had ever seen on any human. The lower part of his arms appeared to belong to an average size man. Until it came to his hands and then once again, they were a greater size and appeared as if they did not belong to him.

He had on trousers but even that did not stop Nyght from noticing something about his legs. They appeared to be the same length as hers. This might not mean much, but since she was still only fifteen, she figured that at some point the man's legs had just stopped growing. That is upward because the girth of his upper thighs was about the same as his upper arms. The middle of his legs was that of a normal human, but his calves looked as if they did not belong on the man either. They were not quite as wide as his thighs, but they were wider than a normal human, and Nyght was sure that if they were not, the man's leg would not support the weight of his body.

The next feature Nyght noticed about the man's lower body was the fact that he was not wearing any shoes. Most weapon makers wore thick leather boots because of the sparks from their forges flying through the air as they work. However, this man had no boots on at all. She also saw that his feet seemed to be too long for his height.

She moved her eyes to his body and the best way she could describe the one she was observing was someone had placed a set of arms and legs on a barrel and taught it to walk. He was not fat and from his appearance, he was all muscle, and from his chest to his midsection, it appeared he was as solid as a rock.

His beard was the same color as his hair and grew so that it reached the middle of his chest.

The last item that made this man stand out from others was his skin. His face, his arms, and even his feet had a brownish tint. She had seen men who when they worked their forge all day, their skin took on a darker color. Nyght had a feeling that no water would remove any dirt from this man because his skin was that color from the day he took his first breath.

"Are ye done ogling me?" the Weapons-Maker asked, and Nyght put her focus back on his face. He was still inspecting the weapon in his hand, and from the way it appeared, he had never stopped looking at it, but he did know she was studying him more than with just a passing glimpse.

"High-Master Wraith sent me here. You are the Guild's Weapons-Maker are you not?"

The man lowered the sword in front of him and placed the tip on the floor. "And ye are the one that took The Trial of the Circle and passed."

They looked at each other. Nyght did not know what to make of the man in front of her. Not only because of his appearance but also because she could sense something about him. It was as if he was not a man at all. As if, the hardness of his body went all the way through to the inside.

He looked at the girl across the room. High-Master Wraith had told him everything about her. Not just about The Trial of the Circle, but about her eyes as well. Of course, he already knew about what part she played in the death of the former Master Viper, but he did not hold that against the child. Viper never needed his help. He made the weapons the assassins used, but since Viper and the assassins like her used their bodies as a weapon, they never had a need for his services. He would not miss the late Master Viper at all, and when he was the one who found her outside in the cold, frozen in that position, he could not stop laughing the whole trip back inside.

"High-Master Wraith said ye have a pair of fighting daggers, and that he ain't seen a set like them before." He stopped talking but the girl did not say anything. "Well?"

"Well, what?" Nyght asked, even though she knew what he wanted.

"Let me see those blasted daggers of yers!"

When he spoke this time, Nyght thought she heard his voice make a grinding noise. As if he had pebbles between his teeth. It was not how he spoke that bothered her; it was what he said. He referred to her blades as "blasted daggers," that, she did not like, and therefore would not do as he had so forcefully asked. He was not a High-Master and even though he may be part of the Guild, she was not going to let anyone disrespect the gift Moon had given her; she turned around and started walking away.

"Where the blast do ye think ye be going?"

Nyght stopped walking but did not turn to look at the man behind her; although, she did give him her answer, "You have nothing to teach me." She then started walking again.

"Wanna bet?"

Nyght heard the question and as soon as he had spoken, she heard the Weapons-Maker coming toward her, fast. If he was an assassin, with the noise his feet were making every time he placed one on the ground, there was no way he could sneak up on an enemy. Especially not Nyght. She waited until she knew he was exactly the distance away she needed him to be and when she was ready, she quickly turned around, bringing her arms out of her cloak along with her daggers. She raised them just above her head and away from her, crossing the blades to form an X while at the same time she moved her left foot forward a step to give her more support. She did this to stop the sword the Weapons-Maker had brought down on her as she turned around. She was sure he had planned to slice into the top of her head, but since she was so quick, he only came within four handbreadths of his target.

Even he knew she allowed him to get that close.

They held that position. His sword extended out in front of him with the blade over the top of her head and she with her blades stopping the sword from coming any closer. Each of them knew that either of them could break the hold at any moment but each of them knew this was the opportunity for the other to measure their opponent.

Nyght had not had any real test with her daggers against another being. This was her first. She was sure of their strength because Moon would not give her a weapon and then have it break after one use. Her daggers might hold out, but her arms would not. The man with the sword had sturdy muscles and since she could see his bare arms, she could see that his strength would hold out longer than hers would. She would have to give in soon, not because of her skill, but because his strength was much more than hers. That did not mean she would not hold out for as long as possible.

The Weapons-Maker knew he could force the

child into submission or into making the next move. He was only using a small portion of his strength, and at any moment, he could simply put pressure on his sword, and the child would either have to move out of the way or would end up with a slice in her head that would end her life, but he chose not to. He did not want to kill the child; he wanted to see just how well she handled herself. Not physically. It did not matter how strong a person's body was. If their will was weak, they would break long before their body came to its end.

Even though he was much older than the child, much, much older, they were about the same height. In fact, the child was a bit taller than he was. That did not bother him; most humans are. With their height about the same, as she was looking into his eyes, he was looking into hers. High-Master Wraith told him about the child's eyes but not even High-Master Wraith knew her eyes would not have any effect on him. Not just because he was not an assassin and had never killed another living being, but because of what he was.

High-Master Wraith had also told him about the fighting daggers the child carried. Weapons were why the Weapons-Maker lived. He had been making them as soon as he was able to hold a hammer. He was only five when his father placed a hammer in his hands but since then he had made quite a few beautiful pieces: swords, knives, axes, bows, lances, shields, and a number of other weapons the assassins of the Guild required for their assigned task. During his entire life, he had never seen weapons like the ones the child was using to hold back his attack.

He took his eyes off hers so that he could examine them better. The one in her right hand was pale white which matched the color of her skin. The one in her left hand was black, and for as long as he had been making weapons, he still could not tell the ore used to create the items he was admiring. Since he had an intimacy with weapons, even ones he did not make himself, he could tell that wherever those weapons came from, they were one of a kind.

He then remembered the name High-Master Wraith had called the child. It was Nyght. Then with his affinity to weapons, he knew how the child had come upon those weapons. He knew they were a gift. A gift from one that when fully showing was just as pale as the child herself. "So, ye serve Moon do ye?"

Nyght did not know how this man knew what he had said which caused her to think that maybe it was not a good idea to play anymore. Maybe this man had something against Moon, and if that was true, then he might have something against her. She made the first move.

With her two daggers crossed she held the sword at bay and slid them down the length of the blade. This kept it away from her but at the same time allowed her to force the blade upward and away from her as she moved forward. She knew she would not be able to make any type of attack because as soon as she moved the daggers, the blade would come down. By moving forward and forcing the sword upward, the man had to step back, or he would be too close to his opponent and in close quarters his sword was useless.

The Weapons-Maker was not impressed with the counter move. It was an easy one to come up with, especially when his opponent used a weapon better suited for close quarters. He gladly retreated from their stance taking more than enough steps backward to put some distance between them. Although, he did not lower his blade. Not because he was afraid of the child attacking, but because he did not want her to think their little match was over. In fact, it had only just begun.

The Weapons-Maker quickly moved forward, and from the appearance, it seemed as if he would completely close the distance between the two. However, when he came within a single stride of Nyght, he swung his sword out in front of him coming from his right. He was aiming for her midsection and even though he did not want to kill the child, he was not going to make it easy for her to survive.

Nyght saw exactly what the Weapons-Maker was trying to do. With the height at which he was holding his sword, it forced her to protect her midsection. She figured her opponent would expect her to either use her daggers to block the blade from making its complete swing or for her to step out of its reach. She chose the second option but added something of her own to her defense.

Just before the sword was less than a half of a handbreadth away from her side, she forced her body back enough so the blade would not connect with her. Instead of placing her daggers down in front of her to block the sword, she waited until it was just in front of her left side, and then she put her blades against the sword's outer edge. She used her own blades to push the sword on its path causing it to move faster than its wielder wanted it to. As the daggers pushed the sword away, the Weapons-Maker's arms went with the sword causing his body to follow the path of the sword. As the tip of the sword reached the right side of Nyght's body, she stepped forward to begin her counterattack.

The Weapons-Maker was still not impressed with the move the girl had completed. It was a typical defense move to what he had tried to do. Now that his sword was more to his left, his right side was unprotected, and he had no problem in seeing that the girl was aiming for it.

Since she had forced his sword and body to swing to his left, he continued in that direction and was quick enough to spin completely around with the sword leading the way. When he was facing the girl again, his sword was once again in motion to slice into the child's left side.

Nyght saw the blade once again coming toward

her left. When she forced it away from her, she tried to close the distance between her and the Weapons-Maker so that she would have the advantage with her shorter blades. As he turned, her opponent stepped back first with his left foot, then halfway through his turn he stepped back with his right, putting him over a pace away, facing her. With the length of his arms as well as the length of his weapon, he once again had the advantage.

Nyght saw what he was doing before he even made it halfway through his turn. In that amount of time, she flipped the daggers in her hands so that the tips were pointing toward the floor. When the sword reached her left side, she had them out in front of her and slightly to her left to meet the blade.

When the weapons made contact, she felt the jolt from their weapons connecting and knew that even if this was some test, the Weapons-Maker was putting his strength behind each attack. The only thing she did not know was if he was using every bit he had. He might be holding back to go easier on her, or he might just be keeping some in reserve. Nyght knew his strength was the only advantage her opponent had over her, but it was not one that would decide the outcome. She only had to get closer to him to end the match before her strength gave out to her opponent.

As soon as her daggers stopped the sword, she quickly began her next attack. While using Full in her right hand to hold the sword away from her, she turned her body to her left. She extended her left arm outwards allowing Umbra to lead the way. As she spun, she kept the blade in her left hand at the height so when it came around it would end up in the Weapons-Maker's face, point first.

The Weapons-Maker saw the move she was attempting and knew that with her turning her body, she would bring herself closer to him, along with the dagger. If he had a shield then he would have simply raised it up to block the move, but since he only had the sword, he took a step backward bringing his sword with him. His opponent had put enough pressure in holding his blade in place with her one dagger. She was using it to give her extra support in making the spin toward him. When he pulled his sword away, he took that support from her; and since her body was in the middle of a spin, she had to follow through with it causing her to miss her intended target.

Nyght felt the sword's movement and from it, she knew her opponent had retreated backward. This freed up the dagger in her right hand which she was using to keep the sword away. Now, she could use it in her attack.

As she spun, the blade in her left hand missed its mark but she did not stop her motion. She continued in the spin and brought her right hand around as well, still holding the dagger so that the blade was facing away from the outside of her arm. She moved the blade to the height of her opponent's midsection, but by the time it would reach him, he would have already taken another step backward, so she continued with the spin of her body, bringing her left hand back around toward the Weapons-Maker forcing him to take another step backward.

The name of the maneuver was *The Whirlwind of Blades*. It was a move used by those with shorter swords or daggers to put them closer to their opponent. The person performing the move would force the other person to keep their eyes on the blades as well as their opponent's body. Because at any moment, they could either stop turning and force one of their blades outwards after simply flipping it in their hand or they could bring up one of their legs trying to connect with their opponent's body. The Weapons-Maker knew also that if the person was not careful, they could lose track of their opponent in the breath they had their eyes turned away.

The Weapons-Maker waited for just that moment and when the child's eyes were off him, he stopped moving backward, bent down at his waist, and thrust his sword forward. This counterattack would make the person have to adjust their attack since their opponent's body was now lower to the ground than it had been a breath ago.

Nyght came to another end of a cycle in her turn and as her eyes came around she saw that her opponent was no longer standing upward. He had crouched down and had extended his sword aiming it straight for her midsection.

As she came to the point in her turn where she was about to be facing the Weapons-Maker, she flipped the daggers in her hands so that the blades were now pointing upward. She then brought them both downward crossing the blades in an X. Where they met, she struck the top of her opponent's sword, forcing it to the floor. Since her blades were holding it in place, she could not move them, or her opponent would bring the sword up cutting into some part of her body. She decided that her best move would be to use her blades and force the sword to her right and she would then move to her left, freeing her up for her next attack. She did not get the chance to begin the move.

As soon as the tip of his blade touched the floor, The Weapons-Maker adjusted his hold on the handle so that if he lifted up the blade, it would be facing downward but he did not lift it. Instead, he put more force on it making sure the tip was tight against the ground. He then quickly moved forward. As he did, his body rose up so that he was once again standing but he kept the point of the sword in contact with the ground. This forced the child to take a step backward or her opponent's body would bowl into her. The child's daggers had stopped his blade from moving forward but he had no problem with using it as a fulcrum to push his opponent backward. Even though she was close to him where her daggers would have the advantage, if she tried to strike out, all he had to do was bring the sword up where he would be able to deflect them to the side.

When she had taken two steps backward, he adjusted his hands again so that he was now holding the sword with the blade upward in his right hand. He then continued to move toward the girl but adjusted his blade so that it stretched outwards aiming for her midsection. At the last second, he moved the sword so that the tip of the blade was pointing to his left. With the blade leveled out in front of his body, he rushed forward.

Nyght saw that with the way he was holding his blade, and at the speed he was moving, he would not be able to attack. He would rush her and try to force her backward. She did not have to turn around to look. She knew that her back was toward one of the walls of crates. Her opponent was going to try to pin her between them and the sword. Since she would have to use her daggers to hold the weapon back, she would not be able to use them in an attack until she was free. She decided to move forward herself.

When she reached her opponent, she placed her daggers onto the top of the sword to force him to lower it. If she could, then her daggers would eventually be facing outwards and toward the Weapons-Maker's upper body then she would simply use the cross guards of her blades to keep the sword away from her as she moved the blades forward and into her opponent.

Nyght thought that since he was only holding the sword with his right hand, he would not have the same strength he had when he was wielding it with both. As soon as her daggers met his sword, she knew she was wrong in her assumption. Even wielding the weapon with one hand, the Weapons-Maker's strength was enough to keep her from completing the move. With her daggers on top of the blade, she was able to force the sword downward, but only enough to where her blades were still at an angle pointing slightly upward. She did not have the strength to force the sword any lower, and with the height of her daggers, she would not be able to force them into her opponent's body.

He allowed the girl to lower his sword so that it was just above his chest but not enough to where her daggers were pointing directly at his body. It did not even surprise him when she began to move forward so that he would not be able to pin his opponent against the wall, which was not his plan anyway. The position they were both now in was.

Within the few breaths she was trying to force his sword to lower, as the Weapons-Maker held it in his right hand, he moved his left hand downward and grabbed hold of the braid of his hair, about midway down its length. He then snapped it under his sword and with the speed he used, it wrapped around the child's right wrist. The metal piece at the end of the braid had enough weight allowing it to make two complete circles fastening the braid just below the child's wrist. The look on her face told the Weapons-Maker that she had not expected the move.

Using only his right hand, he pushed his sword up and out causing the girl to step backward. Just before his arm reached the highest it could go, he put more force into the push causing the girl to step back more but not under her own control. When she did this, the braid wrapped around her right wrist went taut, which was the only thing that stopped her from taking another step backward.

When she looked at the Weapons-Maker, he was smiling. She did not say it, but she was impressed with what he had just accomplished. She now knew what the piece of metal at the end of his braid was for. He used it like a hook to lock the braid around her wrist. She thought about the fact that she had cut her hair because of the way Master Viper had adored it and she did not like it. Now she would have to think about growing it out again because what she had just seen her opponent accomplish might come in handy.

Nyght still had her blades in her hands and even though her right hand was not free from the end of the Weapons-Maker's hair, she did not think she was in any worse position than before. Besides, it was only hair; as she had cut hers off, she would now shorten the Weapons-Maker's as well.

When her opponent forced her backward, the braid tightened which was exactly what Nyght needed. She brought the blade in her left hand up and over to slash through the part of the braid just below her right hand. She knew that once she cut it, she would be free. When the dagger's blade struck the braid, nothing happened. The blade just stopped, not even cutting a single bit of the hair.

The daggers had been a gift from Moon and Nyght thought they were special. She had no problem with cutting through the thick books belonging to High-Master Wraith and the Weapons-Maker's hair was a lot thinner than the bindings. So why could her blades not cut through the braid? She put her eyes on her opponent for the answer.

He knew what she wanted to know but now was not the time to give her the answer. He did give her something to think about. "Ye ain't the only one that has been blessed, girly."

The whole incident with the braid only lasted about ten breaths and now Nyght was focusing back on the situation. Even though she did not have the complete use of her right hand, it was not useless. She flipped the dagger in her hand so that the blade was once again, facing away from the outside of her arm. As she made the adjustment, she took one step forward and turned her body to the right. This caused her body to wrap up in the braid as well, but she planned on that.

As she turned, she raised the blade in her left hand up and when she had made a complete circle, she had just enough time to position it at the proper height to block the blade of the sword coming straight for her throat from her left. As her opponent made the hurried move because he knew the closeness would be a disadvantage to him, he did not see the blade in Nyght's right hand.

When she wrapped herself in the braid, she made sure the blade led the way and when she stopped her spin, its tip was pressing against the Weapons-Maker's chest. Directly over his heart. With his sword blocked, he would not have been able to stop the final thrust that would force the dagger into his chest. Of course, Nyght did not know it but if she had tried to end his life, the blade of the dagger would not have even made the slightest cut into the Weapons-Maker's skin. His hair was not the only part of his body blessed.

Nyght did not want to kill her opponent, but with the location of her blade, she ended up with the advantage or that was what she thought. Since the Weapons-Maker had seen the girl in action, he was willing to let her have the win. Her move would not have caused him any harm, but to anyone other than himself, the person would have had the blade go into their chest, and being so close to her, they would have been looking directly into her eyes as they took their last breath. He had to agree with High-Master Wraith, the child was good. No, better than good.

She had come up with a way to use the attack with his braid to her advantage. He was sure she had never seen the move before because of the look on her face when he used it. Therefore, she was able to devise a counterattack at that very moment. A sign of a person who was born to bring death to others.

"I think it's time we had a drink," he said, trying to let the child know that the bout was over. She made no movement that would allow him to believe she felt the same way. "Come now, we can't stay like this. Me weapon at yer neck, and yers at me chest."

"I can, or I can force my blade into you, and when you have your drink, it will flow from a new hole in your body."

The Weapons-Maker had to smile at the comment. Partly because he thought it was humorous but mainly because he knew that since the blade did not cut through his braid, it would not puncture his skin. He did not want the standoff to go on any longer. He never had to sleep, and he had a feeling that if they stayed like this, before she let her eyes close, she would try to make the new hole she had mentioned.

He made the move to let her know that their contest had come to an end by dropping the sword he had in his hand.

Even after the gesture of peace, Nyght was not ready to put her trust in her opponent. Now that the sword was no longer an issue, she moved the blade of the dagger in her left hand so that the tip pressed against the Weapons-Maker's throat. "Your braid," she said to let him know he should remove the last weapon he had used against her.

He still was not concerned about her using her daggers on him but since he wanted to move this meeting along, he slowly moved his left hand upward and brought it to her wrist. He quickly tugged on the metal clip at the end of his braid causing it to un-hook and freeing the child from the binding.

Once free, she still held the daggers where they were for two breaths. She then decided that since the match was over and she had won, there was no need to end the Weapons-Maker's life. She made a spin with her body to unravel herself from the braid but when she ended the spin, she was once again facing the Weapons-Maker with her daggers posi-tion so that if he wished to continue, then she was willing.

The Weapons-Maker turned around and walked over to where he had been working when Nyght had first entered the room. He bent over and lifted a wooden bucket off the floor then brought it back over to Nyght. When he reached her, he pulled the dipper out of the bucket and offered it to her to have the first drink. She did not take it and the Weapons-Maker understood. He then lifted the dipper up to his own mouth and swallowed the entire contents, showing the girl that since he had not been able to defeat her with a sword, he was not going to try to poison her to win their match. He took no offense at what he had to do, after all, she was in the Assassin's Guild, and there was more than one way to elimi-nate an enemy.

When he finished, he placed the dipper back in the bucket and handed it to Nyght. She took hold of it and as soon as it was free from his hand, she had to put more effort into holding the bucket. He had lifted it with one hand with no problem, but when she grabbed it, she had to quickly put her other hand on it while holding onto her daggers and maneuver it so that it would not fall. Just so she would not drop it, she lowered the bucket to the floor. While keeping her eyes on the Weapons-Maker she lifted the dipper out of the bucket and took a drink of the water. Even though the little bit of fighting she had just completed had not even caused her to be a bit thirsty.

"Ye are Nyght are ye not?" he asked.

"Yes, Weapons-Maker," Nyght replied.

"Ye can stop with the Weapons-Maker title. All that High-Master, Master stuff is for the levels above. Me name is Pacton-Settac-Kanig-Gretag-Belain-Dartog." He saw the look on her face when he told her his name. It was one most humans ended up with after he spoke his full name, and before she told him it would be easier to call him Weapons-Maker he gave her another option, "Ye can call me Dart though. That is what the rest of this bunch does."

"So why the long name if you go by Dart?"

Nyght's question did not surprise Dart. She probably did not know much, if anything, about his kind. "Pacton-Settac-Kanig-Gretag-Belain-Dartog is me full name. Belain was me father, and Gretag was his father, and Kanig was his father and Settac was his father, and Pacton was his. When I give me name, I give me past father's names not only because their name is part of mine, but because they are the ones that came before me. So now ye know where I come from."

Nyght understood what he was telling her, but she still did not know where he came from, or at least not literally. "What are you?" Nyght asked, hoping to find out why the Weapons-Maker's body looked as if his parts came from more than one person.

"Ye never seen one of me kind before have ye?"

"I don't even know what one of your kind is."

Dart smiled at her answer. One thing he admired was someone who spoke their mind. If they did, then there was less likely a chance they would be hiding something. "Me da, Belain is a Dwarf. Me ma was human."

"Was?" Nyght asked, hearing the word Dart used in reference to his ma.

"She died, long time ago. Me da raised me here," Dart said and moved his eyes around the room.

"You mean here in this room?"

"Not just this room, the whole castle."

"Your father was the Weapons-Maker of the Guild before you then?"

Dart let out a loud laugh and once he finished, he gave a bit more of his family history. "Me da wasn't just the Weapons-Maker of the Guild. He built the Guild himself." He paused for three breaths then continued, "Brick by brick, piece by piece, all by himself."

Nyght heard what the Weapons-Maker said, she just had a hard time believing it.

TEN

Dart turned to his right and started walking away from Nyght. "Come girl, let me show ye the rest of me place and I will tell ye how the Guild was started."

Nyght watched the Weapons-Maker as he moved across the room. She let go of the dipper which fell back into the bucket at her feet, then followed the half-Dwarf/half-human. She knew what a Dwarf looked like because Moon had seen them before and passed the knowledge to her. From the memories, she saw beings that looked something like Dart only their bodies seemed to be more proportional than his. She took it that his appearance was due to his mixed blood.

Dart stopped at a door and waited for Nyght to reach him. He then looked over his left shoulder to make sure the girl was behind him before he showed her the next room they would be entering. When Nyght stopped, he gave her a smile, turned his head, and then pulled on the handle to the door in front of him. It made a creaking noise as it came toward him. When it was opened far enough, he stepped through with Nyght behind him.

There were torches on stands spaced through-out the room supplying ample light. Although there were too many for Nyght to count, because the room was so big, she could barely see the wall on the opposite side. All through the room there were racks, shelves, wooden barrels, and metal bins full of weapons. So many that not even the biggest army in the nation would be able to use all the weapons in the room.

Nyght did not know what she was most im-pressed with, the size of the room or the number of weapons and armor she was looking at. There were swords of various sizes and designs, axes that were double bladed and single as well as throwing and war axes. Lances and pikes, hammers, maces, and morning stars. "Come this way," Dart said, turned to his left, and started walking. Nyght took one more look at what was in the room then followed the Weapons-Maker.

They made their way through the room and around the weapons kept in a variety of containers. When they finally stopped, they were standing in front of wooden tables waist high that stretched out across the room. Nyght took a step ahead of Dart so she could get a better look at the items before her. She did not know the names of them, nor had she seen any of the items before; that was until she came across something that jogged a memory from long ago.

Curled up on the table were a few of the same

items. Each one was a single wire and at each of the ends, there were small pieces of wood attached. She remembered seeing the same exact item back in the room the man had taken her to when she was younger. It had been under his mattress. It was so long ago that she did not even remember what the man looked like. Except she did remember there was something about his eyes. As for the item on the table, she was sure that was where she had seen it before.

"It's called a garrote." Nyght turned her head to look at him. "Let me show ye how it's used." Dart picked up the piece of wire by one of the wooden handles and the rest of it uncoiled. He then grabbed hold of the other handle and held the wire taut out in front of him. "Ye get up behind yer target and wrap this around their neck." To show her what he meant, Dart positioned the wire around the front of his own throat with his hands behind his head. "Then ye pull tight on the handles and twist, causing the wire to cut into the person's throat. It be the lack of air they die from and not from the slice of the wire itself. Though I have heard of people pulling hard enough that before the victim be buried the ones doing the burying had to reattach the head by sewing it back on their shoulders." At the last part, Dart actually laughed.

Nyght turned and put her focus back on the items on the table. She walked down the row looking at the weapons that were for the assassin's trade. She stopped when she came to a table that had some metal objects on it. She stretched her hand out and picked one of the items up. It had metal spikes on one side that were a third of a handbreadth long. There was a total of twelve spikes. On the other side of the spikes, there was a piece of metal that looked like a handle. As she inspected it, she saw that there was enough open space in the handle where she could slip the entire item onto her hand, and so she did. Once situated, the spikes were on the side of her palm facing outwards. The handle on the back of the item was now against the back of her hand and forcing her to keep her hand and fingers stretched outwards.

She looked down at the table and saw that there was another item just like the one she was holding, as well as two others. All four items were a set. Two she would be able to put on her hands. She then looked at the other two and saw the opening of the handles were wider. Wide enough so that she could place her foot in them even if she kept her boot on. "They are for climbing," she said as she turned her head to look at the Weapons-Maker. It was a statement, not a question. "You place them on your hands and feet. The spikes will assist a person to climb up and down. The only thing is that they would need to have a wall on each of their sides so that they could put pressure on them to make the climb."

"Ye seen them before?"

Nyght gave her answer, "No, I just know what I

could use them for." She then turned her head away and placed the item back on the table with the other three parts of the set. She had never seen grappling claws before. She did not know how she knew to use the item, but she did. She now remembered that the night she left that room she had only taken her knife as she had glanced over the items under the mattress. She did not know how to use any of the other items, so she only took the knife because it was what she needed at the time.

Dart watched Nyght as she looked at the weapons. He knew what she was, but he could tell she had no idea. It was not his place to tell her. That he would leave up to High-Master Wraith. He alone had that right since he and the child had something in common. Dart also thought he had best move their tour along. He saw the girl was looking at the items in front of her and she was probably wondering just how she knew about them, and how to use them, even if she had never seen them before. "Come on," he said and walked away heading further into the armory.

Nyght took one last look at the items around her then followed the Weapons-Maker putting no more thought into the different items.

They walked through the room and finally came to another door. Nyght saw that this one was solid iron and knew that if she tried to open it herself, she would not have been able to budge it. Dart did not have a problem. He placed his hands on the door, but instead of pulling this one open, he pushed it inwards. The door opened and as soon as it had cleared the entranceway Nyght felt heat coming out of the room on the other side. Heat which was more than she had ever felt before.

Dart walked into the room and Nyght followed. Not only was the heat strong, but the light in the room looked strange. It was as if the entire room glowed in an orange illumination. When Nyght stepped inside she could see where the heat and the light were coming from.

In the center of the room, there was a mound of stone that rose up, not from the floor, but out of it. She could tell that it was circular with the lower part wider than the top. She could see the orange glow coming from what was in the mound as well as the heat it was putting into the room.

Dart walked over to the mound, and even though the heat and the smell started bothering Nyght, she had to see what was causing the room to look and feel the way it did.

She walked over and stood next to Dart. When she looked down she saw some type of liquid in the mound. Now that her eyes had adjusted from the light and the heat, she could see the liquid she was looking at was not like anything she had ever seen before. Then memories from Moon came to her. Moon had seen this exact thing only it was never in a room. It came out of the ground, out of the towering mountains that spewed its contents into the air.

"Magma," Dart said and Nyght turned away from the mound in front of her. Not just to see him, but so that she could give her eyes a rest from the heat and the light. "This is where me da started building the Guild."

Nyght turned back to look at the mound of rock and the magma bubbling inside it. The smell was starting to affect her as well. She did not know it but the gases coming from the molten rock were poisonous to most living creatures. All except for Dart and his kind. To them, it was just like breathing air.

Dart saw that Nyght was starting to feel the effects of the gases. "I think ye need a breath of fresh air," he said and Nyght took one more look at the mound in front of her, then turned to leave. When they exited the room, Dart closed the iron door behind him. Nyght continued to walk away to put more distance between her and that place.

They walked back through the armory and came to the room where they had their little skirmish. By the time they reached it, Nyght was feeling better. Since Dart had left the door to the room open, she stepped through with the Weapons-Maker right behind her. "Take yerself another drink of water. That will help clear yer head."

Nyght went over to the bucket which was still where she had left it on the floor, bent over, and pulled up the dipper. As she stood up to take a drink, she could feel her head spinning a bit. As she drank the water, she turned to make sure she could see

Dart. If he wanted to harm her, now would be the best time to do so since the other room affected her physically. Maybe that was his plan from the very start.

Dart saw the way the girl was looking at him and knew she was just waiting for him to make a move to attack her. He gave her a smile then walked over to his left heading toward the grinding stone where he had been working when she arrived.

He walked past it and over to a group of barrels that were tall enough to reach the height of his knees. He pulled one out from the others, turned, and sat down on it so that he was facing Nyght. He then turned his body enough to grab hold of another barrel and pulled it in front of him then used his foot to push it away. Far enough so if the girl took him up on his offer to sit, there would be enough distance between them to make her feel more comfortable.

Nyght knew what the gesture meant and after she finished the bit of water left in the dipper, she dropped it back in the bucket and walked over to the seat the Weapons-Maker provided her with. As soon as she took her seat, he began his story.

"Me da was one hundred fifty as by the count of humans when he left his home and came to these mountains."

"Where was his home?" Nyght asked.

"Where all his kind come from, Below." Dart could see that the child did not understand. "Dwarves don't look at things the way others do. Like when I tell ye me da was one hundred fifty as by the count of humans, it is because we don't be keeping track of seasons or passing of seasons from one moment to the next. We don't be naming our cities or even have maps of them. There are only two places to a Dwarf. That is Below the ground and Above it."

"Then why do you have names?" Nyght asked.

"Because we need to know where we came from. Now let me finish me tellen, without any more questions." Nyght nodded to let him know she would remain quiet.

"Me da didn't know how many human seasons he was when he left; he figured that out many seasons later when he made contact with humans. But when he left the Below, he came to these mountains. He came because he was called." Dart stopped talking and looked at Nyght. Even though she wanted to ask who called him, she kept silent, but Dart answered the question he knew she wanted to ask. "It was Creator that called me da. Called him to these mountains so he could build this place."

Dart stood up and walked across the room to the water bucket. He picked it up and returned to his seat. Storytelling always made his mouth dry is what he would say. When he had swallowed a dipper full of water, he continued. "The mound ye saw in that room was the same when me da came upon it. It was the mound he built the Guild around. All by himself."

Dart had told this story to every assassin who had ever come to the Guild as a recruit. He told it because it was his story to tell and because every assassin needed to know; it was not humans who had built the great Guild. "Dwarves don't sleep, ever. Day and night, me da collected the boulders and worked them into the slabs of stones that make up the Guild. He also collected the iron to make the pipes that run through the entire structure. Them pipes are what ye get yer water from."

Whenever he told this story, Dart always had to explain the water pipes in better detail, just like he was going to do with Nyght. "Me da made the big holders that are attached to the High-Tower as well as each of the other seven towers. There are two of these holders on each. When it snows, which it does all the time in these mountains, the snow collects in the holders. Pipes attached to these holders lead into openings that lead deep underground. The magma below heats the pipes. Some of the pipes are only hot enough to melt the snow so that the water stays cold. Other pipes are hot enough that not only do they melt the snow but keep the water hot enough that it can burn ye. That is how ye get the hot and cold water for yer baths."

Since he had been talking about the pipes and water, Dart knew that this was the part where the person hearing the story would want to know about the indoor lavatory. Like any good storyteller, he gave the listener what they wanted. "Me da also built the system to take the waste we be making down through some more pipes. They lead deep underground as well, only they end up flowing directly into a magma pit, burning the waste away."

Dart reached down and pulled the dipper out of the bucket and took another drink, then replaced the dipper. "Altogether there are three hundred and fifty openings leading under the ground and deep into the Below. Three hundred and fifty and the mound which me da built the Guild around. It is the magma in the mound I use to melt the ore to make me weapons. I do it the same way me da did."

Nyght noticed that when he had said the last part, there was something in the Weapons-Maker voice. Something which made it seem that he missed his dad more than he would let anyone else believe. She did not say anything about it. She just allowed him to continue with his story.

"Me da worked night and day to build the Guild. He was all by himself up in these mountains, so he had no idea how many seasons had passed by the time he finished it." Dart took another drink of water. "But there still were no assassins yet. The first one did not come for many seasons later. But while me da was waiting, he made the weapons the assassins would need. Once the first assassin came here, me da told him he could use the place to establish the Guild, the one wanted to build. Ye see, Creator called me da to build the Guild and the first assassin to bring others to the place. Over the seasons, more and more assassins came and soon me da had almost finished what Creator called him to do."

Dart leaned over and put the dipper back in the bucket then pulled it up to him to take another drink. He emptied it completely then dropped the dipper back in the bucket. "Ye see, me da was the one to build the place but once it was done, he heard the call to return to the Below. The call that all Dwarves hear. Dwarves used to live on the Above but when fighting between the races began to grow, Creator called all Dwarves to the Below and that is where they remain to this day." Dart stopped talking and did not continue.

Nyght knew his story was not over, and even though she agreed she would not say anything, she knew she had to if she wanted to hear the rest of the story. "But not you."

Dart stopped staring ahead of him and put his eyes on Nyght. "But not me." He took a few breaths then continued telling his tale, "Me da had felt the calling of the Below but knew someone had to stay and make sure the Guild was taken care of. Not so much as to repairs and such because me da built it so grand, it will be standing long after the last of us be around. But someone had to stay to make the weapons. He went to the High-Masters that ran the place at the time and asked for a human woman. A woman he could sire a child with."

"And they had you," Nyght said.

Dart nodded his head then continued. "It was me da that raised me. I never met me ma, but since she was human, I know she has been gone for a long while now."

Nyght remembered when he had told her his mother was dead. She thought it was something he might have witnessed, but actually, he had never met her, and it was just the lifespan of a human that made him realize she was no longer alive.

"Me da trained me on how to make the weapons the Guild members use. Not just swords, axes, and bows, but the special items that allow them to do the things they do." He paused a moment then continued, "When I was hundred fifty, me da left. He said I was to stay here and work the forge for the Guild. Then he went back to the Below." He stopped talking.

"And you haven't seen him since?" This time Nyght was asking. Dart did not answer but by the look on his face, she knew he had not. "How long has it been since..." Nyght was going to ask how long it has been since his father had left but decided to rephrase the question, "...since you took over making the weapons for the Guild?"

"Four hundred thirty-two human seasons," Dart answered.

Nyght may not be able to read but she knew how to count and add numbers, and she came up with five hundred eighty-two. Dart was five hundred eighty-two seasons. "So how long do Dwarves live?"

Dart looked at Nyght, smiled, and gave his answer, "Me da said that Dwarves live for about three hundred human seasons, as for me, I will live forever. I told ye that ye weren't the only one blessed."

Nyght remembered him telling her that when she tried to cut his braid. "Me da told me that when I was born, Creator kissed me on the top of me head." To emphasize the part he was talking about, Dart lifted his hand in a fist and gave himself three good raps on the top of his head. "Ye see he blessed me so that I will live forever, that is as long as I don't kill another living being of me own kind or any of the other four races."

This was the part of the story where Dart always had to prove his tale was true. "Here," he said then leaned over closer to the grinding wheel and picked up a sword lying against it. He held the weapon out to Nyght hilt first. "Try to kill me." He said the last part with a smile.

Nyght looked at the weapon and tried to decide if this was another test. If she tried to kill the Weapons-Maker, would he try to kill her for attacking him? She looked at the sword he was holding out to her and decided that even if he did fight back, she had to see if he was telling the truth.

Nyght stood up from the barrel, reached out, and grabbed the hilt of the sword. She continued in her forward motion but suddenly stopped just as the tip of the weapon came in contact with Dart's chest. She looked at him and knew he did not intend to try to stop her. She had to wonder if what he said was true or was he trying to end his life at the hands of another.

For Dart, it was always the same. He would give

someone the opportunity to test his story but even those who took the sword in hand always stopped before they made the final thrust. "I knew ye…" Dart did not finish what he was going to say. Usually, he says to the person with the sword, "I knew ye wouldn't have the courage to try," but not this time. Before he was able to, Nyght forcefully pushed the sword into his chest. Dart had no choice but to smile when the tip did not puncture him. "I was tellen the truth."

Nyght felt the tip of the sword against the Weapons-Maker chest. She had put enough force into her thrust that it should have gone through the half-Dwarf but all it did was place a small slice in the jerkin he was wearing. She brought the sword down and then gave her comment, "Actually, I did not know if you were telling the truth or not. If you had not, then it would have been your own fault if I killed you." The half-Dwarf smiled again. "It was as if I had struck stone."

Nyght flipped the sword in her hand to hold it by the end of the blade. She then extended it out to the Weapons-Maker who took it from her and sat it back down by the grinding stone. "So here I be. All these seasons making weapons for the Guild and now High-Master Wraith has asked me to train ye."

"I do not need to be trained," Nyght said.

"Yeah, right." Dart stood up from his barrel. "Ye may have passed The Trial of the Circle like no one could but an Elf but that doesn't mean ye know how to take on everyone ye will come up against."

"I took you," Nyght said, referring to the match they had in that very room.

Dart had gone easy on the girl during their fight. It did not last long, but even in the short amount of time, he saw that the child had natural talent as well as maybe some supernatural. Even though he had been holding back after witnessing the child's abilities, he figured that if they had truly fought and if a weapon could harm him, he would probably be the one who ended up on the floor with her standing over him.

Dart had been working with weapons for his entire life. His father did not just teach him how to make them, he taught him how to use them. "Have ye ever used anything besides them daggers of yers?"

Nyght raised up her right leg, bent it at her knee, reached into her boot, and pulled out her knife. After she was sure the Weapons-Maker understood her answer, she returned the knife to its place and lowered her leg.

"Two daggers and a knife. Ye going to need to know how to use more than just them if ye plan on surviving. Ye never know when someone might get them blades out of yer hands and then where will ye be?"

"It does not matter because if these blades are ever taken from me then it is only because I am already dead."

Dart did not say it, but he had a feeling she was

speaking the truth. When they had been fighting, he felt something from those weapons. He figured they were a gift from Moon, and if so, then there was more to them and the girl than even he could sense.

Dwarves came from Below where neither Moon nor Sun was a part of their lives. Creator made them and he was the one all Dwarves followed. His father had taught him about Creator and even told him that it was Creator's plan that brought his father up to the Above and his plan to put Dart there for the remainder of his days to work the forge at the Guild.

His father had also explained to him that it was Creator who was calling him back to the Below, but since Dart was only half-Dwarf, the call would never come to him. His father had been wrong about that. When he turned four hundred, Dart felt the call. The call to bring him to the Below where the other Dwarves were. The only problem was that he also heard the call to stay at the Guild. No member of the Guild, now or ever, knew that there were a number of times that their Weapons-Maker had left the Guild and started making his way to the Below. After only a few sun-cycles, the call to go back to the Guild pulled at him and he would always return.

Dart was part of two worlds. His body might be in one, but he knew that if he were to leave to go to the other, he would always hear the call to return to the Guild. The only thing that kept him from falling into despair was the job his father had given him to do, which was to work the forge of the Assassin's

Guild. A job he would be doing for the rest of his life and since he cannot die, he would be doing it for a very long time.

"Dart!" Nyght yelled when the Weapons-Maker appeared to be deep in his thoughts and had not heard her question.

"What!?" he grumbled back to her.

"I asked are we done here? As I said, I need no training on any weapons." Nyght lifted her daggers in front of her. "These are the only weapons I will ever need."

Most assassins had their preferred weapon of choice but all of them learned how to use a variety of weapons to a certain extent. "Tell ye what. Ye pass me test and I will concede to not training ye."

"I already passed The Trial of the Circle. I am sure High-Master Wraith sent me to you to show me that I needed training, but I do not."

"Then ye shouldn't have a problem with passing me test," Dart said and smiled. If she refused the test, then she would have to admit she was not so sure of herself. If she failed the test, then she would have to admit she needed training. If she passed the test, well, Dart thought he would have to see her pass it first.

"Very well, I will take your test," Nyght said.

"Good, follow me," Dart said, stood, then turned around. He walked over to a door that was on the wall close to the grinding stone. He opened it and stepped through; Nyght was right behind him.

"This be me training room. Since the Masters

train the new assassins, the only ones that ever use this place are the ones that want to get some extra practice to keep their skills up or ones that want to try out a new weapon."

Nyght looked around the chamber. She saw different areas made up to resemble different terrains. There was one area covered in dirt and one area covered in water. There was even an area that had trees scattered around, actual trees. She was going to ask how they could grow on this level of the Guild but decided that unless they had something to do with the test the Weapons-Maker wanted to give her, then it did not matter.

"Follow me," Dart said and walked further into the room.

They stopped in an area that had multiple targets off in the distance. Nyght saw that this was an archery range where someone could come and practice with the bow and arrow. Nyght never had any interest in the bow, and she did not have one now. Even though she had never used one, if the test required her to do so, Nyght knew she would be able to pass it. Just because she had no interest in the bow did not mean she did not know how to use one.

"Wait here," Dart said, then continued to walk away from her. He moved off to the left and went over to something that looked like a small wooden stool. It had three legs and a top that looked like a seat, but on one of its sides, it had something that looked like a wooden crank.

He took the stool-like object, walked over, and placed it a pace in front of one of the large square targets made from wood. He then walked over to his right and Nyght saw what he was moving toward. A rack that had an assortment of bows. When he chose one, she thought he would bring it back to her and that the test would consist of her using the bow, but instead, he walked back over to the small stool.

Once there, he placed the bottom of the bow into the top of the stool and then bent down and turned the crank. When done, he let go of the bow and Nyght now knew that the crank tightened the pieces of wood, which were holding the bow in an upright position, with the string of the bow being in a straight line.

Dart inspected his work then came back over to Nyght. "From where we are, it is exactly twenty paces to the bow."

"What's the test?" Nyght asked, not seeing what the Weapons-Maker had planned.

"Simple," he said with a smile, "Cut the string." Then with movement quicker than what Nyght would have expected from the half-Dwarf, he reached behind his back, pulled out a knife, and threw it toward the bow. From where they were standing, Nyght had no problem with seeing the knife strike the string, cutting it in two.

Dart gave her one more look then walked over to the bow. He loosened the crank and pulled the bow free then walked over to the board the bow was in front of and retrieved his knife.

When he was back with Nyght he held the bow up with his hand in the middle, allowing the two pieces of string to hang loosely downward. Before Nyght could say what she noticed, Dart spoke it. "Oh yeah, it ain't just about slicing the string. Ye got to slice it into even pieces." The smile returned to his face.

He then turned and walked back over to the rack of bows. Picking up another one, he went back over to the stool and positioned it as he had before. Once he tightened the crank and secured the bow, he walked back over to Nyght but stood off to her left. "At yer own time," he said.

Nyght tossed the sides of her cloak back over her shoulders and lifted up her daggers. "Uh-uh lass. Ye only get one shot so ye won't be needing yer second dagger. Ye miss the first time, ye lose, and ye get trained by me."

Nyght turned her head to the left to look at the Weapons-Maker, "I would need one dagger, if I wanted only one cut."

Her statement confused the Weapons-Maker, but before he could ask what she meant, she quickly turned her head away from him and threw out her daggers. Both of them at the same time. She had moved so quickly that by the time Dart moved his head to follow them, both daggers were already sticking into the wood beyond the bow. He also saw that the piece of string at the top of the bow was shorter than what he had made with his throw. He took his eyes off the target and looked at the girl. She was staring at the target; she knew exactly what he was thinking.

Dart did not walk to the target, he ran, because he had to see if what he thought the girl had just accomplished was what actually happened.

When he reached the bow, he first lifted the string hanging from the top. He then knelt down and lifted the piece of string at the bottom. There was no doubt about it, they were of equal length. He then stepped around the small stool and looked behind it. There lying on the ground was the remaining portion of the bow's string. He bent over and picked it up. Even though he did not have to, just so he could see it with his own eyes, he held the third piece of string up to the piece at the top of the bow and without a doubt it was the same length as the first and so it was with the bottom piece as well.

He stood there looking at the three pieces of string. The skill that it would take to cut the string into three equal pieces was beyond even himself. He had to use the clamp to make sure the bow did not move, but once a knife cut the string, there would not be enough tension on the string to make a second one. That meant that when she released her blades, she hurled them so that they both sliced the string at the same time. If either blade had been traveling at a slower speed, by the time it reached the string, the first blade would have made its cut, removing all the tension.

Not only had she cut the string into three pieces, but they were all of equal lengths. Her throw not only made the blades reach the bow at the same time, but in the exact place she wanted them to be.

Dart, caught up in what he witnessed, did not even realize that Nyght had walked by him and re-trieved her daggers. As she turned and headed back to where she had made her throw, she said, "You can tell High-Master Wraith that I do not need to be trained." She then continued to walk away.

Dart turned his head to see her, then looked back at the string and the bow. He knew that if he spent the rest of his life trying to do what the girl had, he would have a challenging time accomplishing it. He might be able to get the blades to make contact at the same time, but to cut the string into three even pieces would be nearly impossible. At least for him, and anyone else in the Assassin's Guild. He did know of one group that might be able to duplicate the same results, but he would have to see it to believe it.

He dropped the string on the ground and walked away from the bow. He did not have any animos-ity about what she had accomplished. He was a Weapons-Maker, and even though there were oth-ers who were more skilled with the weapons he made, there were none in the Guild. Until now.

Nyght was still some ways ahead of him, so he was watching her as they both made their way out of the chamber. High-Master Wraith had sent the girl to him so he could show her that she still had something to learn from the Weapons-Maker. Dart knew that there was nothing he could teach the child. Not even what High-Master Wraith had suggested and that was humility. No, the only one humbled that day was Dart himself. He could only hope that someone else would be able to teach the one called Nyght that lesson.

ELEVEN

This was the seventh shop Selby walked into since he and his new friend Dodge arrived in Yorkington early this morning. It only took seven sun-cycles at a steady ride to travel from Sarzanac to Yorkington, but they had been on the road for over twenty cycles of the sun looking for the history of the girl they both knew. Dodge, because High-Master Wraith assigned him the task; Selby, because he just needed to know.

When they left Sarzanac, they made for the nearest town. Once there and when they were sure they would not be able to find out any information, they decided they should move on to the next location. Since they did not know where the girl had come from, they had to check every city, town, and village, until they came up with some bit of information that would lead them to wherever the child had been.

Now after six other shops, Selby once again would see if he could find what he was looking for.

As he stepped completely into the shop, the small bell over the door rang as he closed it behind him letting the owner of the shop know someone had entered. He stepped further inside and acted as if he was interested in purchasing one of the many items available. He had a reason to be there, but it was not to buy a piece of clothing which was what the shop supplied.

"May I be of assistance?"

Before Selby turned in the direction the voice had come from, he prepared himself so that his performance would be more genuine. When ready, he turned to face the woman. "I hope you can," he said, making sure he had a smile on his face and a gleam in his eyes. "I am looking for my sister." From the look she was giving him, Selby knew she had not expected his reply.

"I'm sorry but I am the only one here at the moment."

Selby did not show any reaction to her comment because the one he was looking for was nowhere near the small shop let alone Yorkington, so he continued with his well-rehearsed performance. "Forgive me, ma'am, I may have caused you some confusion. No, my sister was not here today or even yesterday. You see, due to an unfortunate incident, I have not seen my sister since I was only five seasons and she but three. I am now seventeen which would put her at fifteen." When Selby devised his cover story, the one he would give to anyone he was trying to obtain information from, he decided to include his age now and the girl's. He knew she was at least fifteen because that was the lowest age a person could be to enter the Assassin's Guild. She could not be older than seventeen but since the girl never told him her age, he had decided to go with the lower number so that he would appear to be the genuinely concerned older brother. As for the age he spoke of when he last saw his sister, he just made that part up, like the majority of his story.

"I am sorry to hear your tale," the woman said. "Why would you think your sister would have been here?"

Selby stepped closer to the woman. "I do not know if she has ever entered your fine establishment. I have already checked other shops in the city looking for information that might lead me to her."

The woman looked at him and saw the concern and the love in his eyes he had for the one he was looking for. Both of those items were not part of his act; they were real. "I will help if I can," the woman said with a smile, and Selby knew she was telling him the truth. "What is her name?"

Since he had given the same speech so many times, he was well prepared to give his answer but made sure his eyes became a little watery before he stepped closer to the woman. "I'm afraid that in all the seasons we have been apart I have forgotten her name." He put his eyes on the floor to show the woman that he felt shame for the part of the story he had just relayed to her. On cue, he heard her walk over to him and placed her hand on his shoulder to give him comfort. Before he lifted his head, he made sure the tears in his eyes would be more noticeable while at the same time, he made sure he kept the smile from appearing on his face because the woman was actually believing what he was telling her. When ready, he raised his head and wiped the back of his right hand over his eyes, "Forgive me. I have been looking for my sister for some time and I feel that each day I take a breath is one more day I will not see her again."

On cue, the woman took a hold of his left hand into hers, "You will find her, I am sure of it." She smiled to offer the poor man some comfort. Selby returned the smile to accept it. "I take it that since you have not seen her in so long then you would not know what she looks like now."

"No ma'am. And there is no way to know when or even if she came into your shop. Or if she had, would you have seen her."

"Then why did you come to my shop?"

Selby was ready with his answer. "With what little bit of information I have discovered, I found out that she wore a cloak. I also found out that she obtained this cloak of hers around the time she was twelve seasons of age."

The woman took hold of his hand a little tighter. She thought that what she was about to tell him would only hurt his heart more than what it was, and she did not want to do that. "I am afraid I have sold many cloaks over the seasons. And for me to remember each person would be impossible. Besides, if the cloak she wears did come from my shop, then it is possible someone else bought it for her and your sister might not have even entered here."

What he had just heard did not have any effect on him. Not only was what she said possibly the truth, but the cloak might not have even come from the woman's shop. That was why he had been checking every place that would sell a cloak like the one the girl wore. Selby had put on his performance so many times he had lost count. "I understand ma'am, what you say is possible, but I still have to try and find her. We have been apart for so long and if it takes me the rest of my life to find her, I will do just that." The woman smiled and squeezed Selby's hand a bit tighter. She also had to blink her eyes to stop the tears from coming. Selby had played his part so many times he was almost starting to believe his own charade.

"Is there anything you can tell me about her that would help me to remember if I had seen her or not?" the woman asked, all the more willing to help the young man.

"As I said, I do not even remember her name. And since her appearance would change as she grew older, there is no true description I could give you." Selby paused for a moment, to add to his performance, "Yet there is one feature about her I am sure would remain the same no matter what her age." He stopped and waited for the question he knew the woman would ask.

"And what is that?" she asked with a smile, hoping she would be able to help the young man in his search.

"Her eyes. Her deep eyes." As soon as he had finished speaking, he knew that after all the time he had been searching, he had finally found something. It was the look the woman was giving him that told him she had seen the girl, his supposedly lost sister. The smile left her face and Selby could tell she was seeing the child in her memories. For the first time since he had been putting on his act, he had to change the script. For even he could not hold back the surprise that she knew something. "You have seen her, haven't you?"

The woman did not know what she was feeling. When the young man mentioned that his sister had deep eyes, she immediately remembered the day she sold the child the cloak. She let go of Selby's hand, turned around, and walked away to gather her thoughts. After the child had left, it took her a couple of sun-cycles to put the child out of her mind. The meeting with the girl with the deep eyes was nothing but a memory, until today. The child had done nothing but purchase a cloak and the woman hoped she would never have to see the child again. Because to her, those eyes were not only deep, but when she had looked into them, she saw death.

The woman did not know it, and very few did, but when someone who has taken a life looked into eyes like the girl's, death is what they saw. No one knew the woman operating this particular shop in the city of Yorkington had once been married. Married to a man who drank more than he worked. There were only two things her husband enjoyed. Drinking and beating her.

That was until one day, as he was beating her, she grabbed one of his empty bottles, slammed it into his head, breaking it. The bottle, not his head. She had suffered for many seasons from the man, and in the moment, while he was lying on the floor and she was standing over him with the broken bottle, she leaned over her husband and shoved the shard of the broken bottle into his throat. He stayed there because he was too drunk to move and that was where he bled to death.

She buried his body that night behind their house. Since everyone in her small village knew what the man was like, when he came up missing, no one put any effort into searching for him. Since all the people in the village felt sorry for the poor woman who had suffered at his hands for so long and now had abandoned her, they did not say anything when she packed up her few belongings and left the village to start a new life.

Selby knew that with the reaction the woman had given, she had seen the girl before. He just did not know why she was acting the way she was, but since this was his first lead, he did not want to interrupt the woman from her thoughts, so he waited until she turned back to face him. "Yes, I have seen your sister." When she spoke, she was afraid to look at the man two paces from her. Even though she had looked into his eyes before, she did not want to take the chance she would feel the same thing she had when the child had come into her shop. She knew siblings could share certain traits, and just maybe his eyes were the same as his sister's eyes and she had not noticed.

"When did you see her?" Selby asked since she had confirmed his suspicions.

The woman thought for a moment then answered, "A little over three seasons ago." Even though it had been a while, the woman had no problem remembering.

With what she had said, Selby knew they were talking about the same girl. The person had deep eyes, the cloak, and the time she purchased the cloak was around the same time she arrived in Sarzanac.

Selby walked over to the woman and noticed that she positioned her head so that she was not looking at him. He thought it was strange but did not have time to wonder about how she was acting. "Can you tell me anything that might help me find her?" Once again, his words were not part of his previous performance. Since it was the first time he had come close to finding out anything about the girl, he was being genuine with his questions as well as the feelings he had for asking them. Here was his chance to find more information about the girl.

The woman was looking at the floor, but she

raised her head and looked into the young man's eyes. She could not resist the temptation. She had to know if his eyes were like the girl's. To her relief, they were not. She let out a sigh and not even Selby knew why. He thought it was because she was happy to be able to help him. "I don't know if I can help you or not." She saw the look on the young man's face and felt sorry for him. She may not want to ever see the child again, but her brother would do anything to have the opportunity. "She came in, bought the cloak, and left. That was all."

Selby could tell the woman had told him all she knew or at least all she thought she knew. People, even those who think they have told everything about a certain situation, might overlook the slightest detail, but to Selby, the slightest detail could be the most important. "Was there anyone with her?" he asked to walk the woman through the day.

"No, she came in alone."

"What did she pay you with?"

The woman thought for a moment then answered, "Silver, three pieces of silver."

Those two pieces of information would not help him. Selby already knew what the girl looked like even though he had pretended he did not, so he did not ask for a description, and he was not surprised when the woman had not noticed that. Most people do not think the way Selby does. "Did she say anything about where she was going or where she had come from?" Selby asked the question, only looking for the answer to the last part. He already figured that the girl had left Yorkington and went to Sarzanac but where she came from was what he needed to know.

"No, she said very little," the woman said, and Selby knew they were talking about the same person. The girl he had known for three seasons spoke very little to him. "There is one thing I do remember," she said but did not continue.

"What is it?" he asked to find out what she was hesitant about saying.

"Forgive me, I mean no offense with what I am about to tell you but the girl she...she smelled."

Selby did not know how to take the statement so of course he asked, "What do you mean, 'smelled'?"

The woman was embarrassed to be telling this young man, who was obviously a loving brother, what she had noticed about the girl that day and even though she was hesitant, if he wanted to know everything about her meeting with his sister, she would tell him. "I noticed that she smelled as if she had spent her whole life in the woods."

"As in living in a house or a village in a wooded area?" Selby asked.

The woman frowned a bit because she realized she was going to have to explain herself better. "The child, your sister, smelled as if she lived in the woods themselves. That maybe she spent more time in them than she did in any dwelling."

He thought about what the woman had said. He

had grown up on the streets of Sarzanac and understood many sun-cycles could go by before a person had a chance to bathe. When he heard that the girl "smelled" he did not see how it would help him. More than likely, she smelled when she arrived in Sarzanac but since he probably did not smell like a field of flowers, he paid no attention to it.

He took a moment to go over what she had just said and even though the word "smelled" did not make him see a connection to the girl, there was another word the woman had used that made him add another piece to his puzzle.

He looked at the woman, and she was surprised he had a smile on his face. He then walked over to her, took her right hand into his, and shook it. "I thank you ma'am, you have helped me greatly."

She looked at him not knowing how what she had said about his sister's smell would help him. "My pleasure young man, I hope you find her." She meant what she had said. She may not want to see the child again, but it was obvious the young man truly loves her. She just did not know the type of love.

Selby turned to leave, but after two steps, he turned back to face the woman. He pulled his coin bag off his hip and poured some of its contents into his hand. When he picked out the ones he wanted, he returned the others to the bag and placed it back on his belt. He then walked back over to the woman, lifted her hand, and curled her fingers around the coins he had placed in her palm, "For the information," he said then turned and walked out of the shop.

Once gone, the woman lifted her hand and saw what the young man had given her. It was three silver coins. The same amount the girl had paid for the cloak.

Dodge rested on his back, stretched out on his bed in the room of the inn where they were staying. Normally if a city had a Guild House, which Yorkington did, the assassin would stay there, but since he was traveling with a non-Guild member, they did not have that option. Only members of the Assassin's Guild could utilize the facilities.

The fact that Dodge could not stay in more luxurious lodgings like what the Guild offered was somewhat unpleasing to him, but what bothered him the most, was that no matter what place they came to, Selby always insisted they take up residence in a lower part of the city. Dodge did not have a problem with paying a higher fee, especially if it granted him better accommodations, but his traveling companion was adamant about not staying in a place near the area where he had to perform his search. Dodge thought it would be easier and quicker for his companion if they had sought out a higher quality of accommodations because he would be closer to the types of establishments Selby was looking for. Selby would not hear it, so they took up residence in a place well below Dodge's level of comfort.

He was resting his head on his hands behind his head. He had his eyes closed, but since he wanted to get an idea of what time it was, he opened his right eye to see out the small window in the room. Since the filth on it was so thick, it was obvious that the window had gone without a cleaning for quite some time. Dodge was not sure if it was cloudy out or if the window itself was interfering with allowing some of the light to come into the room. Since he figured it was more of the second one, he determined it was not even midday, which if Selby's outing was like all of his previous ones, his partner would not be back for quite some time.

Dodge closed his eye and went back to his rest. Which seemed as if that was the only task he would be doing on this little adventure High-Master Wraith had sent him on.

He was an assassin, and with the job, there were many times he had to look for information concerning what he needed to do. On this adventure, he had someone else who seemed to not only be more than capable of handling it but had more enthusiasm about going at the task. Dodge did not have a problem with hunting down information, but he was an assassin, and his skill for removing whatever person the information pertained to was more to his liking.

Dodge took a deep breath then let it out slowly. With Selby going about looking for anything to lead them to the history of the child Nyght, there was nothing for the assassin to do. He had offered to join Selby on his little outings, but Selby was even more adamant about Dodge not going with him than he was about where they would take their rooms. So that left the assassin mostly hanging around whatever place in which they were staying.

They had been on the road for over half a mooncycle. Dodge knew that what they were doing would take time, but he thought the one known as Captain Selby would be better at finding out information to lead them to their destination. Unfortunately, the good Captain Selby had no luck in acquiring anything to help them reach their goal. The only reason they had left the last city, and the city before that, and the city before that, and the city before that, Dodge paused his thoughts for a moment to make sure he had the count right then added another "city before that" to include all five cities they had visited since they left Sarzanac. The only reason they had left the last places was because Selby decided they would not find out anything about the girl.

The assassin still had not made up his mind on how he felt about this assignment. He loves the Guild and loves working for it even though his current task was not a contract that would use the abilities he learned from his training. He still was going to see it to the end as if it were his first. The only problem was that since Selby was doing all the work, Dodge was growing a bit bored. On the other hand, since Selby was doing all the work, Dodge thought that this was the easiest job he had ever accepted. On the other hand, since his associate was not having any luck in finding something to help them complete it, it was turning out to be the hardest job he had ever taken on. The only thing that kept the assassin from going crazy was the fact that part of being an assassin was having patience. Of course, it would help his patience if he had a more comfortable bed to sleep on.

Since he had been lying on the bed before Selby had left that morning and he was not sleeping anyway, Dodge raised up and swung his legs over the right side of the bed. He reached down and pulled his boots on, then reached under his pillow with his right hand, and removed the knife he had placed there for quick and easy access. He stood up and walked over to the window looking outside to see if maybe he should do a little exploring on his own.

Since Yorkington did have a Guild House, he could go there and at least associate with some of his fellow Guild members. Maybe that would remove some of the boredom he was feeling. Even when he was between assignments he never felt as bored because he knew his next job would not be too far away. Now that he had one, which was going nowhere fast, he was getting restless, and a restless assassin was a danger to himself.

Part of the reason an assassin stayed alive was because they always stayed alert. He did not want to become too complacent because it would be quite easy for an enemy to take advantage of the moment.

Most people think an assassin would not have any enemies. The only thing an assassin does not have to worry about is another member of the Guild taking their life. The rule was in place and followed by all, no assassin of the Guild would take the life of a fellow member. That did not stop any of the many *want-to-be-assassins* who took up the profession of paid killer to try to take out one of the Guild members who had killed a person, or a family member or friends of one of his past assignments wishing to seek revenge or justice. The Guild trained their members to take out their target with no notice; unfortunately, sometimes someone would remember seeing a face that was out of place which would lead the associates of the target to start looking into the unknown face. No matter how careful a Guild assassin may be, with enough time and money, someone could find the one they were looking for.

Even though Dodge did not think he was an assassin with a target on his back, he preferred to stay alert and ready just in case someday he did.

He again looked out the window and decided he would wait until the sun was out of the sky before he left his room. Even if Selby came back with no information, he would be going out again once the sun was gone. Selby had two reasons for being in the city and the night-time was when he took care of the second one.

Dodge walked back over to the bed and sat down on the side. Just as he made contact, he stood up again because he heard someone coming down the hall. They were moving fast so he was not worried that it was the type of person he had just thought about a moment ago, but he did not want his back to the door if they came into his room. As soon as he heard the footsteps stop at his door, he moved his right hand behind his back ready to pull out one of the knives he kept on him. When the door opened, and he saw that it was Selby, he brought his hand back around.

Dodge noticed two things. The first was that his companion was back much earlier than normal and the second was his companion was smiling. "You found something," he said as a statement, not as a question, because he could see by the smile he was correct.

"She was here in the city," Selby said after he stepped into the room and closed the door behind him. He then walked over to the window and looked through it even though there was so much grime on it, it would be difficult to see anything. This was something Selby did every time he returned. He did it to make sure no one followed him back to his lodging. Dodge knew this because he would do the same.

"How long ago?" Dodge asked.

Selby, certain no one had followed him, turned to look at the assassin, "A little over three seasons."

Dodge was quick to process the information, "Around the same time she arrived in Sarzanac." Selby nodded to agree. "How did you find this out?" Selby smiled and Dodge knew what it meant.

When they had left Sarzanac, the assassin had given Selby full control as to how they would find out about the girl's past. When he told Dodge that they would start by finding out where she obtained her cloak, the assassin thought he had just heard the most ridiculous thing in the world because he did not see how finding where the cloak came from would lead them to where the girl had been.

Selby had always been inquisitive, and to be, he had to spot every bit of information no matter how useless someone else might think it was. He told Dodge that he remembered when he first saw the girl, he noticed her cloak was rather new. Even though it was dirty, the color led him to believe she had recently purchased it. Since he found out the girl had come into Sarzanac the night he met her and the cloak was showing some wear on it, then he knew she had not acquired it in the city.

Of course, Dodge made the argument that maybe she had stolen the cloak from someone in the city. Selby was quick to point out that he noticed the ends of the cloak appeared to have a hint of grass stain on them as if the bottom scraped across the ground as the girl traveled over a great distance wearing the cloak. Since he knew the girl had come to the city, Selby was sure she was the one who had made the cloak look the way it did.

Convinced that the cloak was a lead, Dodge questioned Selby on how they were going to find out where the one cloak out of all the ones ever made came from. Selby simply told the assassin that they would ask; and in every city, town, or village they went to, that was exactly what Selby did.

Dodge was quick to bring up the point that it would take them forever to check every shop that might sell a cloak. Selby was quick to let him know they only had to check shops that sold the higher quality cloaks like the one the girl wore. Of course, Dodge did not see why his companion would think that. Selby explained that he could tell by the type of material used in making the cloak that it would come from a shop that did business with people who had the funds to buy a cloak of such quality. The cloak's outer covering was wool, which a lot of cloaks were, but the inside lining was silk. This allowed the person wearing it not to feel the wool against their skin since silk was much smoother. Selby knew, and so did Dodge, that silk did not come cheap, which led Selby to the idea that the cloak came from a shop which caters to a higher clientele.

This led Dodge to ask the question, "Then how did our little assassin acquire it?" They both knew the girl that made her living from killing rats on ships was not, "higher clientele." That was the only question during the entire conversation Selby did not have an answer for, but it was something he was going to find out.

"So now that we know where she purchased her cloak from, where do we go from here?" Dodge asked.

Selby stepped around the assassin and walked over to the second bed in the room, which was his. He knelt down next to it and started going through his belongings. When he retrieved what he needed, he stood back up and unfolded the parchment. He found the area on the map where Yorkington was located and looked at the names of the cities close to where they were. When he saw what he was looking for, he walked over to the side of the bed where Dodge was standing. "Here," Selby said and laid the map down on the bed so they both could look at it.

Dodge had brought the map with him but that was not the reason Selby needed the assassin's help at the moment. He had grown up in Sarzanac and had never left until he went out to find information about the girl. So even though he was the one who had found the information that would lead them to their next destination, Dodge was going to have to help him with where they would be heading. "One of these three cities will be the next place we go to." Selby was pointing his finger at the general area where he wanted the assassin to focus on.

"Why not these other ones?" Dodge asked while pointing at a couple of the cities Selby had not included.

"Because they are not surrounded by any woods." Since he was bent over looking at the map when he said it, he had to turn his head to look at Dodge. The look on the assassin's face told him that he had no idea what he meant. Selby stood back up to give his explanation. "The woman who sold her the cloak said the girl smelled like woods."

Dodge did not hesitate to speak when he heard his friend's last comment. "You are basing where we go next on the fact that the girl smelled like the woods?"

"Yes," was all Selby said, because he did not think he needed to explain any further. Dodge thought differently.

The assassin walked away to take a moment to get control of his rising anger. He had just spent the last twenty sun-cycles chasing down a lead based on the girl's cloak. Even though he thought it was a long shot he went with it. Now they were heading to their next destination because the child smelled like the woods and that was the only lead they had to go on. When he was ready, Dodge turned around to look at his traveling companion. "Would you mind telling me why you believe the smell of the woods is going to lead us to where we need to be?"

Selby could tell that the assassin was starting to lose patience. If he had to explain his way of deducing where they need to go then he would do so. "It is not just the fact that the woman said the girl smelled like the woods but also because the second night she had arrived in Sarzanac, she asked me if there were any woods around the city." Selby thought his explanation would prove to the assassin he was on the right path. He thought wrong.

After Selby stopped talking, Dodge waited for his

companion to continue but since he did not, the assassin asked a simple question, "So?"

Selby was going to have to explain more, and he started to wonder just how the assassin was able to do what he did for a living if he had problems seeing the pieces of the puzzle. "She wanted to know where the woods were because that was what she was accustomed to. I had a feeling then that she wanted to use them to hunt or something like that. With the way she took to killing rats, I figured she had hunted before. That was why I arranged for her to start taking care of the rat problems the ships in port had."

Surprisingly, Dodge started to see what the young man was presenting to him. He walked back over to the bed and looked at the map noticing the area where Selby had pointed a moment ago. Woods surrounded all three cities he had pointed out. The few others in the area were not. "You think she must have visited one of these places surrounded by woods?"

"Visited or may have even lived there?"

Dodge stopped looking at the map and put his eyes on Selby. From what the young man had just said, they might be close to the end of their search. "Which one?" Dodge asked.

"You tell me." Selby could tell the assassin did not know what he meant and put his eyes back on the map, "These three places are the only ones surrounded by woods. Since I have never been out of

Sarzanac, I could not tell you which one we should go to." He then looked back at the assassin, "Do you know which one of the three is the largest?"

Dodge looked at the map, and since he had traveled across this entire region, he knew the answer, "Faulkton is the biggest but why do you think she would choose it."

Selby had his answer, so he bent over, picked up the map, and began folding it while he gave it, "Because she has always gone into bigger cities. She came to Sarzanac which is a decent size. Even though this is my first time in Yorkington, I can see that except for Sarzanac, it is bigger than the other places in which we have stopped."

"You think she stayed in the bigger cities, like Faulkton?" Dodge was not sure exactly why the girl had stuck to the big cities but if it were him, that was where he would go as well. With bigger cities, it is easier to hide because of all the people. In the smaller cities, a single person would stick out more, be more remembered. The only thing he wondered about was how the girl would have known.

"I think that is the best possibility we have had so far."

Even though Dodge heard Selby, he had been deep in thought about how the girl had known to hide in the big cities, so he did not notice the young man had walked back over to his own bed until he looked up and saw he had moved. He turned his head to face Selby who was returning the map to his bag, "So what do we do when we reach Faulkton?" He might have been a capable assassin, but he knew that if he let the young man take the lead in what they were trying to accomplish, he would take the assassin with him.

Selby finished with his pack, stood up, faced the man on the other side of the room, and gave his answer, "We find someone that would have bought whatever it was she would kill to make a living." Right away, he could tell Dodge did not understand. "If she made her living from hunting then she would have had to sell it to someone that could pay her coin."

"But what if she lived in the woods and never went near the city? Maybe she ate the food she killed." Dodge was not trying to poke holes in the young man's plans, but he wanted to see how Selby's mind worked.

"She paid for the cloak with three silver pieces."

"I take it the woman at the shop told you this or did you have some divine vision from Creator?"

"The woman at the shop," Selby said and smiled at the assassin's sense of humor. "Since she paid with three silver pieces, she was making coin somehow. And since she made a lot of coin killing rats, I'm sure she made coin by killing other animals..."

Dodge finished his sentence for him, "Which means she had to have sold them to someone like a trader or a butcher." Selby nodded to agree with the assassin. "Let's get out of this city and back on the road," Dodge said and turned to start collecting his gear anxious to be once again on the move and not stuck in a rundown room in a rundown inn.

"Not yet," Selby said, and the assassin turned around to look at him. "I know you are in a hurry to find where our friend came from, as am I, but I need to take a look throughout this city before I leave. If you want, you can go ahead and start out for Faulkton, I will catch up with you in a couple of sun-cycles."

The assassin knew what his companion still had left to do in the city. He had done the same in every place they had stopped at during their travels. Even though Dodge wanted to continue with his assigned task, he knew what Selby was doing would help his Guild when the time came. Since this was the first time the young man has been out of Sarzanac, Dodge thought it would be best if he stayed with his young friend. "A sun-cycle or two won't hold us up. The girl's trail is at least three seasons cold so two sun-cycles isn't going to make it any colder."

Selby nodded to the assassin to let him know he appreciated the chance to take care of his own business. "Since I have found out what we could about our friend, I am going to head out into the city to have a look around."

"I guess I will just stay here and take a nap," Dodge said.

Selby did not know whether the assassin was serious or was joking, but Selby left the room to take care of the second reason he had left Sarzanac.

Dodge sat down on the side of his bed, removed his boots, placed his knife back under his pillow, then laid down on the bed. He could not help but think that this was still probably the easiest job he had ever taken, then again, maybe it was not.

Since Yorkington was the biggest city Selby had been to since he left Sarzanac, he was glad he got an early start on exploring it. By the time the sun had gone down on the first day and started coming up on the second, he had seen enough. Yorkington would be an excellent place for him to set up another base of operations to go with the one he had already created in Sarzanac. Yes, his dream was coming together nicely.

TWELVE

A moon-mark being in Faulkton and Selby had no success in finding information on the girl. The city was situated with woods all around it. There were also a number of people dealing with the trading of animals, but he could not find a link to them and what he was looking for. Selby was beginning to believe that maybe the girl had not stayed in the city. Maybe she had come from one of the smaller towns in the general region. Since he was already in the city, he would continue until he was sure he had checked every shop he thought the girl could have been to.

He also knew that if he returned to his room again with no information, Dodge might just decide it was time to move on. The assassin understood that information was necessary but when it came to putting the amount of time into obtaining that information, Dodge had run out of patience four sun-cycles ago. Selby knew that if they left before they searched out every single nook and cranny, then they might miss the one thing that would lead them to where they needed to go. Selby was not going to take the chance and even told the assassin that if he did not want to wait in Faulkton, then he could head to one of the other cities. The assassin decided he would stay with his partner even though the only thing Dodge had been able to do so far was lie around in their room and wait. Faulkton did not even have a Guild House for him to go to.

Selby walked out of the trading shop and went further down the street. By the sun's position, he saw that it was going on the fourteenth sun-mark. Plenty of time to find a few more shops and question anyone working in them.

The next one he came to, Selby looked through the window and saw a young man, who appeared to be a few seasons older than he was. Since the man was a young age, Selby thought he probably had not worked at the place around the time the girl had been in Faulkton. That is if she did spend time in the city, but maybe there was someone older in the shop he could talk with.

Selby stepped inside and when the young man saw him he stopped cutting the piece of meat he had been working on, picked up a cloth, and wiped his hands. Not that it probably did much good because the cloth appeared to be even dirtier than his hands were. "Can I help you sir?" the young man asked.

"Maybe, can you tell me who is the owner of this shop?" Selby thought that the young man was only an assistant.

"I am. Been it for two seasons," the man said, and since Selby appeared not to be interested in purchasing anything, the young man went back to cutting the meat in front of him.

Selby had known the girl for over three seasons in Sarzanac. If this man had owned the shop for only two, then there was no way he would have worked with the girl. Since he was in the shop anyway, and Selby was always thorough, he was still going to see what information the young man had, if any. "So how long have you lived in Faulkton?" Selby asked.

"All my life," the man said as he brought down his cleaver in the center of the side of meat.

With that answer, Selby decided to continue with his questioning. It was possible that when the man was younger, he happened to see the girl around. He walked over to stand in front of the counter as the man continued to cut into the meat. "Maybe you can help me?"

The man took a quick look at Selby and then put his eyes back on what he was doing. He was a busy man. He had a lot of work to do and if the man who came into his shop was not going to make a purchase then he was just wasting his time. To be courteous, he did not tell the man to leave, there was always the possibility he would end up buying something. "What do you need?" he asked to get the man to speed the meeting along, so he could leave and allow him to work without interruption.

"I am looking for my sister," Selby said and when

the man brought his cleaver down, he held it against the counter for a moment and gave Selby a look to let him know that his patience was running out. "She would have come through the city a few seasons ago."

The man lifted the cleaver and started cutting the meat again. "Does this sister of yours have a name?" he asked, trying to be polite to a potential customer.

Since the man had started to partake in the conversation, Selby stepped closer to the counter. "No, at least not one I remember." The owner gave him a look which told Selby he was not going to let the meeting continue much longer. Selby decided to speed up his inquiry. "We were separated when we were very young. So young, I do not even remember her name. As for what she looks like, I could not tell you that either. The only thing I can remember about her is that she has deep eyes."

The man put one more chop into the piece of meat, then looked at Selby. "That isn't much to go on and I can't help you so if you aren't going to buy something, I got work to do." He then picked up the cleaver and started cutting the meat again.

Selby could tell he had just been asked to leave and since it did not look as if the man would be of any help, he might as well. "Thank you for your time and good day," Selby said, and the owner grunted his own goodbye.

Once outside, Selby turned right to start his

search for the next place he would look for information. When he was away from the shop, he heard someone shouting, "Hey you!" Since they did not use his name, Selby continued to walk down the street. "You there, the one looking for his sister!" As soon as he heard the last word, Selby knew someone was calling him. When he turned around, he saw the young man he had just been talking with. Selby did notice that he was holding the cleaver he had been using and Selby did not think that was a good sign. He had not taken anything from the store, so he did not know why the man was coming toward him armed.

He positioned his right hand behind him so he would be able to draw his small dagger in case the man was going to use the cleaver for some other reason than chopping meat. He never wore his sword when he walked around a city. He thought that displaying a weapon was asking someone to test your skills and since he was efficient with his daggers, even more so since Dodge had been giving him lessons, he was not worried about dealing with the man coming toward him.

When he reached Selby, the man stopped but did not raise his cleaver. Selby took that as a good sign. "You said she had deep eyes?"

Selby nodded then asked his question, "Have you seen her?"

"No," the man quickly responded, and Selby thought the man was wasting his time, then the man continued, "But when my father was alive and ran the shop, he talked about a girl with deep eyes." The man looked around and saw people were stepping around them. "Why don't we head back to my shop, and I will tell you what my father told me." The man turned and walked back the way from which he had just come. Selby followed.

When they entered the shop, the man did not even go behind the counter. He turned around and began telling Selby what he knew. "Like I said, my father ran the shop before he passed away."

"My sympathy for your loss," Selby said to give the gesture that he was concerned about the passing of the man's father.

"Thanks," the man said then turned around and walked a little further into the shop. When he turned back around, Selby could tell the man had just stopped the tears from reaching the surface of his eyes. He might have had a gruff reaction to Selby just a few moments ago but that did not mean the man did not miss his father. "It was about ten seasons ago my father started telling me about this girl who would come into his shop and sell the kills she had. Rabbits were what she brought in the most; she would also have coons, beavers, and a squirrel every now and then."

Selby heard the man say it was about ten seasons ago, and if the man was talking about the girl he was looking for, then that would put her about five seasons old. Selby had to stop himself from acting so surprised that the girl so young would not only be killing but selling her kills as well.

"He told me she had deep eyes. I didn't remember anything about her until after you left. When I picked up the goose." The man turned his upper body and pointed over to where he had been earlier then turned back to face Selby. "I remember my father saying that the same girl would bring in geese as well. He also told me the girl told him she had killed the birds with only a stone. I thought my father was just telling me some wild tale, you know something a parent would tell a child, so I never really put too much into it."

"Did you ever see her?" Selby asked.

"No. When I did start working in the shop I pretty much stayed in the back and cleaned up. I do know my father would bring some of her kills to me and teach me how to cut them up to sell. With the geese, he would sell the meat and the feathers. They were what my father really made a good deal of coin from. In fact, after he told me the girl had stopped coming around, he never made the money like he did when she brought in her kills."

"Do you know about when she stopped coming around?"

The man lifted his hand and rubbed his chin, "I would say it was about maybe a little over three seasons ago maybe closer to four. My father has been gone for two seasons and the girl stopped coming around almost a couple of seasons before my dad became ill."

Selby now had a time frame to work with. If what the man had said was the truth, which he believed it was, then when the girl left Faulkton, it was not long afterward that she reached Sarzanac. "Do you remember how long she sold her kills to your father?"

"For about seven seasons. That is about how long my father told me the stories. That is if the girl I'm telling you about is your sister."

"I'm sure it is," Selby said with confidence. "Is there anything else you can think of, maybe something your father mentioned like where she lived in the city or if she came from another one?" Selby could see the man was trying to remember.

"No, I don't think so. All I can remember is that my father did talk about her, but I figured he was probably making some of the tales up because I couldn't believe a girl of five seasons could kill animals, nor kill geese with just some stones and no sling."

Selby could not hold back the smile, "This one could and I'm sure that whatever your father told you, he was speaking the truth." Selby saw the man give his own smile when he had mentioned that the man's father had not been lying to him when he was a child. Selby figured the man had told him everything he could remember. He pulled his coin bag off his hip, poured out a few, and picked out three silver pieces. He then walked over to the man and handed him the coins. "For your help," he said, and gave the man a smile, who offered his own thanks with a nod.

Selby then turned and headed for the door, but the man had one more thing to say.

"I hope you find your sister. I have a feeling that with what my father told me, that girl is probably still making a living from hunting."

Selby did not give his reply, he just smiled. He did not tell the man that the girl with the deep eyes was no longer hunting animals. She had moved on to bigger prey.

When he exited the shop, Selby looked around. The area he was in was not where he was going to find out any more information. He knew the girl had been in the city of Faulkton for about seven seasons. That meant she had to be staying somewhere, and even though he did not know the exact location, he knew the type of area he needed to seek out.

He looked up into the sky and saw that he had a few marks before the sun went down. Usually, he would head to a certain area of the city at night when he finished his main task for the day, looking for information concerning the girl. Now that he had more information he could use, he would start his search a bit earlier.

He made his way to the part of the city where he had spent most of his nights since he had arrived. He was always looking for the proper environment as well as the proper people. Since he was only look-ing, he did not bother to talk to any of the people living in the area but now he had a reason.

The section of the city is where the less fortunate

people live. Meaning they had no coin whatsoever. They fed off whatever they could find, steal, or catch and kill. They lived in the many abandoned buildings every big city has even though they did not start out that way. Selby had lived the same way as the people he had seen in the area as well as back in Yorkington and Sarzanac. As he was walking through the streets, he could not help but think about the possibilities he would have. Right now, he was there for another reason.

He continued to walk around until he found exactly what he was looking for. A group of small children were running around in front of a building. The youngest appeared to be about two seasons old and the oldest could not be more than seven. Selby walked toward them but stopped before he was too close just in case they decided they did not want to have anything to do with someone as old as him or as tall. Children learned to stay away from adults they did not know.

He opened the sack he was carrying and pulled out one of the items he had purchased before he left the part of the city where the shops were. He then tossed the item so that when it landed, two of the children saw it. When they stopped running around, so did the remaining ones, and then all the children had their eyes on what had just entered their play area.

The children looked at the item then lifted their heads to look in the direction they thought it had come from. They saw a man standing ten paces away and since he had another of the items in his hand, they knew he was the one who had thrown the item close to them.

When Selby was sure that all the children were looking at him, he took a bite of the apple he was holding. He loves them as do most children. "Would you each like to have one?" he asked and held up the sack to let the children know there were more than just the two they had seen.

One of the children bent over, picked up the apple, and took off running. Selby figured that since the child had his, he wanted to get away before someone told him he had to give it back. Selby did not care about the one that got away, the apple nor the child. Not only did he have more apples, but there were more children.

They came over to him and they all had their eyes on the sack. Selby was sure it was not only because they liked apples but also because the children were hungry. He himself could remember what it felt like to be living on the streets and not have enough food to silence his belly. "I will make a deal with all of you." The children's faces sank a bit when they realized the apples would not be freely given to them and they might have to do some work. Selby could not help but smile because he knew what they were thinking. "Don't worry. What I want you to do will not be difficult." The children's faces all took on smiles and Selby continued.

"I need to talk to someone who has been in the area for about ten seasons. Can you all count to ten?" Some of the children nodded to let him know they could, and some shook their heads to let him know they could not. One child started counting on his fingers. Selby figured that the boy was trying to find out for himself if he could count to ten. "Well, those of you who can't count to ten, go with someone who can." Since the children were so young, if he put them with another, they would work better than if they went alone. "I will give each of you one apple now. And to the ones who can take me to someone that has been in the area for ten seasons, I will give them another apple." Selby paused to give the children a chance to take in what he had just said, "Do we have a deal?"

All the children nodded their heads, then spit. Selby took it as something the children in this city did to seal the deal. He would have preferred a handshake because more than one child ended up spitting on his boots. He also noticed the child who had been counting on his fingers was now trying to get enough spit in his mouth to spit again because his first attempt was running down his chin.

Selby knelt down and started handing out the apples. As soon as a child had theirs, they took off running. When he got to the last child in line, a little girl who could not be more than three, he offered the apple to her, but she did not take it. Selby wiggled it a bit but still, the child did not reach for it.

Selby positioned himself so that his left knee was on the ground, while he rested his arms on his right. "What's wrong?" he asked the little girl.

She hesitated for a moment then quietly spoke her answer, "I don't like apples," she said, and Selby did not know whether he wanted to laugh or give the girl a hug because she was so cute. He looked around and saw the other children had all run off, so he and the girl were the only ones remaining. While still kneeling in front of the girl, he turned to his left and removed his coin bag. He brought it up in front of him, opened it, and looked inside. He then pulled out a copper piece and handed it to the girl who took it with both her thumbs and forefingers, but Selby did not let go and the girl looked at him thinking that she was not going to get the coin. Before he would allow her to have it, he had one thing to say, "You buy something you like, and if you can take me to someone who has been around for ten seasons, then I will give you another one." He still held onto the coin, "Do we have a deal?" The little girl nodded and smiled. Selby let go of the coin and she turned and took off running.

He stood and looked into the sack of apples. He did a quick count to make sure he had enough to give one more to each of the children whether they found a person Selby could talk to or not.

He then walked over to the building the children had been playing in front of and sat down on the steps. He would wait until one of the children returned to lead him to someone that may have the information he was looking for. As he sat there, he could not help but feel nostalgic. He had spent a great deal of time sitting on the steps of his building back in Sarzanac. He then turned and looked at the building that went with the steps and wondered if there was anyone living inside.

He turned back to keep a lookout for the children to return. They would be the ones to bring him the next bit of information he needed. He could have walked around the area and asked any individual the questions he had but the children living in the area would have a better idea of the people around. Even if they were younger than ten seasons, they would make sure they found the type of person the man with the apples was looking for. They wanted apples and he wanted information. Selby knew that some-one always wanted something and someone else probably had it. He would build his dream on that philosophy.

He had not come to Faulkton to work on his dream, but since he was there, he could lay down the beginning foundation, the children.

Two boys were the first ones to return. "Did you find someone?" Selby asked.

The boy on the left answered him. "Yeah, he's down that way," he said as he turned his head and pointed off to his left then turned back to face Selby.

"What's your name?" Selby asked the boy on the right.

"Alec."

"Ok Alec, you are going to be my lieutenant."

"I want to be that," the boy on the left said.

"You can be one also," Selby told him, and the boy turned and stuck his tongue out to the other one. "Alec, I need you to sit on these steps and when the other kids return, you have to tell them that Captain Selby wants them to stay here."

"Who's Captain Selby?" Alec asked.

Since he was only a child and asked a question that had an obvious answer, Selby did not feel as if he had made a mistake in promoting him. "I am Captain Selby, and you are my lieutenant. And if you are here when I get back, not only will I give you another apple, but I will give you a copper piece as well." As soon as he finished, he could tell that the other boy who also wanted to be a lieutenant also wanted a copper piece so Selby was ready, "Yes, I will give you one also." The boy on the left smiled. "Ok Alec you stay here," Selby said and stepped off the steps, and Alec was quick to move into the same spot Selby had just moved from. "You," Selby said to the other boy to get his attention, "You take me to the one you found."

They started walking down the street. When they had moved away from the steps, the boy asked a question, "Captain Selby, what is a loot-en-tint?" Selby had to force himself not to laugh.

The sun had gone down over three marks ago

and Selby still had not found out any more information. The children he had paid were able to find people who had been in the area for about ten seasons but none of the ones he had talked to knew anything about the girl with the deep eyes.

The children had long abandoned him, their interest well into something else since he had run out of apples, so now he was walking through the worst part of the city hoping to find someone that would be able to give him information on where the girl had lived in the city or before.

As he walked past a building, out of the corner of his right eye, he saw something move. Since it was night and he was not in the safest part of the city, Selby turned his head to make sure no one was about to jump out of the alleyway and attack him. With what he saw, he was in no danger. The movement was someone appearing to be making themselves more comfortable with the small blanket they had around their shoulders.

Since he had talked to quite a few people but had not come up with anything useful, Selby decided he would see if the person in the alley would be able to help him.

Selby walked into the alley and positioned himself so that he was standing in front of the person which he could now tell was male. The man was sitting with his back toward the wall of a building and had his knees up to his chest with his head resting on them. Selby had just seen him make a move, so he was sure he was not dead and doubted very much he had fallen asleep so quickly. "Excuse me," Selby said to get the man's attention. When he lifted his head, Selby saw that the man was probably not even fifteen seasons old.

"I don't have anything for you to steal so if you are going to rob me, you will be wasting your time," the young man said and put his head back down on his knees.

Selby had seen this type of person before. Someone who had given up on living even though they have not been alive long enough to be an adult. Living on the streets can kill a person long before their body was dead. Selby knew how to get the young man's attention.

The young man had more life than Selby had expected because when he tossed the copper piece to the ground in front of him, he lifted his head up at once to see if what he had heard was real, which it was. "For answers you might have to my questions," Selby said to explain the coin.

The young man did not reach out to take the coin, "And if I do not have any answers or they are not to your liking?" he asked.

"The coin is yours to keep, as well as more if the answers you give me are helpful."

The young man took another moment to look at the stranger then reached forward and picked up the copper piece, "What do you want to know?"

Usually, Selby would immediately start asking

the questions he wanted answers to, but with this man, his thinking went a bit further. "What is your name to start with?"

The young man laughed, "Well at least I know that answer will be the truth, but I doubt it was worth your copper piece."

"Let me decide on that," Selby said and saw the questioning expression the young man had. "So, what is the answer?"

The young man took another moment then replied, "Tat, my name is Tat."

Selby had a name, to him, that was worth the copper piece already because he had made an advancement in the meeting. "How long have you been living on these streets, Tat?"

"All my life."

Selby heard the sadness in the answer. One more thing he had seen in others like this young man. The street is where they had lived, and it was probably where they would die. A lesson Selby had learned from his time on the street. People the age of this young man usually never were out on their own. Unless something happened, which caused others to stay away from him or the ones he did associate with were no longer around. Selby had a feeling the second choice was part of Tat's story.

Selby had lived on the streets for almost his entire life so the dirt, trash, and other less pleasant things on the ground did not bother him, and because of that, he had no problem in taking a seat directly in front of Tat to continue their conversation. "What happened to them?" The surprised look on Tat's face told Selby he had guessed right.

Tat decided he had talked enough and placed his head back on his knees. That is until he heard another coin land at his feet. He looked at it then back to the man in front of him, "You don't have a problem with tossing your coin around."

"I have coin, what I prefer, is to have an answer to my question," Selby spoke with a bit more authority. If he was going to go through with what he was thinking, Tat was going to have to learn that the one tossing the coin around was the one who decides what was important and what was not. "I'll ask again, what happened to them?"

Tat had an answer, he just did not like thinking about it. For a moment, he thought he could just tell the stranger anything because he would not know the difference, but he decided that maybe he could talk about it. He had not talked to anyone in a long time and this stranger would not be around ever again, so what would it hurt? "Their names were Randolph and Olivia. They were my best friends." Tat lifted his eyes so that he was not looking directly at the stranger but over the top of his head. It helped to tell his story. "Times were tough. The people that ran the city decided they needed to get rid of some of the less desirables. They started by kicking us out of the house we were staying in."

Tat did not know it, but Selby could relate to

the young man's story. There were a few times the people who ran Sarzanac tried to kick him and his friends out of the building they were staying in. Bad people forced him out of his home after the death of his mother and sister. Selby was not going to let that happen ever again.

"A few moon-marks after we were kicked out, we started feeling the real effects. They forced us out during the cold season. Randolph said they decided to do it during that time so more of us would be taken by the cold itself and then there would be a lot fewer of us to get rid of some other way."

"Is that how you lost Randolph and Olivia?"

Tat lowered his head so that he was looking into Selby's eyes. Selby could see that however his friends died, it was worse than succumbing to the weather. "We were starving. Olivia decided to take matters into her own hands. She went and got a job in one of the brothels. Only she didn't tell me or Randolph. When she came back with some coin and food, Randolph asked her where she had got it and she said she had found it. Two sun-cycles later, she just happened to find more coin and more food. That was when Randolph and I followed her."

"To the brothel."

Tat nodded his head. "We snuck inside and found the room she was working in. Randolph loved her and I guess she loved him, that was why she sold herself to get him and me some food. Randolph burst into the room and the man she was with did not like the interruption. Randolph attacked the man, but since Randolph wasn't much of a fighter, the man had no problem..."

Selby finished his sentence for him, "...killing him."

Tat nodded. "The man had a knife, and when he pulled it out of Randolph, he wasn't in the mood for spending time with Olivia anymore, so he stabbed her also." He stopped talking but Selby knew there was one more part to the story. When he was ready, Tat continued, "I was there. Standing in the doorway. When the man turned and looked at me, I ran."

Selby did not say it, but he knew the young man had been running ever since. He also knew he would go through with his plan but first he needed to ask the questions he was looking for answers to concerning a certain girl. Selby thought this was the perfect time to take Tat's mind off his past. To help, he reached into his coin bag, pulled out another copper piece and tossed it at Tat's feet.

"The first two were for answers to your life. The third is for answers to mine." Tat reached out, picked up the coin, and nodded to let Selby know to ask his questions. "I'm looking for information about a girl who might have been in this city. She would have been here for about seven seasons. Possibly from the time she was five until the time she was twelve. She used to hunt in the surrounding woods to earn coin." Selby did not use the story he was looking for his sister and even though he was not going to let

Tat know why he was looking for the girl, he would never lie to him. He then told him the last thing about the girl he knew, "She had deep eyes." When he said it, he waited to see the reaction he would get from others who looked into the girl's eyes. Tat did not react in that manner, so Selby thought he had reached another dead end.

"Well, I don't know about any girl with deep eyes, but a little over three seasons ago, there was a girl that lived in the same building as me, Randolph, Olivia, and others. This girl had claimed the building first, but Randolph made a deal with her that he and all of us could use the three lower floors but the top one belonged to the girl. She was really creepy. Always stayed to herself. Hardly ever came out in the daytime and I know she used to hunt animals because there were a couple of times, she had given us some food."

Selby listened to the description and even though Tat could have been talking about the girl he knew, Selby was not convinced. If he had seen her eyes then he would have been sure they were talking about the same person. "Is there anything else you can think of about the girl?"

Tat took a moment to think. "Yeah, she always carried these two bags with her. I have never seen anything like them. I think she kept her water and food in them, they were black. Randolph told me she had a knife she kept in her boot. He was sure of it because he got a very close look at it when they first met."

There was no doubt to Selby that his new friend was talking about the girl he knew. "Where did she stay, what building?" Selby thought that if he could see where the girl had lived, she might have left something behind to let him know where she had come from.

"The people that run the city tore it down. They felt if there were no more abandoned buildings, there would be no place for people like me to go."

The city of Sarzanac had tried the same tactics but Selby knew that no matter how many buildings they remove, or how many homeless people they kill, cities like Faulkton, Yorkington, and even Sarzanac, will always have abandoned buildings and people needing them. That was a fact of life.

Now that the building where the girl had lived no longer existed, he had lost a possible connection. "Is there anything else that you can tell me about the girl you knew? I am trying to find out where she came from." Selby still was not going to tell him that he was looking for the girl because an assassin had come to him asking for his help. "I mean her no harm if that is what you are thinking."

Tat chuckled. "From what I heard about her, if you did mean her harm, it might be more difficult than you think." Selby had to laugh because Tat was telling the truth. After they shared the laugh, Tat continued. "Randolph had been on the streets longer than any of us. That was probably why he looked out for all of us because he knew what it was like to live like this." Immediately, Selby thought he would have liked to have met Randolph. He probably would have made him a lieutenant. "He said he had seen the girl a few times before we moved into the same house. He never said much about her, but he did think she was different from the rest of us; something which made her seem as if she had a hard life even though she was so young. I remember saying 'No harder than the rest of us,' but Randolph said that she had. He then said if he had to guess she probably came from Bonehaven. I don't know much about the place, only what Randolph said, and he said it was to the north. That is about all I know."

Selby was ready to leave, but he still had some things to discuss with his new acquaintance. He stood up but kept his eyes on Tat who was still sitting. While looking at the young man, Selby moved his left hand to his hip and pulled off his coin bag. He then tossed it and the remaining coins inside at Tat's feet who quickly picked up the bag and stood up. When he finished with his inspection of the contents, he asked his question, "So why are you giving me this much coin for that bit of information I gave you?"

Selby replied, "The three copper pieces were for the information." Selby saw that Tat was waiting to hear what the rest of the coinage was for. "The rest is for my new lieutenant in the city of Faulkton. I need one that is a bit older than the other two I recruited earlier." Tat still did not understand so for the next few marks, Selby explained to him what a lieutenant under Captain Selby was responsible for as well as what Captain Selby expected from his lieutenant by the time he returned to the city which would be on an unknown schedule because Selby still had a task to take care of. He had faith that Tat would do exactly what Captain Selby required of him.

Dodge sat on his bed sharpening one of his daggers. Every time he passed the blade over the whetstone, he thought that if he had to stay in this city for one more sun-cycle, he was going to use the dagger to slice his own wrist just to break up the monotony. Not only was he bored out of his mind, but he had also not seen his partner for a couple of sun-cycles.

Selby burst through the door so quickly that Dodge barely had time to get his dagger up. He also just barely refrained himself from throwing the dagger in his hand across the room and into his traveling companion. In the time they had been together, he had shown Selby some of the techniques the Guild had taught him. Nothing that would get him into any trouble, but enough to help Selby with his dream. Selby was a quick learner, which was apparent to Dodge since he had not even heard Selby walking down the hallway to their room.

Before he could warn his partner about the dangers of bursting into a room with an assassin, especially one who already had a weapon in their hand as well as being bored to death, Selby spoke, "We're heading for Bonehaven," and with that, Dodge started packing.

THIRTEEN

They stood in awe looking at what was before them. They had come to the town of Bonehaven expecting to find the answers they were searching for, or at the very least, something to lead them to the next step in their journey. From what they were seeing, Bonehaven was the end.

Selby walked back over to his horse, opened his saddlebag, and pulled out the map. He unfolded it, and when he was sure he was looking at the area on the map where he thought they were, he walked back over to Dodge. "This must not be Bonehaven. We must have taken a wrong turn."

Dodge heard Selby's remark, but he did not agree with his friend. He looked up to the sky and saw the sun then put his eyes back on the land covered by rocks and boulders. "We passed the sign not more than a land-mark ago stating Bonehaven was ahead." Dodge took a couple steps further, not because he wanted a better look, he could see the destruction down the road from him just fine. He moved closer because he felt as if what he was looking at was not possible.

He had never heard of Bonehaven until the night Selby came back to their room and told him where they needed to go next. When they had looked at their map moon-marks ago, he had seen the town on it, up toward the north. When he read the name Bonehaven on the map, all he thought was that it was just one more town or city they would have to search through for the answers they were seeking. Now standing on the road to the city, but not seeing the city itself, Dodge knew he would find no answers in Bonehaven.

"Look," Selby said and walked up to stand next to Dodge holding the map so they both could look at it. "The map shows that the town of Bonehaven is situated in a valley with high mountains on the side." Selby let go of the map with his right hand and pointed ahead of them. "Those don't look like high mountains but off in the distance there are some so we must not have gone far enough."

Dodge understood what his friend was thinking but he had a feeling that even if they could make their way around the destruction before them, Bonehaven would not be on the other side. It was obvious to the assassin that all the high mountains, supposed to be around the town, were now on top of it. Somehow the mountains, all of them that stood over the town, had crumbled down and covered it. Dodge did a quick count of the land before him and reckoned eight sections looked as if they could have been the base of mountains. He knew what happened to the tops of them.

As they stood there, it was Selby who broke the silence, "What do we do?"

Dodge could tell by the tone of his friend's voice that he now accepted the fact that they were looking at the last place where Bonehaven had been. "We're done," Dodge said then turned around to walk back to their horses.

"What do you mean?" Selby said turning to watch the assassin walk away. "Even if this is Bonehaven it doesn't mean she came from here. Maybe she came from another town farther to the north or from another direction."

Dodge heard Selby walking toward him and turned around. When he reached him, the assassin snatched the map out of Selby's hand. "There is no other place to the north!" Dodge said and fiddled with the map until he had it situated to look at it. After a quick examination, he verified what he thought he had seen before. "Bonehaven is the last place on the map. Everything past this point is nothing but mountain range so there is nowhere else to go." Dodge knew he was not speaking the entire truth. There was one more place on the other side of the buried city, but there was no way to get to it, and no reason to, at least not by going forward.

The assassin did not tell his friend that deep in the mountains was where the true Assassin's Guild resided. Dodge even thought he might be closer to it now than they were to Sarzanac, but he would have to travel all the way back to their starting point just to get to the Guild. When the Guild was first created there were passages through the mountain range that led to the Guild which is the way the first assassins traveled to it. Now with the passing of time, using the magical passage in a Guild House was the only way to get to the true Guild. He handed the map back to Selby and turned around, "We're done. Mount up."

Selby turned and looked at the direction he wanted to go. He then went over to his horse and did as Dodge had said. Only instead of going back the way they had come from he started his horse in the direction of the buried city. "Where are you going?" Dodge yelled.

Selby turned his horse around so that he was facing the assassin, "The answer is down there, and I am going to find it." He then turned his horse and started down the road leading to what once was Bonehaven.

Dodge looked at the sky then at his friend riding away. It would take them at least three sun-marks to get to the devastation and once there he knew they would not be going any further. There was no need to even try but he could not help but feel a bit of hope at what his friend had said. Just maybe they could find out something from the city. Then he thought that it was not a city any longer. It was a tomb.

Dodge had not been accurate in his estimation of how long it would take to reach the beginning of where the city should have been. After about two sun-marks, they had to abandon the horses and go on foot because whatever happened to Bonehaven hurled rocks and boulders halfway up the road.

As they climbed over the obstacles, they were able to see some of the road which gave them a bit of help in making their way in the direction of where the town had been. When they reached an area where the piles of rocks and boulders were higher than the two of them put together, even Selby could tell their effort was useless. "It's gone forever," Dodge said, coming up to stand next to his friend. When Selby looked at him, he could tell what was truly bothering the young man.

Selby needed to know everything. If it was information, then he wanted it. With what they had found, not only did it stop them from finding the answers to what they had been searching for, but it brought up the question as to what happened to Bonehaven itself.

"How come we never heard about this?" Selby asked, more to himself than to Dodge.

"The map is old. Someone just never updated it," Dodge said. "We can head back to the small town we last passed through. Since we knew where we were heading then we did not stop there. Maybe that is where the girl actually came from." Dodge did not believe what he was saying but there was nothing else he could think of.

"Quite amazing isn't it!?"

As soon as he heard the first word, Dodge turned in the direction it had come from and positioned his hand at his back so he could pull forth his dagger if the situation required it. He moved at his usual speed when he felt as if he might be in danger. Selby had turned as well and placed his hand at his own back ready to grab his dagger. He was only two heartbeats slower than the assassin. Selby had learned a lot from his friend in the time they had been together.

They saw the man who had called out to them. He was sitting about ten paces away from them on a mule. Since he was sitting with both his legs hanging over the left side of the animal, the man did not have to put much effort into sliding off its back. He then started coming toward the two.

The man was wearing a tan tunic reaching the tops of his feet, but with each step he took, the sandals on his feet became visible. Around his waist, he had a brown piece of cloth tied. He appeared to be quite a few seasons old if the grayness of his hair was any indication. He had it tied behind him so that it hung down his back in one plait. He was about four handbreadths shorter than Dodge but appeared to be moving quite easily over the rocky terrain. It was also obvious that he had no fear of approaching two people he did not know.

When he reached Dodge and Selby, the man stopped and looked in the direction of where Bonehaven had stood. "Quite amazing, is it not?"

the man said, asking again what he had a moment ago.

Dodge and Selby had already brought their hands out from behind them. One look at the man and they both decided he would not be too much trouble for either of them. "Who are you?" Selby asked.

Before the man could answer, Dodge asked his own question, "And what are you doing here?"

"Ah, both good questions," the man said then turned to his left and walked closer to the rubble blocking all of them from going further. Dodge and Selby turned to keep the man in their sights. "I am just here as an observer. I go about this great land looking for things that might be of interest to me as well as others." The man turned around and looked directly at Selby, "As for your question, my name is Adoni. And you are?"

"Selby."

The man nodded to accept Selby's greeting then turned to face Dodge, "And your name?" Adoni asked.

Dodge gave his answer, "None of your concern."

Selby looked at his friend, then at the man who had just arrived. "Do you know what happened here? What happened to Bonehaven?"

"Well of course I do. I would not be much of anything if I did not know what was going on now would I." Neither Selby nor Dodge knew how to respond.

"So, what happened?" Dodge asked to get

whatever information the man had concerning the area before them all.

"Well, I thought it would be obvious," Adoni said and then smiled at his two new acquaintances. Since neither of them spoke, he continued with his observation of what had happened to the city. "The mountains fell and covered Bonehaven."

Selby just stood there looking at the man. Dodge turned around and started walking back in the direction they had come from. Both had figured the mountains had covered the town, so they were hoping the man named Adoni would be able to explain why. "When did it happen?" Selby asked as Dodge walked away.

"A little over ten seasons. One night, the mountains came crumbling down burying everything and everyone."

Dodge was not sure which part of what the man had said made him stop and turn around. Yes, he had heard the first part about ten seasons, but it was the word "night" which made him think that what had happened in Bonehaven had something to do with the girl Nyght. He looked past his friend who was still facing away from him and even past the man Adoni. All he could do was stare at the mounds and mounds of rubble in front of him. He did not say it aloud, but he asked himself "*How*?" He wanted to know how the child Nyght was connected to what happened to Bonehaven. "If it happened a little over ten seasons ago, how come we have never heard about it?" the assassin asked as he walked back to stand next to Selby. "If something like this happened, why did we not know about it?"

Adoni knew the man was asking him the question and even had a simple answer, "That is a very interesting question."

"I know," Selby said, and turned to look at Dodge who was now looking at him, "Think about it. It happened ten seasons ago. I was only seven at the time and living on the streets of Sarzanac. I had more important things to deal with than what happened so far away. As for yourself, you were probably..." Selby stopped, looked at Adoni, then turned back to face Dodge and continued, "...in training."

Selby was referring to the time Dodge had spent at the Guild learning his trade. He also realized that Selby was correct. He had spent five seasons in the one tower and trained by his Master. He had no contact with anyone else in the Guild let alone anyone on the outside. He never knew what was going on in the world and that would include the destruction of Bonehaven. If this happened when he was eighteen, then when he had completed his training two seasons later, this incident, as well as everything about Bonehaven, had already become a part of history with very few if any ever mentioning it again. He turned his head to look at where the town should have been. He then walked over to Adoni and when he reached him, Dodge took a few more steps to be closer to the destruction. "Did anyone get out in time?" he asked, then looked over his right shoulder directly at Adoni to let him know the question was for him.

"I am sure that if they were within the walls of the city, by the time the mountains began to fall, there was no time for anyone to make an escape." Dodge was not sure if the man had answered his question or not. "I can tell you that it was a caravan that brought the news to other places. As the story goes, the caravan was heading for Bonehaven but when they arrived, they found it like this. The people said they had not heard anything, and I am sure that if they had been close, they would have not only heard the mountains crumbling but seen them fall as well. Even though it happened at night."

Once again, the man used the word "night" which caused his mind to think of the girl they had been searching for information on. Of course, Dodge also thought it might just be a coincidence instead of a play on the word. He then looked over at Selby and remembered the night he had talked to him and invited the young man along. He had used a play on the word "night" in reference to the girl's name. He had told Selby that she had chosen a name but would not tell him what it was, instead, he said, "Maybe one night you two can talk about it." He would not give the names of other assassins, so he phrased the statement to keep to the rule while at the same time, giving his friend a very small clue. Dodge was wondering if this man Adoni was doing the same to him.

"And there is no entrance to get us inside?" Selby asked.

Adoni turned to look at him, "Maybe, if you were the size of an ant but as for the way you are now, you will not be getting into Bonehaven." He then turned and started walking toward his mule, "Bonehaven used to be a mining town." He turned and noticed that the man who had not given his name and the man called Selby were standing together looking at him. "The people who owned it did not live in the town, but when word got to them about what had happened, they came to see just how much of their investments they had lost and what it would take to get the place running again." He took a glance in the direction of where the town should be then back at the two men. "When they saw what you see now, they left and never came back." Adoni turned around and went back to his mule grabbing hold of the reins. "Bonehaven is no more, my good gentlemen. I suggest you go back to wherever you came from and forget about it."

Neither Selby nor Dodge knew what to say. They just stood there as the old man led his mule away from them.

When he had left their sight Selby asked, "So what do we do now?"

Dodge waited for two breaths then started walking back in the direction they had left their horses. "Like the man said, we go back to where we came from." He continued to walk but stopped when Selby grabbed him by the shoulder and spun him around. For the first time since they had been traveling, Dodge was ready to pull out his dagger and end his friend's life. As soon as he saw the look in Selby's eyes, the assassin got control of his anger, especially since it was not toward his friend. Now he spoke in a calmer tone, "It is over, we have come as far as we can." He then turned around and began walking again.

"But we don't have all the answers yet!" Selby yelled to the assassin.

Dodge turned around and saw that the young man was not going to move. Selby was not one to give up on finding information on whatever he was searching for. Dodge knew they had all the information they would ever have. He walked back over to his friend. "We were led to Bonehaven. It is where our journey ends because it is where the girl's journey began." He could tell Selby did not understand what he was saying. "Our mutual friend had something to do with this," he said and extended his arm to point to the destruction he was facing which Selby had his back to. Selby took a quick look behind him, then turned back to Dodge who then continued with his explanation. "I am not sure how she was involved in what happened here, but I am sure, she played some part."

"You're saying she was the one that caused this town to be destroyed?" Selby asked.

Dodge waited for two breaths then gave his answer, "Yes."

Selby stared at him. He knew the girl with the deep eyes was different, but he did not believe she could have caused all this damage. He turned his head to look again in the direction of where Bonehaven should be.

"I do not know what role she played in all this, but if there was one person to walk out of there, either after or before it was destroyed, then it was her." Dodge hoped his young friend would see he was telling the truth or as much as he believed was the truth.

Selby stared a bit longer then turned back to face the assassin. "So, it is over and the only answer we have is that she might have come from Bonehaven, but if that is so, somehow she had a part in its destruction."

Dodge placed his hand on his friend's shoulder. "That is the answer we have come to, and I am afraid the only one who actually knows what happened here, is the girl herself, but I have a feeling she will not be too forthcoming with that information and especially how she was involved."

Selby did not say it, but he knew the assassin was speaking the truth. He turned his head and took one more look at what used to be Bonehaven. He then turned and walked around Dodge heading back to where they had left the horses.

Dodge took a moment to stare at the same place his friend had just been focusing on. He did not know what Selby had been thinking before he walked away, but all Dodge could think of was that for the first time since he had been with the Guild, he was not able to accomplish the task given to him. High-Master Wraith had assigned him to find out about the child's past as well as find out about her parents. In some way, Dodge knew he had succeeded. His search had led him to what used to be the town of Bonehaven, and if the child did come from there, it is possible her parents are still there. Buried under all the rubble. He would go back and tell the High-Master everything he had discovered. Then he would let High-Master Wraith decide whether he had accomplished his task or not. Either way, the journey back to Sarzanac was going to be a long one.

They rode through the gates of Faulkton around the eighteenth mark. They had been on the road ever since they left Bonehaven because Dodge wanted to get back home as fast as possible. "We will take a room for the night, but start again just before the sun rises," he said to Selby to explain what the plan would be.

"I will take the room, but I will not be joining you when you leave."

Dodge stopped his horse so quickly that Selby's had walked a pace ahead of the assassin. He turned his body in his saddle to look behind him seeing the man staring. Selby turned his horse around so that he could face his friend. "I know you want to make it back to Sarzanac as fast as you can so I will not hold you up with what I have to do."

Dodge had a feeling he knew what his friend

was referring to but asked anyway, "And what does Captain Selby have in mind?"

Selby smiled when Dodge called him by the name given to him by his lieutenants. "I will stay here for a little while. Maybe for half a moon-cycle. I can begin working on what I need to do." Before he had left Faulkton, Selby had given Tat very specific instructions on what he needed to have completed before his returned. He was sure the young man had been successful and because of that, Selby, Captain Selby, could move on to the next step in his plan for Faulkton. Even if he only remained for half a moon-cycle when he passed through Yorkington, he was going to initiate his plan there as well and he did not want to hold his friend up for a full cycle of the moon.

"Will you be coming back to Sarzanac?" Dodge asked.

"Of course, that is where my home is," Selby said with a smile.

"You mean your empire," Dodge said to improve on his friend's statement and they both laughed. Dodge put his horse in motion and Selby turned his so that the two were riding beside each other. As they had since they first left Sarzanac. "I will keep the protection of your people in place until you return," Dodge said and looked over to his friend. "Just so you will not have to worry about anything happening." He then put his eyes back in front of him.

"Thank you. When I do return, I will come and

find you. Maybe we can work together at some later time."

Dodge did not turn to look at Selby, "I think you forget who I am and what I do. You do not find me, I find you. Or do you not remember the night in your bedroom?"

Selby gave his answer, "Do you not remember the book I showed you?" Referring to the book with the information about Dodge, other assassins, and the Guild itself. Selby looked to his left and saw Dodge smiling then put his focus back in the direction he was traveling.

"Maybe in your absence I should stop by your room and relieve you of that bit of information, for your own safety." He heard Selby's brief laugh and turned to look at him, "What is so funny?"

Selby turned to look at Dodge, "Before we left, I made sure I hid the book somewhere else. I am even tempted to tell you where because I know you would not believe me."

Dodge stopped his horse and Selby did as well, but they both continued to stare at each other. "Where?" Dodge finally asked.

Selby waited long enough to drag the suspense out, but then gave his answer, "On top of one of the buildings belonging to the Assassin's Guild." He could tell that his friend was surprised.

Dodge was trying to figure out if he was telling the truth or not. Since he could simply ask, he looked around to make sure no one was close enough to hear him, and even then, he leaned closer to Selby before he said a single word. "You mean you hid the book about the Assassin's Guild on top of the Assassin's Guild?"

"Can you think of any safer place, and since neither you nor any of your fellow Guild members go to the top of any of the buildings, then I don't have to worry about them finding it." Having finished giving his answer, Selby put his horse in motion to continue through the city.

Dodge took a moment by himself then set his own horse at a pace to catch up to Selby. When they were riding side by side, the assassin asked his question, "How did you even get on top of one of our buildings?"

Selby kept his eyes forward but gave his answer, "If I told you, then it wouldn't be a secret."

Dodge knew that his friend would never tell. He also knew that even though Selby might have business here in Faulkton and in Yorkington, there was another reason he was not ready to go back to Sarzanac.

Selby had set out on this journey to find out about the girl he had known for over three seasons. Dodge could tell that not knowing about her was bothering the young man in more ways than he was letting on. It was not just about not finding out the information, Selby was hoping to understand her, and by understanding her, then just maybe he could get to know her more than he had before she had entered the Guild. Now he was going to stay away from Sarzanac for a while to come to terms with the fact that no matter how much he tried, he would never know the girl the way he wanted to.

He rode out the gates of Faulkton before the sun was barely in the sky. Selby had not been in the room when he woke, and Dodge was sure he had wanted it that way. The assassin had to admit to himself, even if not to his friend, that the rest of his journey back to Sarzanac would be a bit lonelier.

As an assassin, he would travel by himself on most of his assignments, so when he completed his assigned task, he went his own way with no ties to anyone. This time he had traveled with the young man known as Captain Selby by those working for him. Dodge was sure that if he had not asked the young man to come along, more than likely they both would still be looking for answers. Selby had a way of finding out information that would take others twice as long if not longer. A part of him believed that Selby felt worse than he had when the answers they found about the girl came to an end, but an end is where the journey came to.

Once through the gate, Dodge kicked his horse to get him to gallop a bit faster. He wanted to get to the Assassin's Guild as soon as he could to inform High-Master Wraith what he had discovered.

As for his adventure with Captain Selby, the

assassin had a feeling there would be others the two would share.

Dodge knocked on the door to High-Master Wraith's chamber and then waited. "Enter." Dodge heard the word, but it was barely noticeable through the door, and it was the first time the assassin had heard the High-Master respond in such a manner.

Dodge opened the door and when he had stepped through, he turned so his back was facing away from it, so he could wait to sense the first of the three daggers, which usually came toward him. He had not heard them by the time he closed the door and since High-Master Wraith had always performed the test with him, he was surprised when he turned and saw the High-Master was standing next to the fireplace with a goblet in his hand.

Dodge walked further into the room, "High-Master?" Dodge said to draw the man's attention.

He took a sip from his goblet, then turned away from the fire, "Dodge, I am glad you have returned." High-Master Wraith motioned with his hand for the young assassin to take a seat in one of the empty chairs in front of the fireplace while the High-Master sat in the other one.

Dodge did not know what to think. High-Master Wraith had always tested his skills when he came to the High-Master's chamber but this time he had not. The only thing he could determine was that somehow the High-Master had found out about his failure in the task assigned to him. He did not know who else would have known but he was a High-Master, and they had their ways.

"What did you find out about our friend?"

Dodge relayed his entire journey to the High-Master. From the time he left to the time he returned only five cycles of the Moon had passed. Dodge had expected his task would have taken seasons, but with the help of Selby, he had completed it a lot sooner even though not to the standard he had expected.

When he finished giving his report, he looked at the High-Master sitting across from him. The elder assassin stood up and walked over to the fireplace taking his goblet with him. He gazed into the flames thinking of the tale Dodge had relayed to him. After a few moments, he lifted his goblet to finish the last of his drink and once he had, he looked back into the flames. "High-Master, I am sorry I failed in the task you gave me."

High-Master Wraith turned and faced Dodge. "You did not fail, my friend. In fact, you not only confirmed what I knew but gave me more information than I had before." It was apparent to the High-Master that his statement confused the younger assassin. Before he began to explain, he walked back over to his chair, sat his empty goblet on the table, and took his seat. "I suspected that the child had come from Bonehaven as well as it was probably where her parents had lived and died as well.

Or at least I knew her father was there when it had been destroyed."

Dodge did not know where to begin with the questions he had in his thoughts, so he picked the one he felt would give him the best answer, "You knew about Bonehaven?"

"Yes," the High-Master said, but did not continue.

Dodge was ready with his next set of questions, "Then why did you not tell me about it, about it being destroyed? Why did you send me to find out about the girl in the first place?"

High-Master Wraith gave his explanation. "I needed you to confirm what I suspected. I kept all the information I had from you so that whatever you discovered would confirm my own information. I knew the child's father was in Bonehaven because when he chose to retire from our Guild, he told me where he was going. I am sure that with the type of man he was, he would not have left the city unless he had a good reason. I heard about what happened to Bonehaven over ten seasons ago. When I did, I thought about the girl's father but did not put anything into it. I did not know about the girl until she came to our Guild. That was when I wondered if she was the child of a pupil of mine from long ago. To confirm my suspicion, I asked you to find out where she came from and whether her parents were alive or not." High-Master Wraith sat forward a bit in his chair, "And my friend you have done exactly that."

Dodge thought about everything the High-Master

had just told him. When he had it all sorted out, he could not stop the smile from appearing on his face. The High-Master had known almost everything before he had set him on the task. Dodge knew he had been used but had no animosity to the elder assassin. How could he, he had too much respect for him. Dodge looked at the High-Master, "So what now?" he asked.

"Now I continue to train the girl and in time I am sure she will become a True Assassin. That I have no doubt of, because her father was one of the best and I can already tell she will be just like him, if not better."

Even though it did not happen often, Dodge knew there had been assassins who had children and trained them outside of the Guild. "You believe her father started her training and that is why she is as skilled as she is now."

High-Master Wraith did not know the answer. "It is possible," he said to give something to the assassin. The child showed she had talent even before she came to the Guild, but the High-Master knew it was more of who her family line came from than who might have trained her before she arrived at the Guild. That bit of information was not for anyone else to know.

High-Master Wraith stood up and extended his hand to Dodge, who stood as well and the two shook hands. "I am sure you are in need of some rest after your journey but let me just say that I am very pleased with the information you have brought me."

"Thank you, High-Master," Dodge said and smiled to show that he was pleased the elder assassin was pleased with him.

"And as I said, I will ensure you receive the amount I promised you." He could tell that Dodge wanted to say something. "What is it, my friend?"

"It is about my payment."

"Do not tell me you want more; you were only gone for no more than five moon-cycles."

"No, High-Master, it is not that. It is just that instead of the payment, I wish to ask for something else."

"And what might that be?" High-Master Wraith asked, anxious to hear what the assassin wanted instead of the large sum of coin.

"I asked that the Mantle of Protection placed over Selby and his people be left intact."

"For how long?"

"For until the time comes that our Guild has no need for Captain Selby."

High-Master Wraith thought about the request. "You are willing to forgo the payment I promised you for the Mantle to remain in place to a seventeen-season-old boy who has his eyes set on something he may not be able to reach?"

Dodge did not hesitate to answer, "He will reach it, of that, I am sure."

The High-Master took another moment for

himself. His young friend was about to forfeit a substantial amount and wanted to make sure he understood what he was doing. "You are willing to sacrifice all you have earned for this young man?"

"High-Master, after my time on my journey with the young man, I know what I will gain from his acquaintance will be more valuable to me than what you offer." Dodge had one more point to make that would convince the High-Master to agree to what he was asking. "As well as valuable to the Guild." Like everyone else in the Guild, including himself, High-Master Wraith always did what was best for the Guild and the young assassin knew Captain Selby was someone who was best for the Guild.

"Very well, I will authorize the Mantle of Protection to remain in place until the Guild has no further use for your new acquaintance."

Now that he had agreed, Dodge had to see if he could add a slight adjustment to the original terms of the Mantle enacted when he left Sarzanac. "Might I suggest the Mantle pertain to his present holdings as well as any future holdings he obtains." High-Master Wraith gave him a look to let him know he might be asking too much, "For the benefit of the Guild of course," Dodge said to help persuade High-Master Wraith with what he was asking for.

"Very well, I will see to it."

"Thank you, High-Master. I will take my leave now if you have no further need of me."

"Go, before you turn the Guild itself over to

this Captain Selby," High-Master Wraith said, but laughed.

Dodge left the quarters and headed back to the level that would take him to the transfer door and back to Sarzanac. He was in good spirits. He had not failed High-Master Wraith, which meant a lot to him. His journey to find out about the girl named Nyght had turned out better than he thought it did. Until he realized, he still did not know who she really was.

FOURTEEN

She thrust her dagger into the mannequin for the eight hundredth time that night. Every night for the past four seasons, Nyght would practice her killing technique. She had asked Dart to make her the mannequin, a replica of the upper torso of a human body, including the head. Made from leather, and filled with straw and wool, the entire unit rested on a pole with a circular base so that it remained upright. The pole was adjustable so Nyght could raise and lower the mannequin since she was sure not all of her targets would be the same height.

Each night she went through the same routine. She would hold Full in her right hand and thrust the blade one hundred times into the base of the mannequin's neck, one hundred times under the chin, one hundred times into the right eye, and one hundred times into the chest where a person's heart would be. When she completed the cycle, she would then use Umbra in her left hand and follow the same routine, only instead of the right eye, she would stab the left.

Each of these moves would kill a person within a

few breaths. Even though she knew how to kill, she had not done so in this fashion so the practice would make her body remember the movements, so when the time comes, she would not have to even think about what she needed to do.

For four seasons, she had performed this ritual. In every place on the mannequin where she had made a puncture: the neck, the eyes, under the chin, and over the heart, there was only one hole in each location. With every thrust, her daggers penetrated the exact same spot. If someone were to inspect the entry points, they would think she had only stabbed the object once in each location in the entire time she had used it; but they would be wrong.

When she pulled Umbra out for the last time, holding it by the hilt, she twirled it through her fingers three times then brought it down at her left side and placed it in its sheath so that it rested at her hip waiting for when she would pull it forth again. On her right hip, Full rested in its own sheath.

When she had asked Dart to make her the practice mannequin, he saw she always carried her two daggers in her hands so when he delivered the item she requested, he also presented her with the double scabbard for her blades. Made from leather as well, both sheaths hung from a belt that went around her waist and hooked together in the front. There were straps on both sides at the height of her thighs so that she could secure them there as well. The blades fit comfortably into the sheaths, so when she pulled them out, they came forth with no hindrance. Dart had placed sharpening stones inside the sheaths, so when she removed the blades or returned them, they would strike against the stones so they would not dull. Nyght did not tell him, but the blades would never dull, no matter how many times she used them. She did thank him for the sheaths as well as for the mannequin.

During the day, Nyght spent her time studying. It had only taken her six moon-cycles to learn how to read and write. Afterward, her training consisted of learning about the world and what went on in it. She read many of the books kept in the archives and over the seasons at the Guild, she even learned three of the major languages used in her part of the world. Along with those three, she also learned to speak Gnome and was currently learning to speak Troll. She had thought about asking Dart to teach her to speak Dwarf, but since he had told her he was the only one of his kind in the world Above, she had little need for it.

During her studies, she learned about the race of Elves. Even though the only ones she had ever seen were in the memories Moon had given her, she felt a part of her wanting to learn more about them. She read every book the archives had on the subject, and even discussed them with the Guild Archivist; although the Archivist only knew what she had learned from the books herself. She could only tell Nyght that a long time ago there were Elves in the populated areas of the region. There was an old tale that the first assassin was an Elf, but no one ever confirmed whether that was true or not. When Nyght asked Dart about it, all he said was that his dad never told him about the first assassin to come to the Guild, so he did not know either.

The only current fact about Elves was that when humans crossed the great oceans and went to the lands to the east, they began capturing Elves on the open waters and started using them as slaves. To everyone on her side of the world, it was an appalling way to treat one of the races of the world. Even if a person was doing the most menial task in existence, they received some coinage for it. No one liked the idea of slavery, including Nyght.

On one of the many nights, she and High-Master Wraith sat in front of the fireplace in his quarters discussing many topics, Nyght asked him about Elves. As soon as she mentioned the word, she could tell that it affected the High-Master in some manner, but she did not question him about his reaction.

He did tell her that the Elves live far to the south. No human has ever set foot in their land and when other humans in the world started capturing them and using them as slaves, all Elves in all the lands returned to their home. Some of them still take to the great waters but only in defense of their lands. The Elves had built great fleets of ships to patrol the waters north of where they live to make sure no humans came close to their domain.

Not long after the slavery of Elves began, there were quite a few humans that attempted to invade the Elves' lands, but the Elves killed all the humans, so no one else tried to travel to where the Elves live. The only way to procure slaves now is for the humans to attack a lone ship on the great waters. That and the slaves bred in captivity are how one of the races in the world had become something less than what Creator created them for.

Nyght could tell that what the High-Master had told her bothered him greatly so after that night, she never brought up the subject again. Not only because it bothered him, but also because there was a part of her it bothered as well.

With her nightly practice over, Nyght would join High-Master Wraith in the other room in front of the fireplace for their nightly discussions. She had learned so much from the man. Nothing about using her daggers or even fighting but about the philosophy the Guild followed and how they were a part of Creator's plan. Nyght did not have any feelings toward Creator one way or the other. She had asked Moon about Creator and Moon told her Creator created Moon and Creator was the only being above and beyond Moon.

Nyght could tell by the way Moon spoke that Moon had reverence for Creator, but since Creator had never done anything for her, Nyght looked at Moon as being the one for making her into what she was. To her, Moon was her creator.

Nyght stepped out of her room and walked through the one adjacent to it. She took a quick look at the many books and scrolls belonging to High-Master Wraith but had read all of them herself. Including the ones the High-Master had not.

For the first part of her life, she had no one to teach her things to test her mental capabilities. Now, not only was her body a weapon, but her mind as well. From learning at the Guild, she knew she could accomplish anything she set her mind and body to.

When she reached the outer chamber, she noticed that High-Master Wraith was not present. She looked at the time-marker and saw that it was past the twenty-first mark, the time she and High-Master Wraith would normally meet. She practiced with the mannequin while the High-Master went to his evening meeting, so by the time she finished and came into the outer chamber, he was already sitting in front of the fireplace waiting for her.

She walked over to the chair she used during their talks and sat down. She decided the High-Master's meeting must have run longer than usual so she would wait for him to have their nightly discussion.

Nyght was a very patient person, but when she looked at the time-marker and saw that it was now going on the twenty-third mark, she knew something was not right.

She stood up and her first thought was to check the High-Master's bedroom. Maybe he had come back to his chamber before she had even left her room and had gone directly to bed. It was obvious to Nyght that the High-Master's age was beginning to affect him more and more, especially over the past half season. There were times while they were talking he would break into fits of coughing, and they would have to wait until it passed before either of them continued. She did notice that whatever was in his goblet did help when one of his attacks came upon him. She also knew that he had been drinking from the goblet for as long as he had taken her on as his pupil.

She walked over to the door leading to his bedchamber. In the four seasons she has been in these quarters, she had never entered the room. It was the first rule he had given her to follow, and she had never broken it.

She put her ear to the door but could not hear any noise coming from the other side. Since it was possible that he had decided to go to bed, she did not want to disturb the elder assassin if he had chosen to rest instead of attending their nightly discussion. When the thought came to her, she felt a bit of heaviness in her heart, turned, and went back to her chair by the fireplace where she decided to wait.

The talks she shared with the High-Master would usually last late into the night. Some ending around the time their morning meals arrived at High-Master Wraith's chamber, and on more than one occasion, they continued with their conversation while they ate. Since it was near the twenty-third mark, Nyght had no problem in waiting until either the High-Master returned from wherever he was, or he came out of his bedchamber.

When the time-marker showed that it was now after the fourth mark of the new day, Nyght decided there was no need to wait any longer. The High-Master had not come to the room so she figured he must have gone to his bed before she had left her room. She decided to return to her own and since she was usually awake at this mark, she would either read or practice some more with her daggers. The two things she did when she had time to herself.

As she stood, and was heading back to her room, she turned her head to her left and saw the door to the outer hallway. She did not know why but something came over her to go over to it, so she did. When she reached it, she stood there for a moment looking at it. Normally she only left the High-Master's quarters when she was going to the archives for her studies or to use the lavatory, but something was urging her to open the door.

When she did, she looked out but did not see anything until she looked down. There she saw High-Master Wraith lying on the floor. She now knew why he had not made it to the first room of his chamber let alone to his bedroom.

"High-Master Wraith!" Nyght yelled as she bent down and rolled him onto his back so she could see his face. "High-Master Wraith!" she yelled again since he did not answer. She then lowered her head so that her right ear was against his chest. Even through his clothing, she could hear his heart beating. "High-Master Wraith!" she yelled once more when she lifted her head to look at his face, but he still did not respond.

Nyght jumped up and ran around the circular hallway to one of the only other two doors on the level. She began banging as soon as she was to it and did not stop until the person the room belonged to opened it. "What is the meaning..." High-Master Copper did not have a chance to finish.

Nyght interrupted him, "There is something wrong with High-Master Wraith." As soon as she finished, she turned around and started running back the way she came. High-Master Copper was right behind her.

When they arrived, High-Master Copper pushed Nyght to the side to move closer to the elder assassin so that he could kneel beside him. He placed his right ear over the exact part of his chest Nyght had a moment ago. When he was sure the High-Master's heart was still beating, he raised his head but stayed next to him, "Run and fetch High-Master Grave," he said to Nyght who was standing behind him. When he noticed she had not done as he instructed, he turned his head to look at her, "Now!" he yelled at her. Not because she had not heard him nor because he was angry with her, but because he could tell that the young woman was putting all her focus on the man lying on the floor, and High-Master Copper needed her to help him take care of the one they both had great respect and fondness for.

Nyght snapped out of her thoughts and ran around the circular hallway to the other High-Master's room. When she was gone, High-Master Copper took his friend's hand into his. He was an assassin and even though he had training in how to handle a number of ailments and injuries, he could do nothing for High-Master Wraith. "Did she do this to you?" High-Master Copper asked his unconscious friend, but he was in no condition to answer.

"What happened?" High-Master Grave asked as he came running toward the two.

"I do not know," High-Master Copper said. "Nyght came and got me?" Both turned to look at the young woman standing behind them, "What happened?" he asked her.

"I do not know, I found him like this. Only he was lying face down. I turned him over to check for a heartbeat, and when I heard it, I ran to your chamber."

The two looked at the young woman, but since they had a more important matter to take care of, they put their focus on High-Master Wraith, and not on the one who might have put him where he was. "Let's get him inside his chamber," High-Master Grave said, and they both stood lifting their friend off the floor. Since the door was open, they walked through.

"To the bedchamber," High-Master Copper said, to let the other High-Master know where they should take their friend. "Nyght, open the door."

She ran around them and did as he instructed, then stepped back to allow the two High-Masters to carry the third into the room. She did not follow them because she still remembered the rule High-Master Wraith had given her those seasons ago. She stood at the doorway and since they had not closed the door, she heard High-Master Copper, "Go and fetch the healers, all of them." High-Master Grave ran out of the room, passed Nyght, and ran out the chamber door.

She turned her head to watch him leave, but once he was out of her sight, she turned and put her focus on the bedchamber. High-Master Copper saw her standing at the entranceway and walked over to the door. "Go and wait in your room until you are summoned." He then closed the door to the bedchamber.

Nyght had always been one to do as instructed so she turned and walked away from High-Master Wraith's bedchamber to go to hers. When she entered it, she closed the door behind her, walked over to her bed, and laid down on her back looking at the ceiling. A few breaths later, she raised her right hand and wiped her eyes. When she brought her hand back down, she saw the back of it was wet. She had seen people crying before. She just never had done so herself.

When the door to her room opened, she jumped up out of her bed and saw High-Master Copper. He did not enter the room but only stood at the doorway. "Follow me," he said then turned and walked away. Nyght followed.

When they entered the outer chamber, Nyght looked at the time-marker and saw that it was the eleventh mark. It had been seven marks since she had found High-Master Wraith and she had waited in her room the whole time awake.

When High-Master Copper arrived at High-Master Wraith's bedchamber door, he turned around and looked at Nyght, although he made sure he did not look into her eyes. Something he had become quite good at after four seasons of practice. "High-Master Wraith wishes to speak with you." Before he placed his hand on the door handle, Nyght spoke.

"Is he alright?" she asked and waited for an answer.

High-Master Copper heard the concern in her question, and he even felt bad about having first believing that the young woman was the cause of his friend's ailment. He now realized she cared for the elder assassin the same way everyone in the Guild did. He turned to look at the young woman, "He is awake, but is very weak."

"What happened to him?"

High-Master Wraith had always said his pupil had an inquisitive mind, and apparently, he was right. High-Master Copper thought it might be a good idea to speak with the young woman before she met with his friend. "We do not know what happened to him. The healers could not find anything wrong with him. In fact, he woke up on his own, only three marks ago. When the healers began to ask him questions, he sent them away. High-Master Grave and I have been talking to him for the past two marks, but he now wishes to speak with you. I ask that you keep the conversation brief, because even though we do not know what is wrong with him, in his condition, it is obvious he needs his rest."

Nyght nodded to let the High-Master know she understood.

He opened the door and walked inside. Nyght stood at the entrance confused about what she should do. High-Master Copper had just said that High-Master Wraith wanted to talk to her, but she had not entered his bedchamber since she had arrived at the Guild. Now she was supposed to. "Come in, child," Nyght heard from inside the room and knew it was High-Master Wraith. With his permission, she stepped into the room.

When she entered, she saw High-Master Grave standing next to the bed on the left. High-Master Copper walked over to stand next to him. Sitting up in the bed was High-Master Wraith, and it was obvious to Nyght that the elderly man was not in good health.

"Come closer, child," High-Master Wraith said. Nyght was now over nineteen seasons old and considered a young adult by others, but High-Master Wraith still always called her child.

She walked over to the bed and since the other High-Masters were standing to his right, she went to the other side. When she stopped, High-Master Wraith was looking at her and he was smiling. Without taking his eyes off her, he spoke to the other two High-Masters, "Please leave us."

"Yes, High-Master," they both said at the same time, turned, and walked out of the room closing the door behind them. This meeting was for the two of them alone.

"How are you feeling, High-Master?" Nyght asked.

He turned his head away from her, "I have been better, but I did not call you here to discuss my health."

"Then what did you want to discuss, High-Master?" He turned and looked at her. Nyght noticed he had his eyes focused directly on hers only she could tell that there was something different about his and it only took her a breath to realize what it was. "Your eyes?" she said to ask what was wrong with them but answered her own question, "You are blind." The last part was not a question.

"It is not important, child."

"But High-Master..."

He raised his hand to silent Nyght, and she stopped speaking at the command of her mentor. "I do not know how much longer I have left and there are matters I need to speak with you; ones which you have not come across in any of your books or have heard from anyone else."

Nyght wanted to talk about what happened to him, but whatever the High-Master wanted to say he wanted to do it before he ran out of time. "What is it you wish to speak to me about, High-Master?"

Since he could no longer see, he did not have to worry about the child's eyes and see what he had, all those seasons ago in the other ones, so he continued to look in her direction and answered her question. "About where you come from." He then turned his head and faced the foot of the bed. Thinking about where to begin, and when he decided, he started telling the child the part of her story she did not know.

"You are descended from Elves." He might not have his sight but there was no problem with his hearing, and he heard the child make a slight intake of breath. "It is true. What I am about to tell you is all true. Until this day, I had told only one other. He was once my pupil like you." That was all he was going to tell her about the man with the eyes like hers. He thought it would be best if she did not know that the pupil, he had just mentioned was her father, especially since he was sure she was somehow involved with his death. He took the silence of the child as a sign that she was ready to hear the rest of his story.

"When the five races came into existence, Creator gave the Elves long life but with that, Creator forbade them to take another's life, the same as he commanded the other races."

Nyght was quick to ask her question. "But High-Master we are human, and we take lives, and it is well known that Gnomes and Trolls kill with no concern for anyone but their own races. Isn't that true?"

"Yes, that is true my child, and I do not know the reason why. All I can tell you is what I was told by my father concerning the Elves." He did not tell her about how his father died two seasons before he turned fifteen. It was not long after the passing of his father that he sought out the Assassin's Guild and when he reached the acceptable age, he became a pupil, and over many seasons, became a High-Master.

"How did he learn what he told you?" Nyght asked.

High-Master Wraith smiled again, and gave his answer, "Because, like you, he was also a descendant of the Elves as well."

It only took her a breath to understand what he had just said. If his father came from Elves, it meant High-Master Wraith did as well. It made Nyght feel quite proud to know that the two of them had something more in common than just being assassins. "That means in some way we are related."

He could not see her face but by the way she spoke, High-Master Wraith could tell that Nyght was smiling. "In a way, I suppose we are, only we come from different caste."

"What do you mean?"

With the question, it was time to tell his pupil just what she was, but first he would tell her about himself. "My Elven ancestor was from the caste with the gift of what is called Spirit Walking. They could separate their soul from their body and send it across great distances. They did this to learn about the other races and about events going on in the world. They did it for knowledge." He took a moment to prepare himself for the next part of his tale, "My father could do this as well and he taught me. Only instead of using what I had learned to obtain knowledge as well, I chose to use it in another way."

"You became an assassin," Nyght said to let him know she understood what he had meant, then she said the next thought that came to her. "Spirit Walking. A spirit is like a ghost, and a ghost is something like a wraith and that is why you chose the name 'Wraith' as your assassin's name."

High-Master Wraith smiled again at how astute his pupil was. "Yes, it is a slight play on words, but I like it." The smile then left his face, "But it is because of what I can do and because of how I chose to use it that I am now suffering and have been for the last six seasons."

"What do you mean, High-Master?"

He took a deep breath before he began, a breath that hurt as it passed through his lungs. "The caste of Elves, the Spirit Walkers were not supposed to use their gifts to take a life. I chose to and in doing so, I corrupted my own spirit. And over the past six seasons, my spirit has been trying to leave my body and end my life."

Nyght thought about what he had just said. She remembered that it was four seasons ago, she had come to the Guild, and she specifically remembered one of the first meetings with her mentor. "That was how you were able to strike me with the dart. You used the Spirit Walking."

He smiled again because of how his pupil could figure things out so quickly. "Yes child, that is what I did. When one Spirit Walks, they can take a small item with them. For those that use the gift to learn it usually was something they can bring back with them from wherever they sent their spirit, but for me, I chose to use something that would go with my profession." He thought about all the times he had killed by Spirit Walking and the memories caused him to laugh so hard that one of his spasms came on him, and he started coughing violently.

Nyght had seen the High-Master have one of his attacks before but nothing like what she was witnessing now. She looked around for what the High-Master had always used to calm the coughing and saw the goblet on the nightstand on the other side of the bed. She ran over to it but when she lifted the cup, it was empty. She saw the pitcher sitting on the table as well and figured that whatever the High-Master drank was in it.

When she had the goblet filled, she held it out to

the High-Master. "Here, drink some," she said, and when he reached for the goblet with both hands, since he could no longer see and because Nyght could tell that he hardly had enough strength to hold the goblet, she helped him take a drink. Before he finished, he had drunk half of the contents.

When he pushed the goblet away from him, she held onto it just in case another attack came upon him. When she was sure he was better or at least better than he was a moment ago, she sat it back down on the nightstand.

"Thank you, child. The tonic is the only thing that has kept what is happening to me under control for this long, but I am afraid that even it is not strong enough to keep my spirit with me for much longer."

Nyght turned and looked at the goblet, "What is in it?" she asked, and she could hear High-Master Wraith taking short breaths to answer. She could also hear the wheezing coming from his chest.

"It is something I was told about right after I started feeling the effects of my illness. Before I had even taken on the role as Master. I had not yet discovered what was behind it, so for the first time, I used my Spirit Walking for its true purpose. I allowed my spirit to travel to the land of the Elves and spoke with another Spirit Walker. She explained to me what I was suffering from and gave me the process to make the tonic. I thought that with it, I would be able to continue to use my skills as I had for all those seasons, but in doing so, I only made myself suffer more. Now after so many seasons, my spirit is so unbalanced that it tries to flee my body, more so in the last six seasons and I am sure that in the very near future, it will succeed."

Nyght remembered that she had seen the High-Master drink from the goblet on the day he had given her the test, and as the High-Master thought, she was quick in figuring out why it was that day he had started taking in his tonic consistently going forward. "It was because of the test you gave me. It was because of me, that you had to start drinking the tonic all the time." Once again, she did not phrase what she had said as a question.

High-Master Wraith heard the concern in her statement, but he did not want the child to think that what he was suffering through was her fault. "I was the one who chose to test you the way I did, and I had been taking the tonic long before you arrived."

"But since the test, I have seen you drink it every day," Nyght said.

He did not blame the child for what he had done to himself, but more importantly, he did not want her to blame herself. "I would have ended up in this bed whether you came to the Guild or not. Whether I gave you the test or not, and I will hear no more about the subject." He said the last part to make sure she understood that as a High-Master of the Guild, his judgment on the subject was final.

"Yes, High-Master," she said, to let him know she understood, but deep down, she knew she had a part in what was happening to her mentor.

"Now enough about me. I did not summon you to tell you about my life which will be over very soon so let me tell you about where you come from." She did not speak so he continued. "From what I understand, it was the races of the Gnomes and Trolls to first take the lives of others. The Elves still followed Creator and refused to take the life of another. But at the same time, they prayed to Creator to help stop the ones killing them. Creator answered their prayers. He chose a score of Elves and blessed them." Even though he could not see, he still turned his head so that his eyes were facing Nyght. "He blessed them with death." He stopped to listen to what the child would say.

"I do not understand, High-Master."

As proud as he was of his pupil for being so quick at figuring details out for herself, he was just as proud of her for when she admitted she did not know something. He continued with his story. "He gave those he chose the ability to kill, and they were better than anyone else. Even though there were only a few of them, they were able to defeat anyone who attacked the Elves. The numbers they slew were so high no one knows how many found the end of their life by one of the Elves that brought death. Even though the name of this new caste of Elves is no longer known, lost over so long of time, the meaning of their caste is quite simple." He turned his head so that he was facing the girl again, and then told her the human translation of the name, "It was Death to Death. Those Elves would bring death to anyone who brought death to any Elf." He then turned away.

"What happened to them?" Nyght asked when the High-Master remained quiet.

"The Elves were safe, but something happened to the ones Creator blessed. They became somber and no longer associated with other Elves so eventually those few left the lands of the Elves and lived their lives in other parts of the world. It has been so long ago that probably only the Elves in their own lands remember them since they live for so long. I know because I have a feeling I was meant to. It was something a Spirit Walker of the Elves had told me when I questioned her about my first pupil like you."

"What happened to the other pupil?"

High-Master Wraith gave her an answer just not the complete one, "He died."

Nyght did not think about the other pupil, but she did have a question for her mentor, "How do you know that I am a descendent of one of these Elves?"

He knew she would eventually come to that question. "Your eyes," he said and gave her a moment to think about what he had just told her. "To most people, when they look into your eyes, they see something, but they do not know what it is. The best way they can describe it is that your eyes are deep. Those people have never taken a life." High-Master Wraith took as deep of a breath as he could then continued, "But to the ones who have taken another life, we see death. Not our own, but the death of those we have removed from this world. The more lives we have ended, the more death we will see when we look into eyes like yours."

Nyght heard what the High-Master had said, but her mind was focusing on the first part. He had said that someone who had not taken a life would describe eyes like hers as "deep." She remembered she had used the same word a long time ago. Back in the first town she lived in. It was so long ago she did not remember the town's name, nor the face she had been looking at when she used the word. She could remember the eyes, and she realized the one with those eyes must have been like her. She would have to think more about this when she was alone. It was part of her past and she shared it with no one, not even her mentor. "So, I am descended from Elves, and I am part of this special caste."

"Yes, child."

"Is that why I always wanted to become an assassin?"

The child's father asked High-Master Wraith the same question when he had this conversation with him. "No, my child. You became an assassin because that is what Creator needed you to be. It just so happens that since you are what you are, you will be remarkably good at being one." He was not able to see the smile the girl had. "There is one last piece of history you should know."

"What is it, High-Master?"

He was now about to tell her an even bigger

secret. "The first assassin, the one who had started our Guild was an Elf from the caste that brought Death to Death. So, in truth child, you are the rightful ruler of the Assassin's Guild."

"But you and the other High-Masters are the ones who rule our Guild."

"It was not always the way. With most societies, one individual oversees everything. I do not know what happened to him, but I do know he mated with a human and they had a child. Before the Elf left, never to return, he made his son the ruler. That child was only half-human and lived until he was two hundred seasons. Before he passed away, he made his daughter head of the Guild. And when her time was upon her, she made her son ruler. Unfortunately, he died before he was able to sire a child. That was when the Guild decided to make three individuals rule the Guild. They chose the best out of the assassins believing three individuals would be able to oversee the Guild, as the one from the line of the first assassin would. And even though the High-Masters have continued in the ways of the first assassin, the first High-Masters always believed another of the caste would come along and take their rightful place as ruler of the Guild."

"What about the other pupil with eyes like mine? Wouldn't he have been able to take the ruling position as well?"

High-Master Wraith wished he had known about the first assassin when the other pupil was at the

Guild. If he had, he would have made sure that the assassin did not leave his calling. "I only learned what the first assassin was, after you came to our Guild. It seems that we find the pieces to this puzzle we call life, only when they wish to be found. I found the book about the first assassin and the ones who ruled after him not long after you arrived. It was so long ago that no one remembered him. Not even our Weapons-Maker. Or that is what he says." High-Master Wraith always suspected Dart kept more secrets than the Guild itself.

Nyght knew that the High-Master was telling her the truth. She did not know how she knew but there was something in the way he spoke that moved her deep inside. "I am supposed to be the ruler of our Guild."

"Yes my child, you are. But only after you have proven yourself as an assassin. Until then you cannot lead others."

"I understand, High-Master."

"Good, my child," he said and reached out with his hands. Nyght did not know what he wanted so she took his hands into hers, which is where he wanted them. "I chose to use my gift to test you. You must always remember that the Guild comes first even before our own well-being and desires. The one who formed the Guild, who might have even been your ancestor, knew this and you must carry on the same belief as well as all the other decrees we have followed since the beginning of our Guild.

The first assassin was given a gift from Creator, and that is why, what we do, we do for him."

"Yes, High-Master."

He squeezed her hands in his and smiled. "I know you are the one we have been waiting for. I have told the other High-Masters all of this as well. I will not have long to wait for my end, and the tale of our Guild and your role in it could not die with me. When you are ready the High-Masters will turn the Guild over to your guidance and you will guide us well."

"Thank you, High-Master. I will do my best."

"I can ask for no more," he said then pulled his hands out of hers. "Now let this old man rest." She stood up and walked toward the door but heard the High-Master from across the room. "For tonight might be the night I close my eyes for the last time."

Nyght did not like what he had said so she stopped and turned to face her mentor, and respectfully said, "I am sure High-Master that you will be with us for quite some time." She then turned and left the room. She did not hear what he said after the door closed behind her.

"Not for too much longer, that I am sure of, and thankful for."

FIFTEEN

For half a moon-cycle, Nyght continued with her studies in the quarters of High-Master Wraith. He remained in his bed for most of the time, only leaving it when he needed to use the lavatory. The ones teaching Nyght would give her lessons in the outer chamber next to the fireplace, where she and High-Master Wraith had spent many nights over the past four seasons discussing the philosophies of the world and of the Guild.

For the first three sun-cycles after High-Master Wraith took to his bed, the other High-Masters came to check on their friend but soon he asked them not to return, and having much respect for the eldest High-Master, they did as he wished. The only one he would allow to see him in his condition, which was growing worse with every sun-cycle was Nyght. When the Guild's cook brought their food to their quarters, Nyght would take the High-Master's meals to him. It was Nyght who changed his bed linen when he was not able to get out of it in time to use the lavatory. Nyght took care of him as a child would take care of their grandfather and she was honored to do so.

They still had their nightly discussions but there were times when they did not last as long as the previous ones because High-Master Wraith was too weak to continue. Then there were times their discussions would last well into the morning because the High-Master could not sleep. It did not matter to Nyght because she felt that in the last two moon-marks, she was able to learn more from the High-Master than she had at any other time. To her, it appeared he wanted to pass on his knowledge, and with his age, he had a vast amount of it but little time to do so.

One midday, after one of her teachers had just left and High-Master Wraith was sleeping, Nyght was sitting in her chair by the fire reading. When she heard a knock, she looked at the time-marker on the mantel over the fireplace. She saw that it had passed the fourteenth mark. She completed her lessons for the day, so she was not expecting one of her instructors and it was too early for their evening meals.

She stood, picked up her daggers in their sheaths, and secured them around her waist. She then put on her cloak, closing it around her. Nyght did not think she would really need her weapons, but she always had them in case the need did present itself.

More than likely, it was just someone wanting to see High-Master Wraith, probably one of the other High-Masters themselves. It was only a few sun-cycles ago that High-Master Wraith had requested to see the two High-Masters, so they were probably only there to check on him.

She walked over to the door and when she opened it, she saw a woman she had never seen before; therefore, she did not know who she was. With her arms inside her cloak, she situated her hands, prepared to draw her weapons. "High-Master Wraith is not taking any visitors," Nyght said to the woman. It was the same statement she gave to anyone who came to the door but was not there for her lessons, or to bring her and High-Master Wraith's meals or requested by High-Master Wraith himself. High-Master Wraith had instructed her on what to say.

It took a moment for the assassin to remember why she had come. When the young woman opened the door, she looked into her eyes, and what she saw disturbed her. It took all her training to focus on the reason she was there, "I have not come to see High-Master Wraith. I have come to inform you that the High-Masters request your presence in the Assignment Chamber."

Nyght did not believe she had heard the woman correctly. "I cannot go in there. I have not been given the status of True Assassin. I still have another season of training before I am." Nyght knew the only ones allowed to enter the Assignment Chamber were assassins who had completed their training. It was the room in the Guild where the High-Masters offered an assassin their contract. It was in there the assassin would decide to either take the contract or decline it. Nyght knew she was not ready for that opportunity.

"I am only the messenger, but I do know the

rules of our Guild, especially those concerning the Assignment Chamber, for I have entered the place a number of times. But at the moment, I have been given the task to bring you to meet with the other High-Masters." When she finished giving her explanation, she saw Nyght look back over her shoulder and she knew the reason why. "The other High-Masters have requested your presence. They know High-Master Wraith takes his afternoon rest during these marks and I believe that is why they have chosen to summon you now so you can be back in plenty of time before High-Master Wraith wakes."

Nyght had not left High-Master Wraith's quarters in two moon-marks. She even started using the lavatory attached to High-Master Wraith's bedchamber so she would not have to use the ones on the lower levels of the Guild. She had watched over her mentor all this time and felt as if she was abandoning him.

The assassin could tell what the young woman was thinking. "The other High-Masters are still in charge of the Guild and High-Master Wraith would expect you to honor their summons as if it had come from himself."

Nyght turned her head to look at the assassin and was about to ask, what did she know of High-Master Wraith? But when she looked at the woman's face, she could tell that she had said what she did with nothing but respect for the elderly High-Master. She nodded and stepped through the door, closing it behind her quietly, not to wake up her mentor.

"Since you have never been to the Assignment Chamber, I will lead you there," the assassin said, turned, and walked down the circular hallway to the lift.

They both took it to the ground level then the assassin led Nyght to the lift that would take them to the twenty-fourth floor. She could not help but think that the entire trip had been too time-consuming. If there had been stairs, they could have simply walked down the one level. Nyght even thought that since the distance between floors was not too great, she probably could have used a rope and swung down to the level they needed to go.

When she stepped off the lift, Nyght looked around the circular hallway and only saw a single door on the entire floor, on the other side of the level, opposite where she was standing.

She followed the assassin around the hall and when they came to the door she stopped. "I cannot go in with you. When you are finished, you may return to your quarters without an escort." The assassin was about to turn and leave but stopped to say one last thing. "My name is Ruse; please give High-Master Wraith my best wishes when you speak to him again." Nyght nodded to let the assassin know she would do as she had asked then her escort turned and walked away.

Nyght waited until the assassin was halfway around the circular hall before she took her eyes off the woman and placed them on the door in front of her. The High-Masters had summoned her, so she figured she had no need to knock. She opened the door and stepped inside, closing the door behind her.

About forty paces away from her, three men sat behind a large table. High-Master Copper was sitting in the middle with High-Master Grave on his left. The third man, one she had never seen before, was sitting at High-Master Copper's right.

Since they were waiting for her to come to them, she started walking forward. There were ten steps she had to descend first which put her on a lower level than the door to the room. She saw the stone table, long enough so that all three of the men were sitting on the opposite side of her. When she came to a halt, out of the corner of her eye, she saw the brazier on her right made of the same stone as the table. It stood high enough to reach the height of her waist, and even though she was a pace away from it, she could feel the heat from the fire burning in the center.

She had never been to this room although High-Master Wraith had explained to her how the proceedings went inside the Assignment Chamber. Once summoned, the assassin would wait for the High-Masters to present them with a contract by sliding a piece of parchment across the table. It would have three pieces of information: the name of the person, the last known location of that person, and the cost of the contract. If the assassin did not wish to accept the contract, they would slide the parchment back across the table, turn around, and walk out of the room. If the assassin did accept it, they would pick up the contract, turn to their right, and place the contract in the fire of the brazier. Then they would turn and leave the room to fulfill the contract not speaking a word because there was no need for them to do so.

Nyght had stopped less than half a pace away from the table, and since there was plenty of light coming from the torches around the room as well as from the fire to her right, she had no problem seeing the parchment sitting on the table in front of High-Master Copper.

She did not know why the High-Masters summoned her, but from what she was seeing, it appeared to her that they were about to offer her a contract even though she still had a season to go before she received the title of True Assassin. She thought for a moment that maybe she was there for some other reason and the piece of parchment on the table had nothing to do with her, but when High-Master Copper slid the parchment toward her, she knew what was happening.

She moved closer to the table, reached out, and picked up the parchment already positioned so that when she looked at it, she could read the writing on it, so she did.

When an assassin came into the Assignment Chamber, neither they nor any of the High-Masters presenting the contract ever spoke a word. It had been that way since the beginning of the Guild. Nyght was the first to break that tradition. "No!" she said, having taken a few breaths to get control of herself after reading what was on the parchment. "I will not do this or allow it to be done." Even though she had not accepted the contract, she did not return it to the three men, nor did she place it in the fire to her right. She held on to it with her right hand while she moved her left hand inside her cloak to take hold of the hilt of Umbra to prepare herself for what happened in the next few moments.

High-Master Copper was leading the meeting. Usually, High-Master Wraith would sit in the center chair behind the table, but since he was no longer able to perform his duties, the task fell on High-Master Copper's shoulders, and since this was the first contract he had to present since he accepted the lead role, it was his responsibility to deal with the situation. Even though, he was not looking forward to it.

The tradition of no words spoken within the Assignment Chamber had come to an end. High-Master Copper, as well as High-Master Grave, did not hold it against the young woman standing before them. In fact, since they knew who and what she was, then it was her right to end the long-standing practice. With new leadership, there are always changes. Since she had spoken, High-Master Copper knew he would as well.

"This is Master Spar," High-Master Copper said, gesturing with his right hand to the man at his side. "He will become the new High-Master." High-Master Copper introduced the man so Nyght would know who was attending the meeting.

"High-Master Wraith is the third High-Master of the Guild." Nyght stopped looking at High-Master Copper and turned her head to look at Master Spar before she said her next statement. "And High-Master Wraith still lives."

The High-Masters had informed the Master about the young woman named Nyght. They had told him about who she was and what she was to the Guild. They also told him that he should never look into her eyes. Since this was the first time he had seen the child, he had to concentrate on following the High-Masters' directions and he was glad the child finally stopped looking directly at him because he so much wanted to see if what they told him was true, but at the same time, he was hesitant to do so.

"Yes, High-Master Wraith still lives," High-Master Copper said to get the child to focus back on him, "And that is why Master Spar, still holds the title of Master. There can only be three High-Masters at a time, and until High-Master Wraith is no longer with us, he will retain the title."

"And this is your solution to your problem!" Nyght tossed the parchment back onto the table where it landed halfway between her and High-Master Copper. "You want me to kill him, so you three can proceed with whatever plans you have. Nyght took the last half step to stand directly against the table and leaned over it, "I will not do it, nor will I allow you to send another."

High-Master Copper made sure he kept his eyes off the child's eyes, and he said a silent prayer to Creator asking him why he was the one in this predicament. Because he was now the eldest High-Master, he would have to lead the Guild and it meant performing duties, even if it was something he did not wish to do. "You do not understand what we ask of you, so I will explain."

Nyght was trying to decide if she would let the man explain or draw her daggers, kill the three in the room, then rush to High-Master Wraith to let him know what his so-called friends were planning against him. She decided that she would give the High-Master a chance. A very slim chance. She was still leaning over the table and since the writing on the parchment was facing upward, she ran her eyes over it one more time to keep her anger fueled. The only information on it was the name, High-Master Wraith, and his last known location, which was the Assassin's Guild. Nyght was surprised the three con-spirators had not put down the amount of coin they were willing to pay. Since she had decided to allow the soon-to-be-dead High-Master Copper to explain what all of this was about, she stood up, and took a step back.

High-Master Copper did not know how this

meeting was going to proceed. The young woman did not know it, but even he had a problem with the request, as did High-Master Grave and Master Spar. All three knew that what the Guild required of them, they would do. Now he had to show the young woman she needed to do the same.

"High-Master Wraith is dying." High-Master Copper began, and when he saw the sneer on Nyght's face, he knew he needed to hurry his explanation along. "His death is an embarrassment…"

"To you or the Guild?" Nyght asked interrupting the man.

High-Master Copper sighed and gave her his answer. "To High-Master Wraith himself." Even though he was not looking at her eyes, he could tell that his reply confused the child. "An assassin brings death to others. It is what they are; it is who they are. When their time comes to leave this world, if they should die because of old age, then they can accept it. For we are all victims of time itself, so there is no shame in dying in bed after many seasons in service to the Guild and Creator. If an assassin meets their end at the hands of an enemy, then that is also acceptable, for if they lose their life to someone who was better than they were, then it is an honor to die by their hands."

He bent his head down for a moment before he continued. When he was ready, not only did he raise his head up, but he sat straighter in his chair. "High-Master Wraith is an honorable man. One I have great respect for, and I can say without doubt, that High-Master Grave and Master Spar feel just as strongly as I do."

"Then why did you place a contract on him?" Nyght asked and moved her hands inside her cloak so that they were resting on the hilts of her daggers. The answer the High-Master gave would determine if he lived when he finished speaking it.

"I, nor anyone in this room placed the contract on High-Master Wraith."

"Then who did?" Nyght asked, wanting to know the name of the person she would be meeting with next.

"High-Master Wraith himself," High-Master Copper said to answer her question.

It was the way he said his name, with sadness and regret in his voice, which made Nyght realize he was telling the truth. She just did not know what to say and apparently, High-Master Copper was at a loss for words over what they had been discussing. High-Master Grave saw the turmoil his friend was going through and spoke for the first time. "High-Master Wraith has enacted what is known as 'The Assassin's Honor.'" He gave High-Master Copper a chance to speak but since he remained silent, High-Master Grave continued, "As you know, the Guild has the rule that no assassin can take the life of another assassin."

Nyght knew the rule as well as all the rules that governed an assassin's actions, "Then why are you trying to make me break our rule?"

High-Master Grave continued to explain, "If an assassin comes to a point in their life where they can no longer provide the services which they have for so many seasons, because of an injury or a sickness, then the assassin can invoke 'The Assassin's Honor' as a final request. They will take a contract out on themselves so they can die at the hands of another assassin. In doing so, they retain the honor they would have lost if they were to die in a less honorable way because of an illness or injury."

High-Master Copper, now having composed himself, spoke again. "The words 'Assassin's Honor' has a double meaning in itself. The one the contract is for keeps their honor in death, at the same time, it is an honor for the one who gives them their death allowing the assassin to die as they lived. Honorably."

Nyght understood, although she did have a question, "Why don't one of you do it? You all have known High-Master Wraith longer than I have and I am not even a True Assassin yet. I still have a season to go before I am granted the title."

High-Master Copper turned to his right and nodded to Master Spar who nodded back then pulled a parchment out which he had been holding in his lap. Rolled up and tied with red twine, Master Spar slid the parchment to the other side of the table toward Nyght. "When the High-Masters came to me and explained what was going on with High-Master Wraith, I myself did not believe any of what they told me even though I have great respect for the both of them. When they told me about you, about who you are and what you will become, even though I had never met you until today, I knew they were speaking the truth. And when the day comes that you claim your rightful place as ruler of our Guild, I will be right beside them offering my loyalty and service to you and the Guild."

Master Spar stood and walked around to the other side of the table picking up the scroll he had offered to Nyght to take but did not. "But when they told me about what High-Master Wraith had asked of them, I refused to believe them. I am only a Master and I have no right, nor would I ever think of going against an order given by them or High-Master Wraith. At the same time, I could not ask High-Master Wraith about what his fellow High-Masters had told me because that would be an act of disobedience as well. If I asked him and he informed me that he had given the instructions for his death then it would have shown that I had doubt in his decision, and I would have shown him more dishonor."

Master Spar looked at the scroll he was holding then to the young woman standing in front of him but made sure he did not look into her eyes, "They came to me the day after High-Master Wraith told them of 'The Assassin's Honor' which was ten sun-cycles ago. I spent the first nine in the Archives looking for anything referring to 'The Assassin's Honor' because they also told me they had only heard it from High-Master Wraith when he told them of his plans. I asked them to give me a chance to find out if what High-Master Wraith had asked of them was in fact a rule of our Guild." Master Spar stopped and even though the topic being discussed was a somber one, he had to smile at what he was about to say, "Or was High-Master Wraith just taking control of his life and decided to leave this world under his own terms convincing the High-Masters that an ancient edict actually existed to allow an assassin to take another assassins life." Master Spar extended his hand to offer the scroll to Nyght. When she took it, he walked back around the table and took his seat. "I understand you might think we could have written the scroll in one day, but I assure you, we did not."

Nyght had just been thinking the exact same thought. When she undid the string that kept the scroll rolled up, she looked at it and could tell that the parchment and the writing were very old. She had spent the last four seasons reading anything she could and had spent so much time with books, parchments, and scrolls that she could tell if they were recent or created some time ago. The one in her hands belonged to the latter so after reading the heading on the scroll, "The Assassin's Honor," she knew it dealt with what they had been discussing.

She let go of the end of the scroll and the entire parchment rolled back up, taking the form it had remained in for so long. She then looked at the three men, "You still have not told me why you are asking me to do this. All of you have known him longer." She had asked the question before Master Spar spoke, but she never received an answer.

High-Master Copper gave her one. "Part of the particulars of 'The Assassin's Honor' is that the person who takes the contract out on themselves selects the person who will assassinate them. We did not choose you; High-Master Wraith did." Nyght did not say anything so High-Master Copper continued. "Even though the honor of the assassination could go to someone the person has known for a good portion of their life, the person can also choose one they feel is the best assassin. Or they may even choose one of their own pupils. I have a feeling all three of those reasons led High-Master Wraith to choosing you for this honor."

"I may be his pupil, but I have only known High-Master Wraith for four seasons, and I have not even had my first contract so I cannot be the best." Nyght gave her rebuttal, only she did not know if she was doing it to let the three men know she was not the one to take on the contract, or to convince herself, that she was not worthy of it.

High-Master Copper gave her his opinion about what she had said. "You are his pupil. As for only knowing him for four seasons, it is not the quantity of time people spend together which lets them get to know one another, but the quality. We all know that for the last four seasons, you and High-Master Wraith have spent not only a great quantity of time together, but it was of great quality. As for the last standard, I have a feeling High-Master Wraith feels you are the best, and if you are not now, one day he believes you will be." High-Master Copper looked to his left then to his right then put his eyes back on Nyght to finish his statement, "As we all do."

Nyght looked at the three men then looked at the scroll she was holding. "And if I choose not to fulfill the contract?"

High-Master Copper did not say it, but that was his and the ones sitting with him, worst fear. "It is a contract, and like all contracts offered by the Guild, it can be declined." He saw that Nyght was about to speak and even knew what she was going to say, so he quickly spoke up, "But if you do," he said before she could decline the contract, "I must tell you that since High-Master Wraith chose you, then we cannot offer this contract to another. And since this is a matter of honor, we cannot go to him and tell him that you have declined the honor, and if you go to him saying you will not do it, then you will only add more to his dishonor."

"But he will at least remain alive," Nyght said to let the others know what she preferred.

"But not for long," High-Master Grave said, "We do not know what he is suffering from and if he does, then he will not tell us. He has refused any help from the Guild's healers, and it is obvious from the last time we saw him that he will not last much longer. If whatever is wrong with him is what he dies from, he will know that in his last moments of life, he died with no honor."

Nyght did not know what to say or do. She understood it all, but having to take the life of the one who had taught her so much was weighing on her. She had spent the last four seasons with High-Master Wraith, and even though she had not needed any training in how to use her blades, he had given her the training she needed to survive in the world. She had sat and listened to him, asked him questions, and in the past half moon-cycle, she had even taken care of the ailing assassin. After what he had done for her, she could only think of him as she did Moon, as a father. She knew a person only had one true father, but with what Moon had given her and what High-Master Wraith had as well, she felt blessed to have two she could use the word "Father" to describe.

Nyght remembered that High-Master Wraith had told her the reason behind his sickness, something that he did not even share with the other High-Masters or anyone else within the Assassin's Guild that she knew of. They did not know about how he could Spirit Walk and therefore they probably do not know that he is descended from Elves as she is. They shared that secret together and maybe he decided to let her know, just for what he wanted her to do. Maybe because what they had in common connected them in life, and also in death.

"I do not envy the decision you are forced to make," High-Master Copper said to bring the child out of her thoughts. "And I will not lie to you, but if High-Master Wraith had chosen me as the one to do this honor, I am not sure if I would be able to accept the contract myself."

"Nor I," High-Master Grave said.

"Nor I," Master Spar said as well, adding to the other two's sincerest truths.

They were now waiting for her answer, and she knew what it was. She walked over to the table and placed "The Assassin's Honor" scroll down. She then picked up the contract, turned to her right, walked over to the brazier, and placed the contract into the flames. She watched as the contract turned to ash knowing that the life of High-Master Wraith was now in her hands.

She remembered what her mentor had relayed to her. That once an assassin accepted a contract and placed it into the fire, they were to turn and walk out of the room, so that was what she was going to do, but before she had taken a step toward the door, High-Master Copper spoke. "There is no monetary compensation for this contract." Nyght turned to look at the man and was about ready to tell him that accepting coin for what she had just agreed to do sickened her, but she saw he had more to say, so she remained quiet. "And we would never offer any, but with the task you have accepted, you show, you do have the honor 'The Assassin's Honor' so offers, and that of a True Assassin." He stopped speaking and all three of the men stood. "As of this moment, we all agree that you have completed your training and grant you the title of True Assassin." They all bowed their heads to Nyght, and she bowed back.

"There is one more part of 'The Assassin's Honor' we need to address with you," High-Master Grave said, and Nyght wanted to tell them that she has had enough of "The Assassin's Honor" but did not. "When an assassin has fulfilled the contract given under 'The Assassin's Honor' the assassin takes on the title of Honorable Assassin," the High-Master said.

Nyght had a question for the three men, "And how many alive have the title?"

All three looked at each other then they all faced the young woman. High-Master Copper answered the question, "None." Then all three gave another bow.

She returned the bow then turned and walked out of the room. She knew where she had to go.

When she reached the bedchamber of High-Master Wraith, she opened the door and looked inside. She saw that he was still asleep and since he was still lying on his side with his back to the fireplace to the left of the room, Nyght figured he had not woken up in the time she had met with the two High-Masters and Master.

High-Master Wraith would sleep on his left side. He had told her it was easier for him to breathe, because when he slept on his back, he felt as if his chest was caving in on him. Nyght closed the door, walked over to the fireplace in the outer room, and sat down in a chair.

She sat there until there was a knock at the door. She looked at the time-marker on the mantel and saw that it was just after the eighteenth mark. The person at the door, sent by the Guild's cook, was bringing hers and High-Master Wraith's evening meal.

She went to the door, opened it, and accepted the food from the assassin who had delivered it. As soon as she had the serving tray in her hands, he gave Nyght a quick bow with his head, then turned and walked away. Even though she did not know the assassin's name, she had seen him before and he had brought her the meals in the past, but never had he bowed to her.

She put the incident behind her and carried the tray to High-Master Wraith's bedchamber. She held the tray with one hand so she could open the door with the other. When she stepped inside, she saw High-Master Wraith already sitting up in his bed, prepared for his evening meal. "Good evening, High-Master," she said to greet her mentor.

"Good evening, child. I can smell the venison stew from here," he said to let her know what they would be eating this evening.

"Your sense of smell is as strong as ever, High-Master," Nyght said to give the elder assassin a bit of praise even though they both knew his sense of smell and hearing did not make up for the loss of his sight.

She sat the serving tray across his lap and re-moved the cover over his bowl of stew. She then took her own bowl and sat down in the chair she kept next to the bed where she ate her meals and the two of them would talk. While they ate, High-Master Wraith would normally talk to her about a subject he wanted her to learn, but on this evening, they ate in silence. Nyght did not know how the High-Master felt about the quietness, but for her, all it did was allow the thought of what she was going to do to run through her mind. A part of her was even glad the High-Master had lost his sight, because if he could see her face, she was sure he would be able to tell what she was thinking.

When she saw he had finished his dinner, she placed her empty bowl on the tray then removed it from across his lap. She headed for the door, but when she reached the foot of the bed, she turned to look at her mentor. "High-Master Wraith," she said to let him know she had a question for him.

"Yes, my child," the elderly assassin said, for her to continue.

"Do you have anything else to teach me?" Nyght knew she could not talk about "The Assassin's Honor" with High-Master Wraith. If she did mention it, it would not have the honor it was meant to, so she came up with the question she had asked and waited for the answer.

High-Master-Wraith took a deep, wheezing, breath then answered, "I have nothing else to teach you, my child." He then positioned himself in his bed so that he was once again lying on his left side.

Nyght took one more look at the man she had learned so much from, even from the statement, he had just made. She could tell by the way he spoke; High-Master Wraith was tired. He was ready to leave this world and life behind him. Being who and what he was, he would fight as long as he could against what was killing him, just as any assassin would. If they saw the one attacking, they would never surrender to their enemy. The same way the High-Master would never surrender. Even though eventually he would lose to his sickness but when he did, it would be without honor.

Nyght walked out of the room and when the door closed behind her, she put her back against it trying to decide what she was going to do. The decision was not about whether or not she would fulfill the contract, she knew she would. No, at that moment she was trying to decide if she was going to cry or if she was going to throw the tray she had in her hands across the room because she was angry. It only took her a breath to reject both of those options.

She decided she was going to do what High-Master Wraith had trained her to do and that was remove all emotions. An assassin did not kill out of anger, hate, grief, or vengeance. They kill because Creator needs them to and now Creator needs her to kill her mentor. Even though Nyght did not follow Creator, she knew that when High-Master Wraith left this world, Creator was getting a very good man and the greatest of assassins.

Nyght walked through the room and to the door of their quarters. When she opened it, she placed the tray out in the hallway so it would be there for whomever the Guild's cook sent to retrieve it. She then closed the door and went to her room. Once inside, she closed the door, took her daggers out of their sheaths at her sides, and then climbed into the center of her bed and sat. She crossed her legs in front of her and crossed her arms across her chest placing her blades upward and across the front of her shoulders. She then bent her head down, closed her eyes, and waited.

She did not know how long she had stayed there, but when she lifted her head, she knew she had waited long enough. She climbed out of her bed and once standing, she slid her daggers into their sheaths.

She then went through the room next to hers and into the outer chamber. She went to every candle in the room and blew them out. Next, she went over to the hearth and extinguished the fire. The room was now completely dark, but since she had spent so much time in it and had no problem seeing without any lights, she knew where every object was and avoided them easily to make her way to the door of High-Master Wraith's bedchamber.

She cautiously opened the door, moving slowly herself so not to make a sound. She only opened it wide enough to slip inside, which she did. She had made the outer room dark so no light would come into the bedchamber because it might have awakened her target. Which is what High-Master Wraith was from the moment she accepted the contract, and as an assassin, she had no feelings one way or the other toward her target.

She closed the door just as slowly as she had opened it. Once shut, she made her way around the left side of the room keeping close to the wall. She had her cloak on and kept it closed as much as she could, and since it was black, it would make it harder for anyone to see her, not that anyone else was in the room that could. The only light in the room was coming from the fireplace, and it had died down in the time since she had left the High-Master after they had finished their meal, the flames were so low they hardly produced any light at all.

She continued around the room until she lined up directly with the High-Master, more specifically his back and his neck. He was still lying on his left side facing away from her. When she started moving toward her target, she moved just as slowly as she did when she had opened and closed the door. High-Master Wraith had taught her that there was no need to rush in ending a target's life. They were already dead; they just did not know it. Now she understood what he had meant. From where she was, the High-Master was already dead. She was just filling in the gap that would take him to his death.

When she reached the side of the bed, she removed Full from its sheath on her right hip. She then slowly knelt down so that her eyes were looking directly at the back of the High-Master's neck, just at the base of his skull. She then lifted Full and with a single, swift, and precise thrust, she ended the target's life.

When the blade entered the body, she pushed it in far enough so that she knew the target had no chance to survive, then removed it from the body. Since she had practiced the killing stroke for the past four seasons, she had no problem with performing it at a level that would have even impressed her mentor even though she no longer had one who was alive.

She stood up, looked at Full, and noticed that there was not a single drop of blood on the blade. She was sure it was because of who had given her the dagger and its counterpart. With the contract fulfilled, she could walk directly to the door, which she did, opened it, and then closed it behind her. She then went to her room, laid down on her bed, and went to sleep. She did not even shed a tear for what she had done. High-Master Wraith had trained her to be an assassin and she would not dishonor him by adding emotions to her kill.

If Nyght had taken a moment to go to the other side of the bed, she would have seen the smile High-Master Wraith had as he lay there. Whether it had appeared when he had fallen asleep or just before the blade entered the base of his skull, was known only to him.

The next morning, Nyght opened the door and took the tray from the assassin who had brought hers and High-Master Wraith's morning meal. The same as she had done many times before. The only difference this day was that by the time the assassin had made it to the lift to take him back to the kitchen, he heard someone shouting at him. "Get High-Master Copper and High-Master Grave, High-Master Wraith is dead." The assassin ran to High-Master Copper's door, but the High-Master was already out in the hallway as if he had been waiting by the door, waiting for some sign.

The courtyard outside the High-Tower of the Guild stayed at a comfortable temperature even though outside the walls of the Guild, it was cold enough to freeze a person within a single mark. The wizards of the Guild had placed the spells over the entire area so everyone could attend the funeral of High-Master Wraith.

The news of the fate of High-Master Wraith took no time to spread through the Guild. In fact, it seemed as if everyone already knew that when they woke that morning, the atmosphere would be a lot more somber.

Guild members were the only family each of the assassins had so everyone knew what was happening to High-Master Wraith. Maybe not the reason why, but they knew he was dying in a way that would steal his honor, but they also knew his pupil, the one called Nyght would make sure the High-Master would go to his next life with honor. They also knew she was no longer just Nyght. She was now, Honorable Nyght, and she is a True Assassin.

Dart had built the funeral pyre in the middle of the courtyard. Lying on that pyre of wood was the body of High-Master Wraith. All the assassins, currently at the Guild, and a great number from other locations that could attend had come to see the final passing of one of the greatest High-Masters who had been a part of their Guild.

They all stood around the pyre, waiting. High-Master Copper, High-Master Grave, and High-Master Spar stood three paces away from the crowd. High-Master Copper, being the eldest, was the one holding the torch that would set the pyre on flames along with High-Master Wraith's body. Instead of walking forward to ignite the wood, he turned around to face the crowd. Standing directly behind him, he saw Honorable Nyght looking at him. He walked over to her and held the torch out for her to take, "Would you do the honor?"

Nyght nodded and took the torch from his hand. She then walked forward past the other two High-Masters who had stepped aside not only so they could watch her, but to allow her to proceed to the body of her former mentor.

When she reached the pyre, she placed the end of the torch against the wood close to the High-Master's head, then she did the same at his feet, and then one last time at the center of his body. The wood quickly caught fire because of the oil Dart used and soon flames consumed both the wood and the body of High-Master Wraith.

Nyght did not turn around to go back to where she had been standing when she took the torch from High-Master Copper. She did step backward moving to her original spot, but she never took her eyes off the pyre. High-Master Wraith deserved that honor.

When she was back with the other assassins, High-Master Copper, and the other two High-Masters joined her. She was not sure if what she did next was something she was supposed to do or not, but it felt like the right thing to do.

Without taking her eyes off the flames, she knelt down so that her right knee was on the ground. She did not have to look to know that not only did the High-Masters follow her action, but so did every assassin who was watching the last moments of High-Master Wraith. They remained in that position until the body had turned completely to ash. Not a single assassin spoke a word. Not a single assassin made the slightest move. Not a single assassin shed a tear. Every assassin would miss High-Master Wraith.

SIXTEEN

Nyght woke because of the banging noise coming from somewhere. She sat up in her bed but did not sense that whatever had awakened her was a threat; she still stood and dressed and secured her sheaths around her waist. She might not be in danger, but with the exception of when she went to bed, she always wore them. Even in bed, she kept her blades at her sides.

The last thing she put on was her cloak. She has had it since she was twelve seasons old, but since she had grown in height, the garment barely passed her knees. She had become used to the way it covered her from head to toe and she had even thought about finding one that did, but for right now she wanted to find out what, or better yet who, was making the banging noise.

When she walked into the outer chamber of High-Master Wraith's quarters, she looked at the time-marker over the fireplace. She saw that it was just past the eighth mark. Usually, she would have been up by now and taking care of her mentor, but since she and the other assassins had just attended his funeral yesterday, there was no need for her to rise so early. Especially since she had only gone to bed on the fourth mark of the day having stayed up thinking about her now former mentor.

Nyght heard the banging noise coming from out in the hallway. She walked over to the door to exit the chamber and when she opened it, the noise became even louder. She stepped out into the circular hallway and began to follow where the sound was coming from. When she came to a stop, she was standing in front of High-Master Copper's quarters. She did not know whether she should interrupt the High-Master or not, but since the noise was loud and the Guild had already lost one High-Master, she did not want to end up finding out that something happened to another.

She banged on the door, but as she did, the noise from inside the chamber sounded as well and Nyght was sure that whoever was in there had not heard her knocking. This time she waited until there was a pause then knocked again, only this time she also called out, "High-Master Copper, are you ok?"

When the banging did not start again, she figured that High-Master Copper was coming toward the door. When it opened, Nyght was surprised at who answered.

"What's the problem Nyght?" Dart said standing with the door open toward him and holding a very big hammer.

"What are you doing in here?" Nyght asked

then gave a follow-up question, "Does High-Master Copper know you are in his chamber?"

The right corner of his mouth curled upward at what he had heard, "Do ye think I would be doing what I be doing if High-Master Copper had not asked me to do what I be doing."

The way he answered was typical of the Weapons-Maker. He seemed to use more words than necessary but since Nyght had spent time with him over the seasons talking with him as she had with High-Master Wraith, she had no problem with understanding what he was saying and asked her next question, "What are you doing?"

To answer her, Dart took a step back to allow Nyght to enter. When she was in the room, he pointed over to her right, so she turned her head to look in the direction. She saw the wall he had pointed to but what the Weapons-Maker wanted her to notice was the huge hole in the center of it which he had made. Nyght turned her head to look at Dart, but she still did not understand, so he closed the door and started walking over to where he had been working.

"The High-Masters came to me three sun-cycles ago. They asked me to begin working on this level and explained to me what they wanted me to do." He stopped walking and turned to face Nyght. "They said I would know when to begin."

Nyght looked at the Weapons-Maker and understood what he meant. Dart said the High-Masters had come to him three sun-cycles ago. That would

have been the day before they had summoned
Nyght to the Assignment Chamber. She knew what
they had meant when they told Dart he would know
when to begin; they were referring to High-Master
Wraith's death. So even before she had agreed to
what they had asked her, they had planned for whatever was going on in this room. She did not feel they
had forced her into doing what she did; they just
knew she would. Now she wanted to know what
the Weapons-Maker was doing specifically. "Why
have you made a giant hole in High-Master Copper's
wall?"

Dart turned back around and made his way over
to the wall where he had been working. "They told
me about who you are." He then turned around to
look at Nyght. "Even though they didn't have to because I knew from the moment I saw yer eyes."

Nyght was ready with her next question, but it
had nothing to do with this room. "Why didn't you
tell me then, if you knew?"

"It was not me place," he said then faced the
wall and started striking his hammer at the edges
of the hole, knocking more of the mortar and stone
away. Between swings and hits, he continued to talk
to Nyght. "With who ye are, it is Guild business, and
more to the point it is Elf business." He struck the
wall again making more stone fall to the ground in
front of him.

"Are you not part of the Guild?"

Nyght asked her question when Dart was in

mid-swing and it caused him to stop with his hammer in the air over his head, but he lowered it to respond although he did not turn to look at her. "I am Dwarf; I am part of nothing which is part of the Above," he said referring to the world the Dwarves stayed away from.

Nyght walked over to Dart. He had lifted the hammer into the air again but before he could bring it forward Nyght placed her hand on his shoulder and stopped him from continuing. He turned his head so that he was looking at her over his right shoulder. "You are also part human and humans do belong in the Above and in the Guild," she said then removed her hand. This was not the time to discuss whether the Weapons-Maker fit in or not; he would have to decide so she changed the subject. "You still have not explained what you are doing."

Dart lowered his hammer and turned so that he was facing Nyght. To him, it was obvious. He was not going to get any work done with her there so he might as well tell her and then she would let him get back to what he was doing. "The High-Masters want this room and the entire level put back the way it was before."

The answer did not tell her enough, "What do you mean the way it was before?"

Over the seasons that he had known Nyght, Dart learned that she was going to ask questions until she had run out of them so he decided it would be easier and quicker to just tell her everything all at once. "The High-Masters have given me the task to put this level back the way it was when the Rulers of the Guild had been here. This whole floor was their living quarters. When the line of the Rulers ended and the High-Masters took charge, they had me da divide the level into three separate, but equal sections, and they moved into them. Now that a Ruler has returned, they want it put back the way it was so that the Ruler can once again have it to himself." Dart gave a quick smile then corrected what he had just said, "I mean to herself."

Nyght could not believe what she had heard. There was a part of her that caused her to think the High-Masters had used her to get rid of her mentor because he was old. She was able to force that down because she could tell they did care for the elderly assassin. Even with his death, she did not think they would just turn over control of the Guild to someone who had not even fulfilled their first contract. At least not her first true contract. Now Dart, someone she had come to trust just a little bit less than High-Master Wraith, was telling her that the High-Masters were going to make this entire floor hers.

"Now can I get back to me work?" Dart asked and turned to face the wall and the hole. He brought his hammer up over his head but before he could let it fall forward, Nyght spoke again, and he halted his swing.

"But I am not the Ruler yet." Nyght waited until Dart turned back around to face her again before she continued. "High-Master Wraith said that I would have to prove myself to the other assassins."

"And ye will. And when ye have, ye will rule the Guild and the High-Masters will step down without hesitation. That is why they have assigned me the task of putting this level back the way it was. Me da was the one to divide it so I am the one that un-divides it for ye." Dart turned around again to continue with what he was doing before he answered the door, something he was regretting now but before he even raised his hammer, Nyght spoke.

"No!" she said, and once again Dart turned to face her.

"No, what? Ye aren't the Ruler. Well, I can tell ye, ye are."

She realized Dart had misunderstood what she had meant. "I do not mean that I am not the Ruler even though I am not yet. When I said 'No' I was referring to what you are doing. You are not to make this room or this level back into what it was when the Guild had one Ruler."

"Yeah, I am," Dart said because he was not going to go against the High-Masters' request.

"No, you are not," Nyght said to let him know what she wanted.

"Yeah, I am!" Dart said more forcefully.

"Am I or am I not the Ruler?" Nyght said thinking she would put an end to the back and forth debating.

As usual, Dart was ready with his answer, "Ye are

but even ye said ye are not yet. So therefore, since ye are not yet, I do not yet have to do as ye say."

Nyght could not stop the smile from appearing on her face, but she still needed the Weapons-Maker to stop what he was doing, at least for the moment. "Then I ask you in memory of High-Master Wraith that you do what I ask until I have a chance to speak with the other High-Masters."

Dart knew she had outthought him. There was no way he would deny the request she had just made. "Very well, but I don't want to be involved in any dispute between the High-Masters and yerself. I just make the weapons and keep the Guild up to specs. Assassins' affairs are for assassins alone."

Nyght smiled, "Thank you," she then turned to leave the room but stopped before she reached the door and turned back to face the Weapons-Maker. "You were not here during the time of the First Ruler?"

He had no idea why she would ask the question, but he gave his answer, "Me da said he left after about one hundred human seasons. It was as if the First Ruler organized the Guild and trained the first assassins, but when he felt the Guild would be able to continue without him, he left. Not even me da knew where he had gone."

"Thank you," she said then turned and left the room.

Dart had no idea what the young assassin was planning to do but something inside him told him that the young woman known as Nyght would never take the role of Ruler. He did not know why, but he had a way of sensing when things were not right in the world, and something was not right with Nyght. That he was sure of.

It was just past the eighth mark so Nyght knew the High-Masters would still be in their morning meeting with the Masters of the Guild. Even though she would someday be Ruler of the Guild, Nyght decided it would not be proper to interrupt the meeting, so she waited in the hallway for it to be over.

While there, Nyght began to think about how her life had turned out. She thought about how she had started out working in a brothel, cleaning floors, and now here she was an assassin, and one day she would be Ruler of the Guild. She had known when she heard the word assassin that she was destined to be one, but now, she was going to be something she had never even dreamed of.

Nyght did not let what she would become change the person she was. She was still an assassin and even when she became the Guild's Ruler, she would not rule the other assassins. To her, a person should never rule their family and that is what the Guild was to her. Even though she does not know the names of every assassin, they are her brothers and sisters. They are the ones who had given her the life she has now. The life she had wanted for so long. She raised her head to look up at the ceiling, "Thank you, High-Master Wraith," she said and ended with a smile.

When the door to the room where they were holding the meeting opened, Nyght watched as the Masters exited. As soon as each of them saw her, they greeted her the same way, "Morning, Honorable Nyght."

High-Master Wraith's funeral had just taken place yesterday, but ever since then, every assassin who saw her would greet her with the title, Honorable Nyght. The High-Masters had told her that when she fulfilled "The Assassin's Honor" she would receive the title of Honorable, but she did not think they would call her that directly.

After the last Master had walked out of the room, High-Master Copper came out as well, "Honorable Nyght, is there something you wish?" The way the High-Master spoke her name, as well as what he had asked, Nyght heard the respect he was giving her. The same way he addressed High-Master Wraith and a part of her did not believe she deserved so much respect.

"May I speak with you and the other High-Masters, High-Master Copper?" Nyght asked.

"Of course, Honorable Nyght," he said then adjusted his stance to let her enter into the room he had just exited.

When she walked inside, she saw High-Master Grave and High-Master Spar sitting, but as soon as they saw her, they both stood up and greeted her, "Good morning, Honorable Nyght," they said together.

She returned the greeting, "Good morning, High-Masters,"

"Honorable Nyght wishes to speak with us," High-Master Copper said standing to her right.

"If that is ok with you?" Nyght added. She did not want the High-Masters to think she was trying to overstep her position.

"Why of course," the other two High-Masters said at the same time.

Nyght saw that they were waiting for her to begin, but since she had never really addressed the three High-Masters before, as their next Ruler, she felt a bit unsure of how to begin. She decided it would be best if the High-Masters were a bit more relaxed because they seemed to be nervous; probably because they had no idea why she wanted to speak with them. "Please, have a seat," Nyght said and High-Master Grave and High-Master Spar sat down in the chairs they had been sitting in when she entered. She then turned to her right and nodded to High-Master Copper for him to join his fellow High-Masters. He nodded and walked over to his chair and took the seat between his two companions.

Nyght walked over to stand a pace away from the edge of the table. She did not take a seat because she did not want the High-Masters to think that she had come there as someone who was over them. That was the last thing she wanted, but she did come there for a reason. "Dart has told me that you have instructed him to remake the twenty-fifth level back into the way it was when the Guild had one Ruler."

The High-Masters turned and looked at each other, then turned back to face Nyght. High-Master Copper was the one to speak for all of them. "We have assigned him the task, yes."

Nyght asked a simple question, "Why?"

Once again, the High-Masters exchanged looks but did not say anything to one another. When they were through, they again looked at Nyght and High-Master Copper answered her question, "We know that when the Guild had a Ruler, his or her quarters was the entire topmost level. We wanted to return it to the way it was back then so that it would be ready for when you fully take on the role as Ruler. Since we are not sure how long it will take our Weapons-Maker, we thought it would be best for him to begin with the renovations immediately."

"And we have already assigned others to help us remove our belongings to one of the lower levels with living quarters," High-Master Grave added.

"We can talk with the Weapons-Maker and get his best assumption on how long it will take him to finish if you wish it to be done in a specific time frame," High-Master Spar said.

"I do not want it to be done at all," Nyght said and saw that she had confused the High-Masters. They looked at her then at each other. It was obvious to

Nyght that they did not understand what she wanted or why she was speaking with them. "Why do you want the level to go back to the way it was?"

They all turned to face her, and High-Master Copper gave their answer. "As I explained, so it can be the way it was when the Guild had one Ruler, and now that we will have a Ruler once again, then you will need to have your quarters as they were before."

"I do not need an entire floor for myself. Nor do I ever wish to rule the Guild by myself."

They looked at each other again then High-Master Grave said what they were all thinking, "That is what the Ruler is for, to lead us and the Guild."

Nyght had a lot of respect for the High-Masters, but she saw that she was going to have to make sure they did not set her up to be the only voice in what happened with the Guild. She had spent much time with High-Master Wraith. Not only did she listen to what he would teach her, but she also watched the way he worked with his fellow High-Masters.

They respected him for being the eldest of the three, and yes, it was obvious he had more knowledge and wisdom than any other of the High-Masters, but Nyght also saw that he did not use that knowledge to gain power. He would quickly accept a suggestion or idea from one of the other High-Masters if he thought they had made a wiser decision than he would have. When he did believe his way of handling a situation was the best solution, he would always present substantial facts that led him to his decision, and when done explaining, the other High-Masters understood his reasoning as well as why High-Master Wraith was a great High-Master.

He did not try to take control of the other High-Masters, and even when he did lead them in a certain direction, he did it so they would learn and gain knowledge as well. Now thinking about it, Nyght could see that High-Master Wraith was preparing his counterparts for the time when he would no longer be with them. Maybe he had even allowed her to witness those times he met with his fellow High-Masters so she would gain knowledge as well. To herself, she thanked High-Master Wraith again.

By listening to the three High-Masters sitting on the other side of the table, she knew she was going to have to be like her mentor. She would have to lead them, but she would not rule them. She stood up straighter before she began, "The Guild does not need to return to the way it used to be. I am referring to the twenty-fifth level and any other aspect of the Guild."

"But now that we have a Ruler again, there is no need for the three of us to be High-Masters," High-Master Copper spoke, but the other two nodded in agreement.

Nyght did not agree with them. "There will always be a need for High-Masters because that has been the way since the last Ruler, and in the time of the High-Masters, the ones before you and yourselves, they have brought the Guild to where it is today. And just because the Guild will have a Ruler, we cannot forget or toss aside all the good the High-Masters have done."

All three of them nodded at what she had said. Not just because she had given them and their pre-decessor a grand compliment, but because they knew that when the young woman took the position as Ruler, she would rule them well.

"What do you suggest, Honorable Nyght?" High-Master Spar asked.

She was now ready to discuss what she had come up with when she had spoken with Dart. "I suggest we do make renovations to the twenty-fifth floor." She saw the confusion they had by the looks on their faces. First, she had said she did not want to make the changes and now she said she did. Nyght let them think about it for a few breaths then contin-ued. "However, instead of making the three cham-bers into one, I suggest we make the three chambers into four. Three for the three High-Masters and one for the Ruler. Together, all four of us will take the Guild into a new era. One, which is better than when there was only one Ruler, and one that will be bet-ter than with only three High-Masters. We four can lead and guide the Guild far better than I ever could alone. And I will need your seasons of experiences as assassins, Masters, and High-Masters. I am still young and do not have the knowledge the three of you possess so I will need your guidance."

They took a moment to look at the young

woman. Each of them was astounded at how well she had led them to a solution. As if they had heard High-Master Wraith speak the words himself.

High-Master Copper stood, as did the other two High-Masters, and then he spoke, "As we will need yours, Honorable Nyght." All three gave a quick bow with their heads and she returned the gesture.

Nyght was satisfied with what they had accomplished but it was time for her to move forward herself. "High-Master Wraith informed me that I would have to prove myself to the Guild, and for that, I will need to accept a contract. Something to show the other assassins I am worthy to accept the title of Ruler."

"We have discussed this among ourselves as well and when a contract has come to us, we will offer it first to you," High-Master Copper said.

"Are there no contracts available?" Nyght asked with disappointment in her voice.

"I'm afraid there are times when even an assassin must wait until their services are required." High-Master Grave said, and he could tell that their future Ruler was eager to accept her first contract.

"There is the one," High-Master Spar said, and the other two High-Master looked at him. "Forgive me High-Masters, for I am of the least of you, and if I have spoken out of turn then I apologize."

"What is it, High-Master Spar?" Nyght asked, not understanding the confusion.

All three turned to look at her. "It may not be a coincidence..." High-Master Copper said.

High-Master Grave was the one who finished the statement, "...but the will of Creator."

High-Master Wraith had talked extensively about Creator. Nyght sat and listened to his lectures, but she still had never been one to believe that Creator was the one she followed. Even though Moon and her did not talk the way they used to before she had come to the Guild, Nyght still followed Moon. Even so, she was very interested in what the High-Masters were referring to. "What is the will of Creator?" she asked.

The High-Masters turned and looked at one another and then the two nodded to High-Master Copper to explain. "Two sun-cycles ago, we received word that someone was interested in purchasing the services of our Guild."

"Someone wanted a contract completed," Nyght said to let the High-Masters know she understood, and by the excitement in her voice, she let them know she was interested in taking it.

High-Master Copper continued, "Yes, it is a contract but there are a few conditions that will need to be adhered to and we have not finished discussing it to decide who would be best for the assignment."

Nyght took a step closer to the table, "I see no better time to discuss the matter than now," she said with a smile and the other three in the room smiled as well. She gestured with her hand for the High-Masters to take their seats, while she remained standing so the meeting could continue.

They all sat, and High-Master Copper began to explain. "Usually when we are reviewing the details of a potential contract, we do not invite the assassin we are planning on offering it to, to join us, but since you will be the Ruler, and will be attending the meetings, I suppose there is no better time to start than now." Nyght bowed her head to accept the generous statement and then he continued.

"A Rolling Contract is put in place when an individual has requested a number of targets to be removed over a period of time. In this instance, the buyer wishing to purchase our services has requested that his brother be the first target. He is a very powerful and wealthy duke. But this duke has two sons who are to be targets as well. One is of seventeen seasons of age and the other is of fifteen seasons."

Nyght now understood why there was the need for the Rolling Contract and to let the High-Master know that she did, she explained. "Since one of the edicts of our Guild is that we will not take the life of anyone under eighteen seasons, the contract will remain in place until the youngest son reaches the proper age and can be removed as with the first son when he becomes eighteen as well."

"That is correct," High-Master Copper said. "The youngest is only fifteen so the contract will be in place for three seasons. Therefore, the member of our Guild who accepts it will have to remain attached to the contract until it is fulfilled."

"Is there a reason why I should not be offered this contract?" Nyght asked.

"The location of the targets is on the other side of the world. In lands far to the east across the great ocean," High-Master Grave said. "And even though we have Guild Houses in those lands, the person who wishes to purchase our Guild's services lives on this side of the world. His father banished him many seasons ago, so it is obvious as to the reason he wishes to see the death of his brother and his brother's sons. With them out of the way and with his father already deceased, he is the only one remaining to inherit all the family has."

High-Master Spar continued with the conversation, "Since it is our Guild who will directly accept the contract, then we will be responsible for assigning the assassin. And if an assassin accepts the contract, it cannot pass to another unless the one who has taken on the contract is unable to fulfill it."

High-Master Copper spoke next. "The assassin will have to be away for a total of three seasons. If you were to take the contract, then you would be away from the Guild for that amount of time and you are our Ruler."

"Not until I prove myself," Nyght said to let the High-Masters know she was going to do exactly that. "Is there anything else about the contract?"

"Nothing specifically, but since the contract will take the assassin to lands far to the east, they will have to speak the language they do."

Nyght remembered High-Master Wraith telling her that even though the people living on the other side of the world originally came from these lands, because of the separation over time, their language had changed greatly. "I can learn the language," Nyght said to let the High-Masters know she was willing to do what was necessary to obtain the contract.

"But it would take you at least a season to learn the language," High-Master Spar said.

High-Master Copper respectfully corrected his fellow High-Master. "Being new to the High-Master position, you do not know that our Honorable Nyght already knows three of the local languages as well as Gnome and I believe she is studying Troll as well," He looked back at Nyght and smiled to get confirmation if what he had said was true.

Nyght nodded to let High-Master Spar know that High-Master Copper was correct. "I should be able to learn the language within two cycles of the moon."

"Another sign that this is the will of Creator," High-Master Grave said, and it was obvious to Nyght, that he was the most devout of the three.

"What is a sign?" Nyght asked.

High-Master Copper answered. "We have begun some initial planning and we have found that the next ship sailing for the lands east will not be leaving for another two moon-cycles."

Nyght did not say it, but she was starting to

believe High-Master Grave was correct in saying that it was the will of Creator. "Is there anything else I need to know?"

The three High-Masters exchanged looks then turned back to Nyght, "Only the amount the contract will be for which is something we have not decided on as of yet, but I assure you, that with what the buyer is requesting, the cost will be quite substantial," High-Master Copper said.

Nyght did not care about any coin she would receive, at least not as much as she cared about taking on her first contract. "If it pleases the High-Masters, I would like the opportunity to prove to you, and my fellow assassins, that I am worthy to be Ruler of the Guild by taking on this contract."

They exchanged looks once more then all three of the High-Master stood at the same time. High-Master Copper spoke but he said what all three of them were thinking, "We have no doubt you are worthy, Honorable Nyght." She bowed her head to accept the praise and respect and they returned the gesture, then High-Master Copper continued, "Of course, we will need to follow standard protocol and once our cost is delivered to the buyer and if he chooses to agree to what we are asking, which I am sure he will, we will need to offer you the contract in the Assignment Chamber."

"I would be honored to do so. And this time, I will adhere to our tradition and not speak." They all smiled at her last statement. When the moment was over, she continued with a couple more items she wished to address with the High-Masters. "If you would indulge me for just a few moments more, I wish to discuss other matters with you and I ask that if you feel what I am suggesting will not benefit the Guild then do say so." Nyght needed to discuss her concerns with the High-Masters, but she did not want them to agree to them just because she was to become the Ruler. She needed them to be honest with her so she could learn as well as lead.

"By all means, Honorable Nyght," High-Master Copper said, and all three High-Masters sat back down, giving the floor to the young assassin.

"First, I believe we should assign a team to search through the Guild's archives to look for anything that pertains to the time when the Guild had a Ruler. Even the three of you did not know about 'The Assassin's Honor' until High-Master Wraith spoke of it. If that information went missing for so long, there might be more that could help us move the Guild forward. Even if we choose not to use the information, at least we will be able to know what took place in the past, which can help us in the future."

Before she had even finished speaking, all three High-Masters were smiling. "I believe that is an excellent idea," High-Master Spar said. "As I was looking for information concerning 'The Assassin's Honor' I came across other items which I did not know existed."

"If the others agree, High-Master Spar," Nyght

said to address the High-Master individually, "Would you be willing to oversee the search for any lost knowledge?"

High-Master Spar stood, "If my fellow High-Masters do so agree, it would be an honor, Honorable Nyght."

"I agree," High-Master Copper and High-Master Grave said at the same time and High-Master Spar turned and bowed to his companions, then sat back down.

"Thank you, High-Masters," Nyght said to let them know she appreciated their support then she moved on to her second request. "I also believe it would be beneficial to the Guild if someone, perhaps one of the Archivists themselves, sit down with Weapons-Maker Dart and document every bit of information he has. He has been at the Guild longer than any of us and I am sure he has witnessed plenty. I do know he was not present during the time of the First Ruler, but his father was and might have passed some information on to him."

Once again, the three High-Masters were impressed with what the young assassin had brought to them. Each of them gave a silent prayer to Creator, thanking High-Master Wraith for teaching their future Ruler so well.

"I will see to it," High-Master Grave said. He always liked the Weapons-Maker and thought he alone could be the one to document whatever Dart could tell him.

"I have only one more thing to ask of the three of you." Nyght's voice took on a somber tone.

"What is it, Honorable Nyght?" High-Master Copper asked.

She took a deep breath then spoke, "I ask that a new rank within the Guild be established." Now the High-Masters did not know what to say and so they remained quiet anticipating the young assassin's next statement. "I would like the rank to be that of Esteemed. It would be similar to the title of Saint which a priest obtains after they pass from this world but while they were alive, performed great services. We would grant the title Esteemed to members, who have shown great service and gone above the call of duty and have left us. Whether they were an assassin, a Master, or even a High-Master." She stopped to allow one of the High-Masters to ask the question she knew they were going to.

High-Master Copper asked, "And who do wish to be the first to take on the title?" He as well as the other two High-Masters knew the answer.

Nyght held her head up high, and with as much respect as she could put into her voice she answered, "High-Master Wraith." She took a moment to swallow the lump in her throat so she could continue. "If you agree to what I ask then I request High-Master Wraith be known from this day forward as Esteemed-High-Master Wraith."

Once again, all three High-Masters stood and

High-Master Copper answered for all of them, "I think that would be most acceptable." They again gave a quick bow with their heads and Nyght gave one to them. "May I ask what led you to initiate the idea for Esteemed-High-Master Wraith?"

For Nyght it was a simple answer, and she gave it, "So that all of us have someone we can strive to become like." She needed to say nothing else on the matter. "That is all I desired to ask of you, and I thank you for allowing me to do so."

"It was our honor, Honorable Nyght," High-Master Copper said.

"If there is nothing else you wish to speak with me, I will take my leave and wait for your summons to the Assignment Chamber."

High-Master Copper looked at his two companions, then back to Nyght "I believe we have nothing at this time."

She gave one last bow with her head, and they did as well. She then turned and walked out of the room. Not hearing the short conversation between the High-Masters.

"Esteemed-High-Master Wraith knew what he was doing when he chose to take her on as a pupil," High-Master Grave said, already using the new title of his old friend.

"Yes, she will be a great benefit to our Guild," High-Master Spar said.

Even though High-Master Copper was devout, maybe not as devout as High-Master Grave, he still gave his opinion of the one who had just left. "Thank Creator for bringing that one to us."

Both High-Master Grave and High-Master Spar did, "Thank Creator," they said together.

SEVENTEEN

Nyght did not have much to pack on the day she was leaving the Guild. The ship was not sailing until the next sun-cycle, but she had something she needed to take care of before she started her journey to fulfill her first contract.

For the last two moon-cycles, she prepared herself. She learned the language spoken in the lands on the other side of the great waters. She also finished learning Troll. Not that she was planning on having any dealings with them, but she had chosen to learn the language as well as Gnome because they were different. When Esteemed-High-Master Wraith told her she was a descendant of Elves, she wanted to learn their language as well, but there was no one within the Guild who could speak it. Elves had not been in her part of the world for a very long time, and when they left, so did their language. Nyght knew that in the lands to the east, the people used Elves as slaves. Just thinking about it made her conscience burn with hatred for the way some people would treat others.

Apart from the slavery, Nyght was looking

forward to traveling to another part of the world. More importantly, she was eager to sail on one of the big ships. When she lived in Sarzanac and had worked at removing rats, she did not have the opportunity to take to the great waters. She had to remain in the city and prepare for the time she would enter the Guild; now having completed the task, she could cross the oceans.

Something about the great waters called to her. She knew Moon was the Guardian of the great waters and since she was so close to Moon, she felt the connection between Moon and the life the great waters contained.

Nyght spent the morning doing the one thing she had been doing every night. Since she was not going to be able to take the mannequin with her, she spent the good part of the morning practicing with her daggers. She altered between the thrust to the neck, the eye, under the chin, and the heart. She walked around the mannequin and when she came to the part of it that she would attack, she moved her daggers with speed and accuracy. Even after many seasons, each area on the mannequin only showed one entry point per section. She continued to perform her exercises until she heard a knock on her door.

As soon as she pulled Full out of the right eye of the mannequin, she twirled both her daggers through her fingers. After the third spin, she brought them down to her sides and into their sheaths. She turned to face the door to her chamber, "Enter," she said, standing in front of the mannequin.

Dart walked into the room and saw Nyght standing there with no expression whatsoever. He knew she would be leaving in a few marks to undertake her first contract; one that would keep her away from the Guild for over three seasons. Usually when an assassin accepts a contract, there is very little discussion about it or the assassin. Since this particular mission was for the future Ruler of the Assassin's Guild, everyone in the tower as well as every assassin in every Guild House in every city, knew not only about the contract but also about Honorable Nyght.

"I take it ye will not be taking that practice dummy with ye on yer trip?" Dart asked and ended with a smile.

"If it was small enough to carry with me, then I might." Nyght turned around and looked at the object of discussion. She placed her hand on the shoulder and thought about how many marks she had spent using her daggers on the mannequin practicing her killing thrust. "But I will have to find something else to practice on while I'm away." She turned and Dart saw the smile she had on her face. He knew she was referring to the targets of the contract.

"Well, when ye return, I will make sure it will be waiting for ye in yer new chambers." While Nyght prepared for her departure, Dart had continued to reconstruct the top level of the Guild. Mostly he was still tearing down the walls of the other two rooms and clearing away the rubble. The two High-Masters had taken quarters on the levels below but since Nyght was going to be leaving, she stayed in Esteemed-High-Master Wraith's quarters, but not his bedchamber. Which when she returned, would be hers. She had asked Dart to make the room where she had lived for over four seasons to remain, as well as the room adjacent to it where Esteemed-High-Master Wraith had kept a good portion of his books. Of course, Dart had no problem with the request. He told Nyght he could use those two rooms as the beginning of the rebuilding to allow all three High-Masters and the Ruler to have their quarters on one level. "Will ye be leaving tomorrow morning?"

Nyght looked at the Weapons-Maker then turned away. Not because she did not want to answer the question, but because the answer bothered her more than she thought it would have.

She was now nineteen seasons old. Before she came to the Guild, she had lived a life where she did not depend on anyone but herself. She had been on her own since she was five. She had lived in places with others, people like Randolph, Tat, and Olivia, in the first town she had come to and then with the others in Sarzanac, others like Keyota, and Selby. In all that time, she had kept a certain amount of distance from them and not just physically.

When she came to the Assassin's Guild, something changed. Part of it was herself, but more of it was because in all the seasons she had been on her own, she had never found people that were like her. Not until the Guild accepted her, not just as an assassin, but also as family, and now she had to leave.

"My ship leaves tomorrow morning, but I will be leaving tonight," she said as she walked over to her bed keeping her back toward Dart, as well as her eyes, trying to keep tears from rising. "I have something I need to take care of before I set sail."

"As do I," Dart said behind her.

She did not know what he meant, and unfortunately, the conversation required her to turn to face him, but only after she made sure there were no tears in her eyes. When she was facing the Weapons-Maker, he turned and went back out the door which he had not closed when he entered. When he came back in, he held a bundle in his hands that was wrapped in a tan cloth and tied with string around the middle. He walked over to Nyght and extended the package to her. He did not speak but she knew he was offering her what he was holding.

Nyght took the bundle, turned, and placed it on the bed. Before she started to undo the string, she took a deep breath to control her emotions. She then removed the string, flipped the bundle over, and opened the ends of the cloth. When she saw the item inside, she could not tell what it was, only that it was made out of cloth and was black. She grabbed the top of the item and lifted it up. As she did, it unfolded and when she had raised it up so that she was holding the top part at eye level, she looked down and could now tell what the item was.

She took another moment to get control of her emotions, and when she was ready, she grabbed the item with both hands and twirled it around her. When it settled, she connected the top clasp located at the bottom of her throat. She moved her hands downward and felt another clasp, then another further down. She did not bother to check to see if there were more because she knew there would be. She then turned to face the Dwarf who had taken a step back to allow her to try on the cloak he had made for her.

She looked down and saw that it went all the way to the floor, so much that it went past her boots, and with the front of it completely closed, not even they would show. She then lifted her hands and pulled the hood of the cloak over her head. Once situated, the edge stopped just a little past her eyes so that she could see clearly when her head was raised completely. She then tilted her head down enough to test her sight. As her head lowered, the hood of the cloak adjusted a bit so that it rose up just enough so she could see by only raising her eyes. The hood also sat off her ears so it would not interfere with her hearing, which was evident when Dart spoke.

"I saw that ye had outgrown the one ye came with. When ye first arrived, ye were no more than a big toe taller than me be. Now ye are four hand-breadths and some more over me."

Nyght pulled the hood back over her head. She wanted to say something but could not. Not because she did not have the words, but because the lump in her throat stopped the words from coming any further. She lifted her right hand, reached over to her left shoulder, and felt the material. When she had bought her first cloak, it had felt just as smooth as the one she was wearing now. Over the seasons, and with all the use she had gotten out of it, it had become rough and ragged. Although she loves the one she had for all those seasons, the one she just received was worth more than the three silver she paid all those seasons ago. Since she still had not spoken, Dart continued.

"I figure ye won't be doing anymore growing. So ye ain't got to be worrying about the bottom reaching your top." Dart chuckled to keep his own tears out of his eyes. "I also put in some pockets on the inside." Nyght moved her hands and felt for what Dart had told her and she found four on each side of the cloak. "There are also two in the back. I figure ye can find something to go in them." Nyght moved her hands and found the two pockets at the back of the cloak. She did not know what she would use them for, but she would find something, just so the Weapons-Maker's work did not go to waste. "There is one more thing ye might find very interesting." Dart walked over and when he was standing directly in front of her, he reached behind his back and brought forth his own knife. "With yer permission?" he asked.

Nyght did not know what the half-Dwarf was going to do, but even though he was standing in front of her holding a knife, the thought that he was a danger to herself never even crossed her mind. She trusted him just as she trusted all those in the Guild. Since she was still trying to get over the way the gift was making her feel, she did not feel comfortable talking so she gave the Weapons-Maker a nod to let him know to continue.

Dart extended his left hand, the one without the knife, and lifted up a part of the cloak, making sure the material was taut. He then jabbed the knife downward onto the cloak. It did not go through. He looked up and saw that Nyght had seen the act as well but was unsure of what had happened. To give another demonstration, Dart took the knife and folded the material around the blade. He then pulled on the knife trying to cut the cloak but failed to do so. He looked back at Nyght, let go of the cloak, and took a step back to explain. "No ordinary weapon can cut through it. No knife, no sword, no arrow. Now I am not too sure how it will stand up to a blessed weapon. If ye want, ye can try yer own daggers, but I wasn't going to be the one to ruin it before ye have a chance to see the cloak whole."

Nyght lifted her hands and raised up the cloak to get a better look at it. Now that she had heard what he had said, her curiosity overcame her emotions to remain quiet. "What kind of material did you make it out of to cause it to resist a weapon?" she asked the question but did not look at the half-Dwarf.

"Well, it ain't the material that makes it resistant to weapons."

Nyght had to look up and her eyes asked the question, "Then what does?"

"Me own hair." He saw the confusion on the young woman's face. "One hundred of me own strands of blessed hair be woven throughout the material; from the top of the hood to the bottom of the hem. Seeing how the hair not be attached to me no longer, it not be as blessed as I be, so that's why I warn ye about going up against a weapon that has been blessed as well."

As much as Nyght wanted to test her daggers against the cloak, she would not. If the day came when a blessed weapon encountered the cloak, then she would know. Until that day, she would treasure the gift. If the day ever came, it would be the last day of the one who damages it. Nyght knew she had to say something to thank the Weapons-Maker and show how much she appreciated the gift, "I will wear it with honor."

"Ye do me honor that ye wear it," Dart said to return the meaningful words. They stood there for a few breaths and to break the emotional silence, Dart spoke, but he did so in the language spoken on the other side of the world. "Three seasons be a long time to not be coming back to the Guild Castle."

Nyght smiled at hearing the foreign language. There were only a few people in the Guild that could speak it. The Archivist who taught her was one of them, and so was Dart, who had learned the language, even though he had never left the Guild and had not learned it from the Archivist. To keep in practice, when she had learned enough of the language, Dart would communicate with her to help with her learning. "It will go quickly, and then I will return," she said in the foreign language as well. She had no problem with speaking the words but the difference between it and her own language was that she spoke it with a heavy accent. It would be obvious to any who spoke the language as their natural dialect, but since Nyght did not plan on talking much to anyone and only if it was necessary, then she did not have a problem with the difference. Nyght continued in the foreign language, "Three seasons is less than what I have spent at the Guild, and I will use the time to learn more about the world and bring what I know back with me."

Dart did not speak the words he wanted to. It was not his place. The feeling that the one who was to become the Ruler of the Guild would not be returning was still strong in him. He may have lived and worked at the Guild, but he was not an assassin, and whatever he was feeling, was not for others. "I'm sure ye will see a great many things," he said speaking in the foreign language.

Nyght thought there was something in the way the Weapons-Maker had said his last statement, but she decided it was due to the situation. She herself was making sure she kept her emotions from surfacing. Even though all assassins had them, it was a matter of self-control not to allow others to see them. "I am sure I will," she said in their own language, then turned around as if she had to take care of something. "I will not miss the constant noise of you demolishing the walls to this level."

Dart knew she was referring to the work he was doing in preparation for her return and taking on the role of Ruler, but even though he did not think she would be back, he did not say it. "Me work will be complete way before ye come back to the Guild." He said it in a way where he was hoping the young woman would see that he might know something that neither she nor anyone else in the Guild did. With her answer, he knew he had not succeeded.

"I am sure that when I see what you will finish, I will be no less impressed than when I look upon any creation of yours." He simply gave a slight bow with his head to accept the compliment. "How are you and High-Master Grave coming along with your telling of what history you have of our Guild?"

"Well in the two moon-cycles we have been at it, we have gotten up to..." Dart took a couple of breaths to think about his answer then gave it, "... me third season of life."

Nyght was surprised at what she heard. She had suggested to the High-Masters that they document everything the Weapons-Maker knew from the time he had been at the Guild. The High-Master and Weapons-Maker had begun two moon-cycles ago and they had only reached the point when he was three seasons old even though they had been meeting every day. "I take it you remember more than most of us when we were so young."

Dart let out a solid laugh, "I remember the day I came out from between me ma's legs."

Nyght could not stop the smile from appearing on her face, but at the same time, she did not want to picture in her mind what the half-Dwarf had just said. With his physique, his mother would have had a very difficult time in birthing him, and even though she has been dead for quite some time, Nyght felt sorry for the woman. "Maybe you two can stick with just the Guild related topics. That should speed the task up a bit."

"Well, since me whole life has been spent at the Guild, every memory I have concerns the Guild. And besides, I think High-Master Grave likes the stories I be tellen."

Nyght wanted to ask the half-Dwarf just how much he was embellishing those stories but decided not to. If he and High-Master Grave were enjoying the task, then let them continue in their way. "Well hopefully by the time I return, you will have passed the first twenty seasons of your life."

He gave the best answer he thought he could give, "By the time ye return, I be sure we will," and they gave each other a smile. "Yer voyage across the great waters will take about two full cycles of the moon. If there be any on board the ship that speaks the language to the east, ye should take the chance to get some more practice. If there be no one, then ye need to speak it to yerself every day. Take one of these books ye be reading and read it in the language. Two months is enough time to let some of what ye learn escape ye."

"I will be fine. I have not forgotten the other five languages I have learned so I will not forget the last one either." As she spoke that statement, she alternated with every word using a different language. She could tell by the look on the Weapons-Maker's face that she had confused him. Even though he knew every language she did, not even he could have changed from one language to another so fluently with every new word she had spoken.

To show her that she did not know everything, the next statement he made was in Dwarven. Nyght knew he had just spoken in his own language but since she could not speak it herself, she did not know what he had said, so he translated for her. "I said, if ye be so good, then how come ye ain't been able to learn how to speak like a Dwarf?'"

Nyght smiled and gave her answer, "Because I would have to knock out all my teeth then hold them in my mouth just so I could sound like one." They both laughed but they also both knew that was what the language of the Dwarves sounded like. "When I return, I will have you teach me your language. That way you will have someone to converse with in your own sound of rocks falling down a mountainside." Once again, they shared a smile.

Dart knew after what she had just said it was time for him to leave. He had not talked to another soul in his native language since his father had been at the Guild. After he left, Dart did exactly what he had instructed Nyght to do, and that was to talk to himself in his own language so he would not forget it. Not that a Dwarf ever forgot anything, but Dart was afraid that since he was half-human, then one day he would forget what it was to be a Dwarf. It was his only fear. She had offered to learn his language when she returned, but Dart knew that was not likely. Not about her learning his language, but about her coming back to the Guild. "Well, I got work to be doing. Have a nice voyage," he said, turned, and walked to the door. Before he left the room, he turned back to look at Nyght. "It was an honor to know ye," he said to tell her how he felt.

"The honor is mine, Weapons-Maker of the Assassin's Guild," Nyght said and bowed her head quickly, but when she raised her eyes, she saw that the Weapons-Maker had already left. She was sure he had heard her, but like her, he too was keeping his emotions hidden. It was the way of the Guild.

Now alone, after the tender meeting as well as the precious gift she received, she could feel how much she was going to miss being at the Guild. She was going to miss being with her family.

Nyght spent the rest of the day in her quarters undisturbed except for the hammering going on down the hallway from Dart working. Even though she had told him she would not miss the noise, every time he paused, she held her breath just waiting to hear the next strike from the Weapons-Maker's hammer.

When it was time to make her way to the level that held the traveling corridors that led to Guild Houses in other cities, Nyght stood and took one look around her room where she had lived for over four seasons, and now it was time for her to leave. As much as she wanted to, she also wanted to stay, but she remembered something Esteemed-High-Master Wraith had told her once, "It is the way life is. Always moving forward. Some part must come to an end so another can begin." Now thinking about it, she realized that more than likely her mentor had been talking about his own death.

To take her mind off the thought, she walked to the door to her room and opened it. Before she stepped out, she turned and took one more look at the part of her life coming to an end. During her time at the Guild, she had not acquired much. Only a few sets of clothes, two of which she was taking with her. She also acquired some books that were given to her by Esteemed-High-Master Wraith, her most favorite she had in one of the pockets on the inside of her cloak. Since she had the new cloak, she had tied her old one around the practice mannequin sitting in the middle of the room. She figured it would not be going anywhere and the cloak seemed to fit the mannequin perfectly.

She then looked over to the small desk. The one where she had spent many marks reading. The same one she had fallen against when Esteemed-High-Master Wraith had sent the dart into her shoulder causing her to sleep and wake up with a very bad headache. She smiled at the memory but at the same time felt sad, because it was of her mentor who was not there to see her leave.

The memory gave her the strength to walk out of the room and close the door behind her. She had to leave because she had to move forward. That was what Esteemed-High-Master Wraith had trained her for and she would not let him down.

Nyght walked out of the room. She had on her cloak with the book inside it. Under the cloak, she had her daggers secured inside their sheaths and she had her knife tucked in the top of her boot. Besides the mannequin and her old cloak, she left two other items behind.

They were what every assassin received when they accepted their first contract. Both items were black. One was a bag the assassins could carry items in. If that item was food, then the spell on the bag would prevent it from spoiling. The other was a waterskin that kept water fresh. She left those items because she would not need them. At least not those particular ones.

Nyght took the lift to the ground floor. Before it even arrived, she saw what was waiting for her. When the lift stopped, she waited three breaths before she stepped away from it. She did this to keep control of her emotions. As she moved forward, she looked at the gathering of assassins present and covering the entire level.

As she walked, the crowd moved as well, making a path for her to move to the lift that would take her to the level of the transport corridors to take her to Sarzanac where her ship would be leaving when the sun rose. She had told the High-Masters she would be leaving the Guild this night, so they must have been the ones to arrange the gathering.

As she walked forward, the crowd of assassins adjusted their positions so as not to interfere with her movements. When she reached the lift to take her to the tenth floor where the transport corridors were, she turned around before she stepped onto the platform. She saw the assassins were all looking at her. Positioned at the front of the crowd were the three High-Masters. To keep her eyes on them and theirs on her, instead of turning around, she took a step backward onto the lift. As soon as it started to rise, everyone attending, including the High-Masters, knelt placing their right knee on the floor, and then all bowed their heads. Nyght knew they would stay in that position until she was well beyond their sight.

When the lift reached the tenth floor, just before

she stepped off, she looked down and saw the assassins were still kneeling with their heads bowed. She then looked across the opening to the other side of the circular hallway. There she saw Dart standing. He gave her a nod and she gave one to him. She then turned and walked to the door marked for Sarzanac. She opened it, stepped inside, and closed it behind her.

Dart stood there looking at the closed door. The Weapons-Maker did not believe he would ever see the assassin known as Nyght again. He knew from the first time he saw her that her life would be more than just being an assassin. He was the one who had secretly placed the book written by the First Ruler in Esteemed-High-Master Wraith's study when he was alive, and the girl had first arrived. Mixed in with all the other books, but not so much out of sight where the High-Master would not find it, while at the same time, he would think he had just stumbled across it.

When Nyght had come to him and they fought, Dart felt that the time had come for a Ruler to take their place at the Guild. He did not see it in the one that came before her. He knew that child would never be Ruler of the Guild. Only now, he did not believe that station was part of Nyght's destiny either.

Before she opened the door she had come to, Nyght pulled the hood of her cloak over her head. While she had been at the Guild, even wearing her old cloak, she very seldom kept her head covered.

Now, she was about to walk back into the world she had left behind over four seasons ago. Even if it had remained the same, she had changed. Not just the color of her skin; now she was an assassin.

Ready, she opened the door and stepped through. As soon as she passed the exit, the atmosphere of Sarzanac came back to her. The sounds, the smell, the feeling.

She took a moment to look around but saw no one, so she stepped away from the door, making sure to close it behind her. She had come out of a different building than she had entered all those seasons ago. That door had taken her directly to the tower where she was to train. Now that she was a True Assassin, she could use the other passageways that led to the cities the Guild Houses resided in.

Not every city with a Guild House was accessible from the Guild Castle. Sarzanac was because it was the only city to take in new recruits. If a person wanted to become an assassin and train at the Guild but lived in another place, they still had to come to Sarzanac, just as Nyght had.

She walked to the end of the pathway and came to the street. Even though she had not entered this building the day she entered the Guild, she knew exactly where she was. The house was on the same parcel of land as the building where she had entered to get to the Guild. She had just come out on the side of the parcel.

She turned to her left and started walking. She

reached the corner and turned left again. When she made it to the middle, she saw the house she had entered over four seasons ago. She saw the steps she had to walk up. She saw the wooden beam situated on the ground where she had once stood. She looked up and saw the balcony where the Masters stood to make their selections. She could not help but think about Viper and how that particular Master had made the wrong choice, at least in reference to the dead assassin. For Nyght, everything turned out better than she could have hoped for.

She moved closer to get a better look and was standing a few paces from the edge of the street. Even lost in her memories, she still did not have a problem with sensing someone coming up behind her and she even knew who it was. "I believe you owe me a story." She waited a moment then turned around. Standing behind her was the first assassin she had ever met. "So how did you get the name Dodge?"

The assassin had known Nyght would be leaving this very night. All of the other assassins in Sarzanac, as well as other cities where the Guild had a house, had gone to the Guild Castle to pay their respects to Honorable Nyght, their future Ruler. Dodge decided he would rather have a moment alone with her. "I believe I told you that if you were to survive five seasons, then I would tell you. By my count, it has only been a little over four." He smiled but made sure he did not look into her eyes. Once had been enough.

"I take it you are not going to tell me your story."

"Not at all, you just have to wait one more season."

Even though Nyght was curious, she had a feeling she would not be hearing the story behind Dodge tonight. "I will be gone for three seasons. When I return, I expect to hear your story, or you can expect to feel my blades."

"Then I will humbly await your return, Honorable Nyght," Dodge said then bowed at the waist, stood back up, and stepped to the side to allow her to continue on her way.

She had not seen Dodge since the day she had entered the Guild. He might have been present at Esteemed-High-Master Wraith's funeral, but since she did not want to talk about that day, she did not bring it up. She gave him a bow as well and then walked out into the city. Just because she had not seen him in over four seasons, it did not mean they did not have a connection. Not only was he the one to recruit her, but he was also an assassin. Which meant he was family. One more she was leaving behind.

Dodge watched as she walked away. He knew where she was going and in the days before she had entered the Guild, more than likely, he would have followed her, but not tonight. He could have even told her what she wanted to know but he felt it was best for her to find out on her own. The only thing he did not know was how she would take the news.

Since it was dark out and she was an assassin, she was sure her presence went unnoticed. There were sentries at the steps of the building as well as some down the street to the left and to the right. The only difference now is that the sentries were a lot older than when she had left four seasons ago. Even though she wanted to get inside the building, she did not want anyone to see her. That was one of the first lessons of an assassin. An assassin seen is a dead assassin.

She went back down the alley and made her way around to the other side of the parcel. The building next to the one she wanted to enter belonged to the same people who had obtained it a while back. She knew this because she was there when they had taken it over.

She came up to the side of the building but stayed out of sight of the two sentries standing guard. She placed her left hand on the hilt and called its name to activate the power of the dagger. "Umbra." She saw herself covered in shadow. She had experimented with the power of the blade while at the Guild, but only when she was alone, not even telling her mentor what her blades could do. This was the first time she used the blade's power in a manner to her profession.

She kept her left hand on the hilt of Umbra inside her cloak. If she let go, the shadow surrounding her would dissipate. She then moved up to the building and started walking toward the door on the side. Once there, she quietly opened the door and stepped inside. The sentries were facing away from the building to watch for anyone who tried to enter. They did not see the shadow that had passed behind them. Even if they had, to them it was only a shadow.

Once inside, she kept her hand on Umbra to keep her in shadow. Since it was night, almost everyone in the building was out in the city. This made it easier for her to sneak up to the top floor. She had been inside this building before, so she knew exactly where she needed to go.

Once there, she walked over to the door that would take her to the roof. When she opened it, she saw the stairs leading upward. Still in shadow, she walked up to the top and opened the door leading to the roof. Since she did not see anyone, she opened the door further, slowly, but only enough so she could slip outside. As soon as she was through, she closed the door behind her.

Now completely outside, she saw the two sentries stationed on the roof. They were facing away from the door. Like the sentries downstairs at the side door, they kept their focus away from the entrance that Nyght used because they did not expect an attack from that direction. Which was not going to happen at the moment because Nyght went there for a different reason.

She looked across the way and saw the edge of the building. The sentries to her right were still looking away. Since she knew she was going to have to jump when she reached the edge of the building, she broke out into a run making no more noise than she would have if she had been walking. She did not learn this skill at the Guild; it was a part of her. It was in her blood like her father and their ancestors. Nyght moved the same way when she was younger and hunted in the woods. Only now, she knew why she was so good at what she had done all those seasons ago.

She ran across the building and when she reached the edge, she jumped onto the building she wanted to enter. Since the distance was no trouble for her, when she landed, she continued with her run. Only stopping when she had made it to the center of the rooftop. There were no doors leading inside, which was the reason there were no sentries on this roof. She did see some on the roof of the building on the far side of the one she was on. Between the four sentries on the two buildings, they were supposed to look out for anyone trying to get inside this one. On this night, they failed.

Nyght entered and exited the room on several occasions when she had occupied it, so she had no problem with hanging onto the edge of the roof while she used her dagger's blade to slide the latch at the bottom of the window to the side. She then opened the window outwards allowing her to push the shutters on the inside, inwards, giving her access to her room. Once inside, she closed the window and the wooden shutters.

She quickly looked around and even though everything looked the same as when she had left, she had a feeling someone had been in the room. She did not know that Selby and Dodge had come to the room not long after she entered the Guild, but she still had a feeling someone had been there.

She ignored her suspicions because she figured that if someone had come into the room, they would not have left the two items she was looking at. There, still lying on the blanket, exactly where she had left them, were her two bags. Even though the High-Masters had given her ones that were brand new, she had decided that when she left Sarzanac she would take the last two items she had brought with her all those seasons ago. She has had them for as long as she has had her knife.

Before she left the room, she walked over to the wall opposite where her blanket was and knelt down. She then removed her knife from her boot and used the blade to pry open the third board from the center of the wall. Once it was free, she moved it to the side and placed her arm inside the hole. She extended her hand to the left and upward then felt around for the pieces of string she had secured to a metal hook she had forced into the inside part of the wall. When she had a hold of the six pieces, she unhooked them and then pulled her arm out of the hole along with the string. She continued to pull and soon she was pulling six bags through the hole.

These were the bags she kept her coin in. Every

time she earned some, she would put them in one of the bags. Then with one end of the string tied to the metal hook in the wall, she attached the other end to one of the bags. While she had her arm inside the hole, she tossed the bags further into the hole. If someone did find the loose board, the bags would be away from the opening. The piece of metal inside the wall was not directly next to the hole, so someone would not think to run their hand on the inside of the wall to look for it. What she had come up with to keep her coin safe worked because after four seasons, all six bags were still there.

Now that she had her bags of coin, she replaced the strings back in the hole and placed the board back into position. She would never be using the hiding place again, but as an assassin, she had to make it appear that no one had ever been there. Even though someone might notice the missing waterskin and the other bag, it did not matter because those were what she had come for and what she was leaving with.

She made her way to the level below, once again using Umbra to keep her in shadow. She did not have far to go but she wanted to make sure no one saw her. When she reached the room she wanted, she took a quick listen with her ear against the door but did not hear anyone inside. Since it was still early out, she figured the room would be empty, so she opened the door, stepped inside, and moved to the corner just to the left of the door. She was able to see the bed in the center of the room. Then she waited.

When someone finally came in, Nyght was surprised at who it was. "You are not the one I was expecting."

The person turned around and already had a sword out, "But I will be the one to end your life for being here," the female who entered said.

The words meant nothing to Nyght. She could have killed the one standing in the middle of the room before she even had a chance to draw a breath to yell for help, but Nyght did not go there to kill anyone. Even though it had been over four seasons since she had seen the woman, Nyght had no problem recognizing her. "Would you kill the one who saved your life once before?" Nyght said. She then stepped out of the corner. She had removed the shadow of Umbra when she had first entered the room, but since the room was already dark, the natural shadow in the corner kept her hidden.

Once out in the open, Nyght still had her cloak around her, and the hood pulled over her head. That did not stop the woman in the room from recognizing who was in the room with her. She had known someone seasons ago who wore a cloak almost like the one she was looking at and it was that person who had saved her life by killing the man about to kill her. "It's you, isn't it?" Keyota asked.

Not only did she have her hood up, Nyght had her head tilted down slightly. The last time she had seen Keyota, not only had her skin been a normal color, but she did not know if Keyota had ever killed anyone. Now that Nyght knew what happened to anyone who looked into her eyes and had taken a life, she did not want this woman to see "Death" as Esteemed-High-Master Wraith had put it.

The next thing Nyght knew, Keyota dropped her sword and came running over to her. When she reached the assassin, Keyota threw her arms around her neck and hugged her. Nyght did not know how to react since it was the first time that anyone had ever hugged her. The closeness alone made her feel uncomfortable, but for some reason, she knew Keyota needed this. Nyght allowed the emotional woman to stay attached to her for about four breaths, then raised her arms and politely pushed the woman away from her, "It is good to see you as well."

"I can't believe it is you. I saw you enter the Assassin's Guild, but I didn't think I would ever see you again."

Nyght was beginning to regret coming to the room. She had only wanted to see one person. She had not planned on talking to anyone else, so she decided to see where that person was. "Where is Selby?"

Keyota did not take offense to the question so quickly asked. She knew the girl, now a woman, was one of few words. "He is not here. He has gone to Duxburough."

Nyght had learned a lot at the Guild. One of

those things was the location of almost every city, town, or village in this part of the world so she knew Duxburough was to the south of Sarzanac. "What is he doing there?" Nyght asked.

Now at ease with the person in the room, Keyota turned around, walked over, and picked up her sword. She then turned back around to answer the question. "The same thing he is always doing. Setting up another Guild House."

"Guild House?" Nyght asked because she had no idea what the woman was referring to.

"I take it you haven't heard. You just returning and all. Selby has made quite a name for himself. That is Captain Selby."

"Captain?" Nyght asked even more confused. When she lived there, the nickname "Captain" was not something Selby ever accepted even though everyone called him it behind his back. Now it seems that is his title.

"That is what he goes by now. Since he always called us his lieutenants, we started calling him Captain. When he established the Barter Guild, he kept the name as his title."

"Barter Guild?" Nyght asked, becoming more confused as the conversation continued.

"Yeah, the Barter Guild. That is what we all work for, with Captain Selby being the one in charge. It was something he had been working on even when you were here. He just never told anyone about it. A few sun-cycles after you left, he left as well. We know he had gone north. When he came back, he pulled all of us together and told us his plan. That was the start of the Barter Guild. The first two houses after Sarzanac were in Yorkington and Faulkton."

Nyght heard the names Yorkington and Faulkton. She did not think anything about them except that they were two places she had been as well. She asked her next question. "And just what is it the Barter Guild does?"

Keyota smiled and gave her answer, "We barter." Since her guest did not say anything, Keyota continued with her explanation, "Mostly information. You know how Captain Selby is always looking for information about anything and everything. Well, he has turned it into a business. If someone wants to know something, they get in contact with one of our Guild members. If we have the information they want, then we will sell it to them. Sometimes we give the information in exchange for other information. But no matter what, we get something. Another thing the Guild does is acquire items others might have an interest in. We don't steal, because it would interfere with the Thieves Guild and Captain Selby does not want to go to war with another Guild. What we do is purchase the item and then sell it to the individual at a greatly higher rate. You know, it's business."

Nyght listened to the entire story, but she still had trouble believing it. She had always known that Selby wanted information, and in all the time she had associated with him, he was planning on building his own Guild, yet never told her. With that thought, she put her mind back on why she was there, "When will Selby be back?"

"Don't know. He doesn't spend much time in Sarzanac. That is why he gave me his bedchamber. Since I oversee the Sarzanac Guild House, he said I should have the best room." Keyota stopped for a moment, then said what she knew to be the truth. "He has not spent much time in Sarzanac since you left." It was then that Nyght lifted her head up enough, so her face was showing more. Keyota saw the color of her skin. "What happened to your face?" she asked. Not just because like Selby, she wanted to know all information, but she had always cared about the one she wanted to be like."

Nyght was quick to answer, "Nothing." Since Selby was not present, there was no reason to stay any longer, so she turned and walked to the door.

"Is there something you want me to tell Captain Selby?" Keyota asked as Nyght opened the door.

She thought for a moment. She had come back to let Selby know she had completed her training at the Assassin's Guild and that she was going away for about three seasons. She also was going to tell him that after she returned, she would like to see him again. She was not certain what she meant by those words, but it was what she wanted to say to him face to face. Since he was not in the building or in Sarzanac, there was no need to. Nyght did answer Keyota's question. "No," then walked out the door.

Instead of going out the way she came, Nyght went downstairs through the building and out the front door. She had moved so quietly the sentries posted out front did not even notice her until she walked past them and then they only saw the back of the cloaked figure.

She made her way to the docks and found the ship that would be leaving for the lands to the east in the morning. She walked up the plank and presented the voucher the Guild purchased for her to board the ship. It was not like the ones she worked on killing rats, although there were some on board. *The White Squall* was a passenger ship. It was bigger than the cargo ships and some of the space below was for the passengers so they could have their own quarters and privacy. The ship also had its hold filled with supplies because the voyage across the great water would take over two full cycles of the moon.

Once Nyght was in her quarters, she sat down on the bed. The ship would not depart until morning. She had planned on spending the time until then talking with Selby, telling him everything about her, and she did mean everything. Since he had moved on, there was no reason for her to wait for him. Instead, she would wait on the ship. In the morning, she would be leaving Sarzanac behind her and everything that went with it, including Captain Selby.

Moon had waited for many seasons for what was happening with Nyght. Moon was not Creator; therefore, Moon could not directly control the way events unfolded. Moon had to be patient and wait. Now, Moon has been rewarded for waiting.

Moon had chosen the one called Nyght for one reason and now she was heading to the lands where Moon needed her to be. Moon just had to be patient for a little while longer.